LEANING FOR
FREDDY NAROWE

"There's something I want to say t

"So? Spit it out."

She stood close enough th
plastering her shirt to her breasts. The scent reminded him of glistening bodies and damp sheets, the image so strong that he clenched his jaw.

"That kiss didn't mean anything to me either! Absolutely nothing."

He stood rock-still as if she'd hauled back and smacked him between the eyes with a fence post. He'd been so focused on assuring himself that kissing her had meant nothing to him that he hadn't considered her point of view. Now it made him fighting mad.

The next time he kissed her—and there would be a next time—his kiss would damned well mean something to her. He'd make sure it did.

Please turn the page for more about JENNY JONES—*and*
Maggie Osborne . . .

"You will find Jenny Jones . . . to be the sort of heroine modern women want to identify with. Jenny lives by the code of the West—her word. This female cowpoke, wrongfully imprisoned for thievery, dresses like a man, shoots like a man, and cusses more than most men I know, yet she retains a subtle sweetness and naiveté."

—**Kate Ryan, Amazon.com**

AND EVEN MORE PRAISE FOR MAGGIE OSBORNE . . .

"Wit, style, and class. Maggie Osborne is a storyteller who consistently delivers all three."

—**Nora Roberts**

"Maggie has surpassed even her own high standards with Jenny. . . . She's written an absolute keeper this time around, a book I won't hesitate to recommend to all our romance readers!"

—**Merry Cutler, Annie's Book Stop (Sharon, MA)**

"4 1/2 stars, highest rating. . . . Her talent for creating legendary characters is reaffirmed as readers recognize her innovation and power on every page."

—*Romantic Times* on *The Seduction of Samantha Kincade*

"A wonderful story that will steal your heart. Don't miss it."

—**Heather Graham** on *The Wives of Bowie Stone*

"An absolutely, positively must-read . . . A very moving story . . . filled with characters you'll remember long after you read the final page."

—**Walden's Romantic Reader** on *The Wives of Bowie Stone*

"A beautiful romance that echoes with a fresh, unusual, and poignantly moving voice."

—*Affaire de Coeur* on *The Wives of Bowie Stone*

Published by
WARNER BOOKS

MAGGIE OSBORNE

······································

The Best Man

WARNER BOOKS

A Time Warner Company

WARNER BOOKS EDITION

Cover design by Diane Luger
Cover illustration by Leslie Wu
Border illustration by Michael Racz
Hand lettering by David Gatti

Warner Books, Inc.
1271 Avenue of the Americas
New York, NY 10020

Visit our Web site at
http://warnerbooks.com

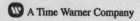 A Time Warner Company

Printed in the United States of America

First Printing: April, 1998

10 9 8 7 6 5 4 3 2 1

To the two Georges in my life. I love you both.

The Best Man

Prologue

This here is my last will and testament, me being Joe Roark, owner of the King's Walk Ranch located seven miles south of Klees, Texas.

The thing is, none of my three daughters is worth a sick spit. Not a one of 'em ever showed a lick of interest in the ranch that paid for all them fancy dresses. I'd as soon leave all of them nothing but a hearty good riddance, but if I do that, then everything I worked my whole life for will go to my fourth wife, Lola Fiddler Roark, and she ain't worth a sick spit either, her being the most recent and the most annoying of my wives.

This here lawyer fella, Luther Moreland, says I can leave my ranch and my worldly goods to charity and cut 'em all out if'n I want to, but that's a hell of a thing, now ain't it? That a man should work his whole entire life to benefit some charity folks who don't know his name and don't care, and who don't know what a hard thing it is to have daughters instead of sons. Even if the worthless women in this family sell the ranch and spend the gains of my sweat and labor on furbelows, which is exactly what I expect, at least it will be family driving a stake in my dead heart and not strangers.

I been thinking about this problem ever since I got sick and I got some things to say about it.

If I got to choose between my useless daughters and my worthless wife as to who gets to squander the fruits of my life's work, then I guess I'd pick my own blood, my daughters. They been disappointing me longer than Lola, but a man expects more of his wife, so though the period has been shorter, Lola's caused more than her share of misery and upset and I aint happy about that or her.

So here's what I come up with and Luther says I can do it. I leave my ranch, my money, and all my worldly goods to my worthless three daughters, but they got to earn it. They got to prove they're as good as the men I wish they'd been. They got to walk in my boots and learn what ranching means, learn what it meant to be me, Joe Roark.

Luther's going to write this up in big legal words and write separate pages with the details, but here's the gist of it, and now I'm talking directly to Alexander, Frederick, and Lester, my daughters. If you three want to get a penny of my estate, then here's what you got to do. You girls got to drive a herd of longhorns to market in Abilene, Kansas. The three of you got to deliver and sell 2000 beeves at the end of the drive. And you got to work that drive like you was the men you should have been.

Luther will explain everything, and he'll release enough expense money to cover the journey and hire on a trail boss, a cook, and nine drovers. A successful drive requires at least twelve hands, so you three got to make up the difference. This aint going to be no cakewalk, it's a work trip. If any one of you aint got what it takes to join up and work your share, then you forfeit any claim on my estate.

If those what join in the cattle drive fail to get them steers to Abilene and sell 2000 of them, then my fourth and worst wife, Lola Fiddler Roark, gets everything.

May the best man win.

CHAPTER 1

Listening to the talk around town, Dal Frisco could believe that Joe Roark's funeral was the biggest event to happen in Klees, Texas, since the war ended five years ago.

As every business in town was closed as tight as a new bottle of whiskey, and he had nothing to do until the interviews began Monday, Dal stood on the hotel porch and watched Roark's hearse roll past. From the line of buckboards, horses, and gigs, it appeared that no one in the county wanted to miss seeing Roark lowered into the ground.

Actually, he supposed that included him. It wasn't every day that a dead man offered the living a second chance. When he considered Roark as a possible benefactor, he felt like he ought to join the procession to the cemetery and take his hat off for the man. He was shaved, shined up, and sober; and there wasn't anything else to occupy his time.

By the time he overtook the tail end of the cortege, most of the buckboards and wagons had reached the cemetery. Falling into step behind the mourners, Dal angled around for a view of the gravesite when he reached the assemblage. He didn't care about seeing

Roark's expensive brass-fitted casket, but he did want a look at Joe Roark's daughters.

He spotted them at once and knew who they were because they had the polished look he expected from a rich man's daughters, and because they were the only seated mourners. When the first prayer began, Dal pulled off his hat and held it against his chest. He gave Roark's casket a passing nod, then turned his attention back to the daughters.

They looked like delicate, high-strung types who carried smelling salts in their fringed wrist purses. He could have believed they were society women who had never set foot on a working ranch. If Dal had been a lot less desperate, he would have turned his butt around and headed back to San Antonio.

The same dispiriting thought had crossed his mind yesterday when he'd recognized a half dozen other trail bosses in town, undoubtedly sniffing around the Roark job like he was. No right-thinking employer—even three ignorant women—would trust a herd to Dal Frisco if he could hire Shorty Mahan or W.B. Pouter. He should just turn around and walk away. He might have done it except he suddenly noticed a detail he'd missed on the initial once-over.

One of the daughters was sitting in a wheelchair.

Shock stiffened his shoulders and he stared. Accepting three greenhorn, coddled society women as hands on a cattle drive lay just barely within the realm of imagination. If he hired experienced men, the best of the best, to fill out the outfit, he figured he might be able to take up the slack and work around the women. Maybe. If he was luckier than he'd been in the past. But putting a woman in a wheelchair in the middle of a cattle drive would be sheer insanity. No trail boss in full possession of his senses would consider such an invitation to disaster.

That thought stopped him cold. One man's disaster was often another man's opportunity.

Craning his neck, he skimmed a thoughtful glance over the crowd, looking for Mahan and Pouter. Only a desperate man would agree to take a woman in a wheelchair on a seven-hundred-mile cattle drive. And last he'd heard, Mahan and Pouter were a long way from desperate.

Feeling more hopeful, Dal stepped behind a woman short enough that he had a clear view of the daughters over her bonnet. They didn't look enough alike to be related, let alone be sisters, he decided, but every one of them appeared more elegant in her black funeral clothing than most of the women standing around him. If Joe Roark had been the kind of man who cared about such things, he would have felt proud that his daughters were putting him down in style.

He also noticed the sisters were dry-eyed. Either they weren't the type to display emotion in public, or their father's passing hadn't plucked too deeply at their heartstrings. Or it might be they were furious at the old bastard for tying their inheritance to a cattle drive.

A different man would have said the Roark daughters were beautiful, but Dal didn't care for the patrician superiority of the blonde in the wheelchair, nor the sullenness of the one he guessed to be the youngest. The middle daughter, however, riveted his attention. Her black hair and green eyes fit the description he'd been given of Frederick Roark, the daughter who had run off to join a touring theater company. She was definitely a beauty, and bold, too. Instead of fixing her eyes on her father's casket, she scanned the mourners as if she were looking for someone.

Dal didn't believe the widespread conviction that actresses were whores who could spout Shakespeare, but he did know that a woman who defied her father and threw away her reputation to run off with a touring company was defiant, willful, and reckless. This daughter was trouble.

Her slow scan of the mourners reached him and paused, probably because he was staring at her. But most men would stare, and most would experience the same shock of electric connection that he felt when their eyes met and held.

He should have looked away when she caught him inspecting her, but he met her gaze head-on, admiring thick lashed, emerald-colored eyes and smooth milky skin. A full lush mouth. Eyebrows a shade lighter than black curls framing the oval face beneath her hat.

Whatever she saw in his expression, it caused her to raise her chin a notch, square her shoulders, and narrow her gaze into a flashing spit-in-your-eye glare. He could almost hear her thinking. "Stare all you want, cowboy, I don't give a damn about your opinion." If it hadn't been inappropriate, he would have laughed. Instead, he shifted his gaze to the sullen daughter.

Faint shadows circled the dark eyes she fixed on her father's casket, but at least she was paying attention to the recently deceased. As Dal watched, a man standing behind her leaned and whispered something in her ear. She didn't look up, but her eyelids fluttered and she stiffened. Her gloved hands clenched in her lap, then she nodded.

The man placed a proprietary hand on the top rung of her chair and touched his watch pocket. A brief victorious smile twitched his lips, suggesting he was pleased that the preacher was about to plant Joe Roark. Most likely he was Ward Hamm who, according to the hotel clerk, had commenced a serious courtship of Lester Roark.

Finally, Dal turned his attention to the sister who worried him most, the one in the wheelchair. It only took a moment to squash his hope that the wheelchair was a temporary measure. Without glancing down, she dropped a gloved hand to the wheel beside her armrest and made a slight adjustment. That kind of unthinking motion was the result of long familiarity.

Frowning, he moved a few yards so he could see her feet. One tasseled black boot peeped from her hem and her skirt lay flat on the right side, suggesting that she was missing one leg, probably from just below the knee. The question was, could she ride a horse?

Scowling, he lifted his gaze. This daughter was the aristocrat in the bunch, and by elimination, she had to be Alexander Roark Mills, the oldest of the three. For a price, the hotel clerk had informed him that Mrs. Mills lived back East in Yankee territory, and she had buried her husband last spring. The clerk had not mentioned that she was confined to a wheelchair.

Her honey-colored hair was parted in the center and swept back into a stylish knot beneath the brim of her hat. Black pearls at her throat and ears caught the weak glow of the winter sun. Although she kept her face turned toward the preacher's droning voice, Dal had a clear view of high cheekbones, a sharp thin nose, and a firm clean profile. Unlike Frederick, this sister did not wear her emotions for all to see, but her stiffly erect posture suggested an excess of pride. This sister would be difficult to second-guess, and she would not easily admit to a mistake.

As the pallbearers lowered Joe Roark's casket into the ground, Dal patted his vest pockets, looking for a cigar, and he gave the Roark sisters a final once-over.

Not one of them looked capable of performing a task more strenuous than lifting an embroidery hoop. He doubted any of them had ever ridden a cutting horse or coiled a lariat. It wouldn't surprise him to learn that the closest they'd been to a longhorn was the beef on their supper plates. Two years ago, he would have walked away from this job and never looked back.

Once the service ended, he stepped out of the way as the mourners filed past the seated sisters, murmured a word or two, then dropped a handful of Texas dirt on top of Joe Roark. That's when he spotted a woman he hadn't noticed because she'd also been seated, but on the near side of the grave opposite the sisters.

The only person unaccounted for was Roark's wife, but Dal doubted this woman could be the wife because she was wearing dark grey, not black weeds. Moreover, the auburn knot on the nape of her neck didn't show a speck of grey as he would have expected on a woman old enough to be the mother of three grown daughters.

Then he noticed the way she held one shoulder a little higher than the other, and the way her head tilted toward the high shoulder. He'd known a redheaded woman in New Orleans who held her shoulder and head like that. He'd never forget her.

Curious, he walked through the headstones, circling around behind the sisters, delaying the moment when he looked at the face of the seated woman in grey. It couldn't be Lola Fiddler. Joe Roark might spend a week in Lola's bed, but he would never have married a woman like her.

But damned if it wasn't the same double-crossing Lola Fiddler who had almost gotten him killed. She was dressed expensively and wearing more paint than she'd worn in the past; otherwise, marrying a rich man hadn't changed her much. She was still brazen enough to show cleavage at her husband's funeral and wear what she damned well pleased—including a smug expression that announced she didn't give a cow chip what the good citizens of Klees thought of her.

As if she sensed someone watching, she raised her head and ran a glance over the people moving past the gravesite. Her gaze slid over Dal, then came back, and her eyebrows lifted in recognition. If she was surprised or dismayed to discover him at her husband's interment, nothing in her expression revealed it. In fact, Dal thought he identified a flash of amusement in her eyes and the flicker of a tiny smile. His own eyes narrowed, and he bit down on his back teeth.

Slowly, he lifted two fingers to his hat brim, offering the minimum gesture of courtesy. Lola being Lola acknowledged his salute by dipping slightly forward, enough to expose a deeper glimpse of cleavage. A low hissing buzzed down the line of mourners. The widow Roark was obliging the town gossips with enough scandal to fuel tongues for a long time to come.

Dal flipped his cigar toward a fallen headstone, pushed his hands in his pockets, and glanced at the sisters again, hating it that his future depended on them.

On the other hand, the Roark cattle drive had just gotten a lot more interesting. Learning that Lola Fiddler was Roark's widow gave him an added stake in helping the Roark sisters earn their inheritance. When he'd ridden into Klees, he'd needed this job. Now he wanted it too.

"There has to be a way that we can get our rightful inheritance without going on a cattle drive," Freddy said again, scowling out the parlor window. In the distance she saw two King's Walk hands riding after a half dozen longhorns. She could easier imagine herself strolling down Main Street in her shimmy and stockings than she could visualize herself chasing cattle.

"You were there when Luther Moreland read Father's will," Alex said from behind her "There's nothing ambivalent about Father's last wishes or about the list of instructions and conditions he drew up. Unless we do this, that woman gets everything."

The heavy draperies framing the windowpanes were dusty and permeated with the odor of cigar smoke. For a moment the smoky smell was so strong that Freddy could almost believe Pa stood behind her, looking out at his land over her shoulder. Pressing her lips together, she turned away and walked to the fire flickering in the grate, extending her hands to the flames.

"Even if we agree, how can we possibly succeed?" she asked Alex and Les. "That's what makes me so furious. Pa knew we couldn't turn ourselves into cowhands. Lola's going to get everything in the end." She waved an angry hand indicating the ranch house, the barn and outbuildings, the land and the cattle. "Damn him. It isn't fair!"

"Please." Les raised a hand to her temple. "Pa's two days in the grave. If you can't say something nice, don't say anything. And must you be so coarse? You know swearing offends me."

"Well pardon me. I certainly wouldn't want to offend your tender sensibilities." She rolled her eyes, but the truth was she didn't care what Les thought. Long ago she had decided since everyone in Klees, including her own family, thought she was an immoral woman, she might as well behave like one, "You can quit defending Pa, it won't do you any good now."

"Just shut up! All you ever did was embarrass Pa or

turn your back on him. You wouldn't even live here at the ranch. Oh no. You had to have a place in town." Les stood and clenched her fists in the folds of her skirt. "You could at least have come out here for Sunday dinner!"

"And talk to that creature he married? Do you know what they say about her in town?"

"Do you know what they say about *you* in town?"

"Stop it," Alex said in a tired voice. "They'll hear you screaming down at the barn."

Color flamed up from Freddy's throat. "I didn't like you telling us what to do when we were children, and I don't like it now!"

During the two weeks that Alex had been home, the three of them had slipped backward into childhood habits. From her lofty position as the oldest, Alex judged, criticized, and issued orders. She had re-arranged the funeral plans and had decided when Luther Moreland would read the will. It had been Alex who persuaded Lola to vacate the ranch and obtain a residence in town at least until the inheritance was decided. Alex who insisted that Freddy stay at the ranch until everything was settled. Freddy and Les had stepped aside and let her take the lead.

Freddy made a sound of disgust. Alex was still lording it over them, still taking charge. It didn't matter that the decisions Alex had made were sound, it mattered that she had come home after a five-year absence and taken control as if she'd never been gone.

Alex folded her hands in her lap and studied Freddy's hot face. "I would rather that you didn't air personal grievances when we know the household staff is listening."

"Why are you addressing these remarks to me? Was I talking to myself?" For as long as Freddy could re-

member, it had always been: Take care of the baby.
Long after Les ceased to be a baby, that had still been
the refrain. Take care of Les. Protect Les. She was sick
of it.

"You start these things, Freddy," Les said, her chin
coming up. "You're not happy unless everything is
stirred up around you!"

"Do you suppose the two of you could stop bicker-
ing long enough to discuss the problem we're facing?"
Alex rolled to the tea table Senora Calvos had laid for
them and poured herself another cup of tea from the
silver service that had belonged to her mother.

Suddenly Freddy's anger seemed overblown and
petulant, a reversion to childhood. But they were no
longer children. Observing her sister, Freddy tried to
imagine what it would be like to spend the rest of your
life in a wheelchair. To know you would never dance
again or spin around in a new gown. She watched Alex
place her cup and saucer in her lap and roll the chair
toward them, trying not to spill her tea. Even the small-
est tasks that Freddy took for granted were now chal-
lenges for Alex.

Freddy drew a breath and struggled to be more sym-
pathetic. "How can you even consider undertaking the
ordeal of a cattle drive," she asked curiously.

Alex glanced at her. "I'm entitled to a third of
Father's fortune. And I'll do whatever I have to do to
make certain that Lola doesn't get her hands on
Father's money."

"Are you saying that Payton didn't provide for
you?"

"Not at all." Alex's neck stiffened. "I have my
home and a modest income."

Freddy guessed that Alex would rather have endured
torture than admit her life in Boston was less than the

image of perfection she had painted in her infrequent letters home. She also guessed that "a modest income" would not support the life Alex had led before Payton's death. But Alex would never admit to anything as vulgar as a lack of funds.

"It's my understanding that Father paid the expenses on the house you rented in Klees after he married Lola. He paid for your clothing and food, paid the salary of your housekeeper."

"If you're suggesting that I need Pa's money, you're absolutely correct." Freddy lifted her chin. "I hated living off of Pa, but I didn't have a choice." At age twenty-seven, she had given up hoping that she could rise above the six months she had spent with the theater troupe. No decent man was ever going to propose marriage to her, and she had no way to support herself.

For a brief while she had thought that maybe Jack Caldwell . . . but no, she would never tell her sisters that Lola's latest escort was a man whom Freddy had been seeing on the sly. Jack was a humiliation she did not want to share.

"It's your own fault," Les commented sharply. "You should have considered your future before you ran off with those actors. But you never think about consequences."

"Believe me, I'd rather be a spinster than settle for someone like Ward Hamm!"

Les jumped to her feet, crimson pulsing in her face. "You can't stand it that I'll have a husband and you never will. You've always been jealous of me!"

Freddy's mouth dropped. "Jealous of you? Whatever for?"

"Because I'm going to be married, and you never will be. You were always resentful that my mother lived

while your mother and Alex's died. And you hate it
that Pa liked me best!"

"Pa didn't like any of us! You're deluding yourself
if you think differently. He wanted sons, not us. He
ignored us, tolerated us when he had to, and tried to
control us like we were part of his herd!" Freddy came
to her feet, anger shaking her hands. "As for being jealous of you and Ward Hamm, that makes me laugh.
He's a shopkeeper, for God's sake. And a petty tyrant
in the bargain. And"—her eyes narrowed—"isn't it interesting that he didn't come courting until Pa got sick?
One could almost think he's more interested in Pa's
money than in you!"

"You . . . you . . ." Sputtering in fury, Les gathered
her skirts in both hands. Scarlet flooded her face. "I
hate you!" Spinning in a swirl of black skirts, she ran
toward the staircase.

Freddy poured the last of the tea into a cup and
raised it to her lips with shaking hands. The day she
was jealous on account of Ward Hamm was the day
she had sunk to depths beyond redemption. Even Jack
Caldwell—gambler, womanizer, reprobate—was better
than Ward Hamm.

"You owe her an apology," Alex said quietly.

She had forgotten Alex. "I'm so sick of Les always
defending Pa! He ran off every suitor she had, just like
he did to you and me. Given enough time, Pa would
have run Ward off, too."

"Les loves him."

"Really?" Fresh anger infused her cheeks. "Does
it ever occur to you that you could be wrong about
something?"

"You're going to attack me, now?" Alex inquired,
raising an eyebrow.

"Les was prepared to spend the rest of her life running Pa's house, serving as his hostess, hoping to be his companion, then Pa trailed a herd to Sante Fe and brought Lola back with him and suddenly he didn't need Les anymore. That's when Ward Hamm appeared. Les used him to punish Pa. Love isn't part of it; Les picked a man she knew damned well that Pa would detest!"

"Then why hasn't she broken off the engagement now that Father is gone?"

"I don't know." Freddy spread her hands. "It's a mystery."

"Is it?" Alex rolled her wheelchair toward the door. "Or is it possible that *you* could be wrong about something?"

The heat of anger lingered in the room after her sisters had gone. Fuming, Freddy walked to the window, letting the chilly air leaking around the panes cool her face.

They hadn't liked each other even as children. They had been competitive and combative, arguing over which of their mothers Joe had loved most or best, fighting over who got to sit next to him at supper. As they grew into adolescence, they had struggled to assert their individuality and distance themselves from each other. Alex tried to reject the responsibilities foisted on her by her stepmothers. Freddy had loathed being the recipient of Alex's hand-me-down gowns, and she felt forgotten, the attention focused on the oldest or the youngest, seldom on her. Les wanted to be taken seriously instead of having her opinions rejected as trivial because she was the youngest. They had always seen each other as rivals blocking access to Pa, or as obstacles standing in the way of getting what they wanted.

Was it any wonder that they hadn't acted in unison

against Joe's iron fist of control? They had each re-
belled alone. Alex had eloped with a man after hearing
two of the lectures he gave during his tour of the South.
Freddy had joined an acting troupe that came through
Klees. Les had agreed to marry a man with all of Pa's
worst traits and none of his good qualities.

Well, why should she care who Les married or for
what reason? She didn't.

She had her own troubles. Les would have Ward
Hamm to take care of her, and Alex had a home and
modest income. But Freddy had nothing. Without Pa's
financial support, there was a very real and horrifying
possibility that she would have to beg for charity simply to live.

Pressing her forehead against the windowpane, she
gazed out at the range and watched the King's Walk
punchers herding strays back toward the barn and corrals. It was a scene she had witnessed all of her life,
but hadn't paid any attention. Now she did, and her
heart sank.

She knew nothing about longhorns except that they
stank and had vicious-looking horns that terrified her.
It was inconceivable that she could take an active role
in a cattle drive.

But unless she rode into Abilene, Kansas, alongside
two thousand bad-tempered cattle, she would be penni-
less. With no place to live, no place to go. Panic choked
her.

When her breathing steadied, she let herself think
about Jack Caldwell. Even before Pa died, Jack and
Lola were driving out together, scandalizing the
county, not that either of them cared. But Freddy had
cared. Being rejected in favor of her hated stepmother
had shocked her.

At least no one knew. In retrospect, she thanked

heaven that her relationship with Jack had been discreet. She'd felt ashamed of herself for refusing to appear in public with a gambler, and she had intended to change that. Before she did, he'd gotten impatient and started seeing Lola.

Well to hell with him. She didn't need Jack or any other man. All she had ever needed was herself.

CHAPTER 2

"Mr. Moreland, ladies, I've listened to this damned fool proposal and there ain't no way I'd boss this drive. Women got no place on a cattle drive, 'specially a woman in a wheelchair."

"Mr. Connity, we don't have a choice. We can't wink at the rules as you put it and simply go along for the ride," Freddy repeated. She nodded at Luther Moreland, the Roark family attorney. "Mr. Moreland will accompany the drive to see that all conditions are met, and our stepmother is entitled to send along a representative to observe on her behalf. People will be watching. My sisters and I must be active participants, or we lose our inheritance."

Mr. Connity hauled to his feet and stared at each of them in a way that made Freddy aware of their pale, sun-protected skin and smooth, callus-free hands. "Some damned fool might accept you three as full hands, but it ain't going to be me. Afternoon, ladies. Mr. Moreland." He nodded, then walked out of the parlor.

They had interviewed four trail bosses, and all four had turned them down the instant they learned that the conditions of the will could not be circumvented.

"They take one look at Alex's wheelchair and that's the end of it," Les said in a discouraged voice. "Would you care for more coffee, Luther?"

"No thank you," Luther said, rifling through the papers on his lap.

"You're wrong if you think you and Freddy would have no difficulty engaging a trail boss if I withdrew!" Alex said hotly.

Freddy smiled. Alex so seldom lost control that it was a pleasure to watch when it happened.

"Oh for heaven's sakes, I was merely stating an observation," Les said, giving Luther a put-upon look. "No matter what I say, one of them jumps down my throat."

Luther Moreland touched a dark bow tie and cleared his throat. "Ladies, Mr. Connity was our last acceptable candidate."

"Surely there's someone else." When Luther didn't answer, Freddy swallowed hard. "Luther, are you saying the cattle drive won't happen? That it's over right now, and we don't have a chance to win our inheritance?"

Les sat down abruptly and Alex froze. They all fixed anxious eyes on Luther Moreland.

He was a tall man, too thin for his frame, with ears that protruded like handles from the sides of his slender face. Even so, Freddy thought, he would have been an attractive man if he hadn't been so shy in the presence of women. Though Luther had known her and her sisters since they were children, their concentrated attention made him uncomfortable.

Dark color filled his cheeks, and he fumbled with the papers in his lap. "There's one name remaining on the list of candidates, but I cannot recommend this man."

Freddy spread her hands with an impatient gesture. "If there's another trail boss who is willing to talk to us, then send for him. We can't just give up."

"Why can't you recommend him?" Alex inquired, rolling her chair forward.

"Dal Frisco is a drunk," Luther said with a frown. "He lost the last two herds he trailed, and consequently he hasn't worked as a trail boss for two years."

"I've heard that name," Les said, tapping a finger against her lips.

"Frisco claims he's been sober for eighteen months." Luther spoke slowly, disapproval underscoring each word. "But he also said I could contact him at the Lone Star Saloon."

"I remember now." Les looked at Freddy and Alex. "Ward's heard all about the disastrous drives that Luther just mentioned. He warned me that we shouldn't even consider Mr. Frisco."

Luther hesitated. "In fairness, I should mention that Dal Frisco was considered one of the best trail bosses in Texas before liquor ruined him."

"He says he's sober now?" Alex asked in a tight voice.

Les stared. "We can't possibly hire a drunk. Ward would never agree."

Freddy narrowed her eyes. "Ward doesn't have a vote here." Before Les could respond, she added angrily, "Maybe you don't need Pa's money, but I do. And I sure as hell am not willing to let Ward Hamm make my decisions for me!"

Les bit her lip. "I want my share of the inheritance as much as you do. But I don't see why we have to make this decision today. We could print flyers soliciting more candidates."

"Les, all of south Texas has known about your

father's will for at least a month," Luther said gently. "The trail bosses who were interested in this drive have already contacted me. Those whom we interviewed today apparently believed they could get around actually using you three as full hands. There are no other candidates."

Alex looked at Luther, and stated flatly. "Send for Mr. Frisco."

"I agree," Freddy said, annoyed that it was Alex who appeared to make the decision.

"What we're deciding now is whether to abandon the cattle drive and forfeit your father's estate to Mrs. Roark, or, before conceding defeat, at least talk to Mr. Frisco," Luther said, still addressing Les. "I cannot recommend Mr. Frisco, but it's my duty to mention that he's offered himself as a candidate. The decision to interview or hire him is yours, not mine."

It was then that the full impact of the day's business truly made an impression. If Dal Frisco turned them down as the other trail bosses had, they would lose everything. Lola would win Joe's estate by default. Fear flooded Freddy's throat. "What happens if Les won't accept Frisco but Alex and I want to hire him?"

"The majority prevails. I should mention that any of you can withdraw at any time. Should that occur, the inheritance will be split equally between the sisters who complete the drive and sell two thousand head in Abilene."

Freddy folded her arms over her breast and glared at Les. "Fine. If you don't want to talk to Frisco, then withdraw, and Alex and I will split a larger fortune."

"Don't take that tone with me! You don't want to suffer this ordeal any more than I do!" Les threw out her hands. "I just think it would be lunatic to trust our future to a man who has lost his last two herds. We should at least be able to trust the man we hire!"

"Shall we have lunch while we wait for Mr. Frisco to arrive?" Alex inquired tightly.

Freddy couldn't help it. The stress of the morning's proceedings released in a sudden laugh. "The perfect hostess. Alex, it should have been you who went on the stage instead of me."

Alex's response was cool. "I think Father would have preferred that none of his daughters ruin themselves on the stage." Turning her chair toward the door, she paused to give Luther the opportunity to jump to his feet and push her into the dining room.

Freddy didn't immediately follow. Walking to the window, she stood looking out, fighting the resentment that burned in her chest.

Surely Pa hadn't intended that the dispersal of his estate would be decided by an ex-drunk, but that's what was about to happen. If Dal Frisco accepted the job and the conditions that went with it, then Freddy and her sisters at least had a chance to win their inheritance. If Frisco walked out as the other trail bosses had, then Lola and Jack would celebrate tonight.

All saloons smelled the same. Strongest were the heavy odors of sweat and smoke, leather and tobacco juice. Wafting beneath the top layer were the scents of brandied peaches, sandwich fixings, pickles, pig's feet in brine. Then came the tang of the wood shavings and a whiff of gaslight and grease. Floating over all, seducing the senses, was the fragrance of the gods, the fruity ambrosia of liquor.

Dal stood at the bar frowning at the rows and rows of bottles lit by gaslights that burned even during the day. Tall bottles, short bottles, fat bottles, slender bottles. Bottles filled with clear, brown, amber, or golden liquids. Whatever a man was looking for, he could find it in one of those bottles. At least temporarily.

Swallowing, he looked down at the shot glass he moved in wet circles on the surface of the bar. A few of these and he wouldn't care about losing the Roark drive.

Every day for eighteen months, he had walked into a saloon indistinguishable from this one, and he'd ordered a shot from whatever bottle gleamed brightest under the lights. He'd fingered the glass, inhaled the fragrance, imagined the burn on the back of his tongue. He'd clenched his teeth and felt the sweat on his brow. Temptation whispered, and when he didn't listen his stomach twisted.

But he hadn't raised the shot glass to his lips. Not in eighteen long damned months.

"You gonna drink that?" the bartender asked curiously.

"Maybe."

Lifting his head, he gazed into the mirror along the back bar and saw his face peering back at him above a row of gleaming bottles. The Klees barbershop was offering a special this week; a tub, shave, and haircut for two bits. A good soak with lots of hot steam might be just what he needed to clear his thoughts and decide where he went from here.

"Are you Dal Frisco?"

He glanced at a Mexican kid, then looked back at the shot glass. "Who wants to know?"

"Mr. Moreland say to tell you the Roark sisters want to talk to you. Out at the ranch."

So Connity had turned them down, too. If they were finally coming to him, then they had no one else.

Staring into the whiskey, he remembered his last drive. Before he shook off the images, the shot glass was halfway to his lips, the hot whiskey scent fuming toward his brain. Christ. It was that easy to throw away eighteen hard months. He pushed the shot glass away.

A man had to be touched in the head to undertake a cattle drive with three ignorant women, and one of them in a wheelchair. He had to be desperate for a second chance.

"Tell Luther Moreland and the Roark sisters that I'll be there in an hour."

Making them wait told him that he still had a little pride.

"I'll take the job. You got yourself a trail boss."

Aside from the introductions, those were nearly the only words Dal Frisco had spoken. When Luther began to explain the conditions, Frisco had raised a hand and said, "You covered everything when we first spoke."

A rush of relief made Freddy's shoulders sag. The cattle drive would occur. Leaning against the horsehair sofa, she studied the one man willing to give her and her sisters a chance, remembering that she'd observed him at the cemetery on the day of Joe's funeral.

Dal Frisco wasn't handsome in a classical sense, but women would notice and remember his rugged good looks. He was tall, comfortable in his bones, and his gaze was cool almost to the point of insolence. He had a slow glance that set something loose in the pit of Freddy's stomach, something hot and fluttery. Where Jack Caldwell had that oddly smooth look that many gamblers had, Frisco radiated a hard inflexibility that few women could meet without seeing a challenge.

Right now he gazed at them as if taking their measure, and it seemed to Freddy that his steady eyes lingered on her a fraction longer than on her sisters. It irritated her that she responded to his attention.

When Frisco finally spoke, his deep, almost raspy voice startled her. "Can you ride a horse?" he asked Alex, running a glance over her wheelchair.

"I used to ride," Alex answered reluctantly, lacing her hands together. "But I'd be terrified to attempt it now. My right leg was amputated just below the knee." When Frisco looked at the one boot on the chair's footrest, color flooded her face.

"Could you drive the chuck wagon? Do the cooking for the outfit?"

Alex looked uncertain. "I haven't done much cooking. We've always had a cook."

"Mrs. Mills, if you can't ride and you can't handle the cooking, then there's no place for you on this drive."

"You're very blunt," Alex said, sharply.

"Yes, ma'am, I am. Now what's it going to be? Are you coming or staying?"

Alex pressed her lips together and gripped her hands. "I guess I could try." Her chin lifted. "If that's the only . . . I'll do the cooking."

"Start figuring what supplies you'll need to feed twelve hands for four months. In a day or so I'll take you out to a brush popper's camp and show you a chuck wagon." He swung his gaze toward Freddy and Les. "Before this drive starts trailing, I want to see both of you cut a beeve out of the herd, rope a steer, and hit a target with a six-shooter. You've got about six weeks to learn, seven at the outside. We leave the first of April."

Freddy stared in disbelief. She glanced at Les's open

mouth, then back at Frisco. "That's . . . we can't . . . how are we going . . ."

Frisco looked at her with an intensity that made her press backward into the sofa cushion. "In case no one has explained this, here's what you're going to do. You'll herd cattle. You'll ride night watch. You'll handle a stampede when it happens. Not if it happens, Miss Roark, *when* it happens. You'll ford rivers and swim cattle. You'll chase strays." He shrugged broad shoulders. "Before we reach Abilene, you'll have been hotter than you've ever been, wetter than you've ever been, and more exhausted than you believed was possible. You'll be dirty, sunburned, and you'll stink of horseflesh and cowhide. I hope to hell all of you will still be alive. A cattle drive is a brutish, dangerous undertaking, and there are going to be times when you're lonely and frightened. If you think you can't pull your share, if you can't learn what you need to learn, say so now and withdraw."

"We can't possibly learn all that in six weeks," Les whispered. Her face was as white as the lace doilies covering the arms of her chair.

"No, you can't. You'll have to learn most of it on the trail, and I hope all of you learn fast. But unless you can perform the basics before we ride out, you don't go. Those are *my* conditions. If you can't stay in the saddle for ten hours, if you can't rope a steer or shoot at a predator, then I don't want you. Ignorance can get you or someone else killed."

"What if none of us can perform the miracles you're demanding?" Freddy snapped.

He gazed at her from clear blue eyes as cool as a winter sky. "Then I'm out of a job, and you three lose your inheritance. We leave on April 1, or we don't go at all. If we leave any later, the herds ahead of us will have grazed out most of the good grass."

Freddy glared back at him, but she didn't speak. He was calling the shots as if they worked for him instead of the other way around. But he also sounded confident and sure of himself. When he spoke, there was no doubt that he knew what he was talking about.

"You'll handle the money?" he asked Luther. When Luther frowned and nodded, he issued his next directive. "Go over our budget and find me enough money to hire some brush poppers. Five men at a dollar a day for two weeks ought to do it."

"Brush poppers?" Alex asked in a faint voice. She still looked stunned.

"Yes, ma'am. You need to sell two thousand cattle in Abilene. We're going to lose a few along the way, so we'll try to start with about twenty-three hundred if we can. Roark is supplying you two thousand beeves in his will, but he didn't restrict you to that number. Right?"

"That's correct," Luther said.

"We'll pull some extra beeves out of the brush. They'll be wild as hell until we get them road broke, but they'll give you a little breathing room." He glanced at the liquor decanter on the tray near the bookcase. "One thing you all need to understand. You take your orders from me."

Freddy opened her mouth, then changed her mind and made herself remain silent, uncertain why she felt combative when she looked at him. The feeling was instinctive, almost protective, as if the force of his masculinity might overwhelm her if she didn't resist.

"If you don't pull your weight, if you endanger my outfit, then you're out. I'll make the decision, and I'll leave you in the nearest populated area. If you don't agree to this condition, then we don't have a deal."

Freddy stood. "And if you take one drink along this drive, Mr. Frisco, then *you're* out."

His confidence and cool assurance, the way he was laying down rules, irritated her. He should have expressed at least a little gratitude that they were offering him a chance to redeem his reputation when no one else would.

His gaze intensified and a half smile pulled at his lips. "Fair enough." A long slow glance traveled over her black gown up to the curly dark tendrils pulling out of the twist on her neck. His frank appraisal heated Freddy's cheeks and made her mouth go dry, made her want to slap his face. She might have if his stare had lasted a moment longer, but he turned to include the others. "We didn't discuss my fee."

She sat down abruptly, deeply annoyed by her strong reactions to this man.

Luther touched his bow tie and cleared his throat. "What is your fee, Mr. Frisco?"

"I want the steers. Win or lose, whatever those longhorns sell for goes in my pocket."

"What do longhorns sell for?" Alex inquired.

"At current market prices, the cattle should bring roughly thirty dollars a head, depending on delivery weight and condition. That's my fee."

Freddy did the math then joined her sisters in a gasp. Even Luther sucked in a hard breath. "That's sixty thousand dollars!"

"That is outrageous, sir," Luther snapped. "That is not the usual boss's fee."

Dal Frisco nodded. "There's nothing 'usual' about this drive, Mr. Moreland. If we're successful, everyone gets a second chance, everyone gets what they want.

The ladies here get their father's estate, I get a ranch in Montana. Everyone wins except the widow."

"But if we're not successful, if we only manage to get a thousand cattle to Abilene," Alex said through white lips, "then Lola wins Father's estate. And you want to profit even if you turn us into paupers. That is absolutely not acceptable."

Frisco shrugged. "My fee is not negotiable. Take it or leave it."

"I'm afraid the Roark sisters will have to 'leave it,' " Luther said tightly. "These ladies don't own the cattle and won't own them unless they win Joe Roark's estate. Therefore, they cannot pledge them as your fee. According to the conditions set forth in the will, I'm authorized to pay you fifty dollars a month out of the funds allocated for this drive."

Frisco placed his hat on his head and stood. "Then we're through talking."

"Wait." Freddy's mind raced. "If we win, we'll own the longhorns." She thought a minute. "If you're as good as you claim you are, then you'll agree to tie *your* money to the same conditions we're bound to. If we win, you can have the damned cows; we'll give them to you as your fee. But if you can't get two thousand head to Abilene and we lose, then so do you. You don't get the cows, you don't get fifty dollars a month for your time and work, you get nothing. Just like us." Her chin rose and her eyes flashed a challenge. "That's a fair offer, Mr. Frisco."

"I agree," Alex said in a strained voice. "If you're unwilling to tie your fortune to ours, then good day to you, sir."

"You have one hell of a nerve," Freddy couldn't resist adding.

He laughed, revealing a flash of white teeth. "I expect I do." He smiled at all of them. "I'm as good as I claim. I'll run two thousand steers into the Abilene yard." He glanced at Luther. "Draw up the contract, Mr. Moreland. If we take in two thousand steers or more, I get the entire sales price. If we bring in one beeve less, you don't owe me a cent. We all walk away with nothing." He tipped his hat. "I'll be in touch." After a minute they heard the front door bang shut.

Freddy sagged against the sofa back. A rush of confusing emotions pulsed at the base of her throat. "That arrogant so-and-so has forgotten who is working for whom!"

"No, he hasn't," Alex said, leaning her head back and closing her eyes. "From now on Dal Frisco is the boss. We work in his outfit and do as he says." She drew a deep breath. "You had a good idea, Freddy. I feel marginally better that you tied his ridiculous fee to his performance."

Surprise lifted her eyebrows, and Freddy felt an embarrassing rush of gratitude. She didn't remember the last time Alex had paid her a compliment, assuming that Alex ever had.

"He's a tyrant." Les slapped at her skirt as if something unpleasant had settled in the folds. "I don't know how I'm going to tell Ward that we entrusted our future into the hands of a drunk who thinks he's some kind of royalty. And his fee!" A worried line settled between her eyebrows.

Luther stood and began gathering his papers. "Well. He seems to know what he's doing."

"For what we're paying him, he'd better know what he's doing." The odd thing was that Freddy had emerged from the interview believing that he did. She couldn't sort out why he irritated her, which only added to her annoyance. "We are actually going to take part in a cattle drive," she said in a wondering voice. It hadn't seemed possible. It still didn't.

The part of a cowhand would be challenging and physically demanding, but after a minute's thought, she saw how she would play it. The heroine needed to display courage and endurance, needed to be what scripts described as plucky. And learning to rope a steer didn't seem so overwhelmingly daunting when she reduced it to stage business.

Suddenly it occurred to her that Dal Frisco made an unlikely hero for the scenes she was imagining. In fact, this entire cattle drive was stunningly miscast. If the miscasting hadn't been so worrisome and potentially dangerous, she would have laughed out loud.

When she emerged from her reverie, Luther had gone, and her sisters were rousing themselves from a shocked lethargy.

Alex looked at Freddy. "There's no point in moving back to your place in town. You might as well stay on here. This is where you'll be learning to"—she waved a slender, listless hand—"do all those things Mr. Frisco mentioned."

Freddy's heart sank. She had been counting the days until she could leave the ranch and get away from her sisters. Sighing, she said, "I'll send someone to pick up the rest of my things."

How were they going to get through this without killing each other?

CHAPTER 3

How could she possibly manage? Any attempt to visualize herself participating in a cattle drive terrified Alex as much as the fear of losing her share of the inheritance.

"Don't think about it," she whispered, pulling a warm shawl tighter around her shoulders.

Because of a recent cold spell, the night air was chilly, and a slight breeze carried the odor of cattle and manure from the barn to the front porch, where she sat. As a child she had hated the pungent stink of cattle and the unsettling sense of limitless space. She still did. It occurred to her that she had spent most of her life dreaming about escaping from the smells and open spaces of Texas, and she had almost made it.

Lifting a hand to her forehead, she closed her eyes. The differences between the East and West were profound. In Boston, people would be dressing for dinner at this hour, preparing to dine. Here, it was called supper, served indecently early, and no one dressed. Back East, good manners masked a fascinating game of subtleties. In the West, manners and etiquette surrendered to bluntness and convenience. What passed for society in Texas didn't bear thinking about.

What surprised her was how little things had changed during the five years she had been gone. The pervading stench of the cattle was the same, and the brush thickets appeared as dense and thorny. Aside from weathering, the ranch house hadn't changed at all. The only one of Joe's wives to leave no mark on the ranch house was Lola. And thank heaven for that.

She couldn't recall the woman's name without shuddering. What on earth had Joe been thinking when he married Lola? He had condemned his daughters for unconventional behavior, then he'd brought home a woman so far beyond the pale that unconventional didn't begin to describe her. A woman who would wear grey and reveal cleavage at her husband's funeral. Another shudder twisted her lips.

That Lola could end by owning the ranch, the cattle, Joe's property investments, even Alex's mother's silver tea set, made her despair. She couldn't stand the thought.

What was she going to do about the cattle drive? No, don't think about it yet.

She had already dismissed Mrs. O'Shane and everyone but her cook. Her carriage was gone and the matching bays she'd been so proud of. She had discreetly sold all her jewelry except the black pearls and her wedding ring. If Luther Moreland had not included the fare for her journey, she would have had to borrow money to afford the long trip home.

It wasn't fair that her inheritance was in doubt. It wasn't fair that Payton had died and she had lost her leg. She gripped the arms of her wheelchair and fought a scream of outrage that burned in her throat. That she could feel like screaming shocked her, she who had never worn her emotions for all to see. Sometimes it felt as if she had lost more than her leg in the accident.

She had also lost control, lost her famed composure, lost her spirit. These losses frightened her despite knowing that she deserved whatever punishment she suffered.

"Are you warm enough?"

Raising her head abruptly, she watched Les step into the light falling across the porch steps. "The house seemed stuffy tonight," she said. "I wanted a breath of air."

"Usually, it isn't so cold this time of year." Les sat in one of the porch chairs. "I don't know why Pa liked these chairs. I've yet to find one that's comfortable."

It hadn't been enough for Joe to surround himself with cattle on the range. He had to bring them to the house as well, in the form of furniture fashioned out of horns. The ugly chairs and tables made Alex long for her tastefully appointed home in Boston. But unless she won her share of her father's estate, her home would be the next item to be sold. It was the only thing left.

"I'm waiting for Ward," Les said, squinting through the darkness at the road. When Alex didn't comment, Les squared her shoulders. "Ward isn't handsome and polished like Payton was, or worldly, but he has his good qualities."

"I'm sure he does." Until now Alex had forgotten that Les had accompanied her to the lecture in New Orleans where she first met Payton Mills. Slowly twisting her wedding ring around her finger, she remembered that night in New Orleans a lifetime ago. She had been well on her way toward spinsterhood, and beginning to accept that she would never find a man she wanted to marry. Then she had listened to Payton's cultured voice and gazed into his fine dark eyes, and decided she could love him.

"I'm twenty-five," Les said in a low voice. "If I don't marry Ward, I'll end up a spinster."

"You've had suitors," Alex said uncomfortably.

Les fixed her gaze on the dark road. "They were Pa's choices, not mine." She fell silent for several minutes. "I thought Pa needed me."

"I'm sure he did," Alex murmured tactfully.

"Then why did he marry Lola?" Les asked angrily. "Why did he bring her here? Do you know what it was like living with her? She didn't care about Pa." Her face twisted, her outrage still fresh. "She slept through breakfast and often through lunch, and some days she didn't even get dressed. Other days she went to town and didn't come home until late. It wasn't a month before everyone was talking about her. Pa didn't need her! All she did was humiliate him."

"Les . . . Father liked women. In his own way, he even liked us. There was a long gap between the death of your mother and Father's marriage to Lola. He must have gotten lonely."

"He had me!"

"He wanted a wife." There was much about her father that Alex didn't understand, but she did understand that Joe Roark had respected marriage and had genuinely grieved the loss of his three wives. That he had chosen to marry a fourth time hadn't surprised her, only his choice did.

They sat in silence, listening for the sound of a gig coming along the road, until Les asked, "What is it like? Being married? I try to imagine it, but I can't."

"In what way do you mean?" Alex couldn't recall having an intimate conversation with either of her sisters. Part of her wanted to encourage the fragile connection, but part shied away.

Les frowned and plucked at the folds of her skirt.

"Did . . . Payton ever strike you when you disobeyed him?" she asked in a low voice.

Alex sat up straight and gripped the arms of her chair. "Does Ward strike you?" Staring, she watched Les unconsciously rub her left shoulder. "Les?"

"I'm just wondering if a husband might do that. If the wife did something to make him very angry, for instance."

"Payton never struck me." Payton's weapon had been words, and he had wielded them with sharp precision. And oh how his words could wound. There had been times when Alex would almost have preferred a slap instead of the flow of criticism and sarcasm.

"Ward doesn't mean to lose his temper," Les explained, standing and moving to the porch rail. Her pale face disappeared in deep shadow. "But he gets so frustrated. For one thing, the store has lost business since his father died. And you don't know how hard it is for a man like Ward to have to wait on people as if he were a menial. Last week the preacher's wife dressed him down because she found mouse droppings in her sack of coffee beans. And he had to stand there and take it or risk having Mrs. Ledbetter move her business to the new store at the end of Main."

"Did he strike you because he was angry at Mrs. Ledbetter?" Alex asked sharply.

"It's just . . . you can't imagine what it's like to know you were destined for great things but find yourself trapped in a situation you can't escape."

"You're wrong," Alex said softly, touching the hard rubber rim that circled the wheels on her chair. "I know that feeling very well."

"Oh." Les whirled, distress pinching her face. "Of course you know. If anyone understands Ward's anger and frustration, it's you."

Alex considered. Was she angry? Trapped was more accurate. She was trapped in this chair and in a life that had begun to shrink once she realized that every stair step was an insurmountable obstacle. She had stopped repaying social calls shortly after her period of deep mourning when she realized that Boston was a city of steps. Since she could not descend even her own porch without assistance, she had begun to restrict her outings. Consequently, the calls at her own door trickled nearly to a halt. Slowly her home was becoming her prison. There was justice in that, but also despair.

"I think I hear harness and wheels," she said, desperate to escape. She rolled forward. "I'll leave you some privacy."

"Don't go!" Les swallowed, and lowered her voice. "Ward admires you, you know. He'd like to hear about your home in Boston and your life there." She glanced over her shoulder at the gig wheeling into the yard. "After we win our inheritance, we're thinking about moving East."

Alex hesitated. She had not liked Ward Hamm when she first met him during Joe's illness, and she liked him less now that she suspected he had struck Les. But she also sensed that Les was not eager to be left alone with her betrothed. "I'll stay for a moment, then I really must go inside. I'm tired tonight."

They waited in silence while Ward extinguished the lanterns on the gig. If Alex hadn't guessed that Les dreaded telling Ward about hiring Dal Frisco, she would have left at once.

"Good evening, ladies. How lovely you both look tonight."

Les flushed with pleasure as if her betrothed's compliments came widely spaced, but Alex doubted Ward could see either of them well enough to judge their appearance since they waited beyond the spill of light falling through the front door. The compliment impressed her as empty.

As Ward stepped through the light, Alex noticed he wore a broadcloth suit of an uncertain brown that matched the thinning hair exposed when he removed his hat. His collar and cuffs were made of stiff paper but it was a fresh set, not wilted from a day in his general store. Her first thought was that Payton wouldn't have dreamed of wearing paper collars or cuffs, no true gentleman would. Her second thought was that she had turned into a judgmental snob.

Before Alex realized what he meant to do, Ward lifted her hand from her lap and brought it to his lips. The gesture was stunningly inappropriate and presuming. Ridiculous coming from a man who had been wearing a soiled apron less than an hour ago. It was all she could do not to express her irritation by wiping the back of her hand across her skirt after he released her fingers.

"Well, Alex—may I call you Alex? After all, we'll be brother and sister soon." Without waiting for her permission, he continued. "Are you finding Klees as provincial as Les and I do?"

That was exactly how she considered Klees, but she couldn't bear to align herself with an unctuous little shopkeeper with grandiose pretensions. "Actually it's been refreshing to rediscover the charming simplicity of rural life," she lied, a smile on her lips. "I miss Boston's cultural advantages, of course, but a constant round of society can be tedious."

She was laying it on thick and felt ashamed of herself for doing so. It wasn't Ward's fault that she considered him unappealing—his mouth thin and meager, his eyes set too closely together. He was hardly to blame for the fact that she had disliked him on sight. "If you'll excuse me, I'll retire now," she said, smiling at Les and nodding to Ward.

She started to roll forward, but Ward blocked her exit. "I find your observations puzzling, Alex. Surely you recall how smothering it was to live in a rural community composed largely of people of the lesser sort. You did, after all, seize your first opportunity to leave."

His rude reference to her elopement brought a rush of color to her cheeks. And impeding her exit was a petty act that she considered offensive in the extreme.

"Good night, Mr. Hamm," she said coldly, fixing him with the same chilly stare she would have leveled at an errant servant. "Please step aside."

At least he had the sense to grasp that he had offended her. He threw a frown in Les's direction, then moved to one side. "Shall I push you inside, sister?"

His use of the word sister made her wince. "No thank you." Though her arms were tired, she lifted her head and pushed on the wheels. "Good night, Les."

"Good night," Les answered in a toneless voice.

Once inside the door and out of their sight, she paused to smooth the irritation from her brow. Once the cattle drive began, she would not see Mr. Hamm again. Surely she could tolerate him for the few short weeks their acquaintance would endure.

"The whole town's talking about you idiot women hiring Dal Frisco," Alex heard him say. "What in the name of God were you thinking? If you want Lola to have the money that badly, why don't you just hand it to her now? Why wait?"

Ward's tone had altered from obsequious to furious. Alex hesitated, then sighed and shamelessly eavesdropped. The conversation was none of her business, but Les was.

"Oh Ward. It was thoughtless of you to refer to Alex's elopement. I told you it caused an estrangement between her and Pa, and it upsets her to be reminded."

"Are you listening? I'm talking to you!"

"Please, Ward. That hurts."

What was he doing? Alex wished she could see, but she didn't dare move for fear her wheels would squeak against the wood floor.

"Answer me. Why did you hire Frisco after I told you not to?"

"There was no one else. Ward, please. Let go of my arm."

"No one else? Don't you ever use your head for something better than a hat rack? Your Pa was rich. You could have offered enough money that every trail boss in Texas would line up for this job. For enough money, they wouldn't have cared if every last hand was a female. Tomorrow tell your sisters to terminate Frisco and spend whatever it takes to hire someone who isn't going to lose half the goddamned herd while he's in a drunken stupor!"

Les said something that Alex couldn't hear, then she heard the crack of flesh hitting flesh. The shock of it made her jump, and her eyes darkened. Her first instinct was to return to the porch and rescue Les, but she paused with her fingers on the wheels of her chair.

She didn't actually know what she had heard. Had it really been a slap?

In fact, Les was no longer a child but a grown woman, capable of making her own decisions and rescuing herself. If Les felt she needed assistance, all she had to do was cry out.

Her conscience absolved, Alex rolled away from the door, passing the archway that led into the parlor. To her embarrassment, Freddy was sitting on the ugly horsehair sofa, holding what looked like a script in her lap, her head cocked toward the porch window. They looked at each other for a moment, each aware the other had been eavesdropping, then Alex hurried past the archway and entered the hallway.

Inside her bedroom, she removed her shawl and folded it into a bottom bureau drawer. She of all people knew the truth in the old saying: You made your bed, now you must lie in it. Les had chosen Mr. Hamm, and now Les had to deal with the consequences. Alex had problems of her own, which no one was offering to solve for her.

Picking up a cookbook from her bedside table, she placed it on her lap, then rolled to the window and looked out at the land she hated.

Dear God. How was she going to manage on a cattle drive? The coppery taste of panic burned her throat.

Clearly Alex had overheard the same conversation and the same sounds that she had, Freddy realized. Laying aside the script she'd been reading, she leaned closer to the window, but Ward and Les had stepped off the porch and she couldn't hear more than a murmur of voices.

Frowning, she gazed across the parlor at the low fire burning in the hearth. Her instinct was to charge outside and order Ward Hamm off the ranch. But Alex hadn't believed it necessary to intervene. That made her wonder if she had actually heard what she had assumed she had. After all, Les had insisted to Alex that Ward didn't hit her. Maybe the crack of a blow was really just Les or Ward slapping at a bug or a fly. There were plenty of both buzzing around the ranch.

Annoyed at herself, Freddy didn't know why she

was worrying about Les, anyway. If their situations had been reversed, Les certainly wouldn't have worried about her.

Picking up the script, she tried to concentrate, but her thoughts wandered. It was a pity that you couldn't choose your relatives. If she and Alex and Les hadn't shared the same father, very likely they would never have found themselves in the same room. They had nothing in common, seldom liked the same things or the same people. They didn't even like each other.

Leaning her head against the high back of the sofa, she closed her eyes and wished she had not agreed to move into the ranch house for the duration of the preparation for the stupid cattle drive. It irritated her that Alex had taken the largest bedroom, and that Les continually played hostess, seeing to meals and dealing with the housekeeper and maids, then asking everyone if she had made the correct decisions. Once again Freddy felt invisible, inhabiting an unseen place between Her Majesty, the oldest, and Pa's favorite, the youngest.

Well, once this outrageous cattle drive was over, there would be no reason to see Alex or Les again, and that was fine with her.

Setting aside the script in her lap, she wandered down the hallway and stepped outside the back door. The cold night air felt good against her cheeks and throat. Walking past Señora Calvos's kitchen garden, she approached the old magnolia tree that she had climbed as a child. Restless, she circled the tree, then meandered toward the fence that set the house apart from the rest of the ranch, wondering if Jack and Lola were together tonight. Probably.

The problem, she decided, was that she was attracted to the wrong kind of man. Put ninety-nine good, decent men in a room and one son of a bitch, and she'd pick the son of a bitch every time. Sighing, she leaned on the fence rail.

Her penchant for picking the wrong man very likely explained why she kept thinking about Dal Frisco, much as she hated it. What she disliked most was the certain knowledge that Pa would have admired him. Pa wouldn't have cared that Frisco was an ex-drunk. Pa would have recognized a man like himself, a cattleman, a man other men feared and respected. At least that's how Frisco would have been perceived before he lost his last two herds. But Pa wouldn't have put much stock in that fact either. He would have said every man deserves a second chance. Of course, Pa wasn't staking his entire future on Dal Frisco.

Idly she wondered where Frisco was tonight and what a nondrinking man did to amuse himself. Had he already found a lady friend in Klees? It wouldn't surprise her. A man that good-looking, that virile and sure of himself, wouldn't have trouble attracting a certain kind of woman.

A woman like me, she thought with a long sigh. *Damn.*

Well, she'd learned her lesson. No more men, not for Freddy Roark. And especially not a cattleman, perish the thought. She'd grown up with a man who smelled like cowhide and cow manure, who talked cows at breakfast, lunch, and supper. There were cattle in the yard, horn chairs on the porch, and a longhorn's head mounted over the parlor fireplace.

That wasn't what she wanted. If she ever took up with a man again, he'd better be able to recite *Hamlet.* But she wouldn't mind if he looked and moved like Dal Frisco.

"Oh for heaven's sake." One minute she was giving

up men forever, and the next minute she was deciding a future lover's profession and how he should look.

On the positive side, Pa's inheritance opened interesting new possibilities. With a fortune in the bank, she could go to San Francisco, where theater people were not regarded as degenerates. There might be a good man in San Francisco who wouldn't care that she had appeared on the boards.

Of course, she'd sworn off men forever. But aside from that . . .

Dal Frisco popped into her mind again, and she sighed. She was willing to wager her best hat and the pile of scripts she'd collected over the years that Dal Frisco couldn't quote a word of *Hamlet* if his sorry life depended on it. He was insolent, arrogant, and ungrateful. Domineering and demanding; a cattleman. He was one drink away from falling backward into ruin.

He was the best-looking man she'd encountered in years.

And a son of a bitch if she'd ever seen one.

CHAPTER 4

The first thing Dal did was instruct the King's Walk hands to begin branding the two thousand beeves provided in Joe's will. Next, he hired five brush poppers and sent them out to the thickets to cull wild cattle out of the brush. Yesterday he'd heard back from his wrangler, and Grady Cole was on his way to Klees. Once Grady assembled the remuda, Dal would ask him to gentle the horses the women would ride. He didn't want them up on green-broke mounts.

It felt good to be working and productive again, to be juggling a hundred details in his mind. He had a future now; all he had to do was grab it.

Before he cantered up to the ranch house, he reined in and studied the King's Walk spread. The ranch was everything Dal had ever wanted, except he wanted it in Montana.

Touching his heels to his horse's flanks, he rode up to the house, expecting to see Freddy and Les practicing some rope work in the yard. He didn't see Les, but he spotted Freddy between the house and the barn. Damned if he could figure out what she was doing, but he had to admit that she looked fine doing it. The black bodice of her dress fit snugly enough to satisfy a man's imagination and suggested a figure that made him blink twice.

For a long moment he stood beside the fence, enjoying the sight of her and trying to puzzle out what she was up to. She appeared to be drawing lines in the dirt with a long stick, while shielding the sun from her face with a tiny, black silk parasol. When he gave up trying to figure it out, he climbed over the fence and studied the lines she'd drawn in the dirt.

"What are all those chicken scratchings?"

"I am an actress," she answered grandly, twirling her parasol above a little hat that wouldn't have kept the sun off a flea. "I'm blocking a cattle-cutting scene." Stepping briskly past him, she pointed to an X with her stick. "Here is where I enter. The lines near stage front represent the herd. I ride along this line." She retraced a path with her stick. "Then suddenly, a cow—"

"Steer," he corrected, frowning at the lines and x's. "We aren't trailing a mixed herd."

"A steer breaks out of the pack."

"Herd. It's a herd, not a pack."

"See this small x? That's the runaway steer. This larger X is me. The steer darts left, but I'm not fooled, it's not returning to the herd." She dragged her stick along the lines, her brow furrowed in concentration. "I pull back on the reins, and assess the situation. Then I gallop in front of the steer, and he stops, turns, and goes back to the herd." Looking up she gave him a triumphant smile that might have taken his breath away if he hadn't been so flabbergasted.

"Miss Roark," he began. But he couldn't think where to go from there that didn't involve a string of cusswords. Fuming, he grabbed the stick out of her hand and broke it over his knee.

"What are you doing? And how dare you!"

"Come with me." Grabbing her elbow, he half walked, half dragged her toward the corrals behind the barn. Little x's and lines. What the hell was she thinking of?

Outraged, she tried to jerk free, tried to hold on to her parasol and at the same time lift her hem away from splats of manure. Ignoring her indignation, he dragged her forward.

"How dare you lay hands on me? How dare you—"

He almost flung her against the log fence circling the branding corral. "Shut up and watch!" Gripping her shoulders, he turned her around. Instantly, she stopped shouting, stiffened, and sucked in a quick deep breath.

The black steer that burst snorting and bellowing out of the chute was on the small side, but still weighed over a thousand pounds, and the span between his horn tips approached four feet. Through a haze of dust Dal saw three of the King's Walk hands run forward, ropes swinging. Two throws missed but the third was a good catch or would have been if the cowboy had been able to hang on. But the steer hooked left and jerked the cowboy off his feet before charging the men waiting near the bonfire.

"Oh my God," Freddy gasped as the steer ran through the bonfire, scattering men and wood and branding irons without giving any sign that it did more than infuriate him to run through a blazing fire.

Dal leaned an elbow on the corral rail and stared at her white face. "Looks to me like that steer didn't stop on his X like he was supposed to."

She gave no indication that she'd heard. She stood there, eyes wide with shock, her parasol drooping at her side.

Eventually the boys brought the steer down and burned a road brand on his left shoulder. Then a couple of cowboys chased him out the gate, and another steer charged into the corral, a brindle this time, with sharp-tipped horns that gleamed wickedly in the sunlight.

"Well, what a surprise," Dal said tersely. "That beeve isn't following his lines and x's either. And I don't notice anybody stopping and assessing. Seen enough?"

Finally she looked at him, her green eyes as large as lily pads, and nodded. He walked toward the entrance to the barn, hearing her stumbling along behind him. He went directly to the tack room, measured out two coils of rope, then returned to the doorway where she was waiting, her head down, her shoulders slumped.

"I guess you think I'm stupid," she said, blinking down at her soiled hem.

"If you've wasted most of a week drawing lines in the dirt, then yeah, I do." Thinking about it pissed him off. "Have you ridden a cutting horse yet? Done any target shooting?"

"I was waiting for you to tell me what to do!" He spotted the accusation in her eyes. Like he was to blame that she'd wasted a week. "That's what we hired you for."

"No, Miss Roark," he answered, speaking between his teeth, "I was hired to take two thousand beeves to Abilene." He took off his hat and swept a sleeve across his brow, hoping to wipe off the anger along with the sweat. "Frankly, it doesn't take too much sense to fig-ure out that no wild steer is going to follow the little lines and x's of your scene." He stared at her. "I have a suspicion that standing at the corral just now is the closest you've ever been to a longhorn. Can that possi-bly be true?"

"Pa didn't like us going down to the barn. He said it was no place for ladies." The fire went out of her eyes as suddenly as if she'd pinched out a candle. "Oh God. They're so *big*. And the horns . . ." She swayed on her feet and for an instant he thought she was going to topple in a faint. Her eyelids fluttered and when she looked at him again, there was only a hint of her former defiance. "Mr. Frisco, I need my share of the inheritance, but I don't think I can do this."

Well, hell. He didn't want to feel anything for the Roark sisters, didn't want this drive to be anything but a job. But he wasn't so jaded that a beautiful woman couldn't reach him. And her fear reminded him that he wasn't the only one with a lot at stake.

"All right," he said finally, staring toward the dust and shouts billowing up inside the corral. "First, get out of those skirts and get into some pants so you can move."

"I don't own any pants," she explained in a voice that told him he should have known this. And maybe he should have. "Les is with the seamstress now. They're making us some trousers."

Walking away from her, he slapped his hat against his thigh and swore.

He was good at cattle and poker, good at reading a trail. He'd been very good at drinking. But he wasn't good at women. He didn't understand their ways or their thinking.

"If you and your sister don't start learning how to be a puncher *today*, you aren't going on this drive." He stared into her eyes. "If the three of you fail to meet my very reasonable requirements to keep your butts alive, then there isn't going to be a drive, and it's going to cost me sixty thousand dollars and my future. If that happens, I am going to be one pissed cowboy."

"I'm going to be one pissed cowboy, too, Mr. Frisco," she whispered, looking up at him with those huge green eyes. "Because unless this drive is successful, I don't have a future either."

He continued staring at her, fighting a sudden urge to laugh. Standing there in her fashionable black dress with her silly little parasol, she looked about as far from a cowboy as a person could get.

Until this minute, she'd been wearing a chip on her shoulder. Now she looked up at him with a moist appeal in her gaze, stripped bare of her pride. He saw a raw vulnerability that he doubted few people who knew her would have believed her capable of exhibiting.

His swore under his breath. Something about this mercurial woman attracted him almost as much as she irritated him. He put two fingers in his mouth and whistled. A half dozen men turned to look, and he motioned one of them forward, handing him the coils of rope. "Teach Miss Roark how to make a lasso," he said gruffly. "When she learns that, teach her how to use it."

"Wait," she said, her eyes filled with alarm and her voice spiraling upward. She clutched his arm. "I can't . . . those steers are so . . ."

His muscles tightened beneath her fingers. "We won't start with a live one." When she felt his arm harden, she hastily dropped her hand and spun toward the cowboy so she didn't see Dal frown then step back and rub his arm. He didn't want to think about her grabbing him.

Inside the barn he found a pair of sawhorses and carried them outside to the space between the barn and house. Then he went up to the house, and he lifted down the steer head over the parlor fireplace. After a few minutes of tinkering, he'd lifted the sawhorses to approximate the height of a steer, and he'd nailed the head on the end of one, nailed a stick to the other. He beckoned Freddy and the cowboy forward.

This is "Marvin Drinkwater," she said by way of introduction.

Freddy walked around the contraption he'd built, took off a glove and touched the tip of the horns, shuddered, and closed her eyes. Her dark lashes swept her cheeks, a crescent of ink against a milky background. Now what the hell was he doing, thinking about eyelashes?

"All right, Drinkwater," he said irritably. "Work on roping in the morning, and put the ladies up on a cutting horse in the afternoon. I'll get the other one."

As Freddy had predicted, he found Les sewing and chatting with a seamstress from town. When she saw him standing in the sitting-room doorway, her expression altered to one of sullen dislike. So that's how it was. This one was easy to read.

"What happened to your cheek?" he asked bluntly. If she'd been in an accident, he hoped the injury was limited to the bruise on her cheek and hadn't incapacitated her further.

"Not that it's any of your business, Mr. Frisco, but I got up two nights ago and bumped into the edge of my bedroom door." Scowling, she lowered her needle and a length of butternut-colored material.

He gave her the same speech he had given Freddy. And then he waited. When she was finally ready to step outside, he led her toward the branding corral, having decided she needed to see the same demonstration he'd shown Freddy.

The next longhorn came snorting and pounding into the corral, and Les's mouth rounded, her eyes widened, and her hands flew to cover her face. She peeked through her fingers with terrified eyes. When Dal put out a hand to steady her, she forgot that she disliked him and leaned on him gratefully, gasping for breath and trembling.

"I can't," she whispered, staring as three cowboys took down the steer.

The stink of burning hair and scorched cowhide filled his nostrils, and he had to raise his voice above the bellowing outrage of the steer and the shouts of the men. "Yes, you can," he said, offering reassurance that he didn't believe himself.

"No. I can't."

"Not if you don't learn what you need to." Taking her arm, he led her to the side yard where Drinkwater was watching Freddy examine a coil of rope as if she'd never seen one before. Dal handed Les a lasso that Drinkwater had made. "Study the knot. Learn how to tie it."

The two women glared at him as if he were solely to blame for their predicament. He narrowed his eyes back at them because he for damned sure knew they were the cause of *his* predicament. "When I ride in here tomorrow morning, I want to see both of you tie a lasso and swing it." If they had been men, they would have flung an obscenity at him, and he would have returned the compliment. Instead, he walked away feeling angry and frustrated, and calling himself a fool for thinking the one in the wheelchair was going to be his biggest problem.

He found Alex in the ranch-house kitchen, helping Señora Calvos chop onions. At least she was in the general vicinity of where he'd hoped to find her.

"Would you care for a cup of coffee?" she inquired with cool politeness.

"This isn't a social call, Mrs. Mills. If you're ready, we'll drive out to the brush poppers' camp and I'll show you a chuck wagon." The day was slipping away from him.

His instinct was to push her chair, but he didn't. There wouldn't be anyone to push her on the drive, and he needed assurance that she could manage by herself.

At the edge of porch steps she glanced up at him with an annoyed expression. "I'll need your assistance on the stairs. If it isn't too much trouble."

Pressing his lips together, he bumped her down the stairs, then he let her wheel herself to the buckboard that he'd asked one of the hands to bring up to the house.

She halted beside the wagon and fixed her gaze on the horizon, her expression stony. "You'll have to lift me onto the seat."

Silently, he lifted her onto the seat of the buckboard, feeling the waves of humiliation that flowed out of her, then he loaded the wheelchair into the bed of the wagon. The high back and seat were woven of rattan framed by sturdy wood. Hard rubber tires capped the wheels. It surprised him to discover how heavy the chair was.

"I can't spare a man to help you," he informed her as he drove the wagon out of the yard. "The wrangler helps the cook when he can, but it's hit-and-miss. He'll help you only after his own work is done." He glanced at her sharp profile. "Can you push that chair over rough ground?"

"We're about to find out, aren't we?"

They drove the next two miles in silence, then she shifted slightly and glanced at him. "In case you're wondering, my husband's sympathies were Union, but he did not serve in the army."

"The war's over, Mrs. Mills."

"Is it, Mr. Frisco?" She swept a gaze across his shirt.

He shrugged. "No sense wasting a good shirt. You'll see pieces of Confederate uniforms all over the South." He waited a beat then turned it back on her. "In case you're wondering, I served in the Confederate army, but not as a soldier. I served in the Quartermaster Corps, trailing cattle for the troops, usually to New Orleans." Immediately he thought of Lola, and his face darkened. Abruptly, he changed the subject. "How did you lose your leg?"

"You, sir, are an offensively blunt man."

"That seems to be the consensus," he agreed, smiling. "I'm also a man with a lot to do and not much time to do it." For about a quarter of a mile, he didn't think she was going to answer.

"My husband was a professor and a lecturer of some renown." She paused as if she expected him to say something, but he didn't. She lowered her head, fiddling with the braid trimming the bottom of her jacket. "We were late for a dinner party at the home of the university's president. It was raining." Her voice thinned. "The driver was going too fast, and the road was slick. We . . . the carriage went off an embankment and rolled."

"And?" he asked when she stopped speaking.

"When everything was over, my husband was dead, and I was pinned beneath the carriage. My leg was crushed." She pulled her skirt away from his thigh. "I don't remember the amputation."

He thought about her story. "Have you considered a wooden leg?"

"Never!" When he looked at her, high color burned on her cheeks. "My husband is dead, Mr. Frisco. We both should have died that night, but I didn't. I don't want a wooden leg. I don't want to walk again as if that night never happened! Do you understand what I'm saying?"

He had no idea. Was she saying if she couldn't die with her husband, the least she could do was be crippled? Or that her husband's death somehow became trivialized if she went on with her life?

"I don't understand limiting yourself if you don't have to," he said finally.

"If you're suggesting that I enjoy feeling helpless and dependent, that isn't true!"

The color blazing on her cheeks and the ice in her eyes told him that if she'd been able, she would have jumped out of the buckboard. Her chin came up, and she turned her face away from him. "I don't wish to discuss personal matters with you."

"You don't have to talk about your leg if you don't want to," he said. "But you do have to get out of your chair, Mrs. Mills. We'll measure you today for a crutch, and I'll have one of the boys make it for you. Or could you manage with a cane?"

"You have not been listening, Mr. Frisco, so I will repeat myself. I will not use a crutch. I will not use a cane. I can't think of any way to make my position clearer. It would be a sacrilege for me to walk again when my husband is in his grave."

She had a voice that could freeze water when she wanted it to. Clenching his jaw, he peered into the distance, relieved when he spotted the chuck wagon and noticed there was no one in camp. He set the wagon brake, then fetched her chair and lifted her into it.

"All right, there's your kitchen. Take a good look." Leaning against the side of the buckboard, he crossed his boots at the ankle, found a cigar in one of his pockets and lit it.

The ground wasn't too rough here, but she still had a difficult time rolling herself forward over small stones, bumps, and the dry winter grass that caught in the spokes of her wheels. Face grim, she shoved herself forward and stared at the utensils hooked on nearly every inch along the sides of the chuck wagon. There wasn't one of them that she could reach without standing.

"Come around back," he said, not offering to assist her though her arms were shaking from exertion. This entire demonstration was a waste of time if she wouldn't get out of the chair.

He dropped the hinged face of the chuck box and propped the support leg on the ground. She could see above the work surface, just barely, enough that he could show her the drawers and storage bins, none of which she could reach from her chair.

"There's room behind the chuck box to store the outfit's bedrolls and any large items the cook needs," he said, showing her the space. He touched the hoops curving over the wagon bed. "In bad weather, there's a canvas cover." He wasn't sure if she was listening. She was looking at the water barrel hung high on the side of the wagon. It was something else she couldn't reach. "All right, Mrs. Mills," he said, crushing the cigar under his bootheel. "Pretend that you're going to make bread. Go through the motions and show me how you're going to do it."

"You know I can't," she said in a low angry voice. "I can't reach the flour bin."

"That's right." Raising his arm, he lifted a spade from a pair of hooks on the side of the wagon, then handed it to her. "Let's try another exercise. Eleven hungry punchers are coming in for supper and the first thing they want is their coffee. Dig a pit and make a fire."

Pale eyebrows lifted, and she looked at him as if he were insane. After a moment, she drew a breath, then lifted the spade and poked at the ground. Her chair rolled forward, and she juggled the spade awkwardly. After observing several attempts, Dal sighed.

"Isn't there a brake on that thing?" When she shook her head, he swore. "There will be by tomorrow morning."

"I can't dig a fire pit," she said after another couple of tries. She threw the spade on the ground. "I can't do this at all."

"Here's what is expected of a trail cook." Lifting a hand, he ticked down his fingers. "You're the first up, before dawn. You make coffee and breakfast, then call the hands out of their bedrolls. You wash the dishes and pack them away. You make sure all the boys have put their bedrolls in your wagon. You drive the wagon ahead to the noon camp and make dinner. You wash the dishes and pack them away. You drive the wagon to the bedding grounds and make supper. You wash the dishes and prepare for breakfast. If the wrangler doesn't have time to do it for you, you collect wood or chips for fuel, and you refill the water barrel. If any doctoring needs to be done, the cook does it. If there's sewing to be done, the cook does that, too." He hooked his thumbs in his back pockets and rocked back on his boots, staring at her. "Can you handle those duties without getting out of your chair?"

"Why are you bothering to ask?" Even her lips were white. Her hands shook on the wheels of the chair. But no tears brimmed in her eyes, just anger and frustration. "Even if I could reach everything and dig a fire

pit, I don't have the faintest notion how to cook over
an open fire." Lowering her head, she pressed her fingertips against her forehead. "This is hopeless."

"Difficult, but not hopeless," he said, leaning a
shoulder against the chuck wagon. Truly, she was a
beautiful woman, with an elegance of dress and manner
that would have made it impossible to imagine her on
a cattle drive even if she'd had both of her legs. She
belonged back East in her social, cultured world, not
out here on the range.

"I don't know what I'm going to do," she whispered, fixing her gaze on the utensils hanging on the
side of the chuck wagon. "My husband . . . everyone
thought we were . . . but it cost more than you imagine
to keep up appearances, and we . . ." Halting, she
dropped her glove and raised her head. "I need my
share of the inheritance. I can't support myself without
it."

Her gloves had picked up dust from the wheels of
her chair, and touching her forehead had left five dis-
tinct points of dust on her forehead. The smudges made
her suddenly real to him, and he could see what it cost
her to admit she needed something. He stared at the
dust prints on her forehead and remembered how it felt
when your pride cracked, shattered, and fell away.

"I'd give you an assistant if I could, Mrs. Mills. But
we're restricted to twelve men in the outfit, including
you and your sisters. I can't spare one of those twelve
as a cook's assistant without jeopardizing the success
of the drive."

"How can I do this?" she whispered, looking up at
him.

"Get out of that chair," he said, glancing at the dust
prints. "Or don't go."

Turning the chair into the wind, she closed her eyes

and let the breeze cool her face. "I hate this place," she said in a low voice. "The ranch, Texas, the smell of cattle and manure, all the empty space. I hate it more than you can imagine."

He waited, watching the back of her head, and he knew when her pride hit the ground.

"How soon can you have a crutch made?" she inquired in a low, anguished voice.

"The day after tomorrow," he said, standing away from the chuck wagon. He pushed her back to the buckboard. "I'll have a provisioned chuck wagon brought up to the back of the house. Study where everything is and how it's loaded. When my wrangler arrives—his name is Grady Cole—I'll send him up to talk to you. He can tell you what kind of food the outfit will expect. The food on a drive is simple, but it must be plentiful and tasty. Practice cooking those items. Food is one of the few things the boys have to look forward to on a cattle drive."

Alex didn't speak a single word during the return drive to the ranch house.

As if he hadn't had enough woman trouble for one day, he found a note from Lola when he returned to the boardinghouse. Eyes narrowed, Dal read the message twice, then crumpled the paper into a ball and threw it against the wall.

He'd been half-expecting a message from her, so the invitation to stop by her rental house wasn't entirely a surprise. She hadn't been too far from his thoughts since the day he saw her in the Klees cemetery, and he guessed that she'd sent a thought or two in his direction.

Looking back, he was glad there had never been

anything romantic between them, although she'd made it clear that she wouldn't say no. They might have ended between the sheets if he hadn't spent more time on the trail than he'd spent in New Orleans, or if the war had lasted longer or if she hadn't double-crossed him. The times had been crazy.

Long before Appomattox, Dal had known that the captain of the Quartermaster Corp was feathering his nest by diverting supplies gathered to be sent on to the troops. When the end was finally impossible to deny, corruption had exploded into scandalous proportions. It seemed like everyone in the South was scrambling to salvage something for himself, stealing beef, whiskey, tinned food, tobacco, even horses intended for the retreating army, and selling them to the French.

When Lola suggested that Dal was a fool not to profit like everyone else, he had let himself be convinced. The cause was lost. It was every man for himself. Why should the rest of the corps line their pockets but not him? He had let her persuade him to sell his next herd to the French instead of taking the steers into New Orleans to be shipped to the troops.

The first surprise came when Lola's French contact informed him that Lola was holding the money from the sale. Even as he watched the Frenchman ride off with the army's cattle, he hadn't yet grasped that Lola had played him for a sucker.

That realization didn't sink in until the next day, when Emile Julie from the New Orleans City Council arrived to collect the same cattle that Lola had sold to the French. She'd sold the herd twice and pocketed the money. When Julie discovered that Dal no longer had the steers he had paid Lola for, a gun battle erupted. Dal was wounded and one of his drovers died that day. And that was only the beginning of his troubles.

Emile Julie bought a full page in the New Orleans newspaper in which he swore that no one cheated him and lived to brag about it. He publicly vowed to kill Dal Frisco and Lola Fiddler if it took the rest of his life to do it. The crazy bastard meant what he said.

The instant Dal rode into New Orleans, dodging Julie's henchmen, he went to Lola's flat on Royal Street, but the rooms were bare and Lola and the money were long gone.

Yeah, he thought, he had a few things to discuss with Lola Fiddler Roark. But not right away. He'd let her stew a little more, let her wonder if he still wanted to choke the life out of her.

CHAPTER 5

"Please, Ward, just listen." Wringing her hands and stumbling over her skirts, Les followed him down the porch steps and into the front yard. "We don't need Pa's inheritance. We'll have the general store. I'll work beside you, and we'll build it together." Tears spilled down her cheeks. "I can't do this." Halting, she covered her face, shuddering and remembering the steers thundering into the branding corral. She could still smell the hot stink of cowhide, and she was going to have nightmares for weeks about horns that had looked as sharp-tipped as needles.

Ward stopped beside his gig, and even in the darkness she saw his knuckles turn white when he gripped the side door. "That's exactly what your father predicted, remember? He said you'd end up selling sugar and pickles if you married me." Stepping forward, he clasped her shoulders and shook her until pins flew out of her hair. Then he lowered his face next to hers. "You're going on that cattle drive, Les, and you're going to make it work."

"I can't!" She steadied herself by gripping his lapels. "Don't make me do this!"

For a minute she thought he was furious enough to

strike her, but she was so wild and frantic inside that she didn't care if he did. "I can't! I can't do it!"

The edge of hysteria thinning her voice must have reached him because instead of shouting or raising his hand, he hesitated and drew her shaking body into his arms. Petting her, smoothing back her hair, he spoke next to her ear in a tone heavy with patience.

"Les, calm down and think. You're a Roark, too good to work in a general store. You can't end up wearing a soiled apron in a general store, I won't allow that. We deserve better."

Usually when he talked about the difference in their status, it led to an angry explosion about how she was marrying beneath herself, followed by accusations that she thought she was better than him. Then he had to show her that he was just as good, had to prove that her name didn't impress him. He had to punish her for being a Roark, or maybe he had to punish her because he wasn't a Roark. She didn't know what went through his mind when he struck her.

But tonight he didn't react as she expected.

"Les, honey, listen to me. We deserve that money. Now I know it's going to be difficult for a refined woman like you to actually work a cattle drive, but you just have to do it. For us. We've got to prove that your pa was wrong." Resentment sharpened his voice. "We've got to get that money and show everyone that I'm just as good as your pa."

She dropped her head against his shoulder and wept in despair while he talked and talked. Other people had controlled her life for as long as she could remember, why should this time be different? No one ever seemed to care what she wanted. And she always went along, letting other people tell her what to do.

"Are you listening?" He gave her another shake.

"Is it just the money, Ward?" she asked suddenly, astounded by her unexpected bravery. "My sisters think you only want Pa's money." He could so easily prove them wrong. All he had to do was tell her that it didn't matter if she walked away from the cattle drive.

He was quiet for so long that she started weeping again. Of course it was the money. Why else would he want to marry her? She wasn't beautiful like Alex and Freddy, and she lacked their confidence and strength. She would never have found the courage to run off like they had. She had no skills, had difficulty making a decision. Whatever she did, it seemed to be wrong.

"I wish you hadn't said that, Les, because I'm not sure you'll understand the answer."

Even the man she planned to marry thought she was too stupid to understand a plain answer. And maybe he was right. She didn't know anymore. If she was as smart as she used to think she was, then Ward wouldn't always be criticizing her.

"The money's part of it. Now don't stiffen up like that, or I'll get mad." He drew a breath and tightened his grip on her upper arms. "All my life I've known I deserved better than being stuck in a backwater hole like Klees, running a general store." His lips twisted in disgust. "I deserve a fine house and servants as much as you do." He narrowed his eyes on the ranch house.

"Ward, you're squeezing my arms."

"When you said I could come courting, I saw a way out." He stared into her eyes. "Frankly, Les, it hasn't been a smooth courtship from my point of view. First your pa insulted me and tried to drive me away, then he died, and finally I thought we'd be just fine. Then we learned about the damned will. Now you're telling me that you don't want our share of the inheritance."

"I didn't say that." The tears kept falling and she

couldn't stop them. "I want you to have your chance at success, really I do. But I just . . ."

"You see, Les," he interrupted, "I can't support a wife without our inheritance. The store isn't doing as well as it did before Pa died. Pa bowed and scraped, but I won't do that. A man like me shouldn't have to. Now don't cry, it makes you look older."

His comment reminded her that she was long past the age when most girls married, reminded her that Ward was her last chance. If Ward didn't marry her, who would take care of her? Who would tell her what to do? She hated other people controlling her life, but the truth was she had no confidence in her own decisions. She *needed* someone to take her in hand.

Pulling a handkerchief from her cuff, she pressed it against her eyes, trying to stop the flood of tears. "Without the money you won't marry me. Is that what you're saying?"

"I'm only thinking of you." He started petting her again, patting her back. "I can't ask you to work in the store like you were common. I'll walk away before I'd put you through that."

Suddenly she felt so tired that all she wanted to do was return to the house and go to bed. Last week when she'd told him about hiring Dal Frisco, something she couldn't control, he'd gotten so angry that he slapped her hard enough to black her eye. Tonight, when she'd told him about not wanting to go on the cattle drive, she'd expected him to slap her again, but he hadn't.

Opening her eyes, she gazed at the moonlight gleaming on his scalp through strands of thinning hair. "I could get killed," she said in a dulled voice. "I could drown, or get trampled—"

"Nonsense. Frisco is one of the best bosses in Texas. He won't let that happen."

She stared at him. In an about-face, Dal Frisco was suddenly a marvel of judgment and efficiency who would protect her during the drive.

"I'll do it," she whispered finally, defeated. There was no choice, not really. If she didn't agree to go on the drive, Ward would leave her, and she'd be choosing destitution.

"That's my good girl," he said exuberantly, pulling her into his arms. "I knew you'd see reason. And, I was saving this news as a surprise but I'll tell you now what I'm willing to do. I'm going with you! I've already cleared it with Luther Moreland. He says there's no prohibition in the will against me accompanying the drive, so long as I don't help you or the others in any way."

She stared at him in horror. "Ward . . . I appreciate what you're . . . but . . ." He would criticize everything she did. She'd be so self-conscious that she couldn't function.

"Now don't worry about leaving the store with no one at the helm. I'd planned to sell it anyway. And I won't mind the hardships, knowing I'm making the sacrifice for us." When she saw the excitement in his eyes, she understood that the whole evening had been leading to this revelation. "I'll be right there to offer encouragement and suggestions when you need them. It's an inspired decision, don't you agree?"

"Oh Ward. Must you sell the store?" she inquired anxiously. "What if we fall short of the number of steers we have to sell?" She swallowed hard, feeling as if a weight had descended on her head and shoulders.

"You'll have to make sure the drive delivers at least two thousand steers," he said lightly.

Trembling, Les remembered the huge steers pounding into the corral, and her expression went slack. It was inconceivable to think that she could prevent one from wandering off if he wanted to go. She couldn't possibly affect the outcome of a cattle drive. Thinking about Ward's faith in her made her hands shake, and she feared she was about to faint.

Pulling back from her, Ward frowned. "Aren't you going to thank me? This won't be an easy trip, you know. And it won't be cheap. I'll have to provide my own provisions. This is going to be damned inconvenient, but I'm willing to put myself through it for you. For our future."

All she could think about was that he was going to sell the store and leave them without a fall-back position. In the end, it was conceivable that they would both be destitute. And it would be her fault, because he was selling the store to be with her.

"I . . ." she clapped a hand over her mouth and spun away from him. Grabbing her skirts, she dashed around the house toward the privy and made it to the door before she threw up.

It was just stage business, Freddy reminded herself with a heavy sigh, trying again to swing the damned lasso. Her arm ached, and her muscles were sore from yesterday's session.

"Not like that," Drinkwater said, examining Les's knot. "Here. Let me show you again." Les stared at the rope in her hands, then threw it down, burst into tears, and ran toward the privy, her skirts flapping.

"Oh, for heaven's sake," Freddy said to Drinkwater, who was looking after Les like he didn't know whether to give chase or let her go. Les was such a baby.

Drawing a breath, she swung her newly tied lasso next to the ground, trying to get it spinning, then suppressed a swearword when the rope caught in her skirts. Drinkwater played out his lasso and showed her. Again. He made it look so easy that she felt like screaming.

Once more, she fixed the size of the loop before she set it spinning near her feet, careful to keep her skirts out of the way. Then she jerked her wrist and the rope flew up and smacked her hard under the chin. Stars exploded in front of her eyes as she fell to the ground.

She could do this, she had to. On the next attempt she got the damned thing off the ground and over her head without hitting herself in the face. The loop collapsed, but not before it fell over her. She'd managed to lasso herself, but she'd gotten the rope spinning in the air.

"You're spinning it from right to left," a voice said behind her. "Spin it from left to right." Whirling, she stared at Dal Frisco who was standing hip-shot and relaxed, grinning at the rope caught around her waist. He looked at Drinkwater. "Find something else to do, son, I'm taking over here."

Pushing the rope down her skirts and stepping out of it, Freddy coiled it and watched Drinkwater tip his hat, then amble toward the corral. Frisco would have to appear in time to see her lasso herself.

Walking forward, he took the rope out of her hands and inspected her knot. "It occurs to me that we can hit the trail with a few unbranded steers or with a few less than we'd hoped to take. But this drive goes nowhere without at least one Roark sister in the outfit." He looked up as Les returned, holding a hand over her lips.

Frisco spun out Freddy's rope, twirled it on the ground then with a flick of his wrist moved the rope over his head. His elbow came up, the rope dipped down, and he deftly lassoed the steer head that he'd nailed to one of the sawhorses. As he walked toward the sawhorse to retrieve the rope, he called over his shoulder. "When are your trousers going to be ready?"

"Sometime next week," Les answered, rubbing her forehead as if she had a headache.

"Not good enough. I'll send down to the bunkhouse and get some pants up here today."

Frowning, Freddy took back the rope he handed her and extended her aching wrist and arm to twirl it next to the ground. She had the twirling part down pat, even when she reversed the spin as he had advised, so all she had to worry about was snagging her skirts.

Her rope skipped against the dirt and flipped out of control, whipping up and tangling in her skirts again. "Damn it to hell!" She wanted to justify Frisco's confidence that she could learn this. It puzzled her that she wanted him to think well of her, but she did.

He looked up from helping Les. "You learn to talk like that while you were traveling with the theater people?"

Bending, she yanked the rope away from a twist of skirts and petticoats. "I learned words to make a preacher blush just sitting at the dinner table, Mr. Frisco. Pa seemed to think an 'excuse me' wiped cussing out of our memory, but it didn't." She looked up at him while she pushed down her skirts. Lord, her arm ached. "I didn't use those words, though, until after I quit the theater." She shrugged, telling herself that she'd been wrong. She didn't care what he thought about her. "People expect the worst of actors. If a swearword hits the air, all it does is confirm what people are thinking about me anyway. It makes no never mind to me."

"I catch your point, Miss Roark," Frisco said.

Standing behind Les, he covered her hand with his and set the momentum of her twirling speed. Gradually, guiding her hand, he brought the rope up until together they had it spinning over her head, then he tilted her elbow. "Release it," he ordered, withdrawing his assistance.

The rope sailed forward a few feet, and Les's jaw dropped. She stared at the rope, then spun to face Frisco and Freddy with huge shining eyes. "I did it!"

"Keep practicing," Frisco said to Les, before he started toward Freddy. "Of course, there's another side to your argument." He took the rope out of her hands and adjusted the loop, making it look easy. "If I accepted your position about behaving the way people expected me to, I'd be sitting in a saloon right now, pouring whiskey down my throat and feeling sorry for myself because folks only saw the whiskey and overlooked entirely what a fine fellow it was going into."

Freddy stiffened and narrowed her eyes. "I'm not feeling sorry for myself!"

He handed her back the rope. "I didn't say you were. I'm just saying there's another way to look at things." Twirling a finger, he indicated that she should work the rope. His grin made her stomach tighten. "You don't have to like me, Miss Roark. But you do have to obey my orders, so let's see some rope work."

She knew what he was going to do when he walked toward her, then around behind, and to her annoyance, her heart skipped a beat. Coming up behind her as he'd done with Les, he waited until she made herself extend her aching arm, then he covered her hand and wrist with his. For a moment Freddy couldn't move. She stared at his brown hand, and felt the warmth from his palm shoot toward the top of her scalp and down to the soles of her feet.

"Is something wrong?"

He stood so close that she felt the length and heat of him along her back. His boots and legs pressed against her skirts, and his breath fluttered a loose tendril on her cheek. Flustered, she tried to imagine why a cattleman, for heaven's sake, could make her feel hot and shaky inside.

"Nothing's wrong," she said sharply. His palm was square and hard, rough with calluses, and she could feel the strength in his fingers. He had work hands, capable hands, hands that seemed oddly expressive to her.

Fighting to concentrate on the rope and not the peculiar tightness in her chest, she struggled to do as he instructed and smothered a sigh of relief when she got the rope spinning above their heads. When he stepped back to adjust the angle of her elbow, his touch seemed intimate and lingering, and she almost lost the momentum of the spin. She would have if he hadn't immediately called, "Throw it."

The rope sailed forward and she stared at it with the same expression of amazed elation as Les had worn. When Freddy threw back her head and gave a shout of happiness, Dal laughed.

"All right, ladies, keep practicing." Pulling a watch from his pocket, he consulted the time. "Give it another hour on the ropes, then change into the pants I send up to the house. Drinkwater is going to take you riding." When Les's face paled, he raised a hand. "All you have to do today is stay in the saddle for three hours. Those three hours are going to seem like forever. And every day we're going to add another hour."

Twitching the rope in her hands, Freddy watched him stride toward the fence, climb over it, then walk around to the back of the house. Lean wiry men had a willowy grace to them that suggested they might bend in a strong wind. But Dal Frisco had no give in him. His backbone was as steely as his eyes, and that was a problem.

Somewhere deep inside, Freddy had assumed that she and her sisters would go through the motions, but they wouldn't *really* be expected to do much of anything on the cattle drive. The genuine cowboys would do the actual work. She and Les would just ride along beside the herd.

But now, a terrible suspicion was growing that Dal Frisco didn't see it that way.

The brake that Dal Frisco had installed on Alex's chair was a godsend. She found it so useful that she wondered why the manufacturer didn't install brakes on all wheelchairs.

But the brake had not solved the problem of digging a fire pit. And unless she overcame that obstacle, there was no point in even inspecting the chuck wagon that now sat in the kitchen yard. She wouldn't have to deal with the wagon if she couldn't dig a stupid fire pit.

First, she looked around to make sure no one was watching. Then she drew a deep breath and told herself that what she was about to do would not be the first demeaning act in her life, only one more. No one had ever died from humiliation, she reminded herself, then she twisted and squirmed and eased herself down on the ground. Like a worm.

"Stop it," she muttered angrily. "Just do what you have to and discover if it works."

She had enough knee to crawl, and she crawled to the spade, cursing the skirts that kept tripping her up. Gripping the handle above the bucket part, she stabbed at the ground, and discovered she hardly made a dent in the hard soil.

"I see the problem."

Snapping her head up, she discovered Frisco leaning against the chuck wagon, watching. Scarlet flooded her cheeks, and she couldn't breathe.

"I'll be back in a couple of minutes," he said, leaning over and picking up the spade.

After slapping her skirts aside, she crawled to the chair, turned, and rested her back against the wheel on the sunny side. She wondered what Payton would say if he could see her now, sprawled on the ground with her pride in shambles, pinning her hopes on a man she wouldn't have deigned to notice a few short weeks ago. Would Payton take pleasure in her plight? Would he view it as an example of just deserts?

"All right, try this," Frisco said, walking around her chair and holding out the spade. She hadn't heard him return. "I had one of the hands grind the blade into a point." Sitting down on his heels, he showed her. Now the spade's edge looked more like a large trowel. "Let's see if this works better." He sat fully on the ground. "Chop and pry. What you want to do is pull up the sod. You don't have to go deep. Here. Try it."

Finally, she managed to hack out a piece of sod. It didn't look like an enormous accomplishment, but that's how it felt. She rested a minute, letting the heat of exertion recede from her face. When she looked again at the small chunk of sod, her elation faded.

"Give me the spade and I'll show you what you're aiming for. Watch."

He pried out several hunks of sod then turned them grass side down in a circle around the shallow hole he'd created. Alex leaned forward. By placing the sod chunks around the perimeter, the pit was suddenly, almost effortlessly deeper.

"The wrangler will help with the fire pit," Frisco said, studying her. "Very likely you won't have to do this too often, but you need to know how and be able to do it when you must."

"I think I can," she said slowly, hating it but knowing that she was going to be digging holes all over the backyard until she got it right. "Give me the spade."

"You'll have plenty of time to practice," he said, standing up. "Right now, I want you to try this crutch." Reaching over her chair to the other side where she hadn't seen him put it, he picked up a crutch, then extended his hand to pull her to her feet.

"I can't," she whispered, shuddering in revulsion at the sight of the crutch.

"We've already had this discussion, Mrs. Mills. Give me your hand."

Panic tightened her chest. "You don't understand. If I walk, I betray my husband."

A year ago she would have been appalled by what she did next. She pounded the ground with her fists and would have screamed if she hadn't suddenly recognized how badly she was losing control. Horrified, she covered her face with both hands and inhaled deeply. She had to do this. There was no choice. Not if she hoped for a future that included comfort and dignity.

"I hate you," she said softly. "I know this isn't your fault, but it feels as if it is. You're making me do something I swore I would never do, so I hate you, Mr. Frisco."

"Take my hand."

He pulled her upright in one smooth easy movement. Immediately the blood rushed out of her head and his face swam dizzily in front of her eyes. She discovered that her left leg had been weakened during her year in the chair, and suddenly she wasn't sure that it would support her weight. She would have fallen if Frisco hadn't grabbed her. Swaying, she clutched his vest.

"Take your time." He slipped the crutch under her right arm and instinctively she leaned on it.

Gradually the dizziness passed, but now she was aware of the appalling empty space beneath her right knee. No, she couldn't think about that. If she let herself dwell on her missing limb, the scream would come again, and this time she might not be able to swallow it down.

Making herself do it, she released his vest and dropped her right hand to the crutch handle. That felt more secure, but she kept her left hand on his chest.

"When you're ready, we're going to walk over to the chuck wagon. You say when."

Payton was in his grave, but she was going to walk. The thought made her feel sick.

"Put your weight on your left leg, move the crutch forward then swing your leg—"

"I can figure it out," she snapped. Frisco stepped away from her, watching carefully. The dizziness returned when she realized she was standing alone. "I just . . ."

He looked into her eyes. "This afternoon your sisters are going to ride for three hours. When they limp home, they are going to be as stiff and sore as your left leg is going to be."

Something flickered in her chest, responding to the bait he dangled. Eyes fixed on the side of the chuck wagon, she bit her lip in annoyance that she had become so transparent. He knew how competitive she was with her sisters.

She almost fell on the first step. She did fall on the second. Frisco caught her before she hit the ground, scooped up the crutch, and handed it to her when she was upright again.

She progressed slowly, fearfully, and fell again before she reached the side of the chuck wagon. "Will you help me sit down, please?"

He eased her to the ground and placed the crutch beside her. Then he joined her, sitting with his long legs folded Indian fashion. "It'll get easier as time passes and your left leg gets stronger. I know you don't want to hear this, but you need to walk with the crutch as often as you can until it feels secure, until it's second nature."

The enormity of what she had done washed over her, swamping her with a mixture of dismay and elation. "I walked," she whispered, staring at him.

He nodded and smiled. "Don't be afraid of it."

She straightened her skirts on the ground then rubbed the leg stretched out in front of her. "I'm not afraid of the crutch, Mr. Frisco."

"Then why are you resisting so hard?"

She lowered her head and spoke in a low voice of anguish. "I'm afraid I won't want to give it up."

CHAPTER 6

The days turned into a week, then another week and another, and Dal drove the women hard. He knew they were stiff, sore, and hurting, but he didn't have time to waste accommodating aching muscles. By the end of the third week, the road branding was finished and the brush poppers had increased the size of the herd by an additional two hundred head. In the fourth week it rained, and he knew time was growing short.

"Except the women aren't ready," he said to Grady Cole, his wrangler and longtime friend. They stood beneath the barn eaves, watching rain pelt the ground. In another two weeks, like a miracle occurring before their eyes, new grass would blanket the range, and herds all over Texas would head out, moving north.

"Them women ain't never going to be ready." Pulling back his lips, Grady spit a stream of tobacco juice toward a rain-slick rock. "Women weren't meant to cowboy. I've known you most of your life, and I gotta say this is the damnedest thing you ever did agree to."

Dal jammed his hands in the pockets of his slicker and gazed out at the rain. "You know the reasons."

"Reckon I do." Grady removed his hat and scratched his scalp, digging his fingers into a thatch of iron grey hair. "If you wait until them women is ready, you ain't going nowhere."

Dal nodded. "They're making progress. It just isn't enough."

Yesterday Grady had put Freddy and Les up on cutting horses with disastrous results. Both of them had spent more time picking their bruised selves off the ground than sitting in the saddle. Before the day's session ended, Grady had been red-faced and apoplectic, and both women had been aching, black-and-blue, and crying.

But both of them kept getting back on the horses. Dal watched the rain and remembered how it felt to climb back on a mustang who had just tossed you on your butt. As competent hands, neither Freddy nor Les was worth crap and most likely never would be. But he was developing a reluctant respect for their determination.

He was developing the same grudging respect for Alex. She could move from chair to crutch now without falling, and she could use the crutch smoothly. He'd watched her take down all the utensils from the side of the chuck wagon, build a fire from start to coffeepot hanging above it. A pile of rocks was fluffier than her biscuits, but she insisted that she was working on the problem and making progress.

He couldn't fault them for trying.

Still, they kept him awake nights worrying about their state of readiness, trying to think of quick ways to turn them into something nature had never intended them to be. "Les would quit in an instant if the other two did." Les was the weakest of the three, the most fearful, and, in his opinion, the most likely to get herself into serious trouble on the drive.

Grady leaned against the barn wall. "If she don't get

herself killed before we ride into Abilene, I'll eat my socks. And if I don't kill her ass of a fiancé before then, I'll eat your socks."

Dal was still burning about Luther Moreland's decision to allow Ward Hamm to accompany the drive. What the hell was this anyway, a spectator event? It was bad enough that he'd have Moreland and Lola's representative looking over his shoulder.

Frowning, he lit a cigar and blew smoke into the rain. "Alex will need a lot of help from you. Even up on a crutch, there's a lot she can't manage."

Grady squirted tobacco juice through the gap in his front teeth. "That woman don't know how to make a decent cuppa coffee to save her life."

"Unless the coffee can float a horseshoe, you don't think it's worth drinking."

That left Freddy. She learned quickly, but Dal wasn't sure that she learned thoroughly. When she had finally managed to lasso the sawhorse steer by herself, she'd seemed to believe that tossing the rope over the horns one time had accomplished her goal and now she could move on to something else. He had an uncomfortable feeling she believed she was learning parlor tricks that she might someday perform on a larger stage.

A man didn't get to be thirty-two years old without meeting a few women who caught his eye and rattled his equilibrium. But he didn't recall running across one like Freddy, who set his mind and body at odds. Every time he brushed against her, his mind said leave her alone, but his body said take her and tame her.

Grady glanced up at the lights shining inside the ranch house. "We ain't talked about you," he commented, hanging a question mark at the end of his statement.

"I've been sober for over a year," he said, studying the end of his cigar. "When this is over, I plan to buy a ranch in Montana. There'll be a place for you, if you want it." He flipped his cigar toward a puddle, then pulled down the brim of his hat. "I guess I'll have to go get our charges. Doesn't look like they plan to work today."

"Me and the horses will be waiting. Not too eagerly, if you want the God's truth."

Stepping into the chill rain, Dal walked to the house and pounded on the front door. Señora Calvos let him inside, and he asked her to fetch the sisters. When they straggled into the parlor, he stared at their skirts and raised an eyebrow.

"Grady's waiting for you two," he said to Freddy and Les before he turned to Alex. "Why aren't you out back, practicing your cookery?"

They looked at each other, then Freddy pointed to the water dripping off his slicker and answered for them all. "It's raining."

"Why yes, I believe it is. And it's chilly, too. Now that we've discussed the weather, shall we return to the subject at hand? Why the hell are you three taking a day off?" Lowering his eyebrows, he scowled at them. "It's going to rain on the trail, ladies. Your duties aren't going to stop just because it's cold and wet. Now, get moving."

Alex rolled her chair forward a few feet. "I cannot possibly make a fire in the rain, Mr. Frisco." She spoke in the same slightly incredulous tone that Freddy had used.

He lowered his gaze to hers. "So what do you plan to tell twelve starving cowboys when they show up at your wagon expecting a hot meal? That you'll feed them only when the sun is shining, and only if the wind isn't too strong or whenever it happens to be convenient for you?"

"Do tell us, Alex," Freddy said in a pleasant voice. "I'm sure the outfit would rather starve than inconvenience you, but I'd love to hear your explanation of why they should have to."

Alex's eyes narrowed and her lips thinned. "Just shut up," she hissed at Freddy.

Dal was in no mood to sugarcoat any speeches. "Plant an umbrella in the ground over your fire site, dig a pit, and build a cook fire. Get that coffee boiling." He swung toward Freddy and Les. Instantly their expressions altered from the pleasure of hearing Alex reprimanded to stares that suggested they hated his guts. "Mud riding is different from dry riding. Get out there and learn what it feels like." He spread his hands. "What do I have to say to you to make you realize that a cattle drive is a seven-day-a-week, twenty-four-hour-a-day job? We don't stop for aches and pains. We don't stop when the weather turns sour." He jammed his hat back on his head. "Here's how it is. The herd is ready to move. There'll be enough range grass to graze them in about two weeks. But you three are not ready. Mrs. Mills, you have yet to prepare three meals in a day." He swung toward Freddy and Les. "And you two have yet to stay on the back of a cutting horse through an entire session."

"We're stiff and hurting," Freddy said hotly. "We have new bruises every day, and——"

"And none of you have had a single shooting lesson. There are all sorts of predators out there, just looking for a chance to carry home some beef for supper. What are you going to do? Stand there and watch a wolf take down one of the steers you need to get your inheritance?"

"No, Mr. Frisco." Freddy's green eyes flashed. "Since you know everything, I'll call you to come and shoot it, so you can save the steer you need to get your place in Montana."

Her feistiness always made him want to laugh. He liked it that she gave as good as she got. "That might be a workable solution if I planned to ride at your side and nursemaid you from here to Abilene, but that's not how it's going to happen. I could be a couple of miles away. And maybe that wolf doesn't have a taste for beef, Miss Roark. Maybe that wolf would like to improve himself by swallowing a bite or two of actress." He walked past them, heading for the door. "You've got two weeks to show me some reason why you should go on this cattle drive."

He grinned as a wave of hatred hit his back and propelled him out the door.

He wasn't grinning an hour later when Freddy's horse stopped hard and she sailed over the horse's head. If the ground hadn't been softened by the rain, she would have broken her neck. Swearing steadily, he walked over to her, mud sucking at his boots, and looked down. "Get up."

"I can't. I'm dead." She lay on her back, rain streaking the mud on her face.

"Is anything broken?"

"It feels like every bone in my body is broken. And frozen."

He heard Grady shout, "Well, God damn." Before the words were out of his mouth, Les flew through the air and hit hard right in front of Dal's feet. She landed face first and slowly pushed to her hands and knees, spitting mud and shaking. At least they were alive. And he didn't notice any bones poking out of their clothing.

"I detest you," Freddy said in a thoughtful voice, as if she'd thought about it and reached the only possible conclusion. She was still flat on her back, staring up at him.

"I know it, and that's starting to piss me off. This was your pa's idea, not mine." He extended his hand to yank her up, but she refused his assistance. "I'm making this as easy as I can. That isn't a longhorn you're working with, it's a milk cow, for God's sake. And you two have the best-trained horses in south Texas. I don't know what else I can do."

Grady stormed up beside him. "You women ain't gonna be happy until you done give me a heart attack! How many times do I got to tell you. Keep your eyes on the cow! Stop looking at the horse. The horse is going to follow the cow, damn it. All you got to do is keep your butts in the saddle and hang on. Now why is that so dad-blamed hard?"

"Thank you for asking if we're hurt," Les moaned, tears rolling through the mud caked on her face. "We sure do appreciate your concern."

"I know you're hurt, damn it." Grady reached down and jerked her up on her feet. "Do you think you're the first to learn cutting? The first to go peddling over a horse's head?" He spit a stream of tobacco juice. "Now get your butts mounted and go find that cow you done scared off. Drive her back here to where I'm standing, hear me? Shoot fire, I hate working with women!"

Freddy dragged herself out of the mud and hunched over, turning in a circle and groaning. "I'm cold and wet and I hurt all over. I hate this, I just can't stand it."

"The day after tomorrow," Dal said grimly, "you're going to work a longhorn."

Both women stiffened and stared at him. The only parts of them that weren't coated with mud were their horrified eyes.

"Hopefully, you'll live through the experience. And after that, we're going to start some target shooting."

One of them screamed when he walked away, but he didn't look around to see which one.

He rode back to the ranch and around the side of the house. Slumping in his saddle, feeling rain drip off his hat brim and down his collar, he watched Alex.

She was on the ground, trying to coax a flame to life beneath an umbrella. If possible, she was muddier than her sisters. If he hadn't known she was wearing black, he wouldn't have been able to guess the color of her attire for the mud coating it. As he watched, she shook wet clods from her hands, blew on cold fingers, then bent over the firewood again. If a woman could curse with her eyes, then she was cussing up a storm. He rode away when he spotted a flicker of orange and heard her shout in weary triumph.

He had to stop worrying about the Roark sisters being prepared and ready for the drive. They never would be. But if he wanted a chance at his future, he had to take them along anyway.

First, he had to see Lola.

The rain had stopped by the time Dal presented himself at Lola's door, bathed, barbered, and dressed in clean trousers, vest, and jacket, and a string tie. Starlight reflected in the puddles, and the evening air smelled like spring. He'd have been tempted to think it a fine evening if he hadn't been standing on Lola Fiddler's stoop, and if he hadn't been sober.

She opened the door herself and stood looking at him with a half smile curving her rouged lips. The light behind her revealed a plumper silhouette than he recalled, but the added curves only enhanced her charms. Lola was no spring chicken, but she worked at being a woman that men looked at twice, and most men did. Age was making inroads, but she was putting up a fight.

"Well, well," she said in the husky voice he remembered. Leaning forward, not caring if a neighbor watched, she kissed his cheek. "Think you're going to need that peashooter?" she asked, smiling at the holster slung around his hips.

"I ought to shoot you right now."

"Why, Dal honey." She opened the door wider. "Is that any way to speak to a poor grieving widow?"

Taking off his hat, he stepped inside and glanced at her dusky pink gown. "It doesn't look like you're grieving too much."

Laughing, she tucked her arm through his, leading him into a parlor crowded with furniture, potted plants, and geegaws atop every surface. "I never was one for conventions." A man wearing shirtsleeves and a fancy vest rose out of a chair near the fire and reached for his jacket. Lola waved a hand in his direction. "This is Jack Caldwell. He'll be my representative if the cattle drive actually gets under way. Jack, this is Dal Frisco. You've heard me mention him."

Dal hesitated as long as Caldwell did, then reluctantly they shook hands.

"Sit down, gentlemen," Lola suggested, smiling and in her element. "Whiskey?" Lifting a tray holding three full glasses, she carried it to the chair Dal had chosen and held it near his face, letting the dark sweet fragrance drift toward his nostrils.

He looked up at her, speaking through his teeth. "No thank you."

"Oh, that's right," she said, turning to offer the tray to Caldwell. "I heard you went off the sauce." She swept him a look over her bare shoulder. "You sure did used to be a drinking man, Dal honey. We had us some times in those days, didn't we just?"

She didn't miss a trick. Her comments were intended to make his throat burn for just one glass of good old times. And she'd left Caldwell seething and wondering if the times she referred to had involved naked flesh and bouncing bed ropes.

When she twitched her skirts out of the way, he took a long look at Jack Caldwell, instantly disliking the man. He would have known that Caldwell was a card fanner even if Luther Moreland hadn't already told him. Caldwell had the closed expression of a poker or monte player, a man always looking for an edge and the big jackpot. Plus, he had that slick appearance that many gaming men favored. Striped trousers, a maroon vest shot with silver thread, a gold watch chain and a heavy gold ring. Blond hair and mustache completed the picture. Dal wouldn't have trusted Caldwell to give him the time of day.

"Cut to the chase, Lola," he said. "Why the summons?"

She sat down and arranged her skirts, then pushed her lips into a pout. "Can't a girl request an old friend to drop by without being accused of hidden motives?"

"You used me, double-crossed me, damned near got me killed, and then skipped out with the money you owed me." Sitting this close to her, he could see that powder had collected in the lines spraying out from the corners of her eyes and running from nose to mouth.

"Why, Dal honey, clearly there's a misunderstanding here." She waved a hand, airily dismissing his accusations. "Didn't you get my message? Well, I guess you didn't. That explains why you never met me in St. Louis like I asked you to. I waited three weeks to give you your share of the money, then I figured you must not have survived the end of the war."

Dal smiled. "You never left any message."

He tented his fingers beneath his chin and wondered how in the hell he had ever gotten mixed up with her. Had he been that out of control or that starved for a woman's company? "Emile Julie is still looking for you. If he or his men find you, they'll kill you. But I guess you know that."

"Last I heard, Julie was still looking to kill you, too." She brought the whiskey glass to her lips with a steady hand, amusement twinkling in her eyes.

A year ago she would have been correct. But the first thing he'd done after he sobered up was decide he was tired of running, tired of Julie's men tracking him down no matter where he went. Only happenstance had kept him alive long enough to sit down with Julie and buy his way out. The meeting was not a pleasant memory. Pacifying Julie, which meant repaying half of the money Lola had cheated him out of, had cost Dal every cent he could beg or borrow. Julie had wanted him to repay the entire thirty thousand, but Dal had drawn the line at saving Lola's hide. He was willing to buy his own life, but even if he'd had the money, he would have let Julie kill him rather than pay one cent on Lola's behalf.

"Julie hasn't cooled off any," he said, watching her. "He's convinced that we ruined his life, destroyed his integrity, and he believes every single person in Louisiana is still laughing about how you and I played him for a fool."

"That we did," she said, smugly, preening herself.

"You did. I didn't know anything about Julie." Enough time had passed that he could talk about it now. He still burned inside, but he didn't eat himself up with thoughts of revenge. Someday, Emile Julie and his men would find Lola and take care of it for him. "A word to the wise. Don't underestimate Julie and don't think he's forgotten. He's out there, and he's looking for you." She wouldn't believe him. Or maybe she did, but he knew her. She'd outfoxed Julie once, and her expression said she believed she could do it again if the need arose.

"What the hell are you two talking about?" Caldwell asked, leaning forward and twirling his whiskey glass between his knees.

Dal turned his eyes toward the settee. "It's none of your business." Caldwell frowned and stiffened, but he had the sense to keep his mouth shut. Dal looked hard at Lola. "You owe me fifteen thousand dollars."

"Interesting that you should mention money, because money is part of the reason I wanted to see you again," she said prettily, dancing away from any offer to repay the sum she owed him. She waved the whiskey under her nose, letting him see her sniff the aroma before she took a sip. Dal swallowed, almost tasting the liquor on his own tongue.

"We have a proposition for you," Caldwell stated coldly.

Dal kept his gaze on Lola's glass of whiskey. "That's an interesting trick. Caldwell's lips move, but I hear your words."

Caldwell half rose out of his seat, but Lola waved

him down. "Jack and I have . . . an arrangement. Joe's will provided for a representative of my choice to accompany the drive and make sure I don't get cheated. Since Jack has an interest in the outcome, he'll represent me."

"He has an interest in the outcome? Already lining up the next husband?" Dal asked, looking back and forth between them.

Lola gave both men a coy smile. "I'm too fresh a widow to make an announcement at this time, but . . ." She blew Caldwell a kiss. "Of course, I'm not going to stay here sitting on my thumbs while you boys play with my future, not when I got so much at stake. I'll follow the herd but along more conventional routes, and Jack will report to me from time to time."

So Lola would be part of the drive, too, only not as visible as his other observers. Mentally, he traced the stage routes, guessing where she planned to rendezvous with Caldwell.

He withdrew his pocket watch. "I'll give you five minutes to say what you have to say."

"Tell him, Jack."

Standing, Caldwell hooked an elbow on the fireplace mantel. "We know what your arrangement is with the Roark sisters. You get around sixty thousand dollars if the drive is successful and you sell two thousand steers in Abilene."

"Luther Moreland talks too much."

"We're prepared to double that figure if you lose enough steers to fall below the required number. Considering your past history, that shouldn't be too difficult," Caldwell said.

Dal crossed an ankle over his knee, forcing himself not to jump up and break pretty boy's jaw. "Your puppet isn't too tactful," he commented to Lola. "In fact, he's pissed me off. So, which one of you do I tell to go to hell?"

She laughed. "This offer is my idea, I guess you tell me." Leaning forward enough to give him a glimpse down her bodice, she patted his knee. "Now, Dal honey, before you get your balls in an uproar, just consider. Everyone knows you lost your last two herds. And the truth is, it's not likely that you'll bring this herd in either, not with three uppity women working the line. So, this is a generous offer. We're prepared to pay you a small fortune just for letting things happen as they will anyway. All we're asking is that you help things along if a miracle occurs and it starts to look like you might actually bring in the required number of cattle. You make sure that doesn't happen, and we all get rich."

Caldwell tossed back his whiskey and slapped the empty glass on the mantel. "The way I hear it, you're finished. With $120,000, it won't matter."

Lola tapped his knee again. "We'll write up a contract, nice and legal. Not with Luther, of course. Luther can't know about this. The minute I sell Joe's ranch, you get paid. In cash. This is the easiest money you'll ever make, Dal."

Minus a few refinements, like the contract and the amount, the speech was similar to the one she had made to convince him that selling the army's herd to the French would make his fortune. Except he wasn't drinking now.

"I've waited a long time to tell you to go to hell," he said softly.

"Dal honey, you know you aren't lucky, you never have been," she said, holding his gaze. "You'll never get two thousand steers to Abilene, not with three women in the outfit. So why not take my offer and relax? A man has to look after his own interests."

On his last drive, he'd lost a hundred cattle in a single river crossing. But if he accepted her offer and a similar disaster occurred on this drive, he'd ride into Abilene knowing it didn't matter. He wouldn't end up with empty pockets.

"Are you still dreaming about Montana?" she asked, running a finger down the back of his hand.

He stared down at her, seeing the expensive silk dress framing her breasts, and noted the rich fabric covering the chair she sat in. All of it paid for by Joe Roark.

Then he thought about Joe's daughters, stiff and sore, muscles bruised and aching, their hair, skin, and clothing matted with Texas mud. He pictured Alex dragging herself over the ground, and Freddy and Les hobbling out to climb on a horse knowing they faced more hours of sheer agony. Dal didn't believe the sisters had a prayer of winning their inheritance, but if by some miracle they did, they would have done it honestly. So would he.

"You know what you can do with that offer." Picking up his hat, he strode toward the door.

"My offer isn't going away, sugar. You can accept right up to the very end."

Outside her door, he sucked in a deep breath of clear, cool air, then he walked directly to the saloon, pushed through the smoke and noise, and hooked his bootheel on the bar rail. He ordered a whiskey and hunched over it, smelling the fumes and moving the glass in familiar wet circles, thinking about Montana.

Along about midnight, the bartender leaned across the counter to wipe up a spill of beer. "You going to drink that whiskey, mister, or just play with it all night?"

"What's it to you?" Dal snarled, dropping a hand to the gun on his hip.

"Just asking, that's all."

He went back to sliding the shot glass up and down, forming the shape of mountains. Lola had offered him $120,000. But he noticed that she hadn't offered to repay the fifteen thousand that she'd cheated him out of.

Brooding, he let his thoughts drift to the Roark sisters, remembered Freddy sailing through the air and splatting into the wet ground. Thought about green eyes blazing up at him out of a sheet of mud. Her breasts heaving while she sucked air, trying to get her wind back. He had looked down at her sprawled at his feet and he'd wanted to fall on her, rip off the male pants that molded her buttocks, and roll her on top of him. Every time he was near her, he felt like they were circling each other, watching and waiting.

He pushed the whiskey away and rubbed his forehead.

The liquor he'd consumed during his drinking days must have drowned his brain. He'd agreed to a doomed cattle drive that was not going to restore his reputation because he couldn't possibly succeed. And if that wasn't enough evidence that he was stone crazy, here he sat, in a saloon at midnight getting sweat on his brow from thinking about a green-eyed, mud-soaked actress who detested him.

If he still needed proof that he'd pickled his brain, all he had to do was think about Lola's proposition and ask himself what kind of man turned down a no-lose offer?

In some ways, life had been a lot easier in his whiskey days.

CHAPTER 7

On the day the Roark sisters were scheduled to work
their first longhorn, the King's Walk hands started
drifting toward the area behind the pens shortly after
Freddy and Les grudgingly arrived. Until Freddy saw
the men lined up along the fence, her chin had been
dragging, her heart pounding, and, like Les, she was
shaking with dread and half-convinced they were going
to their deaths. But the sight of an audience trans-
formed her. She squared her shoulders and told herself
this was simply a scene to be played, that was all. She
could do this.

"Oh no," Les groaned beside her. "Ward came to
watch." Shoulders sagging, she turned away from the
observers and cast a dismayed look at the ground.

Freddy spotted him standing apart from the ranch
hands. "Just ignore him. We've practiced working cattle. The only difference today is that we're going to
work a longhorn." She didn't let herself really think
about what she was saying.

"We haven't done it without falling off our horses
or making Mr. Cole shout at us." Les lifted her eyes to
stare at the longhorn the boys were bringing out, then
she blinked rapidly, and whispered, "Oh, my heavens.
Look at his horns."

Grady overheard the remark and walked over to them. "That longhorn is a cow. It ain't a 'he.' " He rolled his eyes and looked them up and down. "She's old and ain't got much frisk left in her. Some of the boys over there think of her as a pet almost. Her name's Daisy."

"Daisy?" Now Freddy let herself look. Her heart sank. It looked to her like Daisy was a pair of horns with a thousand-pound animal hanging under them. "Oh, my God."

Frisco rode up to them then, and Freddy stood a little straighter. She wasn't going to give him the satisfaction of knowing that she could barely breathe. Shading her eyes from the sun, she cocked her head and gazed up at him with an expression as confident as she could make it.

"Remember that the horse is going to do the work. All you two have to do is stay on top of him." Frisco's cool blue eyes traveled over her body, then settled on Freddy's face.

"We have done this before, Mr. Frisco," she said, tossing her head.

"And never successfully," he snapped. "Les? Let yourself slide in the saddle with the horse's motion. One hand on the reins. The *loose* reins. And one hand on the pommel."

Grady nodded to one of the boys hanging on the fence. "Bring out the herd."

"Herd? What herd?" Freddy gasped. When she remembered her audience, the hand that had flown to her chest moved on up to adjust a curl behind her ear.

"We're going to put Daisy in the middle of the milk cows," Frisco said, watching her. "You go first. You ride into the herd, cut Daisy out." He jerked a thumb over his shoulder. "Then you run her into that pen. It's your turn after that," he said to Les. Frisco gave them one of those lazy, hard-eyed smiles that rolled Freddy's stomach up in knots and made her face feel hot. "You can both do this. Ride slowly into the herd, let your horse know which cow you want, then let the horse do the rest."

"It's a *longhorn*," Les said in anguish. "Must we have an audience? Can't you send those men away?"

Lifting his head, Frisco scanned the men along the fence, watching them exchanging money, taking bets. His gaze lingered on Ward Hamm before he looked down at Les. "Handling cattle has to be second nature. Most of the time someone is nearby, watching, and it might be your fiancé since he insists on accompanying this drive."

Grady led Freddy's horse up to where they were talking. "Get your butt up there," he said in a matter-of-fact voice.

It was about to happen. And the only way she was going to get through this was to think of it as a performance. Frantically, she reminded herself that she knew her role, and hopefully Daisy knew hers. Wishing she hadn't seen the hands placing bets, she placed her boot in the stirrup and swung up on the horse. And it occurred to her that a short time ago she couldn't have mounted without assistance.

Clinging to this small encouraging realization, she settled herself firmly, trying to look like this was something she wanted to do. For an instant she met Frisco's steady gaze, but she couldn't decipher what she saw in his eyes. He sat easy on his horse, shoulders slumped, his body relaxed as if the hard leather saddle were as comfortable as a parlor chair.

"No theatrics, Freddy," he said in a low voice that

only she could hear. "Just ride in nice and easy, do what we've been practicing, and that's it."

That was the difference between her and most people. She knew good theater. Breathing deeply, she immersed herself in the role. Once again, she was Fancy Roark, ingenue, commanding the role of cattle queen. She'd show Frisco how this scene should be played.

Spinning her horse smartly, thrilled that she knew how to do it, she shouted her opening line and galloped toward the herd. "Yee hah!" She could do this. Daisy was just a prop.

By the time she finished talking herself out of her stage fright, she realized that she should have reached the little herd, but she hadn't. The cows were running as fast as her horse. In all directions. Heading out to the open range. The scene was deteriorating badly.

A man sped past on her right, another blew by on the left. Then Frisco's buckskin cut in front of her. Her horse planted his feet in a hard stop, and only a miracle prevented her from flying over his head. Her heart was the only thing that sailed to the ground. Placing a hand on her chest, she gulped for air, then blinked hard.

Frisco leaned toward her, his teeth bared and his eyes as hard as nails. "You little fool! What the hell do you think you're doing? You ever pull a stunt like this again and you're off this drive, do you hear me? Haven't you learned a single damned thing?"

"I didn't fall off," she said in a wondering voice. She didn't know why her audience wasn't applauding wildly, they should have been.

"Take a good look, Freddy." Anger heated Frisco's face, and his expression was carved in granite. "You just started a stampede and it's going to take the boys thirty minutes to round up those cows." Disgust darkened his stare. "Now get your butt out there and help them. I want *you* to bring back Daisy. You, Freddy. Bring her back here and get her in the pen."

She lifted her chin, furious that he was chastising her when people were watching, and rode away. Before she got Daisy back to the pen and inside, she'd fallen off her horse twice. She'd split out the seams on both shoulders of her bodice, lost her hat, and hair was streaming down her back. She was soaked with sweat and furious.

But she'd brought Daisy back. She'd chased after a longhorn, turned her around, and made the animal go where she wanted it to go. As she slid off her horse, trembling with excitement and exhaustion, she had a feeling that life was never again going to be the same. She had done something that even she had not believed in her heart that she could do.

Frisco rode up beside her as Grady led her horse away. "It was a damned sloppy job," he snapped. Staring down at her, he watched her brush dust and dry grass off her pants.

"But I did it!" A grin widened her lips. She stamped a boot on the ground and spun in a happy circle. "I caught a *longhorn*!" Hooking her thumbs in her back pockets, she rocked back and laughed up at him, her eyes sparkling. She wanted to talk about it, wanted to tell him just how she had done it. But he'd been there, a few feet away, watching everything she did.

"Sometime soon, you and I are going to have a little discussion that neither of us is going to enjoy."

Climbing up to sit on the fence, she cleared her mind and watched Les. Even from this distance, she could see that Les was shaking like an aspen tree. To her surprise, Freddy felt a little sorry for her sister. Especially when she noticed that Ward had moved closer to the fence and watched sharply as if he planned to critique Les's performance later.

Frowning, she watched Les draw a deep shaky breath, close her eyes for a long moment, then ride into the herd of milk cows. Immediately it became apparent that Les was having trouble, too. The cattle didn't gallop off and scatter as they had after Freddy's thrilling entrance. Instead, they moved as a group, with Les caught in the middle.

Swinging her head, Freddy looked for Frisco and studied his expression. He was frowning, trying to decide whether to intervene, as Les and the herd drifted farther away. She thought he was ready to signal the boys to ride out and bring the small herd back when Daisy came out of the bunch with Les right behind her.

Freddy couldn't believe her eyes. Stiffening, she sat up straight and watched Les work the longhorn. Les slid and moved on the saddle exactly as they'd been instructed, her gaze fixed on Daisy, her body moving with the horse's motion. Daisy was riled up from Freddy's run and tossed her horns and tried to break for the open range, but Les was right there, guiding her back, blocking a turn, dodging the horns, and moving her toward the gate of the pen.

Wide-eyed and disbelieving, Freddy watched Les drive Daisy into the pen. And she whirled toward the fence when a cheer went up and the watching men applauded wildly. A frown clamped her brow. They hadn't cheered or clapped for her.

Frisco rode up to where she sat on the fence. "Les did it right," he said coolly, as if he knew what she was thinking. "You entertained your audience—and they'll be laughing at you for a long time—but you didn't do what you were supposed to do."

Embarrassment flooded her throat and face with

bright pink. She couldn't stand the thought that the cowboys were laughing at her and cheering Les. Les! If Frisco had wanted to deflate her and make her feel foolish, he had succeeded.

"Les just fainted!" she said with scorn. Les had slipped off her horse, blinked, then wilted to the ground. Freddy saw Ward climb over the fence and run toward her.

"Every one of those men knows how important it is to obey instructions," Frisco said in a tight hard voice. "Les did what she was told to do. You made a fool of yourself by stampeding the herd."

"You've made your point," she said, snapping back at him and feeling the fire in her cheeks. And she'd learned a lesson that she wouldn't forget. Never again was she going to allow Les to best her. It was humiliating. "I want another chance."

"Not today. Next, all three of you are going to practice shooting."

Suddenly she glimpsed a face along the fence that she hadn't noticed before. She jerked and the crimson deepened in her face. Her hands flew to the tangled hair streaming down her back. "What's Jack Caldwell doing here?"

"Caldwell is Mrs. Roark's representative," Frisco said, casting a contemptuous glance toward the man at the fence. "He'll accompany the drive."

It was one thing to know that Jack and Lola were being seen together, it was another to learn they were involved to the extent that Jack would act as Lola's representative. Her chest contracted, and her stomach hurt. Jack's defection, his betrayal, was now complete.

Sliding off the fence, needing to escape for a few minutes alone, Freddy left Frisco without a word and fled toward the house. She had almost reached the side yard when Jack called to her.

"Aren't you going to say hello?"

Hating it that he had followed her, she turned and reluctantly waited for him to catch up, her heart sinking when she saw him. She had kissed those lips, had tugged her fingers through his heavy gold hair.

"You and I have nothing to say to each other." The rich scent of bay rum enveloped her as he approached, smiling the same smile that she'd found so attractive.

"I know I've got some explaining to do."

"I don't want to hear it," she said. But she veered away from the house and walked toward the old magnolia tree.

Jack followed, tossing his hat and catching it. "Fancy honey, you knew from the first that I'm a gambling man. I have to bet on the filly most likely to cross the finish line. Much as I'd like that to be you, well . . ." He shrugged. "But that don't mean we can't be friends."

"How long were you seeing her?" Freddy asked, leaning against the magnolia tree and folding her arms across her chest. It put her at a disadvantage to know how bad she looked, but there was nothing she could do about it. "Did you start seeing Lola before Pa died? Were you seeing both of us at the same time?"

"Now, you don't really want to know about all that."

He was right. A wave of anger colored her cheeks as she realized she knew the answer. She had suspected he was seeing other women while he was wooing her; she just hadn't imagined that one of them might be her father's wife.

He came up beside her, bringing the scent of hair oil and barbershop and wearing his most charming smile.

"Fancy? Now don't give me that look. We had some good times. No reason we can't have some more."

Suddenly she understood. Choosing Lola wasn't about romance, not with Jack. For him it was always the jackpot. Romancing Lola had to do with Pa's money and who would get it and how he could deal himself in for a share. She had ridiculed Les for being blind to Ward Hamm's greediness, but she had closed her eyes to the same thing in Jack. He wanted Pa's money, and he was willing to accept whichever woman came with it.

Stiffening, she stared at him for a long moment, then she tossed back her hair and walked toward the back door. "Go to hell, Jack. And stay away from me during the drive."

She didn't know which hurt more. That he'd traded her for Lola, or that all he cared about was the money.

The way to punish him for betting wrong was to make sure that he and Lola never got their hands on Pa's fortune. Unfortunately, in her heart she suspected they had an excellent chance of winning. Right now she didn't feel confident about anything.

"I don't see why *I* have to learn to shoot a pistol, Mr. Frisco," Alex complained. Narrowing her gaze, she squinted at the bales of hay he had set up as a target. "I am never going to shoot at anything, so this is a waste of time." She was sick to death of trying to learn new impossible things. Weary of battering her pride against new failures, day after day after day. Dismayed, she looked at the pistol in her hand, surprised by the weight of it.

"I'm in no mood for diplomacy, Alex." Frisco planted his fists on his hips. "We're going to start trailing in about ten days and not one of you is close to being ready."

Les looked up from the pistol she was gingerly holding as if it were something vile. "Mr. Hamm is going to be angry when he hears the drovers calling us by our first names." After sliding an anxious glance toward the barn, she returned to inspecting her weapon.

"There are too many Miss Roarks around here. We're going to use first names." Knots rose along Dal Frisco's jaw and an explosion threatened in his expression. "And we are going to pick up the pace," he said sharply. "Ladies, tomorrow and from now on, you are going to saddle and unsaddle your own horses."

"What?" Freddy and Les said in unison.

"You'll also learn how to make up your bedrolls and pack them, and how to set up a tent in case of bad weather. And you're going to work at holding together a small herd of longhorns." He turned stormy eyes to Alex. "Tomorrow, you are going to prepare breakfast for the household, then drive six miles that way"——he pointed a finger toward the open range—"where you are going to prepare a noon meal before you drive the wagon back here and fix supper."

She hated him. He paid them no respect, treated them like hired help, and he demanded too much. Feeling half-crazed inside, she set the brake on her chair, then lifted the pistol and fired wildly, venting her frustration at the hay bales. Freddy and Les looked at her, looked at each other, and then they, too, fired. Noise and smoke flashed around her, but Alex didn't think a single shot among the hail of bullets struck the hay bales. She didn't care. She fired until all her bullets were gone and the hammer clicked down on empty.

"Stop!" Frisco shouted into a sudden silence. Sweeping off his hat, he threw it on the ground, shook his head, and swore for a full minute. Then he sucked in a deep breath, held it, and finally expelled the air slowly. "All right. You have now fired a pistol and sent bullets flying all over this damned ranch. Now, we will learn about a six-shooter, how to load it and clean it, and then we will try again—and the next time we will fire it correctly."

All three sisters looked at him, and said in unison, "I hate you."

The next morning Señora Calvos knocked on her door and reminded her that she was fixing breakfast in the backyard. Alex sat up and pushed a wave of blond hair out of her eyes, wanting to cuss like Freddy.

And, of course, it was Freddy who was first to criticize the meal that she and Les had been rousted out of bed to sample. "What *is* this stuff?"

"It's sowbelly—bacon to you—fried beef, and eggs since we have them," Alex snapped. The ground was wet from an overnight rain, and she'd had a devil of a time getting the fire started. Grease splattered her dress, and she'd burned the beef. If she lived to be a hundred, she would never become accustomed to handling raw meat; she detested the feel of it. As for the eggs, not one had come out of the skillet with an unbroken yoke.

Les turned a lump in her hand. "I guess this is a biscuit?"

"I usually do better." Lifting her head she stared at Frisco, seething with resentment and frustration. "What do you have to say?"

"Nothing." He chewed. And chewed. "Except, it appears that you probably aren't going to be too popular with the outfit." Raising his fork, he poked experimentally at his eggs.

Freddy set her plate aside. "I'm cold, tired, and I don't like sitting on the ground to eat." Her stare dared Frisco to object. "I'm going back inside."

"You and Les head down to the stables and saddle up," Frisco said, prodding one of the biscuits with a knife. Alex noticed and ground her teeth together.

"When do we get a day of rest?" Les whispered, dropping her head. "I ache all over, and I'm so tired I can't think." Now that the sun was up, Alex noticed a new bruise on Les's jaw. She decided uneasily that the bruise must be a result of working the longhorn. Her mind shuddered away from suspecting anything else.

"You don't get a day of rest." Frisco scanned a slow frown around the circle. "If you're tired, get to sleep earlier."

"Freddy, come back here," Alex shouted. "You don't walk off and leave your plate on the ground. You put it in the . . . in the . . ." She looked helplessly at Frisco.

"The wreck pan," he said to Freddy. "Shake off any leftovers, then put your plate in the pan of water up there on the wagon's worktable."

Thin-lipped, Freddy did as she was instructed, then looked down at Alex. "That's the worst meal I've ever refused to eat. We're all going to starve long before we reach Abilene."

Stung, Alex stabbed her fork into the damp ground. "It won't matter because we won't have any steers left anyway. Not if you run them all off like you did yesterday!" She'd heard about Freddy's idiotic performance.

Alex watched her sister stamp back toward the house, realizing that she had resented Freddy all of her life, and Les, too. While she washed up the tin dishes, feeling sorry for herself, she thought about growing up with stepmothers who hadn't liked her and seldom noticed her. In their opinions, she existed solely to look after their babies.

"What are you thinking about?" Frisco asked, reminding her that he was standing nearby, watching her try to balance on her crutch and wash dishes at the same time.

"Reviewing old grudges," she said, surprising herself by the honesty of the answer.

"It'd be better if you'd review your biscuit recipe instead," he suggested.

She looked up, prepared to take his head off, but saw the twinkle in his eye. After a brief hesitation, she laughed. "I'm never going to be a good cook. I don't have the knack for it."

"Maybe you'll get better with experience," he said, walking down the side of the wagon, checking that she'd retrieved all the utensils and hung them properly. "I know you can't harness the mules to the wagon—"

"No, I can't," she said in a weary voice. There were so many things that she couldn't do.

"So Grady will take on that chore. That's him, bringing up the team now," he added, looking toward the side of the house. "Have you driven before?"

"I used to drive a buckboard into town on occasion." Grady waved at her as he came around the house, leading four mules that didn't look to her untrained eye as if they had been gentled to harness. "That was a long time ago," she said, pressing her hands together and watching the animals. "And it was only two horses."

"But you have some experience. Good. Here's the routine. The minute you're packed up, you follow the pilot to the nooning camp. The trail to Abilene is well marked, so we'll rotate the pilot's assignment. Some days it will be me. Most days the pilot will be someone I trust to choose a good site, usually beside water if we can manage it. And we'll always set up camp to the left of the bedding or grazing ground so the hands know where the food is and where to find their bedrolls. After the pilot decides on the campsite, he'll leave you and hightail it back to the herd."

Her face paled. "I'll be alone out there? On the range?" She couldn't think of anything worse.

"The remuda follows you. Grady won't be far behind."

Her relief was followed by concern. "Just how fast will I be traveling to stay ahead of the herd?" How fast did cattle move? She had no idea.

Frisco grinned and her heart plummeted. "The pilot sets the pace, and your job is to keep up with him. You'll see."

The next two hours were the most harrowing Alex had endured since the accident that killed Payton and crushed her leg. The minute she followed Frisco out of the yard and onto the open range, she lost control of the galloping mules and could only hang on for dear life. The mules sighted on Frisco's horse, and the race began. Alex braced her leg against the wagon's front fender, clutched the reins, and prayed she wouldn't fly out of the seat. The din of pounding hooves and rattling utensils crashed in her ears, she bounced around the seat like dice in a cup, dust plumed around her, and she was absolutely and completely terrified.

When Frisco finally stopped, and she managed to halt her team, she covered her face and burst into hysterical sobbing. He didn't say anything, just leaned against the wheel, smoked, and waited her out.

"I can't do this," she said when she could speak.

She'd lost her hat, the sleeve of her jacket had ripped loose, her leg was trembling violently from bracing against the front fender, and she was certain that she had a dozen bruises. Finding her handkerchief, she blotted her eyes and blew her nose. "That was the most horrifying ride I've had since . . . all I could think about was the accident! And Payton, and . . ."

Now Frisco reached up and lifted her down, handing her the crutch to lean on until he unloaded her chair. "Each one of you insists that you can't do anything . . . and then you do it."

"Not this time. Dal, please. I don't ever want to have a ride like that again." She turned her face toward the side of the chuck wagon because looking out at a sea of open space made her feel dizzy. Too late she realized that she'd called him by his first name. "I kept reliving that terrible moment when the carriage began to tip, and I knew it would go over." Shuddering, she closed her eyes and felt hot tears swim up against her lids. "Then seeing Payton lying there so still, and the rain coming down in his face . . ."

Frisco rolled her chair up behind her. "Do you want me to tell you that you don't have to go? Is that what you're looking for, Alex?" he said, walking around the chair to look at her. "All right, stay at the ranch, go back East, do whatever you want. No one is forcing you to participate. That's your choice. But if you do choose to go on this drive, then stop fighting and do what you have to do."

She sank into the chair gratefully, taking the weight off her leg, which was still shaking. When she'd fought down the tears, she opened her eyes and stared at him. He was sitting on the ground in front of her, his wrists crossed on top of raised knees.

The accident that had ruined her life meant nothing

to him. He didn't care what she was feeling, or how hard it was to do the things he demanded. "All you care about is the money."

He nodded after a minute. "I'm here for the same reason you are."

A flush lit her cheeks, and she looked away from him, embarrassed that a moment of superiority had made her forget that the money drove them all. There was no choice about whether she would participate in the drive, and he knew it. Angry, she pressed her lips together and rolled forward a few feet, hating it that he would watch her crawl out of her chair and creep on the ground. "I'm going to dig a fire pit."

"Good," he said, leaning against the wagon and patting his pockets, looking for a cigar. "Pretend that a dozen hungry punchers will show up in about four hours."

The soil was compacted here and heavier than it was behind the ranch house. By the time she hacked out the sod, she was sweating and her arms ached. But she had a fire pit. Turning to tell him, she realized her position on the ground gave her a good view of the hammock beneath the wagon, the cooney, they called it. A gasp caught in her throat.

"The wood is gone!" The wild ride across the range must have jolted out the supply of kindling and firewood and left it scattered behind them. Her mind went blank, and she couldn't conceive how it would be possible to build a fire.

Frisco lifted down a sack and a stick with a nail exposed at the end. Alex had noticed this peculiar tool before and hadn't a notion what it was or how it might be used.

"You aren't the first cook to find himself without firewood." He dropped the sack in her lap and handed her the stick with the nail. "So, you build a fire with prairie coal."

"And what might that be?"

"Cow pies. The drier the better." When her mouth dropped open, he smiled. "No, the food won't taste like manure, unless you drop some of it inside your pots."

She understood at once. He expected her to roll out onto the range, hook up dried manure, and collect it in the sack. A shudder ran down her spine. After today, she would have no pride.

Hands shaking on the wheels of her chair, she blinked hard and rolled away from the wagon. This was the worst. She had no farther to fall; she had hit bottom.

"Well, Payton. If you were seeking revenge," she whispered, glancing toward the high thin haze floating below heaven, "today you have it."

Expressionless, scarcely aware of the tears slipping down her cheeks, she stabbed a powdery circle of manure with the nail, then scraped it into the sack on her lap.

CHAPTER 8

It was a sullen group that assembled in the ranch house parlor the evening before the drive began. Freddy stood near the doorway with Grady and two of Frisco's top hands. There were nine drovers in the room, all lean, iron-muscled men with weathered faces and work-hardened hands. They studied Freddy, Alex, and Les with sidelong glances and with the same curiosity and doubt as she focused on Frisco and Lola, who sat at the front of the room.

As much as she disliked Ward Hamm, who leaned next to Les on the sofa, his store was a gathering place for the town gossips. The tidbit that he'd passed on to Les was alarming, Freddy thought, looking slowly from Frisco's face to Lola's smirk. She didn't know what to make of Ward's information, but she intended to find out before the herd headed north tomorrow.

Skipping her gaze over Luther Moreland and his ubiquitous lapful of papers, she finally let herself glance at Jack Caldwell. He had been trying to catch her eye, but she had carefully avoided him until she was certain his attention was elsewhere. Tonight he was resplendent in striped trousers, a crimson-brocade vest, and snowy cravat. The contrast between Jack and Dal

Frisco was stark. Dal wore work pants tucked into high riding boots, a faded grey shirt, and a worn leather vest. Yet Frisco was the man her gaze continually returned to.

There was no mistaking who wielded the authority at this meeting. Frisco effortlessly controlled the room though he hadn't spoken other than to greet everyone as they arrived. When he rolled back his shoulders and hooked his thumbs in his back pockets, everyone fell silent and looked toward the front of the room.

"I want everyone in their places at sunup. Caleb, you'll ride pilot," he said to Caleb Webster, and Freddy leaned forward to examine a tall man with pleasant features. "Alex, you'll follow Caleb with the chuck wagon, and Grady will be right behind you with the remuda." Next he spoke to the punchers, assigning them swing or flank positions before he considered Freddy and Les. "You two will ride drag, and I'll check on you when I can."

"What is drag?" Freddy asked. Heat rose in her cheeks as she saw the drovers shift uneasily, and Lola and Jack exchanged an amused smirk. So far Lola had not addressed a single word to her stepdaughters, which was fine with Freddy. She hoped the woman choked on the cup of punch she held in her lap.

"Drag is the tail end of the herd. Your job is to keep the stragglers moving." Now Frisco glanced at Luther and swept cold eyes across Jack Caldwell. "I understand you two will share a wagon and Mr. Hamm will drive his own rig." Frisco focused on Jack. "The rule is, no gambling and no liquor on this drive."

Jack leaned back in his chair. "I've never seen any harm in a friendly game."

"And I've never seen a friendly game," Frisco said. "Break the rule, and you're gone. Mrs. Roark will have

to appoint another representative." Now his steady
eyes settled on Ward. "The same applies to you. With
the added promise that if you interfere with the herd or
with my drovers in any way, you're out. You observe,
and that's all."

Ward puffed himself up and scowled. "Naturally I
expect to spend time with my fiancée."

"If she has the energy to socialize after her work is
finished, I have no objection. But if her work suffers,
I'll warn her. If I have to warn her twice, you're both
out. Is that understood?"

Red-faced and embarrassed, Les nodded. Ward just
stared with resentment.

"Everyone here is familiar with Joe Roark's will.
We're starting this drive with two thousand, two hundred and twelve steers. I wish the brush poppers could
have found us more wild beeves because we're not allowed to purchase replacements for any we lose along
the way. A ten percent margin isn't comfortable, but
that's what we have to work with."

Grady stepped forward. "Can we keep any strays
that wander into our herd?"

"That wouldn't be fair, Mr. Cole, now would it?"
Lola waved a finger at Grady like he'd been a naughty
boy, the gesture enough to make Freddy gag.

"Luther? We need a ruling on this issue." Frisco
waited for Luther to refer to Joe's will.

"There's no proviso against accepting strays into the
herd," Luther said finally.

Lola dug her elbow into Jack's ribs, and he sat up
straight. "As Mrs. Roark's representative, I object.
What's to prevent Frisco or his men from collecting
strays all along the trail? That's cheating." Lola nodded vigorous agreement.

"If we pick up ten strays along the way, that's about five more than I'd normally expect," Frisco said.

Luther spoke earnestly to Lola and Jack. "The only prohibition is against the Roark sisters buying more cattle than they start with."

Lola didn't take the decision well. She flounced her curls and pushed her lips into a pout.

Frisco let his gaze rest briefly on the faces of those who would participate in the drive. "While I acknowledge Mrs. Roark's interest in the drive's outcome, let me remind you that everyone in this outfit works for the Roark sisters. The Roark sisters hired us to get two thousand beeves to Abilene, and that's what we're going to do. I don't have to tell you boys that we'll lose a few along the way, and you know what our margin is. So treat each of those steers like he's the one that will make the difference between success or failure." Rocking back on his heels, he gazed hard at each of his drovers as if he were confirming his choices. "That's it. Before I ride back to town, I want to speak to Les, Alex, and then Freddy. Les? Shall we step outside?"

Ward jumped up when Les did and started toward the door. Frisco leaned in to him, almost nose to nose. "None of my drovers comes with a partner attached at the hip, and that includes Les. I want to talk to her. Not you."

Freddy stepped forward, extending a cup and enjoying Ward's purple-faced anger. "More punch?" she asked sweetly. If he called her sister, she planned to throw it on him.

Glad to escape the crowded, overheated room, Les paused and inhaled a long breath of crisp night air before she followed Mr. Frisco down the porch steps.

"I assure you that Mr. Hamm won't interfere," she said in an anxious voice, struggling against an urge to apologize for Ward. "He's as interested in our success as we are."

Frisco led her to the fence separating the house from the outbuildings and leaned his arms on the top rail, gazing toward the barn's dark silhouette. "You've come a long way and you've learned a lot. But it takes years to make a cowboy, not a few weeks. You've never seen a stampede, haven't swum a herd." Taking off his hat, he pushed a hand through his hair. "There's a lot you'll have to learn on the trail, that can't be helped. The last time I took a herd north, two men died, Les. It's a dangerous undertaking even for seasoned hands, which you aren't." Now he turned his head to gaze at her pale face. "If you have any misgivings, let's hear them right now."

"Every day I tell myself that I can't do this. And frankly, I'm scared to death," she whispered, pulling pieces of splintered wood off of the fence rail. "But I don't have a choice."

His gaze moved along the bruise on her jaw, then dropped to the dark mark around her wrist. "Learning has been harder on you physically than the others, and that worries me. Do you consider yourself prone to accidents?"

The question astonished her until she realized that was how he accounted for the extra bruising that showed up on her face and wrists. "I guess I am," she answered carefully.

He sighed and nodded, then straightened and looked down at her. "Keep practicing the basics. And Les . . . try to hold the socializing to a minimum. A tired cowboy is dangerous to himself and everyone else."

When she reported the conversation to Ward before

he climbed in his gig, he slapped a fist in his palm and swore. "Already he's trying to keep us apart. Well, it won't work." He looked at her. "Aren't you going to wish me good luck?" he asked, one hand on the fender of the gig. "I've sold the store, and I've rearranged my life. I'm making this sacrifice for us, and it isn't easy."

"At least you don't have to herd longhorns," she said lightly, suppressing a sigh.

"Is that a criticism?" His eyes narrowed into a look she knew only too well.

"No," she said hastily, placing a hand on his chest. "I just meant that a cattle drive doesn't sound easy for anyone involved. That's all. I know how hard this will be for you."

And it would be, she reminded herself. Hunched over the seat of a wagon all day would be terribly uncomfortable and lonely. He and Luther and Mr. Caldwell had agreed to share a camp near the main outfit's site, but a man like Ward would never spend a minute in conversation with a low character like Jack Caldwell if he didn't have to, and he considered Luther the most boring individual in Klees. He would need her company after the sun sank.

"Well," he said, stepping into the gig and reaching for the reins, "tomorrow our destiny begins." Occasionally he made grand statements like this one, and it always made her uncomfortable. "I hope the drive is successful. I'll hold you responsible if it isn't."

He tossed out the last remark in a light voice as if he were joshing her. But Les suspected he meant it. Twisting her hands against her waist and chewing her bottom lip, she watched the road until the darkness swallowed his gig.

Slowly, she returned to the house, anticipating her

last night in a real bed for a very long while. With all her heart she dreaded tomorrow.

"Grady tells me that you've been driving the chuck wagon around the ranch like some kind of hell cart, and making him eat five meals a day."

Alex rolled her chair close to the wheel of the chuck wagon and touched the wooden spokes. "I'm taking your advice, Mr. Frisco. Trying to set my fears aside and do what I must." She started every day with a lump of fear clogging her throat and went to bed at night with the same lump, only it felt larger.

Tilting his head back, he considered the stars shining in a black sky. "Going to be clear tomorrow." He let a silence stretch between them while she fidgeted with the wheels of her chair. "This trip is going to be hard on you, harder yet on your pride." She knew he referred to that nemesis of her life, the demeaning fire pit, and the crawling on the ground it necessitated. "Can you go the distance, Alex?"

Could she? Was there a point at which she wouldn't be able to take it anymore? When she would give up?

"I don't have a choice," she said in a low voice. Remembering Ward Hamm's gossip, she lifted her head. "Will you go the distance, Mr. Frisco?"

He laughed. "I don't have any choice either. We've all got a lot riding on the success of this drive."

"In your honest opinion, Mr. Frisco, what are our chances of success?" Her hands tightened in her lap. "I don't wish to put myself through this ordeal if there's no real possibility that we'll succeed."

She had been driving the wagon at breakneck speeds just as he'd said, practicing at handling her terror, and she was covered with bruises and small scrapes. Her fingers were burned from lifting hot pans and lids, her nails broken. Her leg ached and throbbed from standing and walking with the crutch. She was sore all over. Even her eyelids stung from worrying instead of sleeping at night. And all of this had happened before the drive even began.

"I can't guarantee success," he said finally. "Too many things can happen. We're going to lose some beeves, that's a given. I can't promise that we'll get two thousand steers from here to Abilene. But we're going to try like hell."

"I see." She wanted ironclad promises, unbreakable guarantees. But they didn't exist.

"Good night, Mr. Frisco," she whispered, turning her chair toward the back door.

Freddy waited for him in front, rocking on the porch swing and listening to the deep-throated frog sounds of spring. The weather was still fickle, warm and sweet one day, wet and chilly the next, but the days were longer now.

As if her thoughts conjured him, she heard Dal's boots on the porch steps and looked up as he sat in the swing beside her. Instantly she frowned. She had expected him to take one of the horn chairs. Edging slightly away from the muscled heat of his thigh and the scent of leather and cigars and that indefinable clean scent of a man who lived his life outdoors, she arranged her skirts and tried to decide if she should just blurt out the question, or wait for an opening.

"You worry me the most," he said, not mincing words on a cordial beginning. "This cattle drive isn't a theater production staged for your personal amusement or enjoyment. You're not along to provide entertainment for the drovers, you're there to work. And work well, not the half-hearted effort you've been putting in."

Gasping, she shifted to face him. "I'm holding my own!"

He stared at her in the light falling through the window behind them. "You have the most potential, Freddy, but you aren't using it. You let Les set the pace, and you keep up with her, but with your natural ability, you should be able to rope better, shoot better, and ride better."

"Believe it or not, I don't plan to make cowboying my life's work! And I don't need to rope better, shoot better, or ride better to portray those actions on the stage."

"Is that what you intend to do when this is over? Return to the stage?"

"I plan to buy a theater in San Francisco with my share of the inheritance. Wouldn't that be something?" Excitement sparkled in her eyes. "The dream of a lifetime. And it would be my theater, so I could pick whatever role I wanted, and no one could say I wasn't ready to play it." She saw herself standing before a maroon-velvet curtain, bowing graciously and bending to pick up one of the many bouquets showering the stage. The dream was so real she could almost hear the applause.

"None of that will happen unless we get the herd to Abilene."

They were back to the criticism. "I'm not the only drover on this drive," she said defensively. Why did he always have to poke and prod until he made her angry?

"One careless puncher can cost the outfit several hundred steers. I've seen it happen. Or a cowboy who thinks he knows more than the trail boss and thereby makes a fatal mistake. I don't want a maverick on this trip, Freddy. And that's you."

"You can't stop me from going!" she said, anger blazing in her eyes.

"Yeah, I can." They locked gazes. "And I can put you off the drive along the way. My problem is this: Can I trust you to follow instructions?"

There it was, the opening she'd been waiting for. "How do we know if we can trust you?"

His eyebrows clamped into a frown. "I'd say it's a little late to question my reliability. That issue was decided the day you hired me. What the hell are you talking about?"

There had to be something wrong with her, Freddy decided, because the angry intensity in his eyes made her cheeks grow hot and stirred her physically, something she did not want.

Lifting her chin, she looked directly into his steady stare. "Mr. Hamm says he heard that you went to Lola's house. He says you kissed Lola on her front porch, then went inside and stayed for over an hour." Standing, she looked down at him. "Can you explain that?"

"Lay it out, Freddy. Exactly what are you accusing me of?"

"I'd prefer not to accuse you of anything." Oddly, this was true, and it was an about-face from her initial reaction to the news. "My sisters and I prefer to give you a chance to explain. Then we'll decide if this drive actually moves out tomorrow."

Ward's gossip about Frisco and Lola had struck her like a blow in the stomach, and raised confusing thoughts of yet another betrayal. Then she had realized that she had no claim on Dal Frisco nor he on her. Yet, she couldn't bear to imagine him with Lola or any other woman.

"I went to Mrs. Roark's house at her invitation to meet her representative, Jack Caldwell," he said, sitting back in the swing. At once Freddy understood that standing had been a mistake. The light from the window revealed her expression, but hid his.

"Is it true that you kissed Lola?"

With a sinking heart she realized that he remained silent too long. Slowly the air ran out of her chest, and she sat down, wishing she hadn't volunteered for this confrontation. Wishing she understood why Dal Frisco mattered so much and when and how such a thing had happened.

"I knew Lola during the war," he said at length.

She gazed at the hard lines of his profile. "I see." Jealousy burned the lining of her stomach and made her fists clench. Only by reminding herself that her future was at stake did she manage to force those feelings aside.

"No, you don't see," he objected angrily. "Lola and I were business partners in a deal that went sour. Lola double-crossed me and damned near got me killed."

"But you kissed her at the door," Freddy insisted, wishing he'd deny it.

"You know Lola; you figure out who kissed who." Standing, he gazed down at her and the light from the window illuminated the anger thinning his mouth. "If you don't trust me, then you aren't going to believe anything I tell you. But you know my history, and maybe you'll believe that I have a hell of a lot at stake in making this drive successful." His eyes glittered. "You don't have to trust that I'll put your interests first, but you can sure as hell trust that I'll put my interests first. If I don't get this herd to Abilene, I'm finished. There won't be another second chance."

He'd taken offense at her reasonable demand for an explanation, and that made her angry. Feeling at a disadvantage because he was looming over her, she jumped to her feet. "We have a right to know if something is going on behind our backs," she said sharply. "You have to know it looks bad to us, you toadying up to the person who stands to gain if we fail. What were we supposed to think about you going to her place and kissing her?"

His hands opened and closed at his sides as he stared down into her face, then he grabbed her waist and pulled her roughly against him. She felt the heat and the hardness of him, the long muscular power of his taut body. And she drew a quick breath when, wide-eyed, she looked into the angry intensity blazing in his eyes.

His mouth came down on hers hard and hot and deliberate. His kiss was so unexpected that Freddy went limp in his arms with shock. She didn't fight or protest, couldn't move or breathe. No one had ever kissed her like this, selfishly, unemotionally, taking with no thought of giving. This kiss was hungry, domineering, something that seared and scorched physically and left her mind reeling.

When his mouth released her, his fingers dug into her waist, holding her hard against his hips, and he looked down at her with icy eyes. "That should prove that sometimes a kiss means absolutely nothing." He almost shoved her away from him. "Good night, Frederick."

Dal rode directly to the saloon and spent the remainder of the evening staring into a shot glass. If Ward

Hamm had walked through the doors, he would have broken every bone in the bastard's sanctimonious body. Hamm had planted a seed of doubt that would blossom into malignant suspicions if the drive failed to be successful. If the drive failed, people would believe he'd cut a deal with Lola.

Raising the shot glass, he remembered saying that he wouldn't take the Roark sisters unless they were ready. Well, they weren't close to ready. Already he had compromised himself.

Staring at himself in the mirror above the back bar, he looked at the whiskey glass hovering in front of his lips. One for the road, and maybe another, then all the worries went away. He was a few swallows from a good night's sleep.

On the other hand—suppose he actually did drive two thousand head into the pens at Abilene. If he succeeded, he would become a legend. No one would remember the herds that Dal Frisco had lost; and no one would forget the herd that he ran into Abilene against all odds.

Slowly he lowered the shot glass and placed it on the bar. Not tonight.

After spinning two bits across the countertop, he walked outside and released a long breath, looking up at the stars. Tomorrow night he'd see those stars from his bedroll. With Freddy Roark sleeping an arm's length away.

CHAPTER 9

The long road to Abilene began a mile from the ranch house.

Frisco waved his hat at the pilot, and Caleb Webster took off like a bullet, galloping north, with Alex racing her team after him. Freddy's mouth dropped as the chuck wagon flew past her, utensils flapping and banging on the sides, Alex's chair threatening to break from the ropes tying it on top. She flat could not believe that Alex was driving the careening wagon or that anyone could remain seated during such a maniacal ride. She'd had no idea that Alex would have to do something this dangerous and recklessly crazy. Next came Grady Cole with the remuda of twenty relief and night horses. Luther Moreland and Jack Caldwell followed close behind. Completing the advance parade was Ward Hamm, driving a wagon mounded high with heaven knew what.

Next, the drovers arrived, driving in small herds they had been holding together on the range. The small herds gathered into one huge seething bawling mass of horns and hooves. Freddy's heart lurched. She considered herself an imaginative person, but not in her wildest fantasy had she visualized what 2,212 longhorns would actually look and sound like when bunched together.

The sea of horns and the bellowing din rendered her and Les speechless. Shocked into silence, they sat frozen on their horses, watching in stunned amazement as the drovers miraculously blended the beeves into a cohesive unit. When the animals began to move out, the herd formed a brown stream of hide and horns that stretched sixty feet across and over a mile long.

Freddy clapped a hand over her thumping heart. More than anything in the world, she yearned to turn tail and ride back to the ranch house, drop into a deep sleep, and awake to discover this had all been an improbable nightmare.

Frisco appeared, riding out of a dust cloud that swirled ten feet high and extended far out onto the range. "You two fall in at the rear," he ordered, squinting through the dusty haze at the stream of steers. "We'll keep them strung out so they don't get overheated, but we're going to move fast for the next three days to get them road-broke and too worn-out to make trouble. Keep pushing the stragglers and don't let them lag. Also, we've got some cimarrones in this bunch—"

"Cimarrones?" Les inquired in a faint voice. Her face was the color of paste.

"The beeves we pulled out of the thickets and breaks," Frisco explained curtly. "These are wild cattle who don't have a herd mentality yet. They'll be a problem for about three days, then we'll move beyond their home range and they'll calm down some. The point is if you see any muleys peel out and start toward you, turn them back into the herd or we'll lose them."

Freddy watched the wide band of horns moving past her, and thought about trying to change the mind of a wild steer who was determined to go home. She didn't exactly see how she was going to do that. Whoever had first decided that it was a good idea to instruct twelve men to take two thousand cattle to a market over seven hundred miles away had to be a raving lunatic.

Studying her expression, Frisco grinned and leaned a forearm on his pommel. "Would you feel better if I rode up ahead and drew some lines and x's for you?"

She glared at him, then felt her chest tighten. Today Frisco's eyes were a deep cobalt blue, a stunning contrast to bronzed skin and the lock of dark hair that fell forward on his forehead. He had never looked more handsome or virile than he did this minute. He loved what they were doing. Dust coated his hat brim and his shoulders, and already the sun was hot enough to pull sweat out of a man's pores and wet down his shirt. The heated stink of cowhide permeated the air, and the horses were restless and edgy with excitement. Every breath pulled dust into the lungs, and something disastrous could happen any second.

But he loved it. Freddy gazed into Dal Frisco's sparkling eyes and saw his pleasure and excitement, saw that he was as alive at this moment as he had ever been, a man totally in his element. She saw an expression that she wished she had seen after he kissed her. She would have understood his excitement then, would have comprehended the electric vibrancy evident in his tension and anticipation. She didn't understand it now. Frowning, she told herself that she didn't want to think about his sensual mouth or lean hard body either. He'd made it clear that kissing her had meant nothing to him, and it meant nothing to her, too.

"There's the tail end," Frisco said, nodding into the swirls of flying dust, then looking at Freddy. "I'll check back with you later."

Freddy and Les didn't budge as they watched him

canter north, moving up the side of the herd. Freddy swallowed a feeling of abandonment. They were alone now, and she wasn't ready.

"I can't do this. I'm scared to death," Les whispered. "I want to shoot myself."

"You'd miss your target," Freddy answered, absently touching the butt of the pistol on her hip. None of the sisters were remarkable shots, but at least they weren't afraid of guns anymore.

"Oh my God," Les shouted. They had waited too long. Les's horse, afraid of being left behind, reared, then bolted after the herd, which had passed them by. Startled and out of control, Les grabbed the saddle horn and fought to keep her seat as her horse galloped into the haze.

Freddy had only a second to watch, then her horse ducked his head, kicked his hind legs, bucked forward and raced after Les. At the first kick, she flew out of the saddle and hit the ground hard. Dazed and unsure what had happened, only that it had happened faster than she would have believed possible, she gingerly picked herself out of the grass and dirt, gave her head a shake and looked around.

"Damn!" Cursing, she took off at a run, shouting at her horse to come back. This was crazy. She was beginning the drive by chasing after the herd on foot. If she'd had an audience, they would have hooted her offstage.

Within a minute she realized she would never catch her horse. Walker was running full out, cutting up the side of the stragglers and heading north. Freddy wasn't. She'd discovered that riding boots were never made for running and she was losing ground. When she tripped over a prairie-dog hole and fell flat, she struggled to her feet, then sank back to the ground in hopeless resignation. The drive was minutes old and already she was out of it. She had lost her horse, lost her share of the inheritance, and she hadn't come within thirty feet of a longhorn.

"Freddy!"

Looking up, she spotted Les, red-faced and sweating, leading Walker toward her. For a minute Freddy thought she had to be imagining things. Catching her horse would have required some hard and skilled riding. Or fantastic luck. However Les had managed it, Freddy wished she had witnessed the feat. Part of her was elated that she hadn't lost everything. And part of her was disappointed. For a few minutes it had appeared that she had a wonderful excuse to tuck her tail between her legs and walk back to the ranch horse and sanity.

"Thanks, I owe you," she muttered, climbing back in the saddle. The thing that galled her about this incident was Les's role in it. She was not accustomed to thinking of Les as competent or adept. After a lifetime of taking care of Les, it sat wrong to have Les take care of her.

"Hurry up. Look how far ahead the herd is."

"I'll take this side and you be responsible for that side. And stay out of my way," Freddy said irritably. Exactly as Frisco had predicted, about a dozen longhorns were falling behind the main herd, wanting to graze instead of trudge north.

"Stay out of your way?" Les snapped. "You can count on it!"

They glared at each other, then hurried to close the distance between themselves and the stragglers. Freddy's gaze centered on a spotted mouse-colored steer who meandered along at a turtle's pace. She was focused enough that she didn't see trouble coming until she heard the pounding of hooves. When she looked up, six black steers with five-foot horn spans were trotting straight toward her, heading for home with a determined look in their eyes.

"Oh God." Her heart stopped and every muscle in her body went rigid. The sudden convulsive pressure of her thighs signaled Walker forward and her horse leapt toward the oncoming longhorns, an action that almost gave her a heart attack. When the steers saw her racing forward, they scattered, still heading south. "Les?" The shout for help came out as a hoarse croak.

Horrified that she'd appealed to Les—Les!—for assistance, she still looked wildly to the east, hoping Les would respond. But Les was riding pell-mell toward some southernbound steers, terrified and screaming for Freddy.

Freddy whipped her head around to face the oncoming steers and everything she had learned or been told went out of her brain. She stared in panic at the longhorns trotting around her, her heart slamming against her ribs, and she went limp in the saddle, helpless with shock.

Walker couldn't tell the difference between a relaxed rider and one half-dead with fear. Her horse interpreted her collapse as his signal to go to work. For the next twenty minutes, all she did was concentrate on holding on, keeping her seat, and trying to swing her legs away from hooking horns. When it was finally over and her horse drew up in quivering satisfaction, the six blacks were headed north again, moving fast to catch up with the herd.

Sweating and utterly boneless, Freddy fanned her face with her hat and waited for her hands to stop shaking and her heart to climb back into her chest. When she could breathe without making terrible little sounds, she leaned forward and stroked Walker's neck. It was all his doing that the steers had been turned around, not hers.

Regardless of how it happened, she'd had a success, and she hoped that Les had witnessed it. But she didn't see Les. It wasn't until she looked behind that she spotted Les riding toward the herd. In the far distance, two cimarrones were turning into specks, running south toward home.

"You idiot," she shouted when Les caught up, scarlet-faced and streaming sweat. "Thanks to you, we now have two thousand two hundred and *ten* steers! The first morning isn't half-over and you're already lost two steers!"

"I'm an idiot?" Les screamed. "Who lost her horse two minutes into the drive? Who could have helped me but didn't?"

"I was busy over here!" Freddy yelled. Their horses circled each other as they shouted and screamed. "But I didn't lose any of *my* cimarrones! And I'm sick of helping you. I've been helping you all of my life. Well, I quit! From now on, you're on your own!"

They stopped screaming as three longhorns trotted past them, heading home.

"Well *do* something. Or are you going to let three more get away?" Freddy shouted.

"They're on *your* side! If you're so damned good, *you* turn them around!" Without a backward glance, Les cantered after the herd, leaving Freddy to chase down the escaping cimarrones or watch their margin shrink by another three beeves.

She was hot on their trail before she realized that she'd just heard Les swear; she planned to rub it in later. Right now, she had her hands full. After a grim battle of wills, she eventually managed to turn back two of the homeward bounds, but she lost the third.

Wiping sweat from her forehead and swearing, she watched the third steer speed south.

And that wasn't the only problem. A wide distance was opening between the dust from the main herd and where she was now. The stragglers were so far behind they made up a separate herd. Frustrated to the point of forgetting that she didn't know what she was doing, Freddy threw back her head and screamed. Then, vibrating with determination, she galloped up hard and fast on the stragglers on her side, shouting cusswords and mad enough to kick at their lazy hides when Walker rode in close. She went after the two cattle who had tried to escape, spooked them into a run, and ran them right past the stragglers, up the side of the herd, and snarling and kicking, she all but shoved them back into the main bunch. Those damned cattle were going to catch up if she had to kick them every step of the way.

From the side of her eye, she noticed that Les, too, had lost some of her shyness and fear. She was kicking at a straggler in frustration just as Freddy had done, all the while screaming her head off. Freddy didn't have time to think about it. She shot after a pair of stragglers, who looked to her like they were thinking about going home. The hell they were.

When Frisco showed up about noon, Freddy rode up to him in a fury. "Where have you been! We could use some help here!"

"I can see that," he said, his mouth tight. "You have stragglers strung out for almost half a mile."

"You're looking at Les's side. My side isn't strung out that far. So where have you been?"

The steely look that she hated came into his eyes. "Riding drag is the easiest job in the outfit. If you're looking for help to manage a few slow beeves, you ain't gonna get it, friend."

"It's more than that, and you know it. We've been fighting those damned cimarrones all morning!" She would have stabbed a finger in his chest if she could have reached him. "We've lost four steers now. *Four!*" Moisture generated by anger and frustration glittered in her eyes.

"We knew we'd lose a few," Frisco said finally, his mouth grim. He studied her flushed face and the sweat streaming down the sides of her cheeks.

"How can you be so calm?" she shouted, trying to keep her horse from dancing around his. "We've lost *four* before noon of the first damned day!"

"On the plus side, you and Les finally learned to do some cowboying. You've learned more in the last few hours than you learned in six weeks of preparation."

Freddy blinked, startled into silence. He was right. She hadn't once worried about staying on her horse since her disastrous beginning. Hadn't thought about aching muscles in her arms and thighs, or the dust, or anything except catching the escaping cattle before they got too far away.

Nothing was going to alter a healthy fear of wickedly curving horns and the massive size of the cattle, but this morning she hadn't had time to think about being afraid. For the last few hours, she had glared at the fleeing cattle and felt a burst of fury that they were trying to escape, steal her future, and make her look bad in the process. In her heart, she was absolutely certain they were doing it on purpose.

"The main herd is grazing during the noon rest. Bring up the stragglers, then come to the wagon for something to eat."

Les arrived in time to hear Frisco's instructions. "Won't the steers wander off?"

"At least two drovers are riding circle," Frisco said, looking at the hair falling down her back and the blood pulsing in her throat and cheeks. "After Daniel and Peach eat, they'll spell the Webster boys." Slowly, he looked back and forth between them, then touched two fingers to his hat brim and rode toward the campsite that Freddy noticed off to the left of the herd.

"We look like hell," she muttered, staring at Les.

"Did you tell him that we lost four steers?" Les looked as exhausted as Freddy felt. "What did he say? Are we in trouble?"

"He behaved like it didn't matter. It's not *his* inheritance." But his money was also tied to bringing two thousand steers to market, so her snarled statement fell flat.

"Is he going to send us some help?"

"What do you think?" Freddy snapped, turning her horse's head toward the stragglers.

"I can't bear the thought of telling Ward that we've already lost four steers!"

"Then don't tell him," Freddy said sharply, riding off. She was in no mood to hear about Ward Hamm.

If one more thing went wrong, Alex thought she would lose control completely.

During the hair-raising chase after the pilot, her crutch had bounced out of the wagon but she hadn't discovered the loss until the pilot waved her off and she had wrestled her team to a shuddering halt. Shaking and quivering from the horrifying ride, feeling like her bones had rattled loose, she wiped terrified tears from her eyes, unable to move for several minutes. When she finally collected herself, she'd reached behind the seat and discovered the crutch was missing. The shock of it stunned her. Then came the realization that she was stuck.

She could not reach her wheelchair, which was tied on top of the bedrolls and the other supplies she was carrying. She couldn't even climb out of the wagon to the ground. Fresh shock came with the appalling realization of how swiftly she had become dependent on the hated crutch. Now it was gone, and she was helpless.

She was still sitting on the wagon seat fifteen minutes later, blinking hard and feeling hopelessly inadequate when Grady's horses swept past her. As he rode by, he paused long enough to give her a disgusted look before he tossed the crutch up to her.

But now she was so rattled that she didn't pay attention as she climbed out of the wagon. Her skirt caught on the brake handle and threw her off-balance before the material ripped up the back and tore free. She fell flat on the ground just as Luther Moreland and Jack Caldwell drove in to camp. Luther jumped down and ran toward her, but Grady's voice stopped him.

"You of all people should know you can't offer any assistance," Grady shouted, looking past Luther at Caldwell, who was watching carefully.

Crimson with humiliation, Alex managed to pull herself up, frowning as she examined her skirt. It hadn't ripped along the seam, worse luck. The skirt was ruined, and exposing a lot of petticoat. "Grady, where is my bedroll?" She had an extra skirt rolled up inside.

Grady's eyebrows soared as if she'd lost her senses. "You ain't got time for no nap," he snapped. "And I got just five minutes before I need to see to my horses."

He dropped the front of the chuck box for her, and hastily dug a fire pit about fifteen feet from the wagon. At least she was spared that humiliation. "Is there anything else you absolutely got to have right now?"

"Go on with your duties. I'll manage."

The minute he walked away she remembered the firewood tied under the wagon in the cooney. Fanning her face with her hand, trying to calm herself, she looked at the fire pit, looked at the cooney, then cast a pleading glance at Luther.

He spread his hands in a gesture of frustration. "Alex, I can't help."

She refused to believe that he meant it until he turned and strode away from her, refused to concede that she was totally on her own until she saw the flat expression on the faces of Jack Caldwell and Ward Hamm. Sagging, she leaned against the wagon wheel.

At the back of her mind, she hadn't accepted the rules. She had honestly believed that Luther and Ward would come to her aid. No man worthy of the name would stand idly by while a one-legged woman floundered in helpless need of assistance. She had counted on that.

She did not finally release this cherished fantasy until she saw Luther and Jack begin to construct their own noon camp. Even Ward busied himself with the supplies in his wagon, deliberately avoiding her eye.

No one was going to help her. She was alone in this.

For several minutes she didn't move, couldn't think. Luther had insisted the rules must be obeyed and so had Dal Frisco, and she had nodded and agreed. But she hadn't believed it. She'd believed that compassion would outweigh the stupid rules. But that wasn't going to happen.

"Now what are you doing? Watching the grass

grow? Woman, you are already behind schedule," Grady complained, walking up behind her.

"Grady! Thank heaven." If she could have grabbed him without falling down, she would have. "The wood. I need the firewood."

"Then get it. The water barrel sprung a leak and I need to fix it before we lose all your cooking water." He headed for the tools in the box lashed to the side of the wagon.

"Damn!" Blinded by tears of frustration and near panic, she made a fist and struck the wheel. Her fist glanced off the iron rim and struck wood, and a splinter punctured the side of her hand. Yelping, she jerked backward, coming within one wobbly second of falling again. After pinwheeling her arm to regain her balance, she pulled out the splinter and inspected the blood trickling down her wrist. The puncture wasn't deep, but it stung and bled, and she couldn't recall where the medical box was or where she might find something to wrap her hand in. Meanwhile, the minutes relentlessly continued to tick by. Now, she was almost an hour behind schedule.

All right, she would ignore the fact that her cuff was soaking up blood and going the way of her ruined skirt. The firewood was the important thing.

Fetching it was a painstaking and humiliating process. She had to drop to the ground, crawl under the wagon and untie the ropes securing the sling. Then she tossed out the wood she needed and retied the ropes. Crawling back out, feeling helpless and foolish, she used the crutch to climb upright. Then, balancing as best she could, she picked up several pieces of wood, put them in her skirts, and hobbled to the fire pit trying not to drop any. Naturally, she left a trail of fallen kindling behind her.

By the time she finally got the fire going, aggravation made her fingers shake, and she wanted to scream. That's when she realized she had not placed the pot hanger first like she was supposed to do. Without the pot hanger, she had nothing to hang the coffeepot on. And now, with the flames leaping, it would be a difficult and dangerous undertaking to set up the hanger. Lips trembling, she looked toward the observers' camp. Their coffee was already brewed, and they were drinking it as they began preparations for their noon meal.

"Luther?" she called in a shaky voice. "I thought you intended to eat with us."

He walked forward a few steps, then stopped, his expression pinched by the effort to stand aside while she struggled. "I'll take my meals with the observers."

So even an oblique appeal was not going to work. Thin-lipped and furious, she found the pot hanger, assembled it, then decided this task would best be managed from her chair instead of trying to balance on the crutch while she drove the ends into the ground. Thankfully, Grady had brought down her wheelchair without her having to ask.

She sank into it with a sigh of relief, taking the weight off of her trembling leg. Too late it occurred to her that transporting the wood would have been easier if she'd done it in her chair.

At once she discovered that rolling to the fire pit was not that easy. Now that spring rains had greened the range, the grass was growing thick and hard to push through. By the time she reached the fire pit, her arms trembled from the effort of pushing herself over rough ground, and she was wondering if in fact the chair was a better idea than the crutch would have been.

But that was a fine point to ponder at another time.

The problem now was to set up the pot hanger without letting the flames scorch her fingers. Rolling as close to the fire pit as she dared, she leaned over the arm of the chair and pushed a leg of the hanger down through the burning firewood and then, arms shaking with the effort, she managed to thrust it securely into the ground. Now all she had to do was dredge up the energy to finish the task.

Because she wouldn't be able to retrieve the crossbar if she dropped it into the flames, she had to make a very tight circle around to the other side of the fire pit, pushing the chair with one hand and holding on to the cross bar with the other. The heat from the fire and repeated failures brought sweat to her brow, and she felt a spreading wetness under her arms. Disgusting. She hated to sweat, believed it made her appear common.

Pressing her lips together, she struggled to maneuver her chair as close as she dared to the flames. When she finally, finally got herself into position, she rested a minute before she pushed this end of the pot hanger through the firewood and into the ground.

It was Grady who saved her life. She heard his shout and opened her eyes just as the flames flickering along her hem made a whooshing sound and leapt up her skirt toward her waist. Before she could scream or beat at the fire, Grady was there with a bucket of water.

He threw the water on her, spun, and raced back to the wagon for more. Sputtering, soaked from head to foot, Alex slapped frantically at the smoke wafting off her lap. Her heart slammed around in her chest and she thought her head would burst with fear.

Grady ran up and flung another bucket of water on her. Gasping, wiping at her eyes, Alex shoved back drenched tendrils of hair. Horrified, she stared down at herself. Her bodice and skirts were soaked, sticking to her skin, dripping on the ground. An acrid burned odor drifted from the holes in her skirt and in the first layer of petticoats.

Grady knelt beside the chair and waved his hands around like he wanted to raise her skirts but couldn't bring himself to do it. "Are you burned?"

She pulled soggy material away from her knees, sending runnels of water into the dirt. "No, thank God!" She couldn't bear to think how close it had been. "Thanks to your quick action, the fire didn't burn through my underskirts." But what if Grady hadn't been here?

Snapping her head up, thrusting wet hair out of her eyes, she stared toward the other campsite. Luther, Jack Caldwell, and Ward stood like a tableau, coffee cups frozen partway to their lips, their postures rigid.

"Would you have let me burn to death?" Alex screamed. "Because you don't want to interfere? Because of some stupid stupid stupid rules?" They stared back at her, not moving.

Then she dropped her face in sooty hands and burst into hysterical tears.

Grady let her cry while he finished placing the pot hanger then ground the coffee beans and set up the coffeepot, hanging it over the fire. Occasionally she heard him mutter, "Gol-dang it!" But he didn't pat or comfort her like she expected him to.

When the mortifying tears finally stopped, Alex closed her eyes and rested a minute. She needed to dry her hair, which was now falling around her shoulders in soggy strands, and change clothes, and she couldn't imagine how she would obtain the privacy in which to do it.

"Grady?" she called in a small voice. "Will you

fetch my bedroll now, please? I need my toiletries and a change of clothing."

"Miz Mills," he said, coming around to stand in front of her with a frown. "It ain't my place to tell you your bidness, but you got ten hungry boys who's gonna be ridin' in here in about two hours looking for their dinner which you ain't started yet. 'Fore you go fussing with female fripperies, mebbe you better get some dinner a-cooking."

Astonishment widened her eyes. "After all that's happened to me . . . I thought . . . surely you don't except me to fix a meal after I was almost burned to death!"

"Well, ma'am, if you're hinting that I should wrassle up the grub, I ain't about to." He stuck out a whiskered chin and stared at her. "You're the cook, and I'm the wrangler. You don't mess with my ponies, and I don't mess with your chuck, and that's how it is." Anger glinted in his eyes. "Ain't that always the way? Offer a woman a helping hand and pretty soon she wants your whole body for doing her work. Well, I got a job, Miz Mills. I don't have time to do your job, too."

Blinking with disbelief, fresh tears welling in her eyes, she watched him stomp away. She could not believe what was happening to her. If ever there was a lady in distress who needed assistance, she was that lady. Yet four able-bodied men stood within sight and not one was willing to lift a finger to help her.

Pulling a handkerchief out of her cuff, she wrung the water from it, then blotted her face and wiped tears from her eyes. She took her time pushing strands of wet hair up beneath her wet hat, hoping that Grady would reconsider and return to cook the noon meal. He couldn't really expect her to go on wearing a skirt that was ripped up the back and burned full of holes, or ignore the fact that she was drenched to the skin from the top of her head to the tip of her boot.

She waited a full five minutes before she accepted that Grady would not return. Then, teary with self-pity, she forced herself to consider the noon meal. Last night, which seemed like a decade ago, she had planned to cook a roast for the noon meal. But there wasn't time now, so she decided on bacon stew, an uninspired throw-together that she'd been told cowboys actually liked.

Once upright on her crutch, she found the knives and cut a slab of bacon into small squares. The puncture on her wrist opened and bled on her work surface, so she took a minute to wrap her handkerchief around the base of her hand. The wrapping made it awkward to work, but she was beyond caring. She hurled the squares of bacon into a deep pot, hung the pot over the flames, then, being careful not to set herself on fire again, she poured water into the pot, before returning to the worktable to peel what seemed like a million potatoes and slice an equal number of onions. At home she would have insisted that the early carrots be peeled because that was the right and civilized way to do it. But here she just whacked the carrots in pieces and dumped them in with the other vegetables that she would add to the pot when the bacon was half-cooked.

She wasn't up to making biscuits, so she threw together some dough for dumplings. The secret to dumplings, she'd been assured by Señora Calvos, was to roll the dough very very thin before cutting it into squares to drop on top of the boiling stew. Well, today that was not going to happen. If she hurried this chore along, she might have time to change her clothes and do something with the wet hair that kept dropping in her face.

There was no point whatsoever in having standards if a person didn't live up to them. Alex Roark Mills was not a woman who served a meal looking as if she had just crawled out of a burning building. She was a person with superior standards. She would find time to repair her appearance.

But shortly after she dumped the vegetables into the greasy stew water, she glanced up and spotted an enormous dust cloud rising on the horizon. With a despairing heart, she stared at the haze and frantically counted the tasks she had to do yet. There was not going to be a spare minute to fix her hair or change her ensemble.

The herd was coming. And her standards were going.

CHAPTER 10

"What in the hell happened to you?" Dal demanded, climbing down from his horse and handing the reins to Grady. He examined Alex with a hard stare. Her hair hung down in frizzy loops and her skirt had turned into a wrinkled black rag with charred holes that exposed scorched petticoats. A bloody handkerchief wrapped her hand. Picking up a mug, Dal walked behind her to the coffeepot and noticed that her skirt was ripped up the back.

She balanced a hip against the worktable and narrowed her eyes. There was no ice in her gaze today, just fury. "Don't let the fact that I almost died delay the enjoyment of your coffee."

Actually, he wasn't enjoying the coffee. It had that weak, clean-pot, new-grounds taste.

"Cowboys want their coffee first thing." It was hard not to smile. He hadn't imagined she could look this disheveled. She told him what had happened, waving the hand without the crutch, furious tears glittering in her eyes. "I don't see why you're still upset," he commented at the end of her tirade. "You didn't get injured, and a drenching never killed anyone."

"*Look* at me," she shouted, pink blazing on her

cheeks. She waved the bloody handkerchief under his nose. "*I almost burned up!* What more do you want?"

"Dinner for twelve," he answered. He tossed the rest of his coffee on the ground, and watched his point men bring the herd in. He wondered if Freddy and Les had caught up yet. "Better set out the plates," he said absently, turning to inspect the observers' camp. Leaving Alex sputtering, he walked toward the two wagons parked closer to the main camp than he preferred.

As he'd expected, it was a greenhorn's camp. He'd ask Grady to show Luther or Ward how to dig a decent fire pit. He was willing to offer that much assistance.

"How do you think the drive is going so far?" Ward Hamm demanded. Dal noticed a layer of cream atop Hamm's coffee and curled his lip. To a man, cowboys drank their coffee black.

"About as expected." Whiskey would grow on trees before he started reporting to Ward Hamm. He addressed Luther. "From now on, I want your camp farther from the outfit."

"Why is that?" Jack Caldwell asked, leaning against the side of the wagon riffling a deck of cards between his fingers. "You don't want us to see what you're doing?"

"I don't want my men distracted." He frowned at the playing cards, then looked back at Luther. "There's going to be a stampede in the next few days. If we can, we'll turn the herd right, away from the wagons, but that isn't always possible. So you boys sleep with one eye open."

Ward peered at the drovers drifting toward the chuck wagon for their noonday meal. "Who watches the herd while they're eating?"

"I don't have time to explain a cattle drive," Dal

said sharply. The more he saw of this man, the more he resented his presence.

Freddy and Les rode in as he returned to the main camp. They were as wrecked as Alex. Their eyes were reddened from dust, and dust packed every crevice of their skin and clothing. Small muddy lines ringed their nostrils and lips. Loose hair flew around faces that were already starting to scorch in the sun, and sweat soaked their shirts. The first thing they did after climbing off their horses and rubbing their lower legs with groans was pull off thin, fashionable gloves and stare at the blisters rising on their palms.

Freddy looked up and saw him watching. "If you say I told you so, I'll . . . I'll . . ."

He smiled and pushed his hat to the back of his head. "All I'm going to say is maybe you'll listen the next time I make a suggestion. Ask Grady for some heavier gloves."

Stepping up to her, he touched the bandanna tied around her throat, letting his knuckles brush her warm skin. "This isn't a decoration." He pulled the bandanna up over her nose and mouth, watched her green eyes flare at the familiarity. "It's to filter the dust."

"I know that," she snapped, jerking the bandanna back down to her throat. Leaning forward from the hips, she narrowed her eyes. "There's something I want to say to you."

Like hell she'd known. "So? Say what's on your mind."

She stood close enough that he could smell the sweat plastering her shirt to her skin. It didn't smell like a man's sweat, but instead reminded him of glistening bodies and damp sheets. The image was strong enough that he clenched his jaw and stared back at her.

"That kiss didn't mean anything to me either! Absolutely nothing." After glaring into his eyes, she tossed her head and marched toward the plates stacked on the chuck-wagon worktable.

He stood rock-still as if she'd hauled back and smacked him between the eyes with a fence post. Whenever he'd thought about kissing her, and that had been frequently, he'd been so focused on assuring himself that kissing her had meant nothing to him, that he hadn't considered her point of view. Now that he knew her reaction, it pissed him off.

Scowling, biting down on his teeth, he watched her knock the dust from her clothing, then wash her hands and face in the basin on the sideboard of the wagon. Reddened eyes snapping, black hair flying, covered in dust and sweat, she was more appealing right now than she had been in her stylish gowns with every hair carefully curled. His eyes flicked to the damp V between her thighs, and he felt a sudden stirring that irritated the bejesus out of him.

"Get out of my way," she snarled when he walked up beside her. Reaching past him, brushing against his arm and chest, she picked up one of the tin plates.

"Turning into a tough cowboy, are you?" he drawled, stepping back.

"I can take anything you throw at me," she said, looking up and holding his gaze.

She was so full of bristling pride and bravado that she actually seemed taller. When he'd kissed her, he had intended to cut her down to size and teach her a lesson, but apparently it would take more than one kiss to subdue this woman. The next time he kissed her— and there would be a next time—his kiss would damned well mean something to her. He'd make sure that it did.

"Well, my God," she said suddenly, staring past him at Alex. "What happened to you?"

"Just shut up," Alex hissed. Lifting a ladle, she flung a splash of dinner onto Freddy's plate. "You look like a filthy ragamuffin yourself!"

Freddy blinked down at the chunks of bacon and vegetables floating in grease. Puzzled, she looked at Dal then back to Alex. "What the hell is this?"

"It needs lots of salt," Drinkwater commented from near the fire, "but it ain't too bad."

Charlie Singer poked a fork at a dumpling. "*This* is bad," he said unhappily.

"Stew needs pepper, too," Peach said. "Ma'am, you got to put some seasoning in. Salt, pepper, whatever other seasonings you got."

Alex whirled on them and bared her teeth. "When I want a critique, gentlemen, I will request one!" Furious tears glittered in her eyes.

"Just offering a few suggestions, that's all," Drinkwater said hastily.

Charlie Singer stared mournfully at his plate. "She's got the temperament of a cook. Now if she'd just learn to cook like a cook."

Dal watched Freddy carry her dinner a few yards away from the others. She looked around like she was searching for a chair, then she sighed and sat on the ground to eat. There was something wildly erotic about a woman wearing a pair of man's pants, he decided. Usually a man could only speculate about the shape and size of a woman's hips, thighs, buttocks, and legs. Now he could see how she was put together, and the sight of shapely slender curves made his muscles tighten and his thighs burn. Clamping his lips together, he turned a frown toward the herd, sending his thoughts out where they ought to be.

"Dal?"

"Yes?" Looking down at Les, he wondered why the sight of her wearing male trousers didn't make his mouth go dry.

"I don't know if I have to ask permission, but I'm going to the observers' camp to have a word with Ward."

Glancing over her head, he spotted Hamm leaning against the side of his wagon, tapping a boot in impatience. "You can eat or you can go visiting," Dal said, looking back at Les, puzzled by the anxiety in her eyes. "You don't have time to do both."

Indecision puckered her eyebrows, then she sighed deeply and straightened her shoulders. After replacing the plate she'd been holding, she walked toward the observers' camp, dragging her boots. When she reached the wagon, she called a greeting to Luther and Caldwell, then Hamm grabbed her arm and led her behind the team, where they wouldn't be observed. Something wasn't right about that relationship, Dal decided, watching, but he didn't know what it was. Unless it impacted the drive, he guessed it wasn't any of his business.

Alex dropped a ladleful of stew on his plate and gave him a look that dared him to comment. He grinned, then walked over and sat down beside Freddy.

"This is the nastiest stuff I ever ate," she said, making a face as he lowered himself to the ground. "The vegetables are all right, I guess. But the liquid is part grease and part pond scum."

"Tell me something." He didn't look at the material stretched tight across her crossed legs. "Whose idea was it for Hamm to come on this drive? Was it his idea or Les's?"

She tasted the coffee and rolled her eyes in disgust. "How should I know?"

"She didn't tell you?"

Freddy stared at him then laughed. "The last time my sisters and I shared any confidences, we were all wearing our hair down." A humorless smile faded from her expression. "Once this drive is over, my sisters and I will go our separate ways, and I doubt we'll ever see each other again. Believe me, none of us will consider that a great loss." After looking at her plate, she turned it upside down on the ground. "Do you have any brothers or sisters?"

"Ellie is married and lives north of New Orleans. My brother died early in the war."

"Were you close to your brother?" Freddy asked curiously.

"Yes and no. Mac was ten years older, so we didn't have a lot in common during the growing-up years. I guess I idolized him the way younger brothers do." The drovers had called it right. The stew was bland and tasteless, the dumplings soggy, half-cooked lumps. Dal glanced toward the chuck wagon and reminded himself this was only the first day.

"It's odd to think of you as a little boy idolizing someone," Freddy said. "When I was a lot younger I used to wish that my sisters and I got along better. But I outgrew the feeling."

"Are you sure about that?"

"Why would you care?"

"We're just making conversation here," he said irritably. "I never saw a woman bristle the way you do." She had an annoying way of appearing sociable one minute, then slamming the door in a person's face the next minute.

"If I seem touchy, it's because there's something

about you that irritates me. I'm sorry to be rude and blunt, but that's the truth."

"Well, there's something about you that irritates me, too." They squinted at each other, glaring against the sun. "Now here's how it is. I don't give a damn about you or your sisters or whether you get along or any of that. But I do care about this cattle drive. If we hope to succeed, everyone has to work together and that means you three have to pull together."

"We're doing our part," she snapped. The chip jumped back on her shoulder.

"It's too soon to judge. But you and Les sure aren't working as a team. Didn't you tell me you're responsible for one side of the drag, and she's responsible for the other? That's not teamwork, and that could be part of the reason why you're losing cattle."

"I knew you were going to bring that up." An angry flush brightened her sunburn. "No one could have prevented those steers from going home!"

"You're wrong," he said flatly, his gaze on her lips. How in the hell could she claim that his kiss had meant nothing? It was an insult of the highest water. No other woman had ever complained about his kisses. "None of the other drovers lost four beeves before noon."

"Is that so!" She jumped to her feet, clamped her hands on her hips, and glared down at him with burning eyes. Her stance placed him at eye level with her crotch, and he had to force himself to drag his gaze up to meet hers. "Well, we aren't going to lose any more!"

All of the sisters responded to a challenge, but none more than Freddy. The problem with using this observation was that he couldn't predict how she would react, only that she would.

"Freddy?" he called, watching her buttocks move as she flounced away from him. "Come back here and get your plate and cup. We forgot to bring servants to wait on you. So pick up your dishes and put them in the wreck pan to soak."

Face flaming, she glanced at the drovers who had heard his remark and were grinning, then she came back for her plate and cup. Bending close enough to him that she felt the heat of anger rolling off her body, she said in a low, sharp voice. "You don't think any of us can do any real or worthwhile work. Well, you're going to eat those thoughts."

"I hope you're right." He emptied his own scraps on the ground before he leaned back on the sparse grass and finished his coffee. He hoped like hell that the Roark sisters would learn to carry their weight, but in his heart he doubted three women raised as ladies would ever be worthwhile hands on a cattle drive. His plan was to work around them whenever he could.

The problem, of course, and Joe Roark had known it as well as anyone, was that a drive of this size needed every available man. There were areas where Dal could not compensate for the sisters' incompetence. Those were the areas that worried him.

That and thinking about a green-eyed, lush-bodied woman who had walked away from his kiss with indifference. He'd have to do something about that. It was a matter of pride.

By the time Les and Freddy came dragging in for the evening meal, Les felt so exhausted that she didn't know if she had enough energy to lift a fork to her mouth. Her eyes stung from the wind, sun, and constant dust, her tailbone was sore, and her legs and thighs ached and quivered. She could hardly walk after she slipped to the ground, groaned, and handed the reins to Grady.

"Git back here, and take off your saddle," Grady called peevishly. "You women just kill me. Every gol-danged one of you think I got nothing better to do than wait on you hand and foot. Well, it ain't gonna happen, so you can just . . . ."

Tuning out his voice, blinking at tears of fatigue, she reached deep and found enough strength to pull off her saddle before she staggered toward the lanterns hanging on the wagon.

"It's about time you and Freddy showed up," Alex complained. "I could have cleaned up the supper mess twenty minutes ago and been done with it if I hadn't had to wait for you two!"

"We couldn't get the laggards to hurry up, then we had to learn how the steers bed down for the night, and then—" She halted abruptly, hating it that she was always apologizing for one thing or another. It wasn't her fault that some of the steers wouldn't keep up with the herd.

"Just hurry up and eat." Alex dumped something on her plate that looked suspiciously like the noon meal only with additional vegetables tossed in.

Les couldn't be certain because she'd spent the noon break with Ward and hadn't eaten. Her stomach had growled all afternoon. "I was going to tell you how sorry I am that you set yourself on fire and got drenched," she snapped at Alex, "but you're doing such a good job of feeling sorry for yourself that you don't need any commiseration from me."

"Look who's talking!" Contempt pinched Alex's mouth. "Everyone within a mile has been listening to you moaning and groaning since you rode in. And in case that doesn't make everyone feel sorry for poor little you, you're limping and rubbing your eyes. What's next? Tears?"

"Oh shut up, Alex," Freddy said, stepping up to the wagon and reaching for a plate. "I hope you didn't put all your time into fixing your hair and changing clothes instead of doing something about your god-awful cooking. I'm just thrilled that you found time to primp, but we're all going to starve to death if you don't get better at preparing meals."

Alex put down the ladle and brushed back a wave of hair with a shaking hand. "Well, you won't have to starve for long. I figure if you two keep losing steers at the rate you're going, this drive won't last a month!"

Les drew back. "Who told you about the cimarrones?"

"Everyone knows you two incompetents lost four cattle this morning and two this afternoon! What are you doing back there? Picking wildflowers? Exploring every little gully?"

Les's heart fell to her toes when she lifted her head toward the observers' camp. It was still light enough to see Ward pacing back and forth, to see the deep scowl pinching his face. He must have heard about the two steers that got away this afternoon.

Her appetite fled, but she knew she had to eat to keep up her strength. She didn't think about what she was putting in her mouth, she just chewed and swallowed as fast as she could before Ward pulled out his pocket watch, held it to the fading light, then scowled at her.

Already most of the drovers were unrolling their bedrolls and Les longed to do the same, but she dumped her scraps on the ground, carried the plate to the wreck pan, then walked out on the range. "I've been wanting a cup of coffee for the last two hours," she said when she came close to him. "If you'll wait a minute, I'll just fetch a cup and come back."

"I want to talk to you now."

His tone of voice warned that he would only get angrier if she delayed. Well, she had waited this long for something to drink, she could wait another few minutes. Dragging her feet, trying not to limp too badly, she followed as he turned on his heel and strode toward his wagon, which she noticed uneasily was parked well behind Luther and Caldwell's wagon.

"Ward?" she called, hobbling after him, stumbling in the deepening darkness. "Do you suppose I could have a cup of coffee from your pot?"

"Isn't that just like you?" Ward hissed, turning so abruptly that she ran into his chest. "Thinking about your own comfort when everyone else except that smug bastard Caldwell is worried sick about the success of this drive because you and your stupid sister are both so careless and incompetent that any steer that comes your way just keeps going!"

"That's not true," she whispered, stepping back from him. "We must have turned around at least a dozen or more beeves. Ward, we did very well considering this was our first day and considering we've never done this before and didn't really know what to expect."

"You let *six* get past you today! Six, Les." Grabbing her sore shoulders, he shook her so hard that her hat fell off. "At this rate, Lola won't have to wait for Abilene to win." His fingers dug into her arms and he pushed his face so close to hers that spittle landed on her lips and chin. "Don't you care? Don't you ever think about anyone but yourself?" Moonlight gleamed on his bared teeth. "I sold my store! I've shaken my bones to powder driving a team over this rough ground.

I've put up with the company of two men who can't talk about anything but gambling or law torts. And for what? To find out that you blithely let six cattle stroll past you!"

"Please, Ward," she whispered. "I ache all over. I'm so exhausted that I can hardly stand upright, and I feel half-sick because I haven't eaten much today."

"It's always you, you, you, isn't it?" He flung her against the side of the wagon so hard that she knew her back and shoulders would bear bruises tomorrow.

"I'm doing the best I can," she whispered, fighting a flood of tears. "You don't know what it's like back there. It's constant anxiety, and the cimarrones come out of the dust all red-eyed and wild and wanting to go home. Several of them at a time, and it's hard to—"

"Excuses aren't going to replace those steers, Les. Excuses won't get my store back. Excuses aren't going to make it possible for us to marry or put food on the table if we do."

She was so tired that her mind reeled. All she wanted to do was splash water on her face to remove some of the dust, and then fall into her bedroll. Closing her eyes, she leaned against the wagon and let him rail at her, detailing her selfishness, her incompetence, her disregard for him and their future. When she tilted forward and missed vomiting on his shoes by mere inches, he was so disgusted that he slapped her and stalked away without helping her to her feet.

Staggering and wiping her mouth, trying not to cry, she returned to the main camp and the fire, which was burning low now. The coffeepot still hung above the embers, but she was too tired to think about the coffee she had wanted so much an hour ago.

Fetching her bedroll, she carried it over near Freddy, who was already asleep. Silent tears spilled down her cheeks while she struggled to pull off her boots. Then, when she finally and gratefully crawled inside her blankets, she discovered she'd chosen a site scattered with small rocks that dug into her flesh. She was too exhausted to brush the rocks out from under her or move to another place. In less than two minutes she was sound asleep.

She didn't twitch or roll over until Dal nudged her awake a few hours later.

Then she sat up, startled and confused to see stars overhead and the other drovers still in their bedrolls. "What's wrong?"

"Night watch," Dal reminded her in a low voice. "It's your turn. Put your boots on and grab a quick cup of coffee. I'll ride with you tonight, and for the rest of the week."

Blinking, trying to swim out of a deep sleep, she rubbed her back while she watched him return to the fire. Night watch. Now, she remembered about taking a two-hour shift each night. She wanted to weep when she realized this meant they would not have a full night of uninterrupted sleep until the drive ended.

She didn't know how she was going to live through this.

Freddy woke when Les gave her a kick on the way back to her bedroll. Sitting up to rub her leg, she hissed an insult then yawned. "Night watch," Dal called softly, his voice coming out of the darkness. "Grab a quick coffee, then we'll go."

Stretching the kinks out of her shoulders and rubbing her eyes, Freddy stood, then stumbled across a couple of bedrolls on her way to the fire, earning muttered curses and insults for her carelessness. The sharp rebukes were further proof, if she'd needed any, that she wasn't going to be shown any special consideration on this drive.

Silently, she drank a cup of scalding coffee, studying the spangled sky and wondering how she would know when her two-hour shift had elapsed. Unexpectedly, a long-ago memory popped into her head, and she remembered sitting on the porch steps of the ranch house, leaning against Joe's shoulder, inhaling the mingled scents of leather, soap, and cigar smoke while he pointed out the constellations and talked about the stars. Since Freddy hadn't imagined that she would ever need to tell time by the position of the Big Dipper, she had forgotten the incident until now.

How odd. Until a minute ago, she would have sworn there had never been any close moments between her and Pa. Surprised by a sudden lump in her throat, she wondered if there were other incidents, just her and Pa, that she'd forgotten.

After shaking her head, she noticed Dal watching her across the embers glowing in the fire pit. He sat on the ground, his wrists resting on upraised knees, his cup dangling loosely from his fingers. Even at this time of night, he radiated an intense physical energy and presence that made her catch a quick breath and hold it. Tonight, with pinpoints of flame reflecting in his steady gaze, and a new beard shadowing his jaw, he looked hard and dangerous. The sudden hot tightening in her lower stomach startled her, as she had never been drawn to hard men who couldn't quote a line of Shakespeare if their lives depended on it.

Wetting dry lips, she jumped up and walked to the chuck wagon, where her night horse was saddled and waiting, tied to the spokes of a wheel. Dal Frisco's past had nothing in it to recommend him, she thought with a frown, nor did his dream of building a ranch in Montana. As far as she could see, they had nothing whatsoever in common. Yet he looked at her, and she started vibrating as if his gaze set off an inner earthquake.

Irritated, she swung into the saddle, suppressing a groan as aching thigh muscles protested another grueling bout on horseback. "How does this work?"

"There are two guards on each shift. You circle the herd in opposite directions. You're looking for anything unusual, marauders, wild animals, the start of a stampede." A light flared briefly, then she smelled the smoke of a cigar. Freddy had always enjoyed the scent.

"And what am I supposed to do if one of those events occurs?"

"You drive off any wild animals, alert the camp to marauders or bandits, and try to stop a stampede before it starts, which is mostly impossible, so you position yourself to control it." Walking their horses, they rode along the starlit perimeter of the bedding ground. The heat of the animals lessened the spring chill of the night. "On second thought," Dal said, "don't try to control a stampede, you don't know how yet. Observe and learn."

Since this was her initial experience on a bedding ground, there was plenty to observe. First, Freddy noticed the cattle slept on their sides, and they weren't quiet as she had supposed they would be. Every now and then they made strange blowing noises that worried her half to death.

Dal laughed softly. "Perfectly normal," he assured her. "It's also normal for them to stand up along about midnight, graze for a few minutes, then lie down again. What's not normal is for one of them to jump up and start bawling. If that happens, the rest panic, they all start running, and we're into a stampede."

"How did you learn all of this?" She told herself that she didn't care about his answer. Talking helped her stay awake.

"I grew up on a ranch in Louisiana," he said with a shrug. "It was nothing like the King's Walk spread, only about a tenth the size. A better question might be why didn't you learn something about ranching."

"Pa had clear-cut ideas about men and women," she said, watching the light from distant stars slide along the horns of the dozing steers. "Men do this, women do that, and they stay out of each other's areas." They rode so closely together, to facilitate quiet conversation, that Dal's leg occasionally brushed hers. She didn't like that, didn't like being physically aware of him. At least she couldn't see his face clearly and didn't have to struggle against the feelings aroused by the cool speculation in his eyes or that slow smile that lifted one corner of his lips.

"If that's true, then it's strange that your father would throw his daughters into the middle of a cattle drive and expect them to succeed."

"I don't think he did expect us to succeed." It was oddly intimate, riding together in the darkness, talking softly and listening to the quiet rustling of the bedded steers.

"If Joe wanted Lola to inherit his fortune, he didn't have to set up this elaborate contest."

"I don't know what Pa was thinking," Freddy said as they slowly circled the end of the sleeping herd and started up the other side. "Maybe he wanted to punish us. I don't want to talk about him. It makes me furious every time I think about what he did to us!"

"Maybe he recognized something in each of you that you're not seeing yourselves. When you make a horseshoe it begins as a lump of metal that doesn't look like much. But fire and pounding transforms it into something hard and useful. Maybe Joe figured you ladies needed a little fire and pounding and figured you'd get it on a cattle drive."

"I told you I don't want to talk about this!"

Instantly, his hand shot through the blackness and gripped her arm so hard that she felt his fingers crushing her bones. "Don't ever raise your voice on night watch!" Releasing her, he moved ahead, scanning the herd, his silhouette tense against the starlit sky.

Heart pounding, Freddy also peered hard at the herd, and she didn't relax until Dal returned and brought his horse up close beside her. "I'm sorry," she whispered between her teeth.

"We got lucky," he said with an obvious effort at patience.

"It makes me mad when you talk about Pa. You didn't know him." Sometimes she wondered if she had known him. She tended to think of Joe in stark tones of black and white. But her earlier memory of sitting together on the porch steps had shaken that image.

"You're wrong, Freddy. I know Joe Roark through what the man built and how he built it. I see hints of him in each one of you."

She started to tell him that was nonsense, but midway down this side of the herd, a shape loomed toward them and Freddy sucked in a breath, holding it until she saw the shape was only Drinkwater, the other guard. He reined up and reported in a low voice, "Everything seems quiet. There was a moment up front. The brindle with the frayed tail couldn't find his partner."

"A big black with a chipped horn," Dal said.

Freddy peered at him, incredulous. To her the longhorns were as alike as kernels of corn.

"That's the one," Drinkwater agreed, moving away from them.

"What did he mean about partners?" she asked, vowing to look for a brindle with a frayed tail and a black with a chipped horn.

"Longhorns choose a traveling partner for the drive, and then walk and sleep near the partner. Won't settle down until they find each other." They continued riding along the side of the herd, their legs occasionally brushing like magnets drawn together. "The steers also travel in roughly the same position every day. The same animals take the point, the same steers fall into the middle, and the same steers lag behind."

"Sort of like people," Freddy said with a smile, inhaling the sweet smoke of his cigar. It pleased her when he laughed. "Dal?" she said when they had rounded the front end and started up the side again. "Do you really think we'll succeed with this drive? Or is it all just a waste of time?" His long silence made her heart sink.

"We have a chance," he said finally. "If the weather holds, if the rivers aren't flooding, if we don't run shy on good grass and clean water. If we don't lose too many beeves."

She ground her teeth together. "We aren't going to lose any more."

"Yes, we will. I don't want to see you and Les lose any more, but we'll lose some in other ways." On the far side of the herd, they heard Drinkwater singing softly. "We'll lose them because sometimes a few stubborn beeves just won't follow their x's and lines."

This time she laughed. "I can't believe I did that."

She knew better now, but she still tended to think of the drive as an enormous stage production. Dal was the maestro; she and the drovers were the actors; Luther,

Ward, and Jack comprised the audience; the cattle provided the stage business. The story line was clear-cut
and tinged with just enough drama to make it interesting. Only the script was ambiguous, offering too vague
an outline and too much room for extemporaneous action.

Dal laughed softly when she told him her thoughts,
but it was uneasy laugher and his voice was sober when
he said, "Make no mistake, Freddy. There's no script
here. This is real, and anything can happen. You worry
the hell out of me because you approach life as if it's a
role you're playing."

She lifted her head. "What difference does it make,
as long as I play my role well?"

"You aren't playing it well. You lost six steers
today," he said flatly. "You're going to keep messing
up until you stop dreaming and start connecting with
what's real."

It was like being in the touring company again,
standing silently, her cheeks flaming, feeling unjustly
maligned while Maestro Delacroix criticized her performance. Anyone could fluff a line . . . or lose a few
steers. She would have explained this except Frisco
would have argued that today was not a performance,
and she couldn't think of a convincing rebuttal.

"How did you get interested in acting anyway?"

"A touring company came through Klees when I
was nineteen," she said tightly. "In retrospect, I realize
they weren't particularly good. They only did melodra-
mas. But it seemed magic at the time. I knew that night
that I wanted to be an actor."

And oh how she had loved becoming someone different every night. Standing in the wings, awaiting her
cue, she had cast Freddy Roark aside and let someone
else take her place. It was that someone else who

emerged before the gaslights, the shepherdess or the lady-in-waiting or the grande dame or the shop girl. The someone else was never invisible, never overlooked.

And on stage the worst dilemmas were always solved. The father reconciled with the son or daughter, the prodigal was forgiven, the lovers reunited, the villain was vanquished.

That's what she loved about the stage, stepping out of herself into a happy ending. And when the applause came, that swell of approval and recognition was an infusion of life's blood.

"You can't guess how much I miss it," she whispered. Since returning to Klees she had been waiting her life away, waiting for another chance, waiting for an opportunity to step before the lights again. But Pa would have killed her if she had run off a second time, just like she had almost killed him when she ran off the first time. So she had stayed in the little house he rented for her in town, dreaming hopeless dreams and watching her life slip away, day by day.

"If we win, you'll have another chance," Dal said. He ground his cigar against the saddle tree, then flipped it toward the range. The sweet smoke floated away in the darkness. He flexed his shoulders, rolled his head, then shifted on his saddle. "Time to head in."

Abruptly it occurred to her that if she would be tired tomorrow, he would be doubly so. He'd ridden a two-hour night shift with Les then another two-hour shift with her. But she already knew he wouldn't complain. Oh yes, Pa would have taken to this man like cheese on pie.

She, on the other hand, was suddenly so tired she could hardly hold her eyelids open. When they returned to tie their horses to the wheel of the chuck wagon, she sat unmoving on her saddle, her eyes closed, searching for the energy to tether the horse and stumble back to her bedroll for the few hours remaining until dawn.

Strong hands circled her waist and lifted her off the saddle. Dal swung her close to him and slid her slowly down the length of his hard hot body. Freddy gasped, and her eyes snapped wide-open. She gripped his shoulders and stared into narrowed eyes, feeling his powerful arousal as her hips slid past his before he set her on the ground. Holding her tightly against him, he looked into her eyes, and for one breathless moment she thought he would kiss her.

"All the world's a stage, and all the men and women merely players," he said softly, his gaze dropping to her lips. "Except on a cattle drive. Keep that in mind, Frederick." Then he released her and stepped back, touching a finger to the brim of his hat. "Sleep fast."

Freddy's mouth dropped open. He'd quoted from *As You Like It*. My God.

Lips parted, pulse thudding in her temples, she watched him walk away from the campfire and the scattered bedrolls. Damn him. She had lied about his kiss having no effect on her. And she'd be lying now if she claimed that the touch of his body hadn't scorched her mind and flesh.

Feeling confused that she had wanted him to kiss her again, furious that he'd quoted Shakespeare and proved her wrong about him, she strode toward her bedroll, this time managing not to wake any of the other drovers. But against all expectations, it was a long time before she finally feel asleep.

CHAPTER 11

The first stampede erupted on the third night, two miles west of San Antonio.

The noise and shaking earth brought Dal out of his bedroll like he'd been catapulted into the air. He hit the ground running and raced for his night horse. As he'd been expecting this, he was fully dressed, and in less than a minute, he was galloping alongside the terrified herd.

That minute was long enough to notice the drovers exploding out of their bedrolls, long enough to watch Alex jump to her hands and knees and frantically scramble for her chair, to see Freddy and Les freeze in panic. He hoped to hell neither of them joined in the melee.

A sliver of moon shimmered through the billowing dust, pushing the shadows enough that he wasn't entirely blind. Squinting into the murk, he saw a tide of clashing horns and pounding hoofs sweeping past him on the right. Stampeding animals gave off a scorching heat, and he felt it on his face, inhaled the nearly over-powering odor of fear and rank cowhide. Shouting orders would have been futile, swallowed by the din of rattling horns and the thunder of eight thousand hooves churning up the ground. He had to trust that his drovers would perform as a unit even though they couldn't see or hear one another.

Swearing and shouting, trying to squeeze down the herd and hold them together, he rode hard, praying his horse didn't stumble in the darkness. The other drovers would be doing the same, trying to reach the point and turn the lead animals toward the tail of the stampeding herd. Once the lead steers turned into a circle, the cattle would twist themselves into a self-stopping ball and eventually the mass would wind so tightly together the stampede would end.

Thirty minutes after the sun drifted above the horizon, the mill finally ceased churning and his weary drovers began to sort things out and drive the herd back to the bedding ground, which was now three miles behind them. Peach and Daniel rode out to search for animals that might have strayed during the early stages. The first stampede had ended.

Dal removed his hat and wiped sweat from his face, watching Freddy and Les riding toward him, their faces pale in the morning light. His instinct was to instruct them to leave the mopping-up to men with experience. But sitting on the sidelines never made a cowboy.

"What are the injuries?" he asked as they rode up. Injured men and horses would return to camp expecting Alex to patch them up. He hoped she knew how to do it.

"Charlie has a gash on his leg and James broke two toes," Freddy reported.

"I never heard or saw anything that terrifying in my life," Les said in a voice scarcely above a whisper. "I'm sorry we didn't help. We just . . . we just . . ."

"You were right to stay out of it," he said wearily. "Later, I'll review what we did. You've heard what to do before, but now that you've seen a stampede, it will make more sense."

Freddy's green eyes widened and moved beyond him. "What happened to those steers?"

"Winding two thousand steers into a tight ball damages them. A steer will lose more weight in a mill than he would if we ran him from here to San Antonio." He jerked his head toward two dead beeves laying on ruined earth. "Sometimes the center of the mill jams too tight and a few get trampled." He crossed his wrists on the pommel. "We'll graze the herd an extra hour this morning to settle them out. You cowboys ride over there and skin and butcher those dead beeves. I'll tell Alex to hold your breakfast until you're finished."

Their faces blanched beneath sun pinked skin, and they stared at him with huge horrified eyes. Freddy stammered, "You want us to—oh my God—skin and *butcher* two cows?" She stared at him in disbelief. "*Us?*"

"You," he said pleasantly. Today she hadn't bothered pinning up her hair but had tied it back at the neck. A light breeze plucked at the black cascade that fell nearly to her waist. "And it would spare me a whole lot of irritation if you'd remember that we're trailing steers, not cows."

Speechless, Freddy watched him ride away, then she blinked at Les with stunned eyes. "I don't think I can do this," she whispered, still shocked.

Les leaned to one side and her chest heaved. If she'd had any breakfast, she would have tossed it over the side of her horse. "It makes me sick just to think about touching a dead steer."

Freddy waited, praying that Dal would ride back and tell them he'd been joshing. But it didn't happen. "I would rather walk back to Klees buck naked and barefoot than do this."

"I would rather spend the rest of my life in a Mexican jail than skin and cut up a dead steer," Les said, swaying in her saddle.

"I would empty chamber pots for twenty years rather than go anywhere near those dead beeves."

"I'd rather eat a bucket of spiders than do this."

"You're in luck," Freddy said. "Alex is frying spiders for our breakfast."

They stared at each other, then burst into semi-hysterical laughter, laughing until tears ran down their cheeks, until their sides ached and their horses were dancing sideways.

"I can't believe this. Did you ever imagine that we—"

"Never!"

When Freddy finally caught her breath and wiped the tears from her eyes, the dead steers were still there. She brought her horse under control and sighed as deeply as any tragic heroine ever had. "I hate this, I hate this, I hate this."

"We're going to get blood on us," Les said. "They have guts in them. Oh God."

"Damn it." Freddy rubbed her forehead. "We don't have any choice. We have to do it."

Les pounded a fist on the pommel. "I'll take the smaller one."

"The hell you will. This will go faster if we work together." Dal would have been thrilled to hear those words fall out of her mouth. But in this case, he was right. The steers were too heavy to wrestle around alone. She and Les considered each other for a long minute, adjusting to the idea of working together, accepting the wisdom of the idea, but not liking it much.

"All right," Les said, riding up beside her. "But just don't go telling me what to do every other minute. You don't know any more about skinning and butchering than I do."

There was no way Freddy could pretend this repugnant task was a role or stage business or anything else that would help her get through it. She couldn't hide behind pretense this time. She would have galloped for home if Les hadn't been with her.

But if Les wasn't running away, neither would she. But she sure wanted to.

"My sisters are doing *what*?" Alex asked, spinning around, then shading her eyes against the sun. Far out on the range she saw Freddy's and Les's horses and two figures hunched over the dead steers. A shudder passed down her frame.

Dal poured a cup of coffee from the ever-present pot hanging over the fire, then helped himself to one of the steaks Alex had fried for breakfast. "When they signal, you and Grady drive out there and get the meat. Wrap the pieces in slickers and load them in the wagon."

"Oh my God." She was going to have to be part of it after all.

Grady leaned against the chuck wagon, sipping scalding coffee and scowling toward the range. "We better not wait. Better go out there soon and make sure they don't throw away the heart and liver and the other small parts."

Alex placed a hand on her stomach as the air rushed out of her body. "Why shouldn't they throw away those parts?"

"You use those items to make son of a bitch stew. It's a favorite with the drovers," Dal said, looking up as

Luther and Caldwell's wagon returned to camp from a trip into San Antonio. "The tube linking a longhorn's stomachs gives the stew a distinctive flavor," he added absently.

She imagined it did. Alex gripped the handle of her crutch until her knuckles turned white, and her stomach rolled as she thought about touching a stomach tube, or cooking it, or, God forbid, eating such a revolting thing. When she opened her eyes, Dal had gone, walking toward the returning wagon, but Grady still leaned against her worktable, watching her curiously.

"You ain't one of those prisses with a delicate stomach, are you?"

She knew the origins of stewed chicken and bacon and pot roasts, but she'd never been subjected to the starting point of wringing the actual chicken's neck, dealing with a pig, or skinning a steer. Lord. Now she was going to have to touch and cook pieces of a steer that ought to be buried in the ground and forgotten.

"I really hate being here." She had compromised everything she had believed she stood for.

In the few short weeks that she had been relying on the crutch, it had become indispensable, and she detested that. Being mobile again was a betrayal of Payton. She hated cooking, it was a task for a menial, and she loathed everything it entailed. And she despised washing dishes that seemed to multiply into an endless number of dirty cups and plates.

She hated sleeping on the ground near snoring men, some of whom slept in their long johns, hated the lack of privacy, hated performing her toilette at dawn, hated careening over the range fearing for her life. She hated and dreaded those moments alone in the middle of nowhere before Grady arrived with the remuda.

Most of all, she hated having no one to talk to.

Freddy's competitiveness was exhausting, but Alex responded to it, which made Freddy one of the last people Alex would admit fear to. If she tried to talk to Les, she'd end up reassuring Les and find no assurance herself. Grady expected her to take everything in stride and was annoyed by any show of weakness. Dal was too busy for idle chat. The drovers were so far beneath her that talking to them about anything other than what went into their stomachs was unthinkable. She didn't like Ward Hamm or Jack Caldwell.

That left Luther Moreland, who was walking toward her now, carrying a box of eggs he'd purchased in San Antonio. She had known Luther for years, and he was a presentable man, but too shy for easy conversation. A sigh lifted her chest. The aching loneliness she was experiencing on this terrible journey was a taste of what she could expect for the rest of her life.

"I brought you some fresh eggs," Luther said, placing the box on her worktable. "They're packed in sand. I wish I could have found more, but there are more saloons in San Antonio than henhouses. Still, you'll have enough for a couple of breakfasts."

"Thank you." She started cleaning her area, putting away dishes and cups, irritated when Dal returned and took a clean cup that she would have to wash later.

"Did you notice if Caldwell met up with Lola in San Antonio?" he asked Luther.

"I believe he did, yes," Luther said uncomfortably.

Dal squinted toward Freddy and Les, and Alex thought she could guess what he was thinking. They had lost two more steers. Three days into a drive, and they had already lost eight animals. Undoubtedly Lola and Jack were celebrating a promising beginning.

* * *

"How many miles did we make today?" Now that she'd seen a stampede, Freddy wasn't anxious to see another. Dal didn't have to remind her to keep her voice low.

"Not enough with the late start we got. Nine miles, maybe ten."

She hated to admit it, but she would miss him and the scent of his cigars when he stopped sharing her night shift. There was another thing she wasn't eager to concede, but she owed him. "Les and I worked together skinning the steers. It was a horrible, nasty chore and . . ." She bit off describing a task she wanted to forget and hoped never to have to do again. "Anyway. We decided to work together on the drag, and we didn't lose any steers today." She paused, then admitted the rest. "We probably would have lost a couple if we hadn't helped each other."

"The cimarrones are settling in. You'll have an occasional steer who wants to head back to the bedding grounds, but the worst should be over now. For the most part, your job is to keep the laggards moving. And eat dust." A grin sounded in his voice.

His matter-of-fact tone annoyed her. She'd expected him to praise her and Les for deciding to work together and stop splitting their territory in half. But of course he didn't know what a huge concession it was for her and Les to trust each other and try to work together.

They completed a full turn around the herd before either of them spoke again.

"Was that the only line of Shakespeare you know?" Freddy asked. She'd been wrestling this question all day, wondering. Staring in his direction, she watched the end of his cigar flare briefly, then move away from his lips.

"I hate to disappoint you, but I'm an educated man. Part schooling, part self-taught."

"Oh." It did indeed disappoint her. It was much easier to think of him as a simple cowboy, knowing cowboy things and not much else.

"Love is a sickness full of woes," he quoted suddenly in a tone that suggested he was showing off. "Do you know who said that?"

"Well, of course I do." When he waited, expecting her to state the author, she lifted a hand. "I can't think of his name right now." When Frisco still didn't speak, she glared across the short distance separating them. "Listen, even the best actresses can't remember every line or recall the author of every play ever written." She tossed her head and felt her cheeks burning in the darkness. It was appalling to think he might have read more plays than she had.

He laughed softly. "Samuel Daniel. *Hymen's Triumph.*"

She didn't even know if *Hymen's Triumph* was a play or a poem or a story or what it might be. Not for the first time, she silently cursed the disparity between a man's education and a woman's. It wasn't fair that he could quote something she didn't recognize.

His leg brushed hers and she jerked away, angry and seeking a way to hit back at him for quoting a line unknown to her and thus embarrassing her. "Do you think you'll start drinking again?" she asked abruptly. When she noticed him stiffen in his saddle, she smiled, ashamed of herself but also pleased that she appeared to have rattled a man who didn't often get rattled.

"Not on this drive," he said curtly.

"Is it true that you lost your last two herds because you were drunk all the time?"

"Could be," he said after a pause. "Luck plays a

role on any drive, and the skill of the drovers, and the weather, and a hundred other things. My drinking didn't help."

Ordinarily Freddy wouldn't have dreamed of asking or answering personal questions. Somehow, she and Dal had moved quickly into a peculiar intimacy that made her uneasy when she thought about it. And she thought about him a lot during the long hours riding drag.

He surprised her by humming as they rode and then by adding words. In a smooth rich baritone, he softly sang, "Nearer My God to Thee," and Freddy listened in astonishment. Dal had a beautiful singing voice that would have done credit to a professional. He would have been a tremendous asset in the olios following a stage production. She couldn't believe her ears.

At the end of the third verse, she strained to see his face through the darkness. "Are you a religious man?" There she went again, prying into personal areas.

"Not especially," he said, lighting another cigar. She saw him tilt his head back and gaze at the stars, then sweep a glance across the dozing cattle. "But a man doesn't get much closer to God than this."

Freddy understood. Riding night watch made a person ponder the firmament and the sweet earth, brought strange and weighty thoughts into a person's mind.

"The beeves like that song. Here's another one they like."

He sang a version of "Dan Tucker" containing lyrics that bordered on risqué and caused Freddy to clap a hand over her mouth to smother gales of laughter. On the far side of the herd, she heard Drinkwater take up the refrain and wished she could hear the words to his version, too. As Dal had promised, the singing did seem to soothe the steers. A few tails twitched and a few steers made the blowing sound that always startled her, but there was no sign of trouble tonight.

When Dal's voice died away, she felt a twinge of disappointment. That aggravated her so much she blurted out a question which had been bothering her. "Are you brushing against my leg on purpose?" Every time his leg touched hers, it was like a tingle shot out of his chaps and ran up and down her leg. "Stop doing it."

Without a word, he rode ahead. Instantly Freddy felt the darkness close around her as she hadn't before. Now she had a taste of the solitude she would face when he stopped sharing her night shift, and she realized it was going to be difficult riding in circles for two hours alone in the darkness. She had never much cared for the company of her own thoughts.

Urging her horse forward, she tried to catch up, but Dal paced her, staying in front until they headed in at the end of the shift. Angry and disappointed and trying not to show it, she sat on her horse in front of the chuck wagon, half-hoping he would lift her down from her saddle again. But he walked toward the coffeepot hanging over the fire. She sighed and followed.

"This is one of those times when you're really irritating me," she said in a voice soft enough not to wake anyone. Pouring herself a cup of coffee, she sat on the ground near him and glared at the low flames beneath the pot.

"Yeah, well you're irritating me, too. Riding close enough to talk means legs are going to brush occasionally. That's all it means."

"Good, I'm glad you understand that." She hoped he didn't think the light reflecting on her cheeks was a blush. "Why did you quote that line about love being a sickness?"

"No reason," he said shortly. "It just came to mind."

"Well, the fellow who said it was right." She didn't try to repeat the quote because memorizing lines wasn't her strong suit, a failing that had driven Maestro Delacroix to despair. But she always got the gist of her lines. "I don't want to fall into that kind of sickness again."

"Sounds like you're a woman of experience," he said in a light voice. She couldn't tell if he was teasing her.

"Experienced enough," she answered, tossing her head. She'd enjoyed dozens of flirtations, and once she had mistakenly believed she might be in love. The last experience was too humiliating to dwell on, but she never thought of it without thanking God that she hadn't succumbed to a man just because he looked good wearing stage tights. "I suppose you're experienced, too."

"Experienced enough," he said, tossing her response back and giving her one of those slow cool smiles that made her thighs tighten and her heart pound.

"I don't want to talk about this," Freddy said abruptly. She had no idea why she was sitting with him in the middle of the night when she could be in her bedroll grabbing some sleep. Straightening her shoulders, she walked away from him, feeling his gaze on her back.

"Good night," he called softly, his voice floating toward her. She didn't answer.

After crawling into her blankets, she folded her arms behind her head and gazed up at a sky milky with stars. Dal had been showing off. Quoting lines about love, singing. Showing her that he was more than just a cowboy and a former drunk.

She wished she could do something to show him that she was more than just an actress with a ruined reputation who wasn't very good at anything.

When she flounced over on her side, her nose touched a piece of cloth. Sitting up, she lifted the square of material close to see what it was and discovered a new bandanna. Puzzled, she studied the long forms sleeping around her. Who had left this for her?

When she remembered that Luther and Jack had driven into San Antonio today, she turned her face toward their campsite. Luther had agreed that gifts were acceptable and could have explained that fact to Jack, if asked. A glow and the dim outline of a coffeepot above it told her where their fire was, but she saw no movement in the observers' camp.

Pulling the bandanna through her fingers, she considered what to do. She would have to thank Jack for the small gift or reject it. And that, she realized, was why he had given it to her.

"Ward, please. I can't continue to miss the noon dinner." Facing the main camps, Les noticed that some of the drovers had already placed their empty plates in the wreck pan and were lighting cigars. There was no water here, and the herd was restless. They'd move out soon.

Ward's hand flashed forward and gripped her lower jaw. Anyone watching would think he merely touched her face as a lover might do. They wouldn't know he squeezed so hard that she couldn't speak. "What do you and Frisco talk about on night watch? Answer me!"

She clasped his wrist and signaled that he had to

release her or she couldn't talk. "We sing to the cattle ... we talk about the day's events ... he tells me things I need to know." When she saw Ward's eyes narrow, she added hastily, "like how to ford rivers, that kind of thing!" She was so hungry and tired. "Tonight's the last night Dal will ride with me. Tomorrow I'm on my own." And she dreaded the responsibility. "Ward, I have to go. Please." Dal was frowning at them.

"I don't understand you, Les. You act like it's unreasonable for a man to be concerned about his fiancée spending several hours in the middle of the night with another man. You don't appear to welcome my suggestions as to how you can improve your efficiency. You make it seem like you'd rather be with those people than with me."

"Ward, the observers' wagons travel faster than the herd," she said, trying to hold her voice to a reasonable tone. "You arrive before we do, and you've already had your dinner when Freddy and I ride in. We don't have much time to eat because we're the last to get here."

"Your stomach is more important than I am?"

"I'm not saying that," she said, beginning to despair. "But I do need to eat. When I miss dinner, I don't do as well out there. I'm practically dizzy by the time we bring the steers onto the bedding ground. Surely, you can understand—"

"Oh, I understand all right," he said in a low snarl. "I understand that I sold my store to come on a goddamned cattle drive to support a selfish woman who only thinks of herself. I understand that I'm putting myself through hell for nothing." He waved a hand toward his wagon. "I was going to give you a tin of canned tomatoes as a treat, Les, a little gift. What a fool I am. Why did I ever think someone named Roark would care about a mere shopkeeper?"

The mention of the tomatoes made her mouth water, and she swallowed, wishing she had them now because she wouldn't get dinner. Alex would have everything packed away before she got Ward calmed down and reassured.

It went exactly as she predicted. She was still trying to soothe him when Freddy shouted her name. When she glanced toward camp, the fire was out, the coffee-pot packed away, the drovers already gone. The only people still in camp were Alex, holding the reins to her mules; Freddy, waiting with Les's horse; and Dal, watching her with a thunderous expression.

"I have to go," she said, feeling a rush of panic. She murmured, "sorry," as she passed Dal, then swung up on her horse without meeting Freddy's glare.

"Les?" Alex shouted at her. "I've been waiting for you. Come here a minute."

Cowed by Dal's disapproval, she wanted to ride out immediately. But a lifetime of habit made her respond to Alex's imperious command. Trotting up beside the seat of the chuck wagon, she gazed at Alex with plead-ing eyes. "Please, no lectures."

Alex's cool gaze focused on her jaw. "If you let him browbeat you now, he always will." She tossed Les a small bundle, then braced her leg against the seat fender and lifted the reins.

"No one gets special consideration on this drive," Dal said sharply, speaking to Alex. "If Les doesn't eat when everyone else does, she doesn't eat. Don't do this again." He nodded at the bundle Les was hastily tuck-ing inside her vest.

Alex froze him with a withering glance. Les would have given the earth to be able to look as haughty and cold as Alex could when she wanted to.

"That is my sister," Alex snapped. "If I choose the

extra work of preparing a special packet to save her from starvation"—she flicked a look of disgust at Les—"that is my affair and not yours." She slapped the reins across the back of the mules and the chuck wagon shot forward toward the open range.

Tears of surprise, gratitude, and admiration glistened in Les's eyes. She wished she could stand up to people the way her sisters did. Her gaze followed the chuck wagon streaking across the prairie. She couldn't remember ever doing anything to help Alex.

Knots rose along Dal's jawline. "If you continue missing meals, we'll have to talk about it. That's not acceptable, so work it out." He pulled his horse around and cantered toward the herd.

"Bravo," Freddy said softly. She, too, was watching the chuck wagon race away from them. "Sometimes I admire the same qualities in Alex that also make me want to throttle her." She nodded at Les's vest. "The rest of us had the last of the son of bitch stew." A light shudder twitched her shoulders. "I hope she sent something better for you. Not that you deserve it."

They rode out together, trotting into the sun and dust toward the same stubborn beeves who always lagged behind the herd. "You don't understand," Les called. "Ward drives his own wagon, and he has nothing in common with Luther and that gambler. He needs company."

"Fine. Give him company after you eat," Freddy said, swinging in behind the herd.

"That would only be a few short minutes." Once she saw that the situation with the laggards was normal, she eased the packet out of her vest and untied the cloth. Alex had made her a thick cheese sandwich, fragrant with butter. And she'd been given a hard boiled egg, an item so precious that she could hardly believe her good fortune.

Freddy frowned at the egg. "Son of a gun. Maybe I'll miss a couple of meals, too."

"Ward can't seem to understand that I need time to eat." But she had to fix this problem or Dal would. Somehow, she had to make Ward see reason.

Freddy rode beside her, their legs brushing. "In the theater we handled this kind of thing by facing the person who was being obstinate and saying, 'Ward, piss on you'."

Les's head snapped up. She could have chastised Freddy for being vulgar. She could have pointed out that she'd never find the courage to say something like that. Instead, she imagined Ward's expression if she did, and burst into startled, delighted laughter.

Freddy smiled. "Hurry up and eat, then let's chase those stupid beeves back to the herd. I'm in a mood to show those old mossbacks who's in charge back here."

That night they came in for supper only fifteen minutes behind the other drovers, earning themselves a nod from Dal.

Les could feel Ward watching from the observers' camp, but she didn't look in that direction. Falling into step behind Freddy, she washed her face, then filed past Alex to receive her supper. After Alex forked a slab of meat onto her plate, Les looked up. "Thank you."

"Blood is thicker than water," Alex said with a shrug. Then she smiled and touched Les's wrist. "Don't rush off. For dessert we have sizzling hot, melted tallow poured into a plate of black sorghum molasses. Grady's recipe, naturally. He claims the boys love this."

"Tallow?" Les's mouth dropped open. "Animal lard

and molasses?" She and Alex looked at each other, then both burst into helpless laughter.

"I have it on good authority that you have to eat the stuff fast," Alex said with a slight shudder. "Or the tallow congeals and sticks to the roof of your mouth."

Freddy returned in time to hear. "I hope you're writing down all these recipes, Alex, so you can dazzle your fancy friends when you return to Boston." She laughed. "Course it might be kind of hard to find a longhorn's stomach tube in Boston."

"And she couldn't call it son of bitch stew," Les said. "She'd have to call it something more highbrow, like nongentleman's stew." That set them off, and they laughed until they were weak, until they became aware of the silence behind them.

When Les turned, she discovered the drovers were watching. At first she didn't understand. And then she did. This was the first time the cowboys had heard the Roark sisters laugh.

Still smiling, she studied her disheveled, sunburned sisters. For all Freddy's vulgarity and posturing and competitiveness, there were moments when Les truly enjoyed her company. And beneath Alex's stiff pride and standoffishness was a caring woman, more likable than Les had ever imagined.

Laughing with her sisters, glad to be with them, was the nicest, warmest moment she had experienced in recent years.

She had to do it. Freddy had delayed the chore for two days. After supper, rubbing her tongue over the roof of her mouth to scrape off congealed tallow, she slowly walked through the early darkness to the observers' camp. Ward was off somewhere with Les, but Luther and Jack were sitting beside their fire, drinking coffee.

Jack stood. "Evening, Fancy honey. I was wondering when you'd come calling."

Heart sinking, Freddy slipped a look at Luther. His puzzled expression told her that he hadn't missed Jack's familiarity. Now everyone would know that she and Jack knew each other and there had been something between them. Squaring her shoulders, she looked him in the eyes. "Don't call me honey," she said, hoping she sounded as cold as Alex. "And don't buy me any more presents." She pushed the bandanna into his hand.

"Now, Fancy honey, don't be like that. We talked about that, remember? And we decided it wouldn't do any harm to be friendly during this drive. Sort of pick things up where we left off."

She stared at him with disgust. They had been meticulously discreet during the time he was calling on her. She hadn't wanted Pa to get a whiff that she was seeing a gambling man, and she didn't want to give the town gossips something new to hang her with. Jack had said he understood. What she hadn't mentioned was that she had never come to terms with seeing his kind of man. Now he'd spilled the beans in front of Luther.

It got worse. Dal walked out of the darkness between the wagons with Ward and Les behind him. They all heard what Jack said next.

He stepped toward her, waving the bandanna. "I bought this for you in San Antonio. A little token of my affection, Fancy honey. For old times' sake."

She was so angry that she was shaking. "I told you to go to hell once, Jack Caldwell, and I'm telling you again."

He laughed. "You're a feisty little thing, aren't you?

I've always liked that about you." He gave her one of those contrived melting looks that made her want to slap him. "There's a nice moon tonight. How about a little walk out there under the stars? Five will get you ten that I've got some things to say that you want to hear."

"You lose," she snapped. "You have nothing to say that I want to hear, not now, not ever." Turning on her heels, her face flaming, she marched back to the fire where the drovers were sitting, drinking coffee, swapping tall tales.

She hadn't made it halfway when Dal moved up beside her, shoving his hands into his back pockets. "Well, Fancy honey, seems that you neglected to mention that you and Lola share an interest in the same man. You want to tell me again how you don't trust me because I used to know your stepmother?"

"My association with Jack Caldwell was over before I ever met you!"

"An association? Is that what they call it now?" His blue eyes narrowed into slits. "I believe I explained the same was true for me and Lola."

A flush climbed her face. "You can go to hell, too, right along with Caldwell!"

"I expect I will. That's a given." He stared down into her eyes. "Fancy honey."

On his lips, her stage name sounded cheap and foolish, more like a name for a soiled dove. Heat throbbing in her face, she pushed past him to fetch her bedroll, then carried it well away from the fire and climbed inside.

She wouldn't have imagined that it would be this upsetting to have Dal learn that she and Jack had been friendly. And she knew that associating with Jack would only confirm the popular perception that actresses were of low moral character. Even Ward Hamm was more respectable than Jack Caldwell. Decent women didn't invite gambling men into their parlors.

Rolling onto her stomach, Freddy buried her hot face in the crook of an arm. Her impulse was to seek out Dal and explain that she had been lonely, and Jack had been the first to come calling as if she were the Freddy Roark she had been before she ran off with the acting company. From the first minute, she'd known he was no good, but she'd given in to loneliness.

She was still castigating herself when two thousand steers simultaneously jumped to their feet and the ground started to shake. This time Dal would expect her to help control the wild run.

Terrified and trembling, Freddy hopped around pulling on her boots, then ran through a cloud of dust to climb into the saddle and race after the stampeding cattle. It required every ounce of frail courage that she possessed.

CHAPTER 12

The moon was bright enough that Freddy couldn't later claim that she was unable to see where she was going. It was sheer terror that drove Dal's instructions out of her mind and led her to the right of the herd, where the dust and heat wasn't as intense. Only the most experienced men worked the right. By the time she recalled that her assigned position was on the left, it was too late to make a correction.

Freddy's heart lurched. Once the point men turned the lead steers, the herd could circle around, stampeding right toward her. Since she wasn't experienced enough to turn the panicked steers into the next circle, the only thing to do now was take herself out of the action or risk ending up trapped in the center of a mill.

An image of the two dead steers who'd been trampled in the last stampede flashed through her mind as she jerked the reins of her horse hard, heading away from the terrible noise of clashing, clacking horns and pounding hooves. Digging her heels into her horse's flanks, she galloped full out toward the dark emptiness of the open range, praying the stampede wouldn't overtake her.

When her horse stumbled and went down, Freddy

screamed, but she now had enough experience to roll out of the stirrups and off the saddle. In a flash she and her horse were both on their feet, Freddy almost sobbing with gratitude that she wasn't injured. But when she dashed toward her horse, he bolted, speeding away in the darkness. Frozen in horror, she stood stock still, feeling the ground begin to shake beneath her boots.

The drovers had turned the point and the wild, uncontrolled herd was pounding straight toward her.

Relief flooded Dal's chest when he grasped they'd caught this stampede early enough that they would bring it under control relatively quickly. Caleb Webster had already begun to turn the lead steers into a mill.

The big question was, where were Freddy and Les? They should be on the left helping to hold the herd together, but things had a way of going wrong during stampedes.

Leaning over his horse's neck, he caught up with Caleb and the lead steers, and started to press them into a turn. At the head of the run there wasn't much dust and the moon was bright enough that when he glanced ahead, he saw a figure on foot running toward the open range. When he saw the drover fall, he knew the man was as good as dead. He was directly in the path of the oncoming steers and couldn't jump to his feet and run fast enough to avoid getting trampled.

Baring his teeth, Dal spurred his horse and hoped the buckskin could fly, hoped he didn't go down, too. He wasn't confident of anything until Bill and Daniel loomed in front of him, shouting and riding straight at the lead steers. The steers bore left to avoid the men and galloped into the mill. But the drover on foot was still in trouble. The drift of momentum would sweep the herd right over him.

Dal bore down on the man, then reined hard. Leaning, he gripped the drover by the arm and pulled him up. As the drover grabbed him from behind, he had a second to realize it was Freddy, then he urged the horse through the darkness, flying out onto the range, away from the swing of charging animals.

He didn't stop until he was positive they were beyond the herd's drift. Then he sat for a minute letting his heart settle back in his chest. Now he became aware of Freddy's arms wrapped around his waist like a vise, felt her shaking along his back. Away from the din of hooves and horns, he could hear her quietly sobbing. Gently, he pried her fingers open and her arms fell away as if her bones had turned to sawdust. She slipped off his horse and collapsed to the ground, giving in to a storm of weeping.

Swinging to the ground, he muttered a curse, then staggered backward a step when she sprang up and threw herself against him. "My horse went down and ran off and I, oh God, I was so frightened, so terrified, I thought sure I would be killed and the ground was shaking so badly I could hardly stand, let alone run, and they were coming and I couldn't get out of their way and—"

Her arms went around his waist again, hanging on like she wanted to melt into his bones and hide there. She had lost her hat, and the twine tying her hair had broken, releasing wild silky curls down her back and over her shoulders. He hesitated, then wrapped his arms around her trembling body and murmured next to her temple.

"It's over now, and you aren't hurt or injured. Freddy, it's all right." The words came automatically, without thought, because the instant his arms went around her everything became physical. She was electric, vibrating against him, the heat and scent of her searing all thought from his mind. His hands moved on her back, rubbing the taut muscles rising along the valley of her spine, and his chest tightened beneath the crush of her breasts. When her hips moved against his, his body responded with an instant, powerful arousal.

She raised her head, bringing her lips an inch from his. "I'm sorry I lost my horse, he—"

"It happens," he said gruffly. In the moonlight, her damp eyes were dark and bottomless, a mystery as ancient as the earth. Her chest still heaved, each gasping breath thrusting her breasts against him. He slid his fingers to her slender waist, letting his hands rest briefly on the swell of her hips, his breath quickening. And he knew the exact moment when she became aware that she was in his arms, locked against him, knew the moment she felt his hard urgent arousal and understood that he wanted her. Her eyes flared and she gasped softly, her gaze dropped to his lips.

If she had stepped away, the incident would have ended right there. But she was as paralyzed as he was, as ready for this inevitable moment as he had been. She stood motionless, breathing hard as he slid the warmth of his hands up her rib cage, letting his thumbs come to rest beneath her breasts, feeling the weight of soft flesh on the backs of his hands. A low groan scraped the back of his throat as her breath hitched, then flowed over his lips, and her hips returned the pressure of his. His mind exploded.

Instinct overwhelmed him and he dropped his hands to cup the sweet curve of her buttocks and he molded her tightly against his erection. When she felt him rock against her, her eyelids fluttered, a soft moan came from her throat, and her body sagged. Together they sank to their knees, then she opened her eyes and her lips parted. "Dal . . ."

He kissed her then, not gently, not tenderly. He didn't kiss her to comfort her. He took her mouth hungrily, almost savagely, wanting to punish her for having a body that tormented him, for telling him that his last kiss had meant nothing, needed to punish her for letting scum like Jack Caldwell call her honey, and for ever thinking about a man who wasn't him.

This time she wasn't motionless in his arms. Her hands flew to the sides of his face and she kissed him back, suddenly as wild and hungry and crazy as he was. As if she had awakened in the moonlight to find herself alive and needing to feel, she threw her arms around his neck and lunged forward, knocking him flat on the ground. Mouth locked to hers, he caught her by the waist, rolled her over and kissed her deeply, wildly, exploring her lips and mouth with his tongue, catching fire when he felt her pliant body wiggling beneath him. Wrapped together, they rolled on the ground, legs tangling, hands clutching and grabbing, rubbing against each other, driving each other wild and half-mad with desire and touching and moonlit craziness.

He found her breasts with his hands and dropped his lips to her arching throat, tasting dust and woman sweat and a trace of something that reminded him of apples. She tore his shirt at the throat, ripping it downward, and slipped her hands inside, her fingers like brands of fire across his skin. One minute she was straddling him, the next minute he'd rolled on top of her. It was like a dam had burst within them both, releasing a flood tide of desire and urgency. And God help him, he would have taken her right there on the ground with a stampede winding down a hundred yards behind them.

Desperate to suck her breasts into his mouth, he was about to rip open her shirt when a steer ran out of the darkness and galloped past them not six feet away. The longhorn was almost upon them before Dal registered the sound, smell, and the tremble in the earth beneath his knees.

Disoriented and struggling to catch his breath, he jumped to his feet, his first thought that the herd had turned and was thundering toward them, that they were about to be trampled into the range dirt. Another animal was headed in their direction, but it was a horse chasing the muley who had peeled out from the edges of the mill. Drinkwater reined up. "Need a hand, boss?"

"Freddy got tossed. We lost our horses," he growled, noticing that his horse was gone too. "We'll walk in." He watched Drinkwater ride after the muley, then he combed his fingers through his hair and extended a hand to help Freddy to her feet. Hazy moonlight revealed bits of grass and twigs caught in the wild tangles of her hair. Her shirttail had pulled out of her trousers and her lips were swollen. A quick look down at himself revealed a torn shirt and unmistakable grass stains on his knees. He had no idea where his hat or his horse were.

As his mind cleared the full enormity of what he had done washed over him. He'd forgotten about a stampede, for Christ's sake. He couldn't believe it. All the time he'd been rolling on the ground with this woman, the earth had been shaking and men were shouting, and he hadn't noticed.

Shocked, he said the first thing that came into his mind. "This can't happen again."

She looked up from tucking in her shirt and putting herself in order. "Are you claiming what we just did didn't mean anything this time either?" Her chin came up in a warning.

He slid a slow look over her breasts and down her hips. "You know damned well it meant something." And he didn't like it. Sex had no place on a cattle drive. There were enough problems on the trail without stirring women into the mix. What he hadn't anticipated was how seeing this woman every day would get under his skin and drive him crazy.

"Where's our camp?"

"About two miles that way." The drovers were still milling the herd, but the stampede was winding down. In the distance, he spotted the glow of two campfires.

Even though they stood on the open range with nothing near them, she elbowed him in the ribs to move him out of her way rather than step around him. Setting a line for the distant campfires, she shoved past, walking fast enough that he knew she was angry.

"What's eating you?" he asked, catching up.

"It meant something, but it can't happen again. I'm thinking about that."

"It's a long way to Abilene, Freddy. If you and I start something, others are sure to find out about it."

"And you don't want anyone to know that you've taken up with some low character like me?" She spit the words between her teeth. "Well you're no prize either, Frisco. Maybe I don't want anyone to know I almost made a mistake with you!"

"What the hell are you talking about?" He had to lengthen his stride to keep up with her.

"You're like all the rest. You think a woman who's been onstage is easy pickings, so you took advantage of how scared I was."

When he stopped to stare, she moved out ahead of

him. "You're not making sense. I did not take advantage of you!"

"Oh? You can't take advantage of a whore or an actress because they're already ruined? Is that what you're saying?"

This was the thing about women that he most hated. They twisted a man's words into a hangman's knot.

He gripped her shoulders and leaned down to stare into her face. "We're not taking another step until you tell me what the hell is going on here."

"You tell *me* what's going on here!"

"Freddy, I honest to God don't know what you're talking about."

"Well don't worry," she snarled before she wrenched out of his hands. "This won't happen again. You can count on it, you son of a bitch!"

It took him a mile of steady walking, watching her fanny in the moonlight, before he figured it out and moved up beside her.

"The reason I said we couldn't do this again—"

"We won't," she snapped.

"Is because I need to keep my mind on business and so do you. This drive is crucially important to both of us. I can't be distracted thinking about getting you alone somewhere when I should be thinking about tomorrow's problems." Already he suspected that sex could be more destructive than liquor ever had been. Even in his drinking days, he hadn't forgotten a stampede that was occurring a few yards away. He wouldn't have believed such a lapse was possible.

"Like I said. You took advantage of a vulnerable moment, treated me like a whore, and now that you've satisifed your curiosity, you're taking the high road. Making me feel used."

Grabbing her shoulders, he spun her around. "I've

wanted you from the first moment I saw you, and I don't apologize for that. I'm going to be wanting you for a long time to come, and I don't apologize for that either. But nothing is going to happen between you and me on this drive. After the drive . . . that's different." He was starting to get mad himself.

"Nothing's going to happen later or anytime!" She wrenched out from under his hands. "As a matter of fact I was using you. I was acting back there, practicing a scene. So don't flatter yourself that I'm holding my breath waiting for the next time busy dedicated you can find a moment to take your pleasure. What happened was a scene from *Home on the Range*. I've worked out the scene now, and I don't need you anymore."

He was about eighty percent certain that she was lying. Nevertheless, her comments stung exactly as she had intended them to.

"Were you acting with Caldwell, too, Fancy honey?" he said sharply. "Practicing an interior seduction scene?"

When she didn't say anything, he knew he'd scored a point. Jealousy, sudden and hot, burned his chest. He couldn't stand to think about Caldwell kissing her, putting his hands on her. He couldn't tolerate the thought of any man touching her.

"Jack was a mistake," she said finally. "I seem to be very good at making mistakes."

He wanted to know just how much of a mistake Caldwell had been. How far had it gone between them? "Caldwell doesn't seem to think so. From what I heard, he believes the two of you are going to get real cozy on this drive. Pick up where you left off, I believe he said. Just where was that, Freddy? Where did you leave off with that son of a bitch?"

She whirled on him. "Jack's a gambler, a womanizer, a man with the morals of a snake. But he's also the only man in Klees who was willing to be seen in public with me! The only reason no one knew I was seeing him is because I wanted it that way. Not him. Knowing that he didn't give a damn what other people thought about him or me meant the world to me! I'll always be grateful to Jack Caldwell because he came to my door when I thought I was dying of loneliness and he reminded me that some men don't believe every actress is a whore!"

Dal would be picking her speech apart and thinking about it for a long time.

"As for getting cozy with Jack on this drive," she continued, practically nose to nose with him, "that isn't going to happen because he's Lola's next husband and because I don't trust him. I'm finished with him, and, mister, I'm finished with you!"

Dal let her stamp off and followed a few paces behind. Her defense of Caldwell ate at him, and he didn't like it that she assumed he condemned her for going onstage. Finally, he had inexplicably shifted from "This can't happen again" to wanting her so much that his groin ached. It was a relief to reach the campsite and get away from her.

As usual after a stampede, everyone in camp was awake and stirred up. The first person he saw was Jack Caldwell. Caldwell, Luther, and Hamm had come to the main camp and stood near the chuck wagon drinking coffee and watching Alex swab out a gash on Dan Clouter's thigh. Caldwell watched Freddy stride toward the coffeepot hanging over the fire.

Frowning, Dal made himself focus on business instead of taking a swing at Caldwell as he wanted to. He turned his gaze on Daniel Clouter. "How bad?"

Daniel had dropped his pants and long johns so Alex

could doctor the gash, and he stood hunched over, his hands cupped over his privates, his face flaming. "Not too bad," he said between his teeth, sucking in a breath as Alex washed out a four-inch cut with medicinal alcohol. She leaned forward in her wheelchair, her face stony and concentrated on the job at hand.

"Anyone else get hurt?" he asked her, watching Freddy out of the corner of his eyes.

After reporting several minor injuries, Alex looked up. "Are we going to have midnight stampedes all the way to Abilene?"

"Possibly. But you're handling it just fine." Alex continued to surprise him. She wasn't much of a cook, he didn't know if she ever would be, but she did manage to put out a meal. He was beginning to rely on Alex to maintain a cool head in any crisis that didn't directly threaten her. Maybe she fell apart after she'd doctored the boys and after every meal, maybe she wept in the privacy of her bedroll, but when duty called, she grimly did what was needed.

"Your horse came back to the remuda, and one of the Webster boys brought in Freddy's mare," Grady said, coming up to him. Grady grinned at Dan's efforts to cover his privates, then he slid a look toward Dal, jerked his head toward the remuda, and walked away.

Dal followed, ready to choose a fresh mount and ride out to help the drovers untangle the mill. There was no need to explain to Grady how he and Freddy had lost their horses. The only thing unusual about a rider getting tossed during a wild ride in the darkness was that neither of them had brought back an injury to anything but their pride. "I'll take the roan," he said.

Grady nodded, but he didn't walk into the herd of horses right away. "What do you know about that

Caldwell fella?" he asked, biting off a chunk of tobacco and tucking it inside his cheek.

"Enough not to trust him. Why?"

"See that red mustang over there? Got hooked in the first stampede, and she's not healing up like I want her to. Anyways, I was up tending to her right before that old piebald steer jumped up and started running toward Sunday, you know the one I mean."

"Keep talking," Dal said, frowning.

"Just before all hell broke loose, I thought I seen Caldwell walking toward the bedding ground. He'd circled around the camp and was far enough out that I woulda missed him if we hadn't had a moon tonight and if I hadn't just happened to look that way when I did."

Grady spit a stream of juice on the ground, then walked into the herd of horses to fetch the roan, leaving Dal to think about the implications of Caldwell approaching the bedding ground. All it would take to start a stampede would be one loud noise. Or a rock thrown at one of the steers. Stampedes would start for a dozen reasons, but they didn't start for no reason.

The same thought crossed his mind again in the morning when he discovered the result of the stampede was one steer dead and two missing.

"Hell, Dal, we've checked every ditch and gully for three miles in every direction," Drinkwater reported, eating his breakfast while he talked. "You want my opinion, those two missing steers probably joined up with the herd right behind us." He forked some boiled potatoes into his mouth. "You want me and Peach to ride over and check?"

"No," he said reluctantly. He'd lose two drovers for a full day, it would disrupt the other trail boss's operation, and the King's Walk steers might not even be there.

He looked toward the three men sitting around the observers' campfire, his gaze steadying on Jack Caldwell. Stampedes were easy to start, and costly. Steers got lost, men got tired or injured, the outfit suffered. But stampedes were a fact of life on any cattle drive. A bright moon or a drop of rain could start a stampede. An unusual odor or an unfamiliar sound. Because Caldwell had taken a midnight stroll could mean something, or it could mean nothing.

Much as he would have liked to throw him off the drive, he had no proof that Caldwell had done a damned thing except gloat over the lost steers.

He tossed back the last drops in his coffee cup. "Get the drovers moving," he said to Drinkwater. "And keep the pace up. I want those beeves so tired tonight that they can't move."

"Is it true you were seeing Jack Caldwell?" Alex asked curiously, as Freddy brought her breakfast plate to the wreck pan.

Freddy sent a silent curse winging toward the observer's camp. "What of it?"

Alex wiped a rag over a plate and sat it aside to dry in the morning sun. "A gambler, Freddy?" Her eyebrows rose and she rolled her eyes. "How could you?"

"Well pardon me if I've tarnished the family honor once again. Pardon me for being lonely. Pardon me for keeping company with a no-account gambling man instead of one of the hundreds of respectable men who were beating a path to my door."

Angry, she slammed her empty coffee cup down on the chuck wagon worktable hard enough to rattle the stack of clean dishes. Hard enough that the table's support leg shook and disturbed Alex's precarious balance. Her hands flew out of the wreck pan's dishwater and she grabbed for her crutch, but not in time. She fell sprawling to the ground.

Before Freddy recovered from the shock of it, Charlie stepped over Alex, dropped his plate and cup in the wreck pan, and started toward the remuda to choose his horse for the day.

"How can you just step over her?" Freddy demanded, horrified and furious.

"Huh?" Charlie looked back, then down at Alex, who was struggling to reach her crutch. "She ain't hurt, is she?" He peered at her. "Naw." And continued on his way.

"I'll help you," Freddy said, rushing to her sister.

"Just get out of the way." Shoving down her skirts, Alex lifted to her knees, then gripped the crutch and pulled herself up.

"I'm sorry, Alex. Honestly. I wasn't thinking about you balancing against the table."

"Of course not," Alex snapped. "But falling down is nothing new, it happens several times a day." Pink blazed on her cheeks, and she was angry.

"When you fall . . . does anyone help you back up?"

"No, Freddy. They don't." Alex faced her with a hard glare. "Does anyone help you when you get tossed off your horse during the morning rodeo?" She referred to the bucking and kicking that occurred every morning while the riders settled out their horses. "People are falling on the ground every day of this drive. The novelty of watching me fall over has worn off for most of the drovers. Not you, apparently, but most."

She hadn't seen Alex fall that often, and this was the first time Freddy had witnessed the other drovers' indifference to it. She stared at her sister, considering Alex's precious dignity and poise. Regardless how casually Alex tried to treat the incident, it must humiliate her every time she crashed to the ground.

"This is very hard for you, isn't it?"

"Your grasp of the obvious is stunning. And it only took you—how many weeks?—to notice. Yes. This is hard. Damned hard as you might say. Hard in ways you can't even imagine because being so absorbed with yourself, you wouldn't even try!"

"I'm self-absorbed?" Freddy leaned forward, careful not to shake the worktable. "When have you ever given a thought to anyone but yourself? When you wanted something you just took it. Or manipulated everyone around you. Or made us feel stupid with your holier-than-thou superiority. You always had to have things your way!"

Alex's face turned white, and she gripped her crutch. "I'm tired of being blamed for everything that's gone wrong in your life! If you feel stupid, that's not my fault. I didn't tell you to run off with that acting troupe and ruin your reputation and your future!"

"You can run off and that's fine, but God forbid that anyone else does the same thing!"

"It was hardly the same thing! I ran off to get married. You just threw yourself away!"

"I was looking for a future, exactly like you were!"

Dal's hand came down on her shoulder. Freddy knew it was him by the leap of electricity that shot through her body and momentarily stopped her heartbeat. "Les has already ridden out. Grady is holding your horse." His voice was cool, carefully impartial.

But she felt like a foot soldier flanked by two attacking armies, and it infuriated her that he removed his hand before she could order him to. "This started because I wanted to help you get up off the ground," she flung at Alex, hoping to get in the last word.

"No, it started because you knocked me to the ground!"

"That was an accident," she shouted, her face turning red. "And don't you say a word," she yelled at Dal, who stood between them, a frown lining his bronzed forehead. "Or you either," she snapped at Grady when she reached the remuda and found him impatiently waiting for her.

"This ain't the time or the place," Grady said sharply. "You got a beef with your sisters, you save it until this drive is over, you hear me, girl? When the cowboys start fighting amongst themselves, the drive goes wrong. If you want to git along, you gotta get along. Don't forget it."

"Tell that to Alex!"

"I will." He slapped Walker on the butt, and the horse kicked, then bolted for the range, carrying Freddy with him.

When Freddy rode up on the stupid stragglers, the first thing Les said was, "Jack Caldwell?" Censure flickered in Les's brown eyes along with a hint of superiority.

"I didn't know he was seeing Lola, all right? It was a mistake, and I regret it. What do you want me to do? Shoot myself?" Baring her teeth, she galloped toward the stragglers.

Last night she had defended Jack to Dal, and she had been wrong. Jack hadn't kept their relationship discreet to please her. Since Jack was seeing Lola at the same time he was seeing her, it suited him to keep her hidden away, that's why he had agreed to Freddy's plea for secrecy. Oh he'd had everything going his way.

Two women, each of whom had a reason not to want her relationship with him known.

She rode by herself during the morning, keeping her distance from Les, thinking about Jack and men in general, and about Dal Frisco.

Every time she thought about Dal, hot color rose on her throat. Actually she understood what he'd said about not letting the attraction between them explode again. She had pretended not to because that was easier than admitting her own embarrassment.

She'd capitulated to his wildly exciting kisses as easily as if she were indeed the woman of low character that most people assumed she was. She hadn't uttered a peep of protest. The instant she felt his desire for her, her mind and body had caught fire with an answering passion.

With a sigh, she wondered how long she would have to pay for a long-ago mistake. How many years would it take before people stopped treating her as if she'd spent time in a brothel? But maybe she deserved censure. Dal Frisco had taken her in his arms and without a moment's hesitation she had flung herself against his body and behaved as if she hadn't an ounce of morality. Like she was perfectly willing to take those wild kisses to their ultimate destination.

And, oh God, she had been. That's what hurt. His touch, his mouth, his hands had inflamed her to the point of craziness, of wanting him so much that she was dizzy and breathless and unaware of anything but him. Nothing even close to such a thing had ever happened to her.

She wished she never had to see Dal Frisco again.

Two women, each of whom had a reason not to want

CHAPTER 13

By the time the herd reached the Colorado River just
north of Austin, Les had driven the stragglers through
enough spring-swollen creeks that the Colorado didn't
worry her. The only difference with this crossing was
that the river was broader and deep enough that the
men had to take the wheels off the chuck wagon and
float it across.

Les rode forward to watch. She stayed out of the
way, but was close enough to see how white Alex's
face was when she finally drew a deep breath, then
flapped her reins across the mules' backs. The mules
started across the river, pulling the wagon behind them
like a raft while Dal and four other drovers strained on
the shore, playing out a rope tied to the back of the
wagon to keep it from turning in the current.

Unconsciously holding her breath, Les struggled to
guess what Alex was thinking and feeling, tried to
imagine the courage and trust it must take for her sister
to enter the swiftly moving water. Les didn't think she
would have been that brave.

Though she hadn't told them, she was developing a
grudging admiration for both of her sisters. She had
seen Alex dishing out food with tears glittering in her

eyes, but the meal was always ready. Twice now firewood had been impossible to find, and she had glimpsed Alex rolling her wheelchair on the range, forking up dried cow pies to burn. And Alex, being Alex, brought her own standards to the ordeal. She insisted on the men using napkins, and it had been Alex who demanded a latrine tent for herself and Les and Freddy.

And Freddy. Freddy set the pace on the drag, relentlessly nudging the stragglers along even when she and Les had been awake half the night working a stampede. If Freddy hadn't made the first cut when skinning the dead steers, those steers would still be lying on the range. And it was Freddy who sat around the fire with the other drovers, drinking coffee, laughing at their tall tales and sly jokes. Freddy who had learned all the verses to the cowboy songs. Freddy who kept practicing with her rope and gun, who had given the stragglers silly names that made Les laugh.

Once Alex made it safely across the Colorado, Les rode back to the main herd, grazing about a mile from the river. But she continued to think about Freddy.

From the time Freddy had begun to blossom, at about age fourteen, men had flocked around her. It was still happening even though Freddy had thrown away her reputation. Learning about Freddy seeing Caldwell had shocked Les, but hadn't surprised her, as she'd noticed how Caldwell always seemed to be watching her sister. And Dal Frisco, too. Both men stood straighter when Freddy appeared, and a hot speculative look narrowed their eyes. Unconsciously, they became more of what they were. More virile, more handsome, more masculine. Around Freddy, Caldwell seemed sleeker, more casually elegant. Frisco became more rugged, more commanding.

Les didn't understand this. In the past, she had condemned Freddy for leading men on, but now that she could observe closely, she had to admit this was not true. Freddy didn't flirt, didn't carry herself differently in a man's presence, didn't behave differently. If anything, she behaved as if she detested Caldwell and didn't trust Frisco. Yet both men watched her with an expression that burned. And when Dal and Freddy were together, something sizzled in the air, as if a violent lightning storm were about to erupt.

Les bent backwards to be accommodating and attractive to Ward, but nothing hot burned in his eyes except anger or resentment. The hard animal heat she saw when Dal looked at Freddy was not present when Ward looked at her. The closest Ward came to the looks that Freddy inspired was when he talked about the money. Sometimes she regretted her choice, but it was too late to do anything about it. Ward had sold his store; his commitment to her was total.

She sighed as she rode up beside Freddy, scrutinizing her sister carefully. Like Les, Freddy was peeling from too much sun. Her nose and cheeks flaked, as did the tops of her ears and the back of her neck. Today Freddy wore her hair pinned up inside her hat, wore a sun-faded shirt, and dusty trousers and boots. A flame of jealousy scorched Les's throat. Freddy's vivid coloring and vivacious expression made her beautiful even now, when conventional wisdom insisted women required curls and powder and corsets and frippery to appeal to men. It irritated Les that Freddy could attract two men with her hair skinned back, dressed as a man, her skin peeling, and coated with dust and grime.

"Alex and the chuck wagon are already across. So are Ward and Luther and Jack." Les saw no reaction to the mention of Jack Caldwell's name. "Dal will start the herd soon."

Les had come a long way since the drive began. Now she could spend all day in the saddle without feeling crippled by suppertime. She would never be comfortable around the horns, but the beeves no longer terrified her as they had in the beginning. It didn't happen often, but occasionally she experienced a euphoric moment when she felt like a capable woman, a person who was carrying her own weight. "Dal says we'll hold the herd here for two days and let them graze. We'll all have a chance to ride into Austin and have a bath if we like."

Up ahead, the lead steers had accelerated the pace, trotting toward the water. They would wade into the river up to their knees to drink. The herd would follow, bawling with thirst, and sheer numbers would push the lead steers on across the river.

"It should be an easy crossing," Freddy commented, shielding her eyes to peer ahead.

But something went wrong. She and Freddy didn't realize it immediately, but eventually, even with their limited experience, they sensed the time had come and passed when they should have moved up the stragglers. Clouds of dust billowed near the river, and the sound of bellowing and shouting rolled back to them.

"Ride up and see what's happening," Freddy suggested. Her frown said she would have preferred to check things herself. But recently Freddy had been gritting her teeth and following Dal's orders to the letter.

What Les saw first was chaos. The cattle, this close to water, raged out of control, every instinct urging them forward, but strangely, the drovers were working frantically to turn the steers back toward the range.

Puzzled, knowing her best course of action was to skirt the pandemonium, Les rode to the riverbank above the point Dal had chosen for the crossing. Reining hard, she stared and her mouth fell open. What she saw horrified her.

Directly opposite the crossing point, Luther and Jack's wagon sat sunk in mud, at an angle that blocked the animals surging out of the river. Pushed by the herd entering the water behind them, the lead steers had crossed the river, had run into the mired wagon, and had no time to veer around it before the oncoming herd shoved them forward. Blocked, the animals began to back up. Now, those caught in deep water with no room to move forward and the herd coming down on top of them were being pushed under the water. They were drowning.

Feeling like she was strangling, Les scanned the banks of the river, narrow here. Dead cattle swirled in the current, littered the water's edge. Terrified animals thrashed in the river, then went under as she watched. And the herd kept coming, escaping from the drovers' frantic efforts to turn them away from the death trap the river crossing had become.

Frozen by the enormity of the disaster, Les might have sat on her horse staring at the carnage for God knows how long. But suddenly Freddy appeared beside her, swearing steadily, her face pale and stunned. "My God," she whispered.

"Who's watching the tail of the herd?" Les remembered to ask.

"We can round them up later. Right now the boys need help." Dropping forward over her horse, Freddy raced along the bank toward a seething mass of heaving, hooking horns and hides.

Even the thought of joining her made Les feel light-headed and sick. If she sat here one more second thinking about it, she would never do it. Grinding her teeth together, she sucked in a gulp of air, then galloped after Freddy, screaming and shouting as the others were doing. In the dust and bawling madness, she lost sight of Freddy. After a minute she no longer thought about anything except staying on her horse and avoiding the slashing horns and terrified steers.

When the battle finally ended, and they had the herd running toward the previous night's bedding ground and away from the river, Les slumped in the saddle, more exhausted than she remembered ever being. How simple life had been before this drive, how calm and predictable and leisurely. Now here she was, filthy, so tired she could hardly think, sunburned, thirsty, deprived of privacy and any hint of comfort, her nostrils filled with the heat and stink of cattle.

That's what she was thinking as she gradually became aware of an unusual warmth flowing down her left leg, followed by the realization of wetness. When she looked down, sunlight glistened on bright red blood soaking her trouser leg. She stared and blinked, astonished that she didn't recall getting slashed, had felt nothing.

Now she did. Pain, hot and searing, arched through her body, and she gasped and gripped her thigh above the gash in her trousers. Her eyelids fluttered and she swayed and sagged then slipped off her horse, falling to the trampled ground.

Rage shook Dal's body, communicating to his horse, making the animal restless and prancy. The buckskin also reacted with nervous edginess to the sight and smell of the dead cattle strewn along the banks of the river.

"How many?" he snapped, staring at the wagon that had set off this disaster. The near side was smashed. Goods littered the ground. Beyond the wagon the few animals who had managed to get around it grazed on lush spring grasses.

Caleb Webster shifted on his saddle and wiped a sleeve across his forehead. "I count forty-two carcasses. We'll probably find more when we check farther down."

"Son of a bitch!" Dal bit down on his back teeth hard enough to make his lower face ache. "Get Drinkwater and your brother and move that wagon out of there."

Jerking savagely on the reins, he turned the buckskin away from the carcasses, rode upstream to a point where the water was clear and crossed there, emerging on the far side with boots and pant legs dripping.

Grady waited beside his horse, studying the dead steers and shaking his head. "Christ a'mighty," he murmured, then spit a stream of tobacco juice between his front teeth. "We can butcher up a couple, but no way can we make use of 'em all."

"What the hell happened?" Dal demanded, jerking his head toward the wagon. "How did that wagon get there just as we ran the leads into the water?"

"Me and Peach got the wheels back on the chuck wagon and moved it and the remuda off that way." Grady nodded toward the camp in the distance. "Our observers"—he paused to spit, contempt in the gesture—"crossed closer to town. Luther and Hamm rode in together." He pushed back his hat and gave Dal a long expressionless look. "Caldwell drove the stuck wagon."

Dal's thigh muscles tightened like cords of iron and the buckskin danced to one side.

"First I noticed something wrong," Grady continued, glancing at the mired wagon, "was when I seen Caldwell unhitching the horses. With no way to move the wagon, the minute those horses moved out the fat was in the fire." He let a long beat pass and then added, "Course, if he hadn't gotten the horses out, maybe we'd a still wrecked on the crossing plus had us two dead horses."

Without a word, Dal turned and rode toward the campsite. Every cell in his body urged him to close the distance fast and beat the living hell out of Caldwell. He forced himself to proceed at a trot, tried to gain control of his fury.

Accidents happened on every drive. And plain bad luck, that happened, too. But a chain of coincidences? He wasn't a man who believed in coincidence. Yet Caldwell just happened to be driving the wagon Luther Moreland usually drove. And Caldwell just happened to drive it along the riverbank instead of going directly to the campsite. And the wagon just happened to dip near enough to the bank that the wheels sank in mud. And this just happened to occur at the precise spot where the herd would cross and at the exact moment the lead steers entered the river.

He tied the buckskin to the wheel of the chuck wagon, then strode toward the observers' camp. Luther, Ward, and Caldwell stood when he approached and, to their credit, both Luther and Ward were white-faced, and obviously shaken.

Caldwell wore a small half smile. "I guess you're looking for me. Sorry for the trouble," he said smoothly, pushing back the edges of his jacket to hook his thumbs in his vest pockets. "I wanted to watch the crossing. Guess I picked the wrong spot to do it. By the time I realized my mistake," he shrugged, "the wagon was stuck."

It was a lie that couldn't be disproved, so Dal didn't even try. He hit Caldwell in the stomach, then as he doubled over, Dal caught him in the jaw hard enough to lay him out. His fury was so great that he would have kicked Caldwell's ribs toward his spine if Luther hadn't gripped him from behind.

"What happened was an accident," Luther said sharply.

Dal spun and thrust his face forward. "Why the hell was Caldwell driving your wagon?"

Luther's eyebrows rose and a flush darkened his skin, but he didn't back away. "Hamm had some legal questions about the sale of his store and asked if I would ride with him." Luther placed a hand on Dal's sleeve. "You're out of line. It was just bad luck."

He didn't believe it. Eyes narrowed down hard, he watched Caldwell sit up and rub his jaw. "If you pull another stunt like this," he warned, speaking between his teeth, "I'll break both of your legs and leave you to crawl to the nearest town."

Caldwell muttered an obscenity and pushed to his feet. "I won't forget this, Frisco."

"I'll make sure you don't." Dal took a step forward and would have beaten the sneer off of Caldwell's mouth if he hadn't heard Alex scream. When he looked over his shoulder, he saw Drinkwater riding toward the chuck wagon, carrying Les in front of him. Even at a quarter of a mile, he saw the blood glistening on her trousers.

Sprinting back to the chuck wagon, he tossed Alex her crutch, then started opening drawers and bins on the chuck box. "Where are the medical supplies?" he demanded, frustrated.

"Top drawer on the left," Alex whispered, her gaze fixed on the approaching horse. "I'll need a basin of water, the whiskey, a needle and catgut, and bandages."

"I'll get the water," Hamm said, running toward the barrel.

"Get the hell out of here," Dal snarled, looking at the bottle of medicinal whiskey he held in his hand. "Luther? Get him away from here!"

"That's Les," Hamm said hotly, scarlet pulsing in his face. "I have a right to be with her."

"Listen, you pompous idiot. The widow Roark came forty-two beeves closer to winning your fiancée's inheritance today. Do you want to hand over the rest of the herd by being where you're not supposed to be? Do you think Caldwell is going to look aside at any infraction?" His hand tightened on the whiskey bottle. "Get back where you belong."

Hamm backed away, his face red and filled with hate.

Behind him Alex called, "Put her on this sheet." She was up on her crutch, awkwardly shaking out a bedsheet. Drinkwater slipped off his horse and caught Les in his arms when she toppled, then he carried her to Alex. She ripped open Les's pant leg, exposing a long deep gash across her thigh. Dal heard her suck in a sharp breath, then he relinquished the whiskey bottle, took Drinkwater's arm, and led him away from the women.

"What happened?" He knew the answer, but asked anyway. When he heard about Drinkwater finding Les laid out on the ground, he nodded and swore under his breath. "Any other injuries?"

"The usual bumps, bruises, and cuts," Drinkwater said, clenching his fists and turning a grim face toward the river when Les screamed. "Hate to hear a woman hurting," he mumbled.

Dal didn't look toward the sheet either. "As soon as the wagon is cleared out, we'll bring the rest of the herd across," he said, his voice clipped and angry. He listened to Les's screams until she fainted, and he kept thinking it could have been Freddy. Freddy laid out with her thigh gashed open and pouring blood. He wasn't squeamish, but his stomach tightened.

He let another minute pass before he returned to the observers' camp to speak to Luther, passing Hamm standing between the two campfires. Dal resented his presence, but the woman leaking blood all over the sheet was the woman Hamm planned to marry.

He stopped. "She's going to be weak, and she'll hurt like hell, but she isn't going to die."

Hamm glared and his lip curled. "You're not God. You don't know if she'll die!"

"Yeah, I do," he said tersely. "You put men and longhorns together and a few men are going to get gashed. I've seen it before." He continued forward, stopping when Caldwell stood up beside the fire. It pleased him that Caldwell already had a dark bruise rising on his jaw. Luther looked at both men then hastened forward.

"How bad is it?" Luther asked anxiously.

"Bad enough. Laudanum will keep the pain manageable, but she'll be plenty uncomfortable and unable to ride for at least a week. We need a ruling, Luther. Is she out of it? Or do we put her on the chuck wagon with Alex and give her a week to get back in the saddle?"

"What would you do if it was one of the Webster

boys?" Luther asked, examining his face. "Would you leave him in Austin and hire on a new man?"

That was exactly what he would have done rather than move the herd with one man short. On the other hand, he'd already planned to rest the herd and graze them for forty-eight hours. That cut a shorthanded week to five days. He glanced back at the bloody bedsheet.

She'd worked hard, and she deserved better than losing her chance at Joe's inheritance simply because she'd been doing the job and run into a bad-luck beeve.

"I'd let the drover have a say in the decision," he answered carefully. "Is there anything in the conditions of the will that prohibits Les from staying on if she wants to? Anything that says she's out if she can't work for a week?"

"I'll check." Luther looked toward the river. "How many cattle were lost?"

"Forty-two at first count. There'll be a few more."

"That's fifty-three down at the three-week point."

And a long way to go. Those were the unspoken words. Dal rolled his shoulders, feeling the tension between the blades. "Caldwell deliberately caused this disaster. I want him off the drive and right now."

Luther met Dal's unyielding gaze. "I'll warn Caldwell to be more careful in the future, but I can't put him off the drive without hard proof of wrongdoing."

Frustration knotted the muscles in his neck. "What the hell do you want? A signed confession?"

"I need something more than suspicion or ejecting Caldwell will look like bias on my part. If that happened, Lola could contest the outcome and tie up the inheritance for years." Luther turned a pained glance toward Les and the bloody sheet. "I suppose there's no way to keep Hamm away from her."

Something in his voice made Dal's gaze sharpen. "That's another one I'd like to throw off this drive. Say the word and he's gone."

"Les wants him here. Still, he seems to upset her." He dragged a hand through his hair and anger glinted in his eyes. "There's something you need to understand. Joe set very specific rules and guidelines. I can't eject Mrs. Roark's representative based on suspicion, no matter how strongly I might agree with you. If I did that, Mrs. Roark could rightly insist that I be relieved of my duty and replaced. She'd file a lawsuit faster than you can ride around that herd. Bring me proof that Caldwell is cheating, then we can get rid of him. And you can't eject Ward Hamm because neither of us likes him. He's Les's fiancé, and she's entitled to have him here as long as he doesn't interfere with her work. The guidelines specifically allow for Hamm to accompany the drive as long as he abides by the rules set for the observers, which he is doing."

"So we're stuck with the little son of a bitch," Dal said, walking away. He stopped beside the edge of the sheet. Blood was everywhere. On Alex's hands and skirt, soaked into Les's pant leg and the sheet.

"She fainted again, thank God," Alex muttered, brushing the back of a hand across her forehead, leaving a red smear. "If I can keep from fainting myself, I'll finish the stitching. I hate this, I hate this, I hate this!"

He gazed down at a tourniquet and the neat stitches below it, then he kicked at a rock and strode toward his horse. He had a herd to move.

It was only later that he realized he'd been expecting Freddy to abandon the stragglers and come charging into camp. Either she had meant it when she claimed she didn't care about her sisters, or a certain reckless,

willful actress was developing a little discipline and responsibility.

Freddy felt wild inside. First she had heard that Les
was dead, then crippled, then being tended by Alex on
the other side of the river. She frantically wanted to
check it out herself, wanted to see with her own eyes
how badly Les was injured. But she couldn't.

To ensure that no more trouble arose, Dal had ordered the main herd broken into six smaller herds, each
of which would cross the Colorado separately. Freddy
and James worked the last of the smaller herds, riding
circle to hold three hundred agitated beeves together.
James couldn't have held them by himself, so Freddy
was stuck until they crossed the river.

Trembling with frustration, she rode around the
small herd, worrying about Les.

For most of her life she had worried about Les. As a
toddler, Les had been prone to wander down to the
barns and sheds, and it had been Freddy's and Alex's
responsibility to see that she didn't even though they
weren't much older themselves. Then Les had taken to
following after them, wanting to do everything they
did, wanting to dress like they did, wear her hair like
they did. Why that had annoyed Freddy so much, she
couldn't remember, but it had.

She remembered helping Les with her lessons,
showing her embroidery stitches, doing Les's mending
because Les never did it right. Then had come the ado-
lescent years and the arguments began in earnest. Les
had been like a clinging vine that she perpetually
fought to be free of. Even after she returned to King's
Walk following her acting debacle, her perspective
broadened, she had found nothing to admire in Les.

When she looked at her younger sister she saw weakness and dependency, and she saw or imagined she saw Joe's favoritism for his youngest daughter.

In retrospect, it occurred to Freddy that Joe's partiality to Les was understandable, though she hadn't recognized this until recently. Alex had run off to the East and was gone. Freddy had shamed Joe by leaving with the acting troupe. Until Lola arrived, Joe would have seen Les as his housekeeper and the companion of his declining years. Until Les brought Ward Hamm to the house, she had given Joe no reason for disappointment.

Ashamed of the jealousy she had felt, Freddy rubbed her forehead. There was more to Les than she had ever suspected. Until this drive she hadn't imagined that Les could be persistent or determined, or courageous. She had never considered Les good at anything except looking to others to solve her problems.

But now she was developing a secret but growing admiration for her sister. Les moaned and groaned, complained and let every new challenge terrify her, then she quietly buckled down and mastered whatever she had to learn.

Finally, she and James crossed the Colorado, ran their small herd onto the bedding grounds, and Freddy was free to find out what had happened. She cantered directly to Dal, who sat on his buckskin, scowling at the herd.

She rode close enough to grip his sleeve, feeling his muscles tighten and swell beneath her touch. "How is she?"

"Drifting in an ocean of laudanum," he said as she dropped her hand. "Alex put twenty-six stitches in her thigh. She lost a lot of blood, and she's weak, but she'll recover."

The light was fading fast but still strong enough that

she could see the strain etching his face. She gave her hand an unconscious shake, hoping to cast off the hot tingle that touching him had caused. "How many did we lose?"

"Forty-six at last count," he said before he turned the buckskin toward camp.

For Freddy, it had always been a man's eyes that caught her attention, and that's what she'd first noticed about Dal. Blue, blue eyes that could be cool or hot, penetrating or soft. She'd seen strength and character in his eyes, and emotion. He could control his expression and usually did, but his eyes gave him away. Studying him now, she saw simmering rage and beneath it the heat that flickered in the depths of his gaze when he looked at her, heat that licked out at her and dried her mouth and made her stomach suddenly roll and tighten.

Swallowing hard, she brought her horse up beside him. As always, when she saw the campfire glowing ahead of her at the beginning of evening, she started to feel the aches and pains of a long workday. Her forehead, nose, and cheeks felt tight and hot from the day's dose of burning sunshine. Her thighs ached from endless hours in the saddle. Her arms felt like stone weights hanging from her shoulders. This was the lonely time of day.

Keeping her gaze on the campfire, she asked quietly. "Is it true that Jack Caldwell mired the wagon that caused all the trouble?"

"Yes."

Pressing her lips in a line, she nodded shortly and added Les to her list of grievances. If Jack hadn't been careless, Les wouldn't have gotten hurt.

"What happens now?" In the shadowy darkness his profile looked as if it were cast in stone. "Is Les off the drive? That wouldn't be fair, Dal. Les has worked hard, she's learned what she had to learn, done everything you've asked from her. I can handle the drag until she's well enough to work again. I swear I can."

"Luther's checking to see if Joe provided for a situation like this."

"But you'll have a say in it," she guessed. Reaching, she touched him again, letting her fingers linger. Not to persuade, but to comfort herself. That surprised her. "Please don't punish Les for something that wasn't her fault."

It sounded like habit, like she was trying to solve another problem for Les. But that wasn't how it felt. There was no long-simmering resentment beneath her plea, no sense of trying to help Les because Les wouldn't or couldn't help herself.

"Is this another practice scene, Freddy?" The darkness was now deep enough that she couldn't see his expression. "Please, Mr. Villain, don't tie my sister to the railroad tracks?"

She jerked her hand away as if the iron muscles beneath her fingertips had scorched her. "I lied to you that night," she said in a low voice, her cheeks suddenly hot. "I wasn't acting, I just . . ." Her chin lifted and she bit off the words. She didn't want him to know how often she relived his kisses and the touch of his callused hands moving on her skin, driving her wild with desire. "I'm asking you to give Les a chance because she deserves it."

Les understood that she was lying inside a tent. Alex or Freddy had mentioned that rain was moving in from the south and they'd set up tents for everyone. She also knew that she'd been badly injured. Bandages wrapped her left thigh and she was aware of pain surging like a hidden current beneath the warm sea in which she floated. But she didn't remember the actual injury or crossing the river or Alex stitching her. All of the drovers had poked their heads past the tent flap and had spoken to her, but she couldn't recall what they had said, remembered only bits and pieces of what her sisters had talked about when they had crawled inside her tent and held her hands.

"Les. Damn it, are you listening to what I'm saying?"

She opened her eyes and smiled at Ward. The tent flap was tied back and light from the campfire reached inside. She could see his thinning hair and drawn expression. He didn't look like the handsome Prince Charming she had been dreaming of, a man who would carry her away to a house like Luther Moreland's. She had always liked Luther's house. It occupied a grassy corner lot off of Main Street. Tall cottonwoods shaded the porch, and there was a bay window with a large fern placed before the center pane.

"But you don't look like him," she murmured, disappointed. Prince Charming was tall and slender, and you couldn't see his scalp through his hair. He didn't shout, and he never criticized or made a woman cry. Prince Charming didn't wear paper collars and cuffs or a shopkeeper's apron, and he didn't imagine snubs or insults in every glance. Prince Charming never ever squeezed so hard that he left bruises on a woman's face and arms, and he never raised his hand in annoyance or anger. His lips didn't disappear into a tight thin line.

"Les." Ward clasped her shoulders and gave her a shake. "They had a meeting. They said that it's your decision to stay with the drive. They'll give you a week to heal, then you have to go back to work or withdraw.

Are you listening? I told Frisco that you would stay with the drive, but he said he had to hear it from you." Fury pinwheeled in his eyes. "If it's the last thing I do, I'm going to take that bastard down a peg!"

It was such an unlikely, unimaginable possibility that Les laughed. Ward drew back, then lunged toward her face and hissed. "You'll see."

She took his hand and smiled, floating, drifting. "I want to go home." Not to the ranch house, but to a house with a bay window and a fern in the front pane. A two-story house with a cozy parlor and no view of cattle from any window. No furniture made out of horns.

"Les, I'm warning you. When Frisco asks, you tell him you're staying with the drive."

"Staying with the drive," she repeated, frowning, trying to understand what he was saying. Did he want to take her for a drive in his gig? Would he stop in the moonlight, gaze tenderly into her eyes, and kiss her? "Do you love me?" she asked curiously. "You've never said the words."

"Oh, for God's sake. How much laudanum did Alex give you?"

"I want you to look at me the way Dal looks at Freddy."

"This is a waste of time," he said, disgust heavy in his tone. "We'll talk again tomorrow."

She floated above the pain, watching firelight flicker on the wall of the tent. Pretty patterns, like moving wallpaper. She thought Freddy and Alex spoke to her from the opening in her tent. One of the drovers called good night. And then Prince Charming came.

"I've been waiting for you," she said, smiling when he entered her tent and sat beside her. The campfire was low now and didn't cast enough light that she could see his face, but she knew it was him. He held her hand gently and stroked her wrist.

"I'm so sorry you were injured, Les."

Oh yes, that is what Prince Charming would say. He wouldn't talk about meetings or cattle drives. She disengaged her hand and lifted it to touch his face. He covered her hand with his own and pressed her fingers to his cheek, moved her hand, and placed a kiss in her palm. Surprise and delight widened her eyes. "Do you love me?" she whispered. She wanted someone to love her, needed to hear words that she could throw against the pain like a shield.

"I have loved you for years."

"Oh!" Tears filled her eyes because his quiet answer proved that she must be dreaming. Disappointment parted the cloud that supported her and she dropped into a cauldron of pain, groaning and moving her leg. The pain was hot and throbbing and more real than Prince Charming would ever be.

"Rest now," he murmured, smoothing a wave of hair back from her forehead. "Sleep. Don't worry about anything, just concentrate on getting well."

His voice floated softly out of the darkness, tender with sympathy and concern. On some level of reality Les understood that the laudanum had conjured him and formed the words she longed to hear. Her dreaming mind gave him a familiar voice, but it wasn't Ward's.

That was the best part. He was nothing like Ward.

CHAPTER 14

Cold rain collected along the brim of Dal's hat and dripped down the collar of his slicker. There hadn't been much lightning associated with the last day and a half of grey wet skies, and he was grateful. A stampede on muddy ground was something he didn't want to think about.

Riding alongside the herd, he slowed beside Freddy and inspected her through a thick sheet of steady drizzle. She rode hunched up, trying to keep the rain out of her collar, shivering and blowing warm breath down the cuff of her gloves.

"I'm going into town," he said, skimming a glance across the wet tendrils of black hair plastered to her cheek. "Your shift is about over; do you want to come along?"

"It doesn't sound like there's anything to see."

She was correct about that. Austin's location ensured growth, but right now it was still a small frontier town trying to decide if its future lay toward cattle, cotton, or politics. But Austin's lack of amenities wasn't why she wanted to stay in camp. The way she and Alex were hovering over Les gave the lie to her earlier statement that the sisters didn't care about each other.

They circled the herd in companionable silence, listening to the rain drumming against the brims of their hats. When her leg brushed against his, he remembered the night she had accused him of intentionally letting their legs touch. She'd been right, of course. He couldn't be near her without wanting to touch her. She was driving him crazy.

Last night he'd tossed and turned, considering her admission that she hadn't been acting. The truth hadn't surprised him. By now he could tell when she assumed a role.

He wanted to ask her about that night, but he didn't. If she confirmed that she wanted him as badly as he wanted her, a door would swing open that needed to remain closed.

There was nothing here for either of them, he reminded himself, looking at her through the slanting rain. They wanted different things, different futures. He had nothing to offer. If she won Joe's inheritance, she'd leave for the big-city theaters. If she lost, it meant he lost too. Between them they wouldn't have two nickels to rub together.

If he started thinking with the equipment below his belt instead of the grey matter above his eyebrows, then he might get her in bed during this drive, but it wouldn't be an act to his credit. She would believe he saw her as an actress-whore, and that wasn't true. She would believe he was merely using her, and that would be true, because he knew they had no future beyond Abilene.

He'd never burned for a woman as he did for Freddy Roark, but he wasn't a man who used women with no thought for the consequences. And he couldn't see any good consequences for either of them in the long run.

He rolled back his shoulders. "Is there anything you want me to bring you from town?"

"Some licorice if you can find any," she said, licking rain off her lips. "Les likes licorice."

He watched the tip of her tongue slide across her lips, felt an instant stirring between his thighs, then he jerked sharply on his reins and trotted away from her, cursing under his breath.

"When you agreed to meet, I figured you'd pick one of the saloons." Pausing in the doorway, Dal inspected the hotel's second-floor lady's salon.

Lola smiled over her shoulder, then led him toward two chairs facing a coal fire. "I'm a lady now, haven't you heard?" Taking one of the chairs, she smoothed her skirts with gloved hands, then demurely crossed her ankles.

As they were the only occupants in the salon, Dal lit a cigar and studied her through a drift of smoke. Her auburn hair was elaborately curled, and she smelled of something a lot sweeter than cowhide. Powdered cleavage peeked from the braided edges of an amber-colored cape. She wore lip rouge, artificial pink on her cheeks, and her eyelashes were darkened.

He couldn't help thinking about Freddy, hunched and miserable, rain dripping down her collar and face, her trousers and boots streaked with mud. At the end of her shift, she would crawl into her tent and sit there shivering, longing for the hot sun she'd cursed two days ago. Tonight she would sleep in a damp, muddy bedroll.

"The next time your future husband interferes with my drive," he said, drawling the words, "I'm going to send him back to you a lot less pretty."

"Now, Dal honey, you got it all wrong," Lola purred, leaning forward to pat his knee. "What happened with that wagon was a fortuitous accident, that's all."

"Caldwell says you'll give Les one week's recovery time, then she goes back on the line or she's off the drive. I'm asking you to give Les however long she needs. I want it in writing."

"And how is my dear stepdaughter?"

"She's feverish, and Alex says the wound is inflamed. Les needs longer than a week to recover."

"Well, well," Lola said, leaning back with a satisfied smile. "Am I to infer that you don't want to replace Les with an experienced hand because you've decided to accept my offer?"

"I want to keep Les on the drive because she's earned her share of Joe's money."

Anger twisted her lips. "Are you hinting that I didn't? You don't have any idea what it was like being married to Joe Roark! Stuck out in the middle of nowhere with nothing but cows for excitement." She waved a hand. "It's the longest ten months I ever spent! No dancing, no cards, one glass of whiskey a night. And the criticism . . . a lady does this, a lady does that," she repeated in a singsong voice of disgust. "Believe me, I earned every cent that's coming to me!"

He nodded at her cape and gown. "Looks to me like you were paid pretty well."

"Dal, I need this money. There aren't going to be any more rich husbands. I'm running out of time." Turning her face, she looked into the coal stove. "I want to get out of the country, to see Europe in style. I don't ever again want to be forced to depend on a man."

He lifted an eyebrow. "Isn't there something missing from those grand plans? Like Caldwell for instance?"

She laughed. "Jack is useful. At present."

Her sly smile told him however much Caldwell might think he was using Lola to reach the jackpot, Lola was a step ahead. She'd dangle marriage to entice him to help her, but Dal was willing to bet that Caldwell would never see a penny of Joe's money.

"It's all moot, Lola, because you aren't going to win," he said, narrowing his eyes.

"Those holier-than-thou troublemaking daughters are still young enough to find a man; they don't need Joe's money. I do!"

"Joe was their father. They have more of a claim to his fortune than you do."

"None of those sanctimonious little bitches ever did a lick of real work. Never had to worry about supporting themselves or getting along in the world! Never went without. They were spoiled, coddled, and pampered all their worthless lives. They don't deserve to win!"

"They're working now," he said softly. "Nobody's pampering them. They're getting their hands dirty. I'll tell you something else about Joe Roark's daughters, Lola. They aren't cheats. They aren't swindlers or liars, and they don't use people for their own benefit. Win or lose, they'll do it honestly," he said standing and looking down at her. Reaching in his slicker pocket, he withdrew a paper and pencil and dropped them on the tea try. "Caldwell's responsible for what happened to Les. And the way I figure it, he's acting on your orders to make trouble wherever he can, which makes you responsible. So you write Luther a note and tell him that you don't object to Les taking as long as she needs to get well. Do it, or you'll regret it, Lola."

"Why, what a suspicious mind you have." Lola tented her fingers under her chin. "But your request does present an interesting dilemma. If my poor injured stepdaughter stays on the drive, that means you won't replace her with a more experienced hand, and that's good for me. On the other hand, if Les has to withdraw, I'll have the pleasure of knowing the little bitch won't get one red cent of Joe's money. If something happens and the other two have to withdraw, then I'd win by default." A smile curved her lips. "None of those girls have what it takes to go the distance." Her eyes hardened. "I ain't letting her off the hook, honey. Les is off the drive, and good riddance. One down, two to go."

Dal let himself see her for what she was, and feel the hatred that had festered since the end of the war. "Two can play this game, Lola. I'm warning you . . . tell Luther that Les stays on the drive, or so help me God, I'll destroy you. You won't get a penny."

"Oh my, I'm shaking in my boots," she said with a laugh. Standing, she moved to the door, thrusting out her bosom and one hip. "Despite everything, I like you, Dal. You're one good-looking cowboy. How is it that you and me never went to bed?"

"Just lucky I guess." He rolled his hat up on his head and walked past her.

Downstairs in the saloon, he bought a whiskey and pushed the glass around on the counter in front of him. Getting tangled up with Lola had started him on the road that ended inside a bottle. He'd let himself get suckered, made a fool of, set up as a target for murder and revenge. He'd betrayed his principles and ultimately his country.

And Lola had walked away unscathed with a lot of other people's money in her pocket.

He gazed at the amber shimmer topping the whiskey

glass, and saw how the cattle drive would unfold. The mired wagon was only the beginning. This hard-luck drive was going to be plagued all the way to the yards at Abilene. And when it ended, Lola would walk away unscathed, with Joe Roark's fortune in her pocket.

Only this time, he wouldn't be the only human wreckage she left behind her.

When he felt sweat appear on his brow, saw his knuckles whiten around the glass, he pushed the whiskey away and glared at the bartender polishing glasses behind the bar. "Does Austin have a telegraph office?"

"Closest telegraph is in Fort Worth."

He spun a coin across the counter and left the saloon. Outside, he pulled down the brim of his hat and gazed at the rain. He knew how to stop Lola. The telegram he'd send would aim a bullet right at her head. If he was lucky, Emile Julie and his men would head north immediately, and Julie would take care of Lola before something happened to Freddy or Alex. His only regret was that Julie wouldn't arrive in time to save Les's share of the inheritance.

Writing the telegram in his mind, angry that he had to wait until he reached Fort Worth to send it, he stepped into a stew of mud, horse droppings, tobacco juice, and refuse, crossed the street, and entered a penny-candy store. "Licorice," he growled at the man standing behind a high glass case.

Christ, he wanted a drink.

When Alex moved out in front of the herd, it was like driving into an ocean of green, tipped by waves flecked with blues and golds and the delicate pink petals of sturdy prairie wildflowers. Up ahead, she glimpsed strung-out herds grazing northward. To the east lay rolling pastures and neat fields of cotton plants. The Edwards Plateau rose on her left, tinted green by twisted mesquite trees, live oak, and cedar.

Since Les was riding with her, she refused to travel at her usual breakneck speed. This frustrated her pilot, but the slower pace was easier on the leg she braced against the seat fender. Actually, her leg had strengthened to the point that her knee no longer quivered and trembled and threatened to collapse when she climbed down from the driver's seat, and she could have used her crutch all day without feeling undue strain. That realization disturbed her. The mobility and convenience of the crutch were insidious seductions too depressing to think about.

"How are you feeling?" she asked, glancing at the rope Grady had used to tie Les to the seat.

Les's eyelids fluttered, and she fixed fever-glazed eyes on the pilot riding out ahead of them. "So hot. Thirsty." The damp cloth on her forehead had dried in the warm breeze.

"Don't rub your leg," Alex cautioned, frowning. According to the book of home remedies she'd brought on this journey, yeast paste helped against the inflammation drawing a red line along Les's wound, and she'd tried white vitriol, too. After she set up camp, she'd give Les some quinine, try that against the fever making her incoherent at times.

Fixing her gaze on the mule's ears, Alex pressed her lips together and swallowed a scream of helplessness. She wasn't skilled in medical matters, hadn't dreamed that doctoring would form such a regular part of her responsibilities. Already she had splinted broken fingers, cleaned cuts, dosed rumbling stomachs, dispensed liniments for strains and sprains. The challenge of unexpected emergencies kept her in a constant state of anxiety and dread. And she'd been praying that nothing as serious as Les's injury would come her way.

The only good thing about Les's worrisome fever was having company during the ride ahead of the herd and while she set up camp. She detested the terrible forty minutes alone, absolutely alone, after the pilot turned back and before Grady swept in with the remuda.

Sometimes the vast open spaces made her feel so insignificant as to experience utter hopelessness. Other times she felt paralyzed with fear, clinging to the wheels or her worktable, terrified that she would be drawn up, up, up and swallowed by the seamless sky. Always she worried that the pilot would forget where he left her and take the herd somewhere else.

When the pilot waved her off and cantered away, she glanced at Les, then reached for her crutch and leaned over the side to poke the crutch tip at the ground. Her routine began by checking every inch of the campsite for rattlesnakes. The first week out, she had rolled her chair over a snake and the experience had stopped her heart and aged her ten years. It hadn't been a rattler, thank God, but it could have been. The lesson stayed with her.

Climbing down, she adjusted the crutch beneath her armpit, and found her pistol behind the driver's seat before she grimly set off on the twice-daily snake hunt. As always, she silently thanked Dal Frisco for insisting that they learn to shoot.

"Were you firing a gun?" Les asked drowsily when Alex returned to the wagon.

"I got two of them," Alex said crisply. She was leaving a satisfying trail of dead snakes behind her. "I'll get you some water."

Then she would grind the coffee beans and throw

together a quick noon meal of cush and bacon. Cush was leftover corn bread crumbled and cooked until crusty then served drowning in salty gravy. Once she had the cush on the fire, she'd put tonight's beans to soak and check to see if there was anything quick and interesting among the food tins.

Sometimes she waited for Grady to dig the fire pit, but more and more frequently she fetched her sharpened spade, dropped to the ground, and dug the pit herself rather than waste time waiting for the remuda. It no longer bothered her that Luther, Caldwell, or Ward might arrive and see her squirming around on the ground. She didn't care what they thought.

Today, Ward arrived before anyone else and Alex was glad for once to see him. It meant Les wouldn't have to wait for Grady to untie her from the seat and help her to the ground. Ward spread a blanket over the grass and took Les a drink of water. Since no one else had arrived yet, he brought Alex an armload of kindling and wood from the cooney.

"How else can I help, sister?"

"I can manage, thank you." She stared at the wood and frowned, then pulled herself off the ground and onto the crutch.

"Shall I bring down your wheelchair?"

"Grady will do it when he rides in."

"At least I can set up the pot hanger and hang the coffeepots."

"I don't need help or want it," she said sharply. "You know the rules."

Immediately he took offense. She saw it in the way his face pinched and his shoulders stiffened. But she wasn't Les. His posturing didn't move her to apologize, it only annoyed her.

"I'm trying to lighten your burden, sister. And there's no one to see."

In addition to his other disagreeable qualities, he had just revealed himself as a cheat. She lowered her work-table, then gave him a frosty glare.

"I choose to abide by the rules whether or not there's a danger of someone catching me cheating," she said coldly.

A plum-colored flush climbed his cheeks. "It would be better for all concerned if we could be civil to each other. Very soon I'll be the head of this family." He stared at her, letting his words sink in. "You and Freddy would do well to remember who will be managing your affairs."

"I beg your pardon! You will *never* manage my affairs, Mr. Hamm."

"I believe it's customary that—"

"Never," she repeated angrily. "Marrying Les makes you her husband, it does not make you the head of the Roark family, and I will never recognize you as such. If you press the issue, Mr. Hamm, I'll tie up the entire inheritance for years if need be, I'll use every legal means available. I promise that you will *never* manage one cent of my money." His presumption out-raged her.

"I may have to challenge that view. For your own good."

He was such a despicable cretin. "This is not the Dark Ages. You're not marrying one sister and gaining the assets of three." She gave the wheel on the coffee mill a savage turn. "I have two excellent attorneys in Boston, Mr. Hamm. Should you pursue this reprehensi-ble course, I will instruct them to destroy you. And by heaven, I will enjoy it."

He jerked backward from her expression. "You think you're so superior!"

"Yes, Mr. Hamm. I do."

"Well, we shall just see, won't we? We'll just see about that!"

Instantly she thought of Payton lying dead in the rain, and she almost stumbled. How dare she hold herself above Ward Hamm? His crimes were pettiness, unpleasantness, greed, an inflated opinion of himself. Her crime was so much worse.

"If you're so superior," he hissed at her, "then why is Les so ill? She has two more days! That's all. Then she has to go back on the line."

"She can't," Alex said flatly. "I'm sorry that Les will have to withdraw from the drive. She's worked hard and she deserves better." Every word she spoke was true. "But I've done everything I know how, and she's still dangerously ill. As I've told you before, Les could die. Her wound has closed in some spots, it's seeping in others. Her fever rises and falls, but it doesn't fall enough. What she needs is a few weeks in bed with someone knowledgeable nursing her. If you care for her, Mr. Hamm, don't wait. I urge you to put Les in your wagon right now and drive ahead to Waco. Put her in a hotel and find a doctor as quickly as you can."

"Oh you'd like that, wouldn't you, you and Freddy." His eyes closed into slits and spittle flew from his lips. "Then the two of you could split her share. I see right through this."

Alex jerked upright and stiffened. If he had been closer, she would have slapped his sweating red face, would have raked her broken fingernails down his cheeks. "How dare you!" The urge to do violence was so strong that she felt faint with her need to strike him.

"If I have to tie Les onto her saddle, she isn't leaving the drive. You aren't going to get our share!"

Rage immobilized her or she would have swung her crutch at his head.

Three days later, when Freddy heard Ward's shout, she pulled back on the reins and peered through a haze of dust. Les's horse was heading south toward Ward's wagon, moving away from the herd. Les was semiconscious, mumbling, and the only thing holding her in the saddle was the waist harness that Ward had devised and made for her.

Riding after her, Freddy caught the reins and guided Les's horse into a turn, leading the mare back toward the stragglers and the dust kicked up by the main herd. When she spotted a puddle left from last night's brief rainstorm, she jumped off her horse, ran to the puddle and wet her bandanna. She mounted again and reached to give Les a shake.

"I . . . wha . . ." Les licked her lips. "I'm dying, Freddy. Please. Please let me lie down."

Tears cut the dust on Freddy's cheeks and she dashed at them with the back of her glove. "Here, Les. Wipe your face." She pushed the wet bandanna into Les's lap, watched Les stare down at it with a stupid expression. "I can't get close enough to do it for you."

She'd never been as happy to see anyone as when Dal rode out of the rolling dust. Cold anger glittered in his eyes when he looked at Les, swaying and bobbing in the saddle. "This is criminal," he said, speaking between his teeth. He sent an icy stare toward Ward's wagon following behind.

Freddy hit the saddletree with her fist. "I've never

hated anyone as much as I hate Ward Hamm. He's going to kill her!"

Last night's rain had cooled the air, but Les was burning with fever and didn't seem to know where she was.

"Please, Dal. Isn't there something you can do? Is there any way to persuade Lola to give Les another week off the line?" She didn't know if another week would be enough, but it would be better than this. Anything would be better than watching this. "If Lola won't agree, then there must be something we can do to force that greedy, murdering, son of bitch Ward to pull her out of this drive before it kills her!"

"Lola won't budge," Dal snapped, staring at Les. Her chin was on her chest, her eyes closed. Only the waist harness held her on the saddle. "I've talked to Hamm, threatened him; he won't budge either."

Freddy pulled off her hat and slapped it hard against her thigh. Anger and frustration made her chest hurt. "He doesn't have the right to make this decision for her!"

"Luther says he does. Les and Ward have officially announced their intention to marry at the end of the drive. She has given her property, future, and life into Hamm's hands. She has no other male guardian, no close male kin. As her future husband, Hamm is claiming ownership and the right to make decisions that will affect them both."

"Ownership!" Freddy shouted in a strangled voice. The West was far more liberal than the East, but even here conventions prevailed when it was convenient. Releasing a scream, she galloped away from Dal and rode up fast and hard on Mouse and Brownie, the laziest of the stragglers. She ran them a quarter of a mile before she halted to catch her breath and wait for Dal and Les to catch up.

"You're the boss. You could put her off the drive," she said to Dal when he rode up, leading Les's horse.

"Tell me what reason I can use that Hamm won't challenge in court. Give me a valid justification, and I'll put Les off this drive faster than you can quote a line from one of your plays."

"She isn't doing the work! Look at her. She's only half-conscious!"

"Ward will say she was on her horse, in position, putting in the hours." Stretching a hand, he gently pushed Les upright, then swore steadily.

Tears spilled over Freddy's lashes. "She didn't work the last two stampedes!"

"Hamm will say that was because I ordered her not to. He'd be right."

Freddy's leg brushed his. "Put her off the drive anyway, I beg you. Alex and I will sign anything Ward wants saying that we'll give Les her share of the inheritance if we win. She doesn't have to finish the drive, she can go somewhere, and rest, and get well. She'll get her share anyway! Tell him that!"

Sunlight fell across Dal's eyes when he turned his head, making them appear coolly translucent. "Alex already suggested that proposition to Luther, but it won't work. You and Alex don't get to decide how the inheritance is divided. Joe made that decision in his will, and the will says if any of you drop out for any reason, you forfeit your share of the inheritance."

"There must be some way around—"

Dal's sudden laugh made her look up. "If there was any way to tinker with the will and Joe's conditions, you would have hired the first trail boss you interviewed. Believe me, if ever there was a watertight will, Joe's will is it."

Despair made her stomach cramp. "The estate could be distributed, then Alex and I could quietly give Les a share. No one would have to know, just us."

"Ward will never accept a verbal agreement from you and Alex, you know that." Sympathy vied with anger across his expression. His jaw clenched when he looked at Les. "This goes on until she dies or recovers."

Freddy covered her face in her hands.

They both watched Les's slumped figure in front of them. "I'm starting to worry about you, Freddy. You were up most of last night sitting with Les, and spent the other half chasing a stampede. Tired cowboys make stupid mistakes."

"It was dark and raining. That's why I ran into Charlie's horse."

"You ran into Charlie because you were too exhausted to pay attention, and you didn't react fast enough. Because you've only had about three hours' sleep in the last four days. If you want to kill yourself like Les is doing, fine, but you're not entitled to endanger my other drovers."

She was exhausted enough that she only half listened to what he was saying. Her attention strayed to his mouth, and she surrendered to the fascination of watching how he formed words. She thought she knew every detail about him—Lord knew she watched every move he made—but she hadn't noticed the way he pushed some words out, caressed others. A ball of heat uncurled in her stomach, and she wet her lips. If she didn't stop thinking about him, wondering and speculating, she would lose her mind.

"How many beeves have we lost?" she asked, fixing

her thoughts in a different direction. Once she had believed the worst thing that could happen to her was never to act onstage again. Now she understood the worst thing would be to endure this ordeal, then discover at the end that it had been for nothing.

"We lost two steers last night." For the first time, Freddy saw weariness in the tanned lines that gave strength to his face. "That brings us to fifty-nine lost."

"And cuts our margin to 153," she said slowly.

Blinking hard, she told herself fiercely that they would win. Fate wouldn't put them through this then snatch away the prize at the end. *Please God*, she thought, looking at Les through a film of tears, *help her. And let us win.*

Dal leaned against the wheel of the chuck wagon, smoking, listening to the night sounds of a sleeping camp. Caleb and his brother sat beside the fire, drinking coffee and talking quietly, waiting to take their turn at night watch. Freddy and Alex were still in Les's tent. Along about midnight, the steers had pushed to their feet as they usually did about that time, had done a little soft blowing and grazing, then settled down again.

Tonight there wouldn't be a stampede, he had made sure of it, at least as sure as he could be that a stampede wouldn't start by human design. Dal had kept an eye on the observers' camp until midnight; now Grady was out there in the darkness and would stay until dawn, watching to make certain that Caldwell didn't approach the bedding grounds.

Dal should have crawled into his bedroll and gotten some sleep, but he kept running events through his mind. Last night a spectacular lightning storm had terrified the steers, had brought them to their feet and started them running. But the night before, there had been no apparent reason for a stampede.

His gut told him Caldwell was behind the unusual number of stampedes occurring on this drive. There was nothing he would have liked better than to catch the son of a bitch red-handed, but it didn't look like that would happen tonight. Tonight Caldwell was apparently giving himself an uninterrupted night's sleep.

An hour later, still not sleepy, he poured a cup of coffee and sat beside the embers to warm himself. The Webster boys were riding the herd, and he was alone, not fit company for anyone. Smoking he watched Alex crawl out of Les's tent, drag herself into her wheelchair, rest a moment, then roll through the darkness to fetch something from the chuck wagon. On her way back, half-blind with fatigue, she ran a wheel into someone's boot. A man rose out of his bedroll, muttered a curse at her, then sank back down. Alex whispered an apology then touched a hand to her eyelids before she maneuvered around the bedroll and returned to Les's tent.

Alex puzzled him. She used the crutch as skillfully and confidently now as if she'd used a crutch from the beginning. But the instant she didn't absolutely need to be upright, she returned to the chair, which was unwieldy, slow, and agonizingly hard to push through high grass and over rough ground. He'd given up trying to understand why she made it so hard for herself.

He didn't notice that Freddy had crawled out of the tent until he heard a chorus of muttered swearing rising from the bedrolls. When he stood, he saw her reeling toward him, tripping over bedrolls, a tired but radiant smile lighting her face.

She gripped his arms when she reached him, excitement trapping the low firelight in her eyes. "The fever's broken! The fever's broken! Les will make it now! She's weak as a calf, but she's going to be all right!" Throwing her arms around his waist, she pressed her forehead against his chest and wept.

The worst thing he could have done was wrap his arms around her, but he couldn't help himself. Making soothing sounds deep in his throat, he held her, stroked her shaking shoulders, and let her cry out the last ten days of fear and worry and now relief.

When she finally raised her face, he discovered he'd made a mistake. The worst thing was not holding her. It was kissing her. He couldn't help doing that either.

CHAPTER **15**

Her response to his kiss was as shatteringly explosive as her response had been the night she'd lost her horse during the stampede. Dal's mouth came down on hers, hard and possessive, and an earthquake rocked Freddy's body, shaking loose a fiery urgency that bubbled through her bloodstream. Any fleeting thought of resistance melted in the heat between their hips, in the fervor of seeking lips and thrusting tongues.

She'd been mad to throw herself into his arms, crazy to pretend that touching him wouldn't be like setting a match to paper. But somewhere beneath the relief of knowing that Les would live and recover had been the excitement of finding a justification to throw caution and sensibility to the winds and seek the thrill of his arms. She had flown to him as unerringly as a moth to the flame, and deep in her heart she knew where it would lead. At some point, without knowing exactly how or when it happened, she had made a decision that she recognized only now.

A low groan wrenched from his throat, and he whispered her name against her lips. His hands stroked her back, her hips, strayed toward her buttocks then slid away. Beneath the wildness unleashed by his kisses,

Freddy retained enough presence of mind to realize he fought the frenzied arousal she felt in his body and in hers.

So many things had changed since they had walked away from each other the last time. It might have been her instead of Les who was gashed by a needle-tipped horn; she could die without ever knowing him. Now she understood that she might take nothing away from this drive except the memory of Dal Frisco. Most of all, she needed respite from the continual wondering and longing and desire that kissing him before had unleashed. What she felt went beyond wanting him; she needed him.

"Please," she begged mindlessly, tearing her lips from his. Her hands pressed and tugged at his chest. Her hips teased against him. And she felt the heat pouring off of him in waves, felt the powerful iron urgency of his desire answering her own.

"Are you certain?" he whispered, his voice husky and strangled.

She was very sure. She hadn't known it until his arms closed around her, and she felt his ragged breath stir her hair, but she knew it now. "Yes," she breathed against his lips. "Yes, yes."

Lifting her in his arms, Dal carried her away from the revealing glow of the fire, carried her past the sleeping drovers and far out on the range. He set her on her feet in the darkness, kissed her deeply, almost savagely, then strode away from her. "Wait here."

Freddy had a moment to ask if she really wanted to do this. And the answer was yes. In the eyes of most who knew her, she was already ruined. She licked her lips and tasted him there. And the answer was yes. She thought of all the times she had said no. And this time the answer was yes.

Would she regret this one day? Would she look back and ask, why Dal Frisco? No other man had aroused her like he did. No other man had possessed her thoughts as he had. No other had challenged her as Dal did or asked as much of her. No man had made her as aware of her body or as aware of his. There were so many things she admired about him, had come to respect about him. Would she regret choosing him? No.

She heard his boots moving through the grass, then he was in front of her, spreading a blanket on the ground. When he came to her, he gazed into her eyes and placed his hot hands on her waist. "I can think of a dozen reasons why this shouldn't happen," he said in a hoarse low voice. "But you look at me like that, and I can't stop wanting you so much that I ache with it."

"Don't talk." Clasping his cheeks, feeling rough new whiskers beneath her fingertips, she pulled his head down and kissed him hard, parting her lips to let his tongue explore and ravish. When his hands slid to cover her breasts, she gasped and her knees weakened. Sinking, she pulled them both to the blanket, her arms locked around his neck. And she returned his deepening kisses, letting his hands sweep over her, letting her mind spin on wave after wave of sensation.

All her life she had been saying no to eager boys and men—although after her time on the boards, no one she knew believed it. But the truth was that before she'd always hesitated, had inhibitions that here with Dal dissipated into the wide spaces beneath the milky canopy of stars. What they were about to do was inevitable. Her body knew that, and so did she. They had been pulled toward each other from the beginning. On some level that she had fought to ignore, she had always known this moment would come, the question being only when and where.

He pressed her backward, his mouth hot and demanding and electric against hers, his fingers fumbling at the buttons on her trousers. Helpless, almost mindless, fighting for each gasping breath, Freddy surrendered to the vibrations thrilling down her body. She wanted to touch him, wanted to rip at the buttons on his trousers, too, but she couldn't. What he was doing paralyzed her. His mouth nuzzled her breasts through her shirt and teased her nipples into hard buds. His fingers slid into her opened trousers, moving across her tense stomach and then he stroked her center and her mind exploded. She couldn't breathe, couldn't think. His lips and his fingers aroused white-hot sensations that she'd never felt before. Mind swirling, she dissolved in fluid waves and she thought she would faint, believed she might die if he didn't possess her now.

Thrashing beneath him, wild with the desire he skillfully aroused, she didn't know he'd pulled off her trousers until she felt the night air rush over her legs and thighs, then he came to her again, covering a sudden chill with the heat of his bare skin. Instinct lifted her hips and her throat arched and her eyes closed. Gripping fistfuls of his shirt while shudders of pleasure trembled through her body, she whispered his name then tensed and cried out softly as he entered her.

"My God!" Lifting on his elbows he stared down into her face.

The heat and fullness of him inside her was unlike anything she had imagined. There was pain, but only fleetingly, and quickly replaced by an instinctual urge to move, to lift to meet him.

Her eyelids fluttered and opened. "Dal?" She licked her lips. Surely this wasn't the end. Surely there was more.

"You're a virgin," he said hoarsely. "Freddy, for God's sake. Why didn't you tell me?"

It took a moment to understand what was happening. Then she felt a flash of anger fed by disappointment and a feeling of loss as he withdrew and rolled off of her. "I was right," she said, sitting up. "Just like everyone else, you assumed—"

He dropped his head and pushed a hand through his hair, swearing softly. "You told me you were experienced."

She had never felt so foolish in her life, sitting in the dark, half-naked, next to a half-naked man. Feeling half-ravished and wholly frustrated.

"This has nothing to do with some generalized opinion about actresses, so don't put that on me," he warned. "This has to do with you and me and that's all. You said you were experienced, and I believed you."

Embarrassment flooded her face and she peered through the darkness, looking for her trousers. "I meant that I'd been kissed." She wasn't really sure what had gone wrong, only that something disastrous had happened which left her feeling angry and empty.

He stood up, pulled on his pants, then threw out his hands. "Freddy, this isn't how a man takes a virgin, damn it! There's a responsibility that goes along with . . ." He planted his fists on his hips, and looked up at the stars, fading now toward dawn. "Damn it. I apologize. I'm sorry."

"I can't help it that I'm a virgin." Where were her trousers? "Was a virgin."

"You should have told me!"

"You know what makes me mad?" Standing up, trying to cover herself with the tail of her shirt, she stumbled around until she found her trousers, but she couldn't find her boots in the darkness. "For years men have been trying to talk me into doing this. Then when I finally decide to go ahead, you jump back like I just handed you a poisoned apple!"

Dal placed his hands on her shoulders, but she angrily shrugged away from him. "Freddy, for God's sake. A man doesn't deflower a woman on the ground in the open air. That's not how a gentleman does it."

"Since when are you a gentleman?" Where in the hell were her damned boots? Later, she would let herself experience the pain of rejection and embarrassment. Right now anger prevented her from humiliating herself with tears.

"In this matter I've always been a gentleman. Will you stand the hell still and listen a minute?" He grabbed her by the waist and pulled her hard against him. "Listen to me. What I just did was wrong."

She would have slapped him, but he caught her wrist. "If you tell me this didn't mean anything, I swear I'll . . ." She wasn't even sure if she was experienced now or still a virgin. She suspected one deep thrust was enough to ruin her, but she wasn't certain. Either way, the whole thing was a disappointment. Much ado about nothing.

He smothered her threat with a kiss that infuriated her because it ignited the heat again and the wild frustration she had felt when he rolled away from her.

"We are going to do this again, and the next time we're going to do it right," he said grimly, staring down into her eyes. "Not on the ground. Not half-dressed. Not fast."

"The hell we are," she snapped, jerking away from him, reaching deep to locate some pride. "Now you listen. I've been wondering about this event for years, and let me tell you something." She thrust out her chin and pulled back her shoulders. "It isn't much. A woman might do this once to satisfy her curiosity or because she had to, but no woman would do it twice. So you can forget any repeat performance!"

He swore and dropped his head back to look at the sky. "See? That's exactly what I was afraid of. When a man makes this kind of mistake, he can wreck a woman. Son of a bitch!"

Finally, she stumbled over her boots but didn't bother taking the time to pull them on. "I saw Les almost dying and I kept thinking, what if that was me? It could have been. And what if I died without ever knowing . . ." She spread her hands, the boots swinging in a wide arc. "For several years everyone I know has condemned me for ruining myself. The respectable women in Klees wouldn't talk to me, wouldn't call on me or accept my calls." Tears choked her. "But I hadn't done anything. Nothing worse than acting some lines onstage. Then you come along and . . . I just . . . I decided I might as well do what everyone thinks I've done anyway."

"This is my fault. I knew you were exhausted. I shouldn't have trusted a decision made when you're this tired," he said, staring at her. Behind him the sky was beginning to brighten.

"You're wrong. This happened because I was doing what I always do, picking the son of a bitch in the crowd." Disgust twisted her lips, and her voice sank to a whisper. "You're like everyone else. When you rolled away, I felt like something you didn't want to touch, like something dirty and unpleasant. But you got what you wanted. I'm not sure what I got."

"Good God! Freddy—"

But she didn't stay to hear any more. Humiliated, frustrated, and hurting inside, she ran toward her bedroll and, when she reached it, rolled up tight in her blankets and pressed her face into the pile of folded clothing she used as a pillow.

Everything she had told him was true, but the reasons for wanting to surrender to him no longer made sense. She couldn't recall why she had decided it had to be him or what had made her impulsively decide that it had to happen tonight. It was just that Dal Frisco did things to her mind and body that no man had done before. She had experienced flashes of desire, but not to the point where she could hardly think of anything else. She'd always been able to control herself.

Rolling onto her back, she stared up at the fading stars. Well, at least she knew now. The mystery of sex was solved, and if she died on this cattle drive, she wouldn't die a virgin.

But she'd never felt as disappointed in her life. Somehow, she'd expected . . . more.

Dal had planned to rest the herd outside Waco, but now he was in a hurry to reach Fort Worth. Waco had only one shabby hotel, and he guessed that Lola would stay there. A shabby room and the chance of encountering Lola didn't serve his purpose on any level.

Instead of grazing out the herd and giving the hands a visit to town, he swam the steers across the muddy, reddish Brazos River and headed north, in a bad mood every step of the way.

As part of his responsibility, he rode circle on the herd several times a day. A good trail boss rode approximately four times the distance the cattle would travel. He needed to know that he wasn't pushing the beeves so hard that any went lame or developed cracked hooves. And it was his job not to wear out the remuda and bust up the horses by working them too hard. This was part of what he watched for while he rode circle. The state of the animals, the effectiveness of his drovers, the condition of the grass and ground they covered. And Freddy.

He couldn't stop brooding over how badly he'd mishandled the situation. In retrospect he believed that he should have known she was still an innocent. There was a skittishness about her, an unawareness of herself as a desirable woman. Women who had been awakened were not careless about leaving a button undone. They noticed, and they knew the message it sent. Freddy didn't. Experienced women could be as modest as a preacher's wife, but they still had a gleam of knowledge in their eyes that Freddy lacked.

"Damn it."

And he couldn't have performed worse than he had after he made the discovery that she was a virgin. Reliving that moment, he would have given much to change it. He should have slowed things down, should have gotten control of himself, should have focused more intently on her reaction and response, but most of all, he should not have quit.

"Damn it."

Now she thought she had experienced lovemaking, and it was nothing to her but disappointing. Now, she was hardly speaking to him. And it was all his fault.

Tense enough that his shoulders and thighs ached, he rode through the dust toward the drag. Ward Hamm was still trailing the herd where he could keep an eye on Les, which didn't improve Dal's mood. He sent a glare toward Hamm's wagon, then turned in beside Les. Dark circles ringed her eyes and she looked ill with exhaustion, but she managed a smile.

"How are you feeling?" he asked, dropping his gaze

to the rope contraption Hamm had made to hold her in the saddle. "Still need that?"

She touched the rope circling her waist. "Probably not, but it makes me feel more secure to keep it a little longer." Les followed his gaze toward Freddy, riding ahead of them, kicking at one of the stragglers. "Freddy's doing the work back here. It's all I can do just to stay in the saddle all day." She bit her lip and pulled her shoulders out of a slump. "Alex says it will take time, but I'll get stronger every day."

"When we reach Fort Worth, we'll stop for a few days. Get a room in town and spend those days resting." When he saw her glance toward Hamm's wagon, he frowned. "That's not a suggestion, Les. That's an order. Do it."

Not waiting for a reply, he urged his horse forward and rode up beside Freddy. She didn't look at him. "We're missing a red steer with a muddy-looking blaze."

A flash of green eyes cut his way, then swung back toward the tail end of the herd. "If I'd seen a stray, I would have turned him back into the herd."

"I'm not criticizing," he said patiently. "Just asking if you've seen that steer."

"The answer is no."

There was a subtext here, and he didn't like it. "There's good grazing near Fort Worth." Nothing in her stony profile suggested she would be receptive to what he had in mind. "Fort Worth has several big hotels, a couple of them as fine as you'll find in the West." He fixed a look on the stragglers. "You and I are going to stay overnight in one of them."

"The hell we are!" Now she turned a full, narrowed stare on him, her expression battened down like a shutter against a storm. "Never, Frisco. No. It isn't going to happen."

"Yeah, it is going to happen, Frederick. I have a responsibility to repair the damage I've done, and I'm going to live up to it. You have a responsibility, too." She started sputtering and making choking sounds like she was trying to talk but couldn't. "You withheld vital information." Now he looked at her. Crimson pulsed in her face, and her eyes were wide and incredulous. She was dusty and sweat-streaked and the most beautiful creature he'd ever clapped his eyes on. "By doing so, you cheated us both."

"What?" The word emerged as a strangled shout.

"That's right. I owe you better, and you owe me better." She was throwing off sparks that he could almost see. "So make up your mind to it. We're going to a hotel, and we're going to do this thing right. Afterward, you can tell me to go to hell, if you want to. Then we'll walk away, and it's finished." Turning his head, he fixed her with a stare. "But we *are* going to do it. If I have to drag you into that hotel kicking and screaming, I will, Freddy. I'm not going to go through life knowing I ruined a woman. That's not going to happen. I'm going to fix this damage, and, by God, you're going to like it!"

Having said his piece, he kicked his horse in the flanks and cantered up the side of the herd. His speech wasn't the most romantic he'd ever made, but Freddy wasn't like any woman he'd ever known. With her, every damned thing was a struggle or a fight. It pissed him off, and made him wonder what was wrong with him that out of all the women in the world, he had to let this one crawl under his skin.

He was still pondering that enigma an hour later while he was out on the range looking for the red steer with the muddy blaze. The land rolled and dipped and he figured the old mossback might be grazing in a gully. His mind was jumping back and forth between searching for the missing beeve and thinking about Freddy Roark, so he didn't immediately register what he was seeing when he rode up out of a twisting gully he'd been following.

Reining, he took off his hat and fanned his face, squinting into the distance. He made out three long-horns, all cows. And what looked like a naked man walking beside them. Curious, he rode forward, slowing when he came up on the longhorns, not wanting to scatter them. A glance revealed they weren't branded and were free for the taking.

"Are these your beeves?" he asked the man, who stood with one hand on the back of a cow, looking up at him.

The wanderer was naked except for a pair of boots and a loincloth like the Indians still wore, and he was tanned deep brown by the sun. Gunshot wounds were distinctive, and this man had been shot a couple of times in the past. He had a few other scars and scabs and a ragged cut across his rib cage. Long brown hair curled on his shoulders, and a brown-and-grey beard reached to his chest. Expressionless, he glanced at the gun on Dal's hip, then settled his gaze on the old Confederate shirt that Dal wore beneath his vest.

"What's your name?" When the man didn't answer, he asked, "Do you understand English?" Still no answer.

The situation was puzzling on several fronts. Now Dal noticed a pouch and a knife hanging from a thin rope around the man's waist, indicating that he had the fixings to make a fire and skin whatever he could catch to eat. It was strange about the longhorns, too. Taming a longhorn was damned near impossible in Dal's view, but the three cows seemed placid and content, not protesting the man's presence or his touch. Clearly they traveled with the naked man, and he exhibited a definite proprietary air toward them. That was disappointing. Dal would have liked to pick up three extras.

He gave it another try. "That's a nasty-looking cut. Do you need assistance?"

For all the reaction in the man's expression and steady grey eyes, Dal might have been addressing his remarks to the cows. It didn't much matter if the man was deaf or a foreigner who lacked English, the end result was the same. They weren't communicating.

"That's the King's Walk herd over there," he said anyway, jerking his head toward the dust cloud a couple of miles to the west. The boys were taking the beeves onto the bedding ground. "If you want to come in and share a meal, have that cut doctored, you're welcome to share our fire." At this point he didn't expect an answer, and he didn't get one.

After casting a covetous glance at the three longhorn cows, he turned his horse into the sunset and rode toward the herd, keeping his eyes peeled for the old red with the muddy blaze. About a quarter mile from the bedding ground, he spotted the mossback heading toward the herd and cursed himself for wasting several hours. At least he hadn't lost another one.

This was a good time of day. With the herd grazing peacefully, supper only minutes away, they'd covered eighteen miles, and he had the same number of beeves as he'd started with this morning. He was ready for a cup of thick scalding coffee, ready to let the day's tensions drain out of his chest and shoulders.

When he heard hooves, he looked behind and saw the cows and the naked man loping across the range.

Indians could run at that fluid pace, but Dal had never seen a white man who had the stamina for it. Interested, he watched the man run past him and guide his cows into the herd on the bedding ground. And he did something not many men would have done. He followed the cows in among the long-horned steers, which seemed a risky thing for a naked man to do. To Dal's surprise, his presence didn't spook the steers. He walked through the grazing cattle and was waiting on the west side when Dal circled the herd and rode up to him.

"Couldn't resist the supper invitation?" Dal asked. The man didn't answer, but clearly he understood English. Dal rode past him to the remuda and gave Grady the reins to the buckskin.

"Them cows he brought in could have the King's Walk brand on them in about thirty minutes. We got irons in the wagon," Grady commented after hearing the story.

"I don't think he intends them as a gift." Dal walked to the chuck wagon and beckoned the man forward. "I hope you have extra fixings," he said to Alex. "We have a guest. I suspect he's hungry and he needs a little doctoring."

She looked up from the wreck pan and pushed a wave of blond hair off her forehead leaving a smear of soap suds. "He's naked," she said, gripping her crutch and averting her eyes.

Dal grinned. "He doesn't talk much either. Hasn't said a word so far."

When he glanced over his shoulder, the man was standing at the edge of the light cast by the lanterns, staring at Alex as if reminding himself what a woman looked like.

Alex straightened her shoulders and drew a deep

breath, then she opened the bin containing her medical supplies and called toward the shadows. "Come into the light and we'll see what needs to be done."

As with every medical incident, her heart sank and she prayed she would be up to the task. So far, common sense and her book of home remedies had pulled her through, but each time she had to play doctor, she had to battle squeamishness and a profound urge to flee.

"I'll doctor you, sir," she said, pride making her sound more confident than she felt. "But I won't feed a naked man. If you want supper, you'll have to get dressed."

Dal smiled and shrugged. "A wise man doesn't argue with his cook."

"I have standards," Alex explained stiffly. "Which include civilized behavior." She set her medical supplies on the edge of the wagon worktable, then groped behind her skirts, seeking her wheelchair.

"I'll find you a shirt and some trousers," Dal said, grinning. Alex would be Alex. She didn't allow the boys to swear in her presence, insisted on napkins, and woe be to the cowboy who relieved himself within her line of sight.

The man watched Alex settle herself in the wheelchair and snap her crutch into the brackets Dal had installed on the chair. She moved the medical supplies to her lap, then lifted her head with an expectant expression. "Please. Come into the light."

The man hesitated, then he came forward and lifted an arm so she could examine the cut on his rib cage.

Dal watched her clean the gash, then he asked the boys which of them could spare a shirt and a pair of trousers.

It bothered him to notice that Freddy had followed Les to the observers' camp, where she was talking to

Jack Caldwell. A flash of jealousy blackened his heart, and he wanted to stride over there, punch Caldwell, and carry his woman back where she belonged.

Instead, he took a shirt and pants to the chuck wagon, then filled his supper plate and sat with the boys, his back to the observers' camp.

CHAPTER ~ 16

The man's skin was taut and warm beneath Alex's
fingertips. She doctored the cut on his rib cage, then
treated a half dozen smaller cuts and scratches, noticing how lean he was, but muscled and well formed.
Magnificent, really. A blush tinted her cheeks, and she
ducked her head, concentrating on a scratch across his
belly and trying not to peek at his loincloth.

"There's a scrape on your collarbone," she murmured, fumbling for her crutch so she could stand to
reach the abrasion. When the man understood, he
dropped to his knees in front of her wheelchair.
"Thank you," she said, surprised and pleased by his
consideration. Except now he was at eye level, and
his continued intense scrutiny made her feel self-
conscious.

As she worked, she stole occasional glances at him.
The lantern shone directly into his face, revealing a thin
nose, broad cheekbones, and thick-lashed grey eyes beneath heavy brows. If Alex had been asked to guess,
she would have said he was probably in his middle thir-
ties. And she suspected a handsome man was hiding
beneath the long hair and unkempt beard.

Lowering her gaze to his chest, she extended a finger

and gently touched an old scar. "A gunshot wound?" she asked, not looking up because he continued to stare at her face.

There was nothing menacing or threatening about his stare, but his interest and attention made her actuely self-conscious. She returned to his collarbone and applied a soothing paste. "My name is Mrs. Mills, but we're being informal on this drive so everyone calls me Alex. What should we call you?' When he didn't answer, she met his gaze then blushed. "Oh. Dal said you couldn't or wouldn't talk. I'm sorry."

Vividly aware that he hadn't looked away from her, she resisted an irritating urge to pat her hair and wet her lips. When she finished treating him, she closed the lid on her medical box and moved a half roll back. "I'll fix you a supper plate."

Lightly, he placed his fingertips on her shoulder indicating she should stay seated. Surprised, she watched to see what he would do next and smiled when he pulled on the shirt and pants Dal had brought him. "If you had a hair cut and a beard trim, you'd be quite presentable," she said, instantly appalled that she'd uttered such a personal remark.

Sinking to the ground in front of her chair, he folded his legs Indian fashion. Then he touched the scraggly ends of his beard and lifted a lock of long hair, his meaning plain.

Later, Alex couldn't imagine what had possessed her to speak so familiarly or to perform such an intimate service. She could have handed him the shears, but that's not what she did. As he turned in front of her chair to accommodate her, she cut his hair then trimmed his beard close to his jaw. By the time she reached his lips, her hand was trembling slightly.

Blinking, she placed the shears in his hand and fished in the medical box for the mirror she kept there.

"I might nick you," she murmured, feeling a need for some kind of explanation.

Taking the mirror from her hand, he gazed into it as if he hadn't seen himself in a very long time. Finally, he took up the shears, revealing a full lower lip and a well-shaped upper lip. When he finished, he stood and looked down at her, a question in his grey eyes.

"You may have your supper now," she said, smiling. Dressed, with his hair cut and beard trimmed close to his jaw, he was as unnervingly handsome as she had guessed he would be.

Again, he placed his hand gently on her shoulder, telling her not to rise, and helped himself to a ladle of stew and two biscuits. Instead of joining the men around the fire, he returned to Alex and sat on the ground beside her.

She should have finished washing the dishes in the wreck pan, should have laid out the items she would need for breakfast tomorrow. Instead, she sat quietly beside the man and observed him from the corners of her eyes.

He'd taken a napkin, which surprised her, as she always had to remind the drovers. And he handled his knife and fork like a gentleman. He didn't slump. Everything about him intrigued her.

When he finished eating, he slipped his plate and flatware into the wreck pan, then bowed before he sat beside her again, now taking some interest in the campsite. He studied the men sitting around the fire, then looked toward the fire burning at the observers' campsite. Turning to her, he lifted an eyebrow, which she interpreted as a question.

After a brief hesitation, she explained Joe's will and

the conditions, wondering as she did so why she was
revealing personal matters to a stranger. Maybe it was
because she felt a secret outpouring of gratitude for his
obvious interest. She'd never expected a man to show
this kind of interest in her ever again. Or maybe it was
recognizing that tonight, with him beside her, she
didn't experience the aching loneliness that usually
made her feel so hollow inside.

"If you didn't want to talk to me," Jack Caldwell said,
gazing down into Freddy's face, "then why did you
come over to our camp?" A knowing smile opened beneath his gold mustache.

"Coming here had nothing to do with you. Les
asked me to accompany her," Freddy said, noticing
that Les and Ward had disappeared. Probably they had
ducked out of sight to exchange a few kisses. They
were pledged to be married, after all. But it irritated her
that Les had left her alone with Jack. She peered into
the deep shadows between Luther's wagon and Ward's,
wondering if they were hiding there.

"I think about you all the time, Fancy. I see you
over there, watch you singing with the boys after supper." When she didn't say anything, he added in a low
voice. "I miss you."

"You'll have the company of your future bride the
day after tomorrow." That's when they would reach
Fort Worth. And that's when she would have to deal
with Dal's proposition. Pride told her to stick her nose
in the air and refuse to go to a hotel with him. But her
traitorous body yearned to discover if there was more
to the mystery than what she'd experienced.

"You know, I've been thinking." Lifting a hand,
Jack touched her hair. "I sure hate to imagine you com-

ing out of this drive with nothing to show for it. I can
fix that for you."

She jerked away and her eyes narrowed. "What are
you talking about?"

"If I were you, I'd be planning how I could get
something no matter how many cattle make it to Abilene."

"We're going to win!"

He grinned. "No, you aren't. But you don't have to
come out of this with nothing."

"Damn it, if you have something to say, just say it."

"Suppose you let some of those stragglers get lost
along the way, or overlook finding a few strays after
the next stampede. Maybe you aren't as careful as you
might be at the next river crossing and a few steers
get washed away. If you agree to help out a little, I'm
authorized to promise you enough money to set yourself up in a nice cozy theater in San Francisco."

Heat flooded her face, and her hand dropped to the
pistol on her hip. "You bastard. I ought to shoot you
where you stand!"

"I'm just thinking of you," he said in a low persua-
sive voice. "Agree to lose a few steers, and your worries are over. You get what you want no matter how
many cattle you deliver."

Fury shook her body. He was asking her to betray
her sisters and all the effort they had put into preparing
for this ordeal and all the hardships they had endured
since. "I tried so hard to see something good in you,"
she said in a low furious voice. "I wanted to like and
respect you."

Irritation flickered across his expression. "I have to
back the winner. No reason you can't do the same. We
can make this a no-lose deal for you, Fancy honey.
Think about it."

She didn't have a chance to tell him to go to hell. Too many things happened at once.

A light caught her eye and she looked toward the space between Luther's and Ward's wagons. Dimly she registered Luther standing at the end of the wagons holding a lantern. But what fixed her attention was the scene between the wagons.

Les sagged against the side of one of the wagons, silent tears running down her cheeks. Ward stood over her, his face twisted in anger. Horrified, Freddy gasped as his hand descended and he slapped her sister hard enough to snap Les's head to one side.

Luther dropped the lantern and ran into the space between the wagons. Fire spewed out of the shattered lantern and ignited a patch of dry grass. Screaming for help, Freddy raced around the wagons, and stamped on fingers of rapidly spreading flame. In less than a minute, the drovers were there, lifting the tongue of the wagon in greatest peril, pulling in front, pushing behind, moving the wooden wagon bed away from the flames. Grady and a man she'd never seen before arrived with buckets of water. They doused the flames and ran toward the barrel for more water.

Everything happened so swiftly that the fire was extinguished just as Dal pulled Luther and Ward apart. Les had crawled away from the flames and the fighting men and sat on the grass, wiping her eyes. When Alex rolled up beside her, she turned and put her head in Alex's lap.

Freddy had never seen Luther so furious or even imagined that he might be combative or willing to settle something with his fists. Spitting with rage, he struggled to shove past Dal and reach Ward, who already had a bloody nose and a cracked lip.

Luther shouted, "You miserable bastard . . . if you ever raise a hand to her again—"

Dal pushed him back. "What the hell happened here?"

With everyone listening, Luther explained what he had seen.

Dal turned a stare on Ward. "Is that true? You hit a woman?"

Dark color rushed into Ward's face, and he glanced at the silent ring of people watching him, condemnation glittering in their eyes. He glared at Dal. "This is between my fiancée and me and none of your concern."

Dal pushed his face next to Ward's. "Everything that happens on this drive is my business." The expression on his face suggested that a lot of things were falling into place in his mind. As they were for Freddy. Ward was beating her sister.

She watched Les lift her head from Alex's lap and look at Ward. Pain, embarrassment, and exhaustion pinched her face. A nasty bruise had already begun to form on her cheek.

"She's going to be my wife. Les is my property," Ward said belligerently.

Freddy lowered her head and swore.

Dal snarled. "You son of a bitch!" He pushed Ward hard enough that he stumbled and almost fell. Then he turned and strode back to the campfire. The drovers stared at Ward, then followed.

"He'll do it again," Freddy said bluntly when she reached Alex and Les. "Get rid of him."

"Freddy's right," Alex said softly, smoothing a lock of hair off of Les's forehead. "You don't have to take that kind of treatment. You shouldn't take it."

Anguish filled Les's eyes. "Ward sold the store at a loss to come with us," she whispered.

"You don't owe him a damn thing." Freddy sat down on the grass and wrapped her arms around her knees. She wished Luther had broken Ward's nose instead of only bloodying it. "He's hit you. He criticizes you constantly. He's demanding and tyrannical. And he almost killed you, making you work when you were feverish and out of your head."

Alex nodded. "We begged him to let you withdraw. We told him that we would give you a full third of the inheritance even if he pulled you out of the drive as we wanted him to do."

Les's eyes widened and filled with tears. "The two of you would have done that for me?"

"He didn't tell you?" Freddy asked in disgust.

Les peered at the observers' camp. "He told me that he saved our share."

Freddy struck the ground with her fist. "Damn it, Les. It isn't *our* share. It's *your* share."

"I just . . . I . . . What am I going to do?"

"You know what you need to do," Freddy snapped.

"I . . . just can't."

They sat in silence in the shadowy patch between the two campfires. "Well, we can't force you to do something you don't want to do," Alex said finally.

Freddy shook her head. "Before this drive began, I would have sworn you couldn't do anything worth doing. But I was wrong. You should feel proud of yourself, Les. You're working as hard and as well as anyone here. You don't have to bow your head to anyone. Especially not to Ward. Think about that." Standing, she stretched and yawned, wishing she'd told Jack to go to hell. "I've got an early watch tonight."

"I still have to lay out the breakfast things," Alex said, releasing the brake on her chair.

Freddy gripped the handles of the chair and pushed Alex forward. "Who's the man I saw helping Grady and the boys put out the fire?" She waited for a minute then called, "Les? Are you coming? I swear, if you go to him now, I'll smack you myself. Get over here."

The three of them had never worked together as a unit, but it seemed natural to help Alex finish cleaning up from supper while she told them about the guest who was visiting their camp.

Freddy listened, but she noticed they were all distracted. Les kept looking toward the observers' camp and Ward. Freddy's gaze continually strayed to Dal. And Alex positioned herself in such a way that she could see the bearded man who sat silently drinking coffee with Dal.

The men looked back at them.

Alex packed away the breakfast utensils, covered a large bowl of dough that needed to rise before noon, then she slid her crutch under the driver's seat of the wagon. She was preparing to crawl up when she felt strong hands on her waist, assisting her. Once on the seat, she looked into the steady grey eyes gazing back at her.

"Thank you." To her surprise, he walked around the mules, checking the harness, then climbed into the wagon beside her. He would have taken the reins from her hands, but she said, "No," and reminded him that Joe's will prohibited anyone from helping.

Before Dal set off in front of the herd, he rode up beside the wagon. "You're welcome to stay with the drive until we reach Fort Worth," he said, then glanced at Alex. "Do you mind having company? We could give our friend here a horse."

"I don't mind." She braced her leg against the fender and smiled at their guest. "Hang on."

The wild careening ride across the prairie range didn't terrify her as it once had, but she'd never really become accustomed to it. Today, however, with someone watching, she was proud of how well she managed. It occurred to her that she was succeeding, doing what she had to do. A burst of self-confidence straightened her shoulders, surprising her. She hadn't experienced any sense of genuine self-confidence since the accident.

Dal waved her off near a grassy-banked creek and galloped back toward the herd. Grady and the observers' wagons hadn't yet arrived, but today, the vast open spaces didn't frighten her. Twisting on the seat, she found her crutch, poked the tip on the ground to scare away any lurking snakes, then remarked, "I wish I knew your name. I don't know how to address you."

He hesitated, then used a finger to draw something on the seat space between them. When Alex frowned, he did it again. "John! Is that your name?"

What he did next paralyzed her. Reaching out a hand, he patted her flat skirt. Gazing steadily into her eyes, he raised her skirt and petticoat. Shock dried her mouth and her heart slammed against her ribs.

"Don't," she whispered. She wanted to jump out of the wagon, but she couldn't move. Couldn't breathe. Worse, they were alone, and she was defenseless, sitting in the middle of nowhere with a strange man who was pulling up her skirt. Panic stopped her heart, until she realized there was no malice in his gaze. Only a depth of compassion that brought sudden helpless tears to her own eyes.

He pushed her skirt to her lap then looked down at the smooth stump the surgeons had left. And Alex knew agony. This was the first time anyone other than a doctor had looked at what remained of her right leg. She couldn't think, couldn't draw the next humiliated breath. She sat as still as a stone and wanted to die. When he touched her knee she gasped, and cognizance returned with the crimson that set her face on fire.

In a flurry of mortification, shame, and fury, she slapped his hand hard and tried to shove down her skirts, but he caught her wrist and forced her to look into his eyes. Sympathy and compassion, sadness and understanding, that's what she saw, and it crushed her.

Silent tears spilled over her lashes when she realized his touch on what remained of her leg had been as gentle as a lover's. There had been no revulsion in his gaze, no drawing back. She covered her face with her hands and drew a deep shuddering breath.

Gently, he lowered her skirt then took her hands in his. Waiting. "You want to know how I lost my leg," she whispered. She was too confused, too deeply rattled to tell a coherent story. Face flaming, she jerked away from him and lowered her crutch. "Perhaps later."

The shock of what he had done remained with her, and consequently the noon dinner was a slapdash affair, and some of the boys complained. But his steady regard made her nervous and clumsy. She would have preferred not to share her wagon with him in the afternoon, but she couldn't manage a moment alone with Dal to arrange it. So she didn't speak or look at him during the ride to the bedding ground, nor did she address him while she prepared supper. But there was not a minute when she didn't think about the strange incident. She was horrified that he would lift her skirts

and look at her leg, that he would touch the stump.
Stump was such an ugly word that she cringed even to
think it. She couldn't bear that he had looked at it,
touched it.

After washing the supper dishes, she laid out the
items she would need in the morning and finally was
ready to put away the hated crutch and return to her
wheelchair. Instantly John came to her. He pushed her
into the shadowy line where the light from the fire and
lanterns met the night. How odd that he'd guessed that
was where she usually ended the day, away from the
wagon and drovers, but sitting where she could watch
them. He sat beside her and lifted an eyebrow. When
she didn't speak, he touched her skirt where it lay flat
against the chair.

"It was a carriage accident," she said finally, sound-
ing angry. "My husband was killed, and my leg was
crushed."

He continued to watch her, his expression telling her
that he knew there was more.

"This doesn't make sense," Alex whispered, looking into his eyes, "but I feel as if I know you." And
somehow he knew her. "You, too, have known sorrow
and loss." She could see that in his face, in his eyes.
"I wish I knew your story."

He turned his face toward the men sitting around the
campfire. Tonight Freddy was reciting something from
a play, and the drovers were drinking coffee and listening intently. After a few minutes they applauded loudly
enough to show their appreciation, but not loud enough
to startle the steers on the bedding ground.

Alex didn't understand the attraction she felt toward
this strange man. His attention was flattering, and she
supposed the surprise of a man's interest was part of
his appeal. Another part might be the fact that he

clearly had been a gentleman at one time. Perhaps that was why her panic had been short-lived when he raised her skirts. Intuition insisted she was in no danger from him.

"Who are you?" she wondered aloud, letting her gaze travel along his profile and wanting to touch the softness of his beard. He didn't answer, but his gaze was gentle.

They sat in companionable silence at the edge of the darkness even after the drovers began to drift toward their bedrolls. Alex remembered the painful silences that had sometimes opened between herself and Payton, but there was nothing awkward about this silence, nothing edgy or anxious.

It didn't make sense, but she would miss him dreadfully when he left.

"I don't care what Frisco said," Ward stated angrily. "We can't afford a hotel!" He walked to the observers' fire and poured himself a cup of coffee. "We'd have to pay for two rooms and meals . . . if you want to rest, you can do it here."

They were camped a few miles south of Fort Worth. Close enough that Les could see the boomtown in the distance, but far enough away that their herd didn't impinge on other herds that grazed outside the town. The grass was good here and the west fork of the Trinity River offered sweet water and a comfortable crossing. She could glimpse an old abandoned fort on top of the bluff overlooking town.

"We've been on the trail almost two months and I haven't seen anything except dust and the tail end of the herd," she said, looking toward the smoky haze overhanging the town. "I'm longing for a real tub bath and a real bed." And a night that wasn't interrupted by her turn on watch. A night without rocks digging into her back or the sounds of male snoring all around her.

"I've just told you that we can't afford two nights in town," Ward said sharply.

"Luther said the estate would pay for me to stay over and rest." The stubborn tone in her voice made her pulse accelerate. She knew he wouldn't strike her, not with people wandering around both camps, but she saw the vein throbbing in his temple and knew his temper was rising. Fear, strong and habitual, closed her throat.

"You. It's always you," he said with disgust. "You never think about me!"

The words were intended to make her feel guilty, were intended to manipulate and control. She knew that, perhaps she had always known it, but the ploy was effective just the same. For a moment, she stood very still, trying to summon a tiny bit of courage.

"If you can't afford a room," she said, staring down at her boots, "then you stay here. But I'm going." This was the best thing she could do for herself. "I'm so tired. I need the rest."

"Are you defying me?" he asked incredulously. He dropped his coffee cup and his hands opened and closed at his sides.

Exhaustion washed through her body, and her shoulders slumped. She was fatigued to the bone. So weary of trying to please him, of trying to always say and do the right thing, the thing that wouldn't make him angry. Right now she was worn-out enough to say things she might not have been brave enough to say otherwise.

"Why didn't you tell me that Alex and Freddy would have given me my share of the inheritance even if I'd dropped out?" The reason she still felt weak and half-ill was because Ward had decided she had to work the drag even if it killed her. She couldn't stop thinking about that. He had endangered her life even after Alex and Freddy had guaranteed her share of the money.

"Don't be stupid. We wouldn't have seen a penny if you'd dropped out! I see through those two. Believe me, they wanted you gone so they would have a larger share for themselves!"

Before the drive began, he might have convinced her, but not now. Her relationship with her sisters was changing. She liked their company, and she was beginning to respect their courage and determination. She cherished this new connection and growing closeness. More than she wanted to win this contest, she wanted her sisters' acceptance and respect. The realization astonished her and raised a film of moisture to her eyes.

"Are you coming to town with us?" Freddy called.

"I'll be right there." When was the last time Ward had smiled? When had she last felt any tenderness toward him? "Please try to understand. All I want to do is sleep for two days."

For the first time since he'd come calling, she walked away from him without a backward glance and without caring what he thought.

Dal tied John's cows to the tail of the wagon, then helped Les into the back. He would have assisted Freddy except she slapped his hands away. She sat on the far side of the driver's seat, as far from any contact with him as she could get, her hat pulled down over her eyes.

Alex rolled up to the wagon. "Buy as many eggs as you can find." She spoke to Dal, but her gaze fixed on John, who sat in the back of the wagon with Les.

"You can come with us," Dal suggested. He planned to drop John off, check Les into one hotel and Freddy into another, then purchase the supplies Alex needed and bring them back to camp. Then, finally, he would return to Fort Worth and Freddy.

Alex had never impressed him as a fidgety type of woman, but she was now. Her hands moved over the wheels of the chair, across her lap, up to her hair, touched her lips, then returned to her lap. She shook her head. "No, maybe I'll go into town tomorrow with Luther." A small smile curved her lips. "Good-bye, John. Have someone change the dressing on your ribs."

Dal flicked the reins over the horses' backs, gave Grady a wave, and one to Caleb, whom he was leaving in charge of the herd. "You didn't bring a satchel," he said, flapping the reins.

"I don't need one," Freddy snapped. "I'm only doing this because you swore you'd force me if I didn't come willingly."

"That's correct." He pressed his lips together and considered. Clearly, she wasn't going to help relieve an awkward situation. All right, he'd add another stop to his list of chores. She was, by God, going to cooperate, like it or not. He would buy her a pretty nightgown and a ribbon for her hair. "You are one exasperating woman," he muttered grimly.

"Got to hell, Frisco."

"You're supposed to say that afterward, not before."

He let John out of the wagon when the man tapped him on the shoulder. Got Les settled into a quiet hotel away from the main street. He all but shoved Freddy into a small hotel at the other end of town, checked them in as man and wife, which bothered him some, and caused her to lift both eyebrows. Then he ordered her a bath, slapped the room key in her palm, and warned her that she better be there when he returned.

That done, he purchased the supplies Alex had requested. Then he stopped by the telegraph office and sent a message to Emile Julie in New Orleans. Before he drove back to the herd, curiosity prompted him to stop by the sheriff's office where he asked if the sheriff knew anything about the naked man he'd found on the range.

"That's John McCallister," the sheriff informed him, standing beside Dal's wagon, where he could keep an eye on the cowboys whooping it up before they headed north again. He tapped his temple. "McCallister's crazy as a coot. Been wandering around out there since the war ended."

"Union or Confederate?" Five years was a long time to wander alone. Or to live inside a drunken haze. Anyone who said the war was over hadn't served in it.

"Someone said he spent two years in a Union prison. I guess that'd make just about anyone crazy." The sheriff shook his head. "You've seen the last of him. He ranges south of here, never goes north." After a minute he added, "McCallister was a doctor before the war. At least that's what I heard. Hailed from Atlanta."

They talked a while about the herds outside of town and about the town's booming growth, then Dal drove back to camp and let Grady help him carry provisions to the chuck wagon. Between trips back and forth, he told Alex what he'd learned about their visitor. She listened, sighing often, while he looked at the sky. Time was passing, and he was as eager as a sixteen-year-old to get back to the hotel and Freddy.

Alex touched his wrist. "Freddy is tough on the outside, but she's vulnerable inside. Don't do anything to hurt her, Dal."

Surprised, he stared down at her. "Did Freddy tell you——"

She laughed. "Why is it that lovers think no one notices their long looks and whispers?"

A flush of color rose beneath his sunburned cheeks. "Freddy and I are not lovers," he said stiffly. And one night in a hotel wouldn't change that situation. In his opinion, lovers were a couple with some form of commitment between them. That wasn't the situation here.

Alex gazed at him with an affectionate smile. "I didn't like you when we first met. But you're a good man. Freddy could do worse," she added, glancing toward the observers' camp where Caldwell was mounting his horse to ride into town. "Just don't hurt her."

He would have sworn that she would lecture him about morality and standards and ruining women. But she turned away and applied herself to the arduous task of pushing the wheelchair through the grass and over the bumpy ground.

He hesitated a moment, then walked up behind her and pushed her back to the chuck wagon. "I like you too, Alex Roark Mills," he said quietly. "I didn't expect to admire any of the Roark sisters, but all three of you are very special women."

They smiled at each other, then she pressed something in his hand. "Give this to Freddy."

He didn't look at the bottle she'd put in his palm until he reached the outskirts of Fort Worth. She'd sent Freddy a little vial of perfume.

After leaving the buckskin at the stables, he walked to the barbershop for a haircut, a shave, and a hot tub. The sisters weren't the only ones who were changing on this journey.

Certainly he'd never expected to spend a night with

Freddy Roark. Or anticipated that he'd feel nervous about it. Never in his life had he applied himself to pondering and planning an evening or spent so much time trying to guess what a woman would consider romantic.

The responsibility of it weighed heavily on him. After his haircut and shave, midway through his bath, he drew on his cigar then looked over at the man soaking in the tub next to him.

"Women like romance," he said, as if picking up an ongoing conversation.

"The decent ones do," the man agreed with a nod. He tipped the ash off his cigar into his bathwater. "Makes it hard on a man."

"Isn't that the truth." He exhaled a stream of smoke and watched it curl toward the ceiling. "In your opinion, what do women consider most romantic?"

"I don't have a fricking idea."

"Neither do I."

"I believe they like flowers," the other man said after a while. "And poetry."

"Music, too, I've heard."

Flowers, music, and poetry; it was enough to get him started. He'd do fine once they got to the actual lovemaking. It was that all-important buildup that concerned him.

"You're Dal Frisco, aren't you?" his bathing companion inquired.

"Who wants to know?"

"Name's Hal Morely. I got a hundred bucks bet that you'll get your herd to Abilene."

He'd guessed right. A lot of people up and down the trail were watching and had an interest in this drive. Any doubt about staking his reputation on the King's

Walk drive vanished. His name, his livelihood, and his future all rested on winning this contest.

"We're holding our own," he said sourly.

Hal Morely stood and reached for a towel. "It might interest you to know that you got trouble coming. I saw a fella named Caldwell talking nose to nose with Hoke Smyth. Old Hoke's been up before the judge three times for cattle rustling. Looked to me like Caldwell and Hoke were doing a little business."

Dal frowned. "Thanks for the tip."

Nothing would happen while they were camped this close to Fort Worth. Besides, right now he was more worried about a small green-eyed semivirgin who could turn him inside out with a look.

CHAPTER **17**

No decent woman ever sat in a hotel room waiting for an illicit lover to arrive, and Freddy knew it. The longer she waited for Dal to return, the more skittish, anxious, and uncertain she became. She would have fled except she had used her leftover bathwater to launder her trail clothes and they were draped around the room, still wet.

Wrapped in a towel, she sat beside an open window letting a warm breeze dry her freshly washed hair while she chewed a fingernail and suffered pangs of regret for ever agreeing to this tryst. What had she been thinking of? In Frisco's opinion, he was doing right by bringing her here, but he wouldn't have forced her. At heart he was a man of integrity.

Which meant that she was here by choice. Admitting this did not go down well.

There were so many points against him, she thought, brooding. His weakness for whiskey. His past association with Lola. His work history. His similarity to her father. Moreover, Freddy had always rejected the attentions of ranchers. She didn't want to end up stuck out in the middle of nowhere with no one but cattle and cowboys for company.

On the other hand, Dal was educated, and a natural leader. He was confident and strong. He could quote lines from plays and literature. He was ambitious and hardworking; he possessed a certain rough charm. He had dreams.

But the main reason she had agreed to ruin herself once and for all was because he had awakened something inside her. His slow smile and those intense, narrowed, blue eyes dropped the bottom out of her stomach and made her wild with desire. He had hinted there was more than the disappointment they had experienced on the range, and she yearned to know what that might be.

Sighing, she lifted a length of hair to the fading sunlight and gazed around the room. The furnishings were nicer than she had expected to find in a frontier town. The bedstead, desk, table, and chairs were made of polished cherrywood. A chintz settee and armchair added warm splashes of color. The decorative touch she most liked was a painted dressing screen.

Nervously, Freddy clutched her hands in her lap. She wanted to run away. She wished he would get here.

By the time Dal's knock sounded at the door, causing her to jump out of her skin, she had donned her damp clothing with the firm intention of leaving. Where she would go, she didn't know. She only knew that she couldn't wait another minute—she had to get out of here. The bed had grown in size and importance until it totally dominated the room.

"Freddy? Open the door."

She stood on the other side, twisting her hat in her hands, suffering a spasm of indecision. "I think I've changed my mind about this," she said finally. Then she uttered words she had never thought to hear on her lips. "I want to return to the herd."

"Freddy, open the damned door and let me in."

"Did you bring the wagon or a horse? I need a horse." With half a dozen herds camped outside Fort Worth, she worried whether she could find the King's Walk outfit.

"Do you suppose we could discuss this while we're both standing in the same room?" He sounded exasperated and pounded on the door again.

"If I let you inside, you'll just try to talk me out of leaving," she said uncertainly. "Wait a minute. Something's going on under the window."

Leaving Dal standing in the hotel corridor swearing, she returned to the window and leaned out. Two stories below, four Mexican musicians stood grouped around a lantern at their feet. They tipped broad sombreros and smiled up at her, then lifted violins to their chins and played a love song so sweet and filled with longing that it raised a lump in Freddy's throat. "Oh!"

Caught in the music, several minutes passed before she noticed the pounding on the door. "Dal?" she said, crossing the room and placing her hand on the knob. "Did you arrange for the musicians?" It was a nice gesture, lovely really. And she could hardly leave in the middle of their serenade; that would be rude. She was stuck until the musicians finished their performance.

"I swear to you. If you don't open this door—right now—I'm going to kick it down."

She caught her lower lip between her teeth and hesitated, then opened the door wide enough to peek into the hallway. "We're only going to talk, we're not—" She stared at the packages surrounding his feet. "What's all that?"

"Gifts."

Freddy suspected the old warning to beware of

Greeks bearing gifts might also apply to cowboys. Then she realized he didn't look like a work-worn drover tonight.

He wore new store-bought clothing, a dark jacket over dark trousers and a crisp white shirt with a silver string tie. The hat he held in his hands was brushed and clean and his boots were polished to a high gleam. He smelled of good barbershop cologne, and his hair was parted in the center and slicked back with oil.

Freddy's mouth dropped. "You look . . . different." And so handsome that he took her breath away. Tonight his tan seemed darker and his eyes bluer. His shoulders wider and his waist leaner. She was accustomed to seeing him with bristle on his jaw, but tonight he was close-shaven, which made her intensely aware of his mouth and lips.

He stuck his boot in the door and leaned forward, pushing her out of the way, then he carried the packages to the bed and dropped them on the spread before he pulled a pocket watch out of his vest and consulted the time. "Dinner will be served in our room in an hour." For the first time since Freddy had met him, he seemed uneasy and uncertain. "I'm going downstairs so you can dress in privacy. I'll return in forty-five minutes. Here. Alex sent you this."

"Wait a minute," she called. But he was closing the door behind him.

Alex had sent her perfume? Then Alex knew. Scarlet burned on Freddy's face, and she collapsed on the side of the bed, clutching the vial in her hand. Damn. During the course of the drive, she had mysteriously moved from not caring what her sisters thought to caring a lot.

Five miserable minutes elapsed before she thought to wonder why Alex would send her perfume. Removing the stopper, she passed the vial beneath her nose, inhaling a light scent of roses. Could it be that Alex was not the most judgmental woman ever born as Freddy had always supposed? Amazing. She brightened enough to inspect the packages on the bed.

Before she left, which she still intended to do, she might as well discover what Dal had brought her. After she saw the dinner gown and slippers, the nightgown and ribbons, she listened to the music floating up to her window and scanned the opulent appointments of the room.

"Well I'll be," she marveled softly. "Dal Frisco is a romantic." But she liked this unexpected side of him, she decided, holding the gown against her body and turning in front of the mirror. He'd chosen green silk with gold ruffles and trim, and the gown looked as if it would fit. Now, if he had just remembered hair pins . . .

"You are so wishy-washy," she said, frowning at her image in the mirror. "Bought off with a new gown and slippers. And a bottle of perfume." Then she laughed. The gown and perfume were inconsequential. The instant she had seen him, her doubts had settled and her longing to discover how the evening would unfold had returned full force.

This time when he knocked, she opened the door immediately and several people entered the room. First came a boy carrying baskets of spring flowers followed by two waiters pushing a linen-clad dinner table set with fine china and sparkling silver. Then Dal appeared.

He stopped mid-stride, just inside the room, and stared. "My God." A slow narrowed glance traveled over the green gown, paused at her waist and again at her breasts before he met her eyes. "You are absolutely the most beautiful woman I have ever seen!"

Freddy gazed at him with sparkling eyes and a flirtatious glance. This was the first time she had worn anything but black since her father died, and the first time she had worn a formal gown in Dal's presence. The mirror told her that she looked lovely, but she needed to hear and see confirmation; she needed to see herself reflected in his eyes.

For a long moment they gazed at each other, and Freddy felt her mouth go dry and her heartbeat accelerate. If the evening ended right now, she would still remember this moment for all her days. The music, the perfume of the flower baskets, and the hard look of desire in Dal's eyes.

Stepping forward, he touched his fingertips to her cheek, then dropped his hand to her waist and led her toward the table. After weeks of sitting on the ground eating supper out of tin plates, the formality of dressing and dining felt strange. Like a role she was playing. Except she didn't know her lines and his hand on her waist felt warm and strong and would have made her forget her dialogue if she had known it.

Dal held out her chair and she sat down in a rustle of silk and ruffles. A waiter draped a linen napkin across her lap, a second man poured wine into her glass. It was a measure of her nervousness that when she saw Dal cover his glass and shake his head, she forgot his history and asked, "Aren't you having wine?"

"No." He drew a breath. "The sight of you is intoxicating enough."

Her mouth dropped and she stared. Not in a hundred years could she have imagined him uttering such a romantic comment. This was Dal, the man who rode his horse like the animal was part of him, who turned stampedes in the dark of night, who rode out of the dust and sun as if forged from flying dirt and hard sunlight himself. Dal who shouted and cursed and drove his cattle across swollen rivers, who worked himself and his men without pity. She would have sworn there was no softness in this man, no pretty words of seduction.

The instant the waiters removed the warming covers, he gruffly ordered, "Leave us."

Freddy wet her lips and desperately tried to think of something to say to this strange new Dal whom she had never seen before and didn't know. And it occurred to her that perhaps she seemed as strange to him, gowned and coiffed and perfumed and not the woman he was accustomed to seeing either.

She moistened her lips with the wine and inspected her dinner. "It looks wonderful," she murmured, knowing she was too nervous to eat a bite.

Dal gazed at the ceiling for a moment before he cleared his throat and touched his tie. " 'All my desire, all my delight should be, Her to enjoy, her to unite to me.' " He turned his empty wineglass between his fingers, running a caressing glance down her throat to the swell of soft flesh curving above the low scoop of her bodice.

Freddy swallowed, then blurted the first quotation that sprang to her mind. " 'Fie on sinful fantasy! Fie on lust and luxury! Lust is but a bloody fire, Kindled with unchaste desire.' "

Smiling, Dal supplied Shakespeare's next lines, " 'Fed in heart, whose flames aspire, as thoughts do blow them, higher and higher.' "

" 'Pinch him, fairies, mutually; Pinch him for his villainy.' "

He laughed, then spoke softly, " 'There is a garden

in her face, Where roses and white lilies grow; A heavenly paradise is that place, Wherein all pleasant fruits do flow.' "

Astonishment thrilled her. She could not believe these words were falling from his lips, couldn't believe they were trading flowery bits of poetry. She liked it, but . . . it was also a bit overwhelming. She couldn't quite make the transition from herding cattle yesterday to being romanced today. "Dal," she whispered, looking into his hot gaze. "What are you doing?"

"I'm trying to seduce you. Trying to do it right this time," he said simply, letting his eyes go soft in the candlelight. "You're so beautiful, Freddy, so lovely."

So was he. Candlelight warmed the strong bronzed angles of his face, played across his fingers and the backs of his hands. His eyes had not left her since he returned to the room. Freddy was aware of his body, remembered the iron strength of his thighs and his hard flat stomach. But it was his steady gaze that made her go weak inside, made her feel as if her bones were slowly melting. His gaze turned alternately soft then hard with desire, gentled by the words on his tongue then heated with speculation.

Her own body responded with a strange restless tension. She felt damp and overly warm, shivery with nerves and anticipation. Picking up her fork, she pushed at the items on her plate, not seeing them. And she listened as he quoted love sonnets to her, feeling her cheeks grow hot when the poetry skirted close to the subject uppermost in her mind, lovemaking.

Behind him, she glimpsed the bedspread, pale against evening shadows. The music drifting in the opened window was sweet and longing. Tension grew in the pit of her stomach and spread through her body. Her lips trembled and so did her fingertips. When she looked at him across the candle flames, she saw only his eyes and his lips, heard only the words he spoke to her, and she decided if he didn't kiss her soon, she would faint from the need to feel his mouth on hers.

As if he'd read her mind, he stood and took her hand, guiding her to her feet. Standing so close that her skirt wrapped his legs, he brought his fingertips to her face and traced the shape of her cheekbones, her jaw-line, her lips. She closed her eyes and swayed as his fingers brushed down the arch of her throat and came to rest on the tops of her breasts. She couldn't breathe, couldn't think. And when his mouth finally came down on hers, she released a sound of gratitude that was almost a sob.

She would have grabbed him and returned his kiss with force and passion, but he wouldn't permit it. To her frustration, he eased back, keeping his kiss light, holding her at the waist to control her movement. Instead of roughly claiming her mouth as he had done before, he teased her with light kisses across her lips, her eyelids, her temples. But gradually his hands on her waist brought her closer and tighter against his hips, letting her feel the rock-hard state of his arousal.

Wild with desire, she gasped and moaned and pressed against him, trying to capture his lips with her own, but he remained elusive, tantalizing her with a brief touch of his tongue, like a swift brand of fire, then gone. His hands caressed the curve of waist and rib cage, hot against the silk of her gown, burning through to her skin, stroking up and down but not touching her breasts. So teasingly close and then away, leaving her arched toward him, yearning for his hand on nipples that had risen like hard pebbles toward a touch that didn't come.

"Dal . . . Dal . . ." Mindlessly, she whispered his

name as his kisses deepened and became possessive
and deliberate. But slow. Exploring. Teasing. Never
quite enough. Kisses that drank desire from her mouth
and left her frantic with wanting, wanting, wanting.

When she was writhing in his arms, helpless in her
need, his fingers deftly opened the hooks running up
the back of her gown and Freddy collapsed against him
in relief. The sensations rippling through her body,
heat and tension and moisture and anxiety and nervousness and desire, oh the desire that made her shake
and tremble and fear that her legs would give way and
she would fall, these sensations overpowered her and
all she could think about was him, his touch, his next
kiss, taking him inside of her, melding into him and
him into her. She had never dreamed that she could
lose herself so completely in a man's kisses. That
clothing could become an insupportable barrier or that
the world could shrink to the thrill of one man's touch.

She had always believed it would embarrass her to
stand naked before a man's gaze, but it didn't. She
heard his sharp intake of breath and saw in his eyes
that she was beautiful to him. And when he, too, was
naked, she gazed in wonder at his hard male beauty
and the differences between men and women. He, too,
was damp with desire, and his lean body gleamed in
the candlelight. When she stretched a trembling hand
to stroke the dark hair on his chest, his skin was hot to
the touch, as was hers, and he, too, was trembling,
which surprised her.

She thought they would immediately resume where
they had ended out on the range, but it didn't happen
that way. He lifted her in his arms and gently placed
her on the bed, then stretched out beside her and began
to kiss her again while his fingers wandered over her
breasts and waist and hips. She felt his need pressing

against her stomach and instinctively wrapped her legs around him, but he didn't move to enter her as she had expected.

Instead, he trailed his mouth down her throat to her aching breasts and sucked one nipple into his mouth and fluttered his tongue across it, and then did the same to her other breast, taking his time. A lightning thrill of surprise and pleasure raced through her body, searing and electric and unlike anything Freddy had ever experienced. And then his mouth moved lower, to her waist and belly then lower still, until he found her center and she gasped, unable to believe what he was doing, something she had never imagined.

When his tongue stroked across her there, she tensed, intending to push him away, but waves of sensation rocked her mind. And she exploded. The tension that had been building gathered into a molten ball that shattered in a burst of ecstasy. She thought she would faint with the intense pleasure of it, thought perhaps she *had* fainted. Throwing her head back into the pillows, she panted, fighting to catch a full breath and trying to understand what had happened.

And then, Dal was leaning over her, gazing into her stunned eyes, covering her with his hips. When he entered the moist heat of her, she gasped and wrapped her arms around him and raised her legs, her movement instinctive. There was no pain this time, just a blissful fullness that felt so right, so complete. Just pure pleasure, and an urge to meet his slow deep thrusts, to draw him deeply into her.

And she felt it beginning again, that swiftly gathering hot tension that drained the strength from her limbs and scalded her mind and body with a thrilling pleasure so sweet and intense that she couldn't contain it, could only let it sweep her up and up and up on waves of breathless joy.

Clinging to him, struggling to breathe, she held him as his shoulders tensed and he murmured her name, then clasped her hard against him. He held her a minute after his body stopped moving, then he eased to one side and guided her into his arms.

Freddy pressed her cheek against his shoulder, struggling to calm her breathing. Her body was bathed in sweat and the night air from the window felt good flowing across her hot skin.

Never again would she look at a married couple in quite the same way. Now she knew why men and women stayed together through adversity and hardship. Why they needed each other so much.

"I played Madame de Chimay all wrong," she murmured drowsily.

Dal lifted his head from the pillow and blinked at her. "What?"

"She's a married woman in love with her husband. But I didn't understand." She placed her hand on his chest and watched her fingers rise and fall with his breathing. "Now don't take offense. What happened just now was . . ." There weren't words to describe it. "Unbelievable. I had no idea I could feel like . . ." She pressed up against him. "Is it like this always?"

"Damn it, Freddy." Reaching to the table beside the bed, he found a cigar and lit it. "This wasn't grist for your acting mill. This was about doing it right." He reached behind and propped the pillows against the bedstead and leaned against them.

"Oh you did it right," she said softly, inhaling the scent of his skin.

"Then you aren't going to tell me to go to hell?" he murmured against her tangled curls.

"Not yet." She laughed and combed her fingers through the hair on his chest, giving it a gentle yank. "Dal?" she said after a minute. "I'm glad it was you."

So glad that it hadn't been Jack Caldwell or one of the actors she had met or any of the men who had courted her over the years. She thanked heaven that she had waited for Dal Frisco.

"Suddenly I'm famished, are you?"

She laughed, happy and exuberant. Rolling away, she found the nightgown he'd brought and dropped it over her head, then tied her hair with a length of ribbon. When they returned to the table, she felt a moment of unaccustomed shyness. There was something warmly intimate about dining in her nightgown with a half-naked man. This was the sort of thing married people did.

But tonight was not about promises or the future. Tonight was Dal's insistence on making her first real sexual experience a pleasant one. That was all, and nothing more.

"Tell me about Montana," she said, forcing a lightness into her tone. "What's it like? Why do you want to live there?"

Dal took a sip from a cup of coffee that had grown cold, then he grinned. "I've dreamed of Montana for years, but I've never been there." Surprise lifted her eyebrows, then she laughed. "I've seen paintings, and I've talked to cattlemen from Montana. Mostly I want to live there because it isn't Louisiana, where I grew up, and it isn't Texas, where my reputation precedes me."

She understood about reputations. "But you want to be a rancher."

He broke a chunk off the loaf of bread. "It's what I know and what I love."

"Dal? Why did you start drinking?"

"Good God," he said suddenly. "I told the musicians to keep playing until I signaled them to stop. Do you want more music?"

Smiling, Freddy shook her head. "The deed is done. We don't need them anymore."

"Did we *need* them?" When he saw the color in her cheeks, he smiled, then tossed a purse out the window to the musicians below.

When he returned to the table, he glanced at her wineglass. "I told you about knowing Lola in New Orleans. I was in the Quartermaster Corps, Lola was looking for a way to exploit the war and the times. If she hadn't found me, she would have used someone else. But she found me," he said in a hard voice. He told her about the deal to sell his herd to the French, told her about Emile Julie, and Lola skipping out with the money from both sales. "What I did was dishonest. I betrayed what I believed in, and I betrayed my country."

Freddy thought about his story. "At the end, everyone was scrambling to save what they could and put their lives back together." She drew a breath. "I'm not excusing what you did. But anyone who lived through those times would understand it."

"That doesn't make it right. But maybe I could have convinced myself and lived with it. Unfortunately, selling the troop's beef wasn't the worst of it."

"What was?"

"Learning that the Frenchman who bought my cattle sold them to the Union," he said in a voice so filled with pain that Freddy winced. "My herd fed the soldiers who were doing their damnedest to kill my neighbors and friends," he said harshly. "The day I learned what happened to those beeves, I walked into a saloon and ordered a bottle. I didn't put the bottle down until eighteen months ago."

"I'm sorry." They sat in silence for several minutes. Freddy reached a hand across the table and clasped his fingers. "What made you stop drinking?" she asked gently.

"Maybe I'd punished myself enough," he said at length. "I took care of the problem with Emile Julie, paid my share of what Lola and I owed him." He shrugged, and his hand tightened around hers. "The war ended for me the day I saw Emile Julie again. It was time to put my life back together, try to salvage something from a long chain of mistakes."

Freddy leaned forward. "We'll get our cattle to Abilene, Dal. It's going to mean a fresh start for all of us." Now she told him about the deal Jack Caldwell had offered her, getting angry again as she did every time she thought about it. "We can't trust him."

"Lola offered to double my fee if I make sure we don't deliver two thousand beeves."

Freddy's heart stopped. For a moment she couldn't breathe. Then she reminded herself this was Dal, and she knew him. He'd made mistakes in the past, but he wouldn't make the same mistakes in the future. Not a man who had punished himself for so long.

She unclenched her fists. "We should keep an eye on the drovers. I don't think they'd betray us, but who knows? Jack has a talent for finding weak spots."

"Freddy?" Dal said in a thick voice. "Thank you for not asking if I accepted Lola's offer."

She held his gaze, and something warm flooded her chest and made her fingers tremble. The shock of suddenly realizing how much she cared for this man shook her deeply. And for the first time she realized she would be sorry to see the drive end, sorry to watch him ride away toward the high mountain meadows of Montana.

"If you don't take off that nightgown in the next minute, I'm going to rip it off of you," he said hoarsely. "I won't be able to help myself."

"What? We're finished with pretty poetry?" she teased, smiling.

Standing, he gazed down at her with a look in his eyes that sent a thrill of anticipation shivering through her body. " 'Gather ye rose-buds while ye may, Old Time is still a-flying.' "

She knew that one. " 'And this same flower that smiles to-day, Tomorrow will be dying.' " Laughing, she ran to the bed, jumped into the tussled sheets, threw off her nightgown, and opened her arms. He came to her and buried his head between her breasts.

He spent the rest of the night demonstrating that she still had much to learn about the pleasures between men and women.

O n the first day Les slept around the clock, rousing only briefly to peer around the hotel room before she dropped back to the pillow and slept again. Hunger woke her near suppertime on the second day and she ate ravenously from the tray served by the woman Dal had hired to sit with her. They talked for a while, then Les dozed again. When she awoke near midnight, Mrs. Goodnight dozed in a chair beside the window.

Folding her hands on top of the sheets, Les leaned against a mound of pillows and gazed at the moonlight shining in the window. In camp, the longhorns would be standing and blowing about now. The night shifts would be changing. Ward was asleep inside his tent.

Closing her eyes, she lifted both hands to rub her temples. What was she going to do?

She had promised herself that Ward would be happy when they got Pa's inheritance—and the hitting would stop. His temper would vanish when they had the money—and the hitting would stop. Once he felt important, felt equal to a Roark, the hitting would stop.

But in her heart she suspected that she would always be the target for his frustrations and disappointments. And the frustration and disappointment would continue because Ward would never be a man like Pa. He would never be a man that other men respected.

Alone in the dark she could admit that she no longer respected him either. She wasn't sure she even liked him anymore. But what could she do?

He had sold his store and sacrificed everything to accompany her on this drive. And he was her only hope in the event they did not deliver two thousand cattle to the yards in Abilene. If they didn't win, she would be lost without him. Wouldn't she?

It troubled her to recognize that Alex and Freddy would also be lost if they didn't win Pa's inheritance, yet she didn't doubt that her sisters would somehow survive.

Staring at the moonlight, she wondered if she, too, could find the determination and courage to build a life for herself without Pa's money. And without Ward. Such a thought was so foreign that her mind shied away from it. But she forced herself to take a closer look.

After several minutes, she released a long sigh. She couldn't see herself clearly anymore. The cattle drive was changing things, changing her. Smothering a yawn, she eased back on the pillows, surprised that the idea of losing Ward didn't frighten her as it once had.

In the morning, she enjoyed a long tub bath and

washed her hair. Mrs. Goodnight had sent her trail clothes out to be laundered and they smelled fresh when she put them on. When she looked in the mirror, color had returned to her cheeks, not the high gloss of fever, but the pink glow of returning health. Her brown hair had a glossy sheen.

"A gentleman has arrived for you, Miss."

"That will be Mr. Hamm, my fiancé," she said to Mrs. Goodnight, looking around the room to check if she had forgotten anything.

"He's very handsome."

"Ward?" Her eyebrows lifted. Maybe Dal had come for her. She hoped so, as she dreaded riding back to the herd with Ward.

But it was Luther waiting in the tiny hotel lobby. He swept his hat from his head. "Mr. Hamm was engaged, and as I was coming into town anyway, I volunteered to bring you back."

Les understood that his explanation was more tact than truth. Ward was punishing her for exercising her will by withholding his company. She smiled up at Luther, realizing that Mrs. Goodnight was correct. His ears were too large and he turned pink beneath his tan when he spoke to women, but he was indeed a handsome man. Odd that she hadn't really noticed before.

Looking at him now, it surprised her to notice that he was younger than she had assumed, not at all a contemporary of Pa's. "Luther, how old are you?" It was a rude question, but she'd known him so long that she didn't think he would be offended.

"Forty-two," he said with a smile. "Old enough to be your father."

"If so, you must have been a rogue at seventeen." The impulsive comment astonished her as it sounded almost flirtatious. He smiled, and the color deepened in his face.

Picking up her bag, Luther cleared his throat and straightened his shoulders. "It's early yet. And I was wondering. Would you like some supper before we drive back to the herd?"

"If you know a place that will serve a woman dressed as a drover, I'd love to have a meal that isn't served on tin plates." She was in no hurry to confront Ward and be subjected to a monologue targeting her faults and detailing how she had failed him.

Luther took her to a restaurant well away from the gambling halls and saloons that ranged along the main thoroughfare. And she realized at once that he had made prior arrangements, anticipating her attire and requesting a private alcove. His thoughtfulness touched her.

"I don't think the Maître d' approves of me," she whispered after they had been seated away from the view of properly gowned ladies. She wondered how large a gratuity Luther had paid the man.

"You look rested," Luther said, examining her face. "You must be feeling better."

"Much better, thank you." After consulting the menu, she smiled across the table, enjoying the treat of an evening out. "Did anything interesting happen while I was gone?"

"The brand inspector paid us a visit. We weren't in violation, but his official count showed we lost four longhorns that we didn't know about."

Les put down her coffee cup. "Now we have only a 149 margin?" At the beginning of the drive that number would have seemed high. Now it didn't.

"James got struck by a rattler, but he was wearing his boots, so he'll be all right. One of the Webster boys shot a turkey, and Alex prepared everyone a feast last night. And there's some good news. Dal has decided to put you and Freddy into the rotation."

"We don't have to ride drag anymore?" Les asked, surprised and delighted.

"You'll have to take your turn, but you'll also ride flank positions. Dal will never give you ladies the point, but he's indicating that you've served your apprenticeship."

Les raised her coffee cup with a dazzling smile and touched the rim to his. "This is cause for celebration! No more eating dust on a daily basis. No more slogging through churned-up mud." She laughed. "Freddy and I are turning into real cowboys!"

Luther stared at her. "You are so beautiful when you smile." Instantly he flashed fiery red and looked down at his plate. "That was an inappropriate comment, and I apologize."

Thunderstruck, Les blinked at him. His ears were bright and his throat had turned crimson. But what astonished her was what he had said. Not even Ward had ever claimed that she was beautiful. She had lost weight on the drive, but she would never be as slender or curvaceous as Freddy, and she would never approach Alex's elegant beauty. Luther's compliment was so extravagant, so unexpected and deeply appreciated that it raised a lump to her throat and for one humiliating moment she thought she might cry.

"Luther," she said, gazing down at her lap, "you're such a nice man. Why have you never married?" It mortified her that she, who was too shy and unsure to speak to most men, had now asked him two blunt, rude, and personal questions. Although she had looked forward to the time she spent with him when he paid a business call to the ranch, their discussions had centered on books and music and general matters. They had never spoken of personal things.

High color continued to glow on his face, but it didn't occur to him that he could evade her question. He touched his collar, then fixed his gaze on a point above her shoulder. "There was a young lady . . ." he said uncomfortably. "But young ladies should keep company with young men." He gave her a sad smile. "I've never really felt young, and I don't dance or do the things that interest young women. She would have found me too old and too dull."

"Do you really think age matters when two people love each other?"

"It wasn't like that. I never declared myself." He fiddled with his fork. "I considered speaking, but she seemed disinclined to marry. Eventually, she accepted someone else."

"Oh, Luther, I'm sorry." Impulsively, she reached across the table and pressed his hand. When he stiffened, she withdrew her fingers and blushed at her boldness. "Please forgive me for prying into personal matters. I don't know what came over me." She forced a smile. "In so many ways, I don't feel like the same person who began this cattle drive."

From that point they took care to focus their conversation on general topics. By the time they climbed into the wagon, a million stars glittered across the heavens. The air was warm and sweet, and Les took an odd comfort in the sight of the herds gathered onto their bedding grounds, and the low music of cowboy songs floating through the darkness.

"Luther?" she said as their campfire came into view. "Thank you for the most wonderful evening I've had in . . ." She couldn't remember the last time she had enjoyed an evening more. Once Ward had taken her to dinner at the Klees Hotel dining room, but the conversation had not flowed easily as it had tonight. Her stomach tightened at the realization that she would see him in a few minutes. He would be sulky, of course, and angry that she had defied him.

The vitality drained out of her body, and her shoulders dropped. Something had changed the night that everyone saw Ward strike her. She had begun to feel trapped.

But Ward surprised her. He seemed to have forgotten her defiance. After helping her out of the wagon, he nodded to Luther, then gripped her shoulders, vibrating with excitement. "I need to talk to you right now, it's important. Our whole future is at stake."

She watched Luther walk toward the observers' camp, then stepped out from under Ward's grasp. "Could this wait until tomorrow?" She had hoped he might mention that he had missed her, or at least inquire if she'd rested well.

"I said right now, Les." Clasping her wrist, he picked up a lantern he'd set on the ground, then half dragged her out onto the dark prairie and down into a shadowed gully where they couldn't be seen by either camp.

Uneasily, Les sat on the dirt slope of the gully and drew up her knees, facing him. The lantern he set to one side illuminated his excitement, and she tried to recall if she had ever seen such jubilation in his gaze.

"What is it?" she inquired cautiously.

"Remember that Freddy told you about Caldwell making her an offer to lose some cattle? Well, I spoke to Caldwell and demanded the same deal for us. Les, you won't believe what he's offered us!"

Her heart stopped. "Oh, Ward. How could you!" Horrified, she started to rise, but he grabbed her wrist and jerked her back so roughly that she stumbled and fell against the dirt side of the gully. Not taking her eyes from him, she sat up and slowly brushed off of her shirt. This time she didn't search for excuses. "Don't do that again."

"Listen! Caldwell promises that Lola will pay us eighty thousand dollars if we help her win." His pale eyes glittered with exuberance. "Eighty thousand dollars, Les! That's a fortune! Think of it! If you only knew how worried I've been. Our margin is shrinking by the week. With the Red River ahead of us and then the Indian Territory, there's no way Frisco is going to bring in two thousand steers. No way at all!" He looked up and his gaze hardened in the lanternlight. "And we don't want him to. I want the son of a bitch to lose. I want him destroyed. This way, Frisco loses sixty thousand dollars and the last of his reputation. This is so sweet!"

She stared at him in disbelief. "Ward, we can't do this!"

"I know what you're thinking. We're giving up a sum several times that amount." Leaning forward, he gripped her arms, his eyes gleaming feverishly. "Les, we'd both rather have your father's fortune, but don't you understand? It isn't going to happen. Caldwell is smart. He won't let Frisco win. But you and I don't have to lose! All you have to do is look the other way and let a few steers go here and lose a few there. That's all. Don't be overly conscientious at river crossings. Let a straggler wander off. Do it, and our future is assured!"

Jerking out of his grip, she pushed to her feet. "What about my sisters? Do they also get eighty thousand if we lose?"

"Oh, for God's sake, Les, don't be stupid. We don't

care about them. Did I ever tell you the insulting things Alex said to me?" His eyes narrowed. "Believe me, she doesn't deserve a penny. And Freddy? That slut doesn't deserve anything either! Forget about them and think about us! Remember where your duty lies. By accepting Caldwell's offer, we ruin Frisco, and we set ourselves up for life! It's perfect."

"You're asking me to betray my sisters," she said, staring at him as if she'd never seen him before. "You're asking me to forget how hard I worked to learn what I had to learn, asking me to toss aside all the hardship and suffering. Getting gored was for nothing."

"I'm not asking you," Ward said sharply, standing to face her. "I'm telling you." A warning glittered in his eyes. "Try to think smart for once. All the hardships you and I have endured, all the sacrifices we've made, it won't be for nothing, not if we end with eighty thousand dollars. You owe me that."

Her hands were shaking and her words emerged in a stammer. She knew the inevitable end of this discussion unless she hastily backed down. But she thought of Alex and Freddy, and how they had been willing to guarantee her share of the inheritance even if she left the drive. Of course, that wouldn't matter to Ward.

"If we help Lola cheat, then what are we? We become equally dishonorable. And we betray good people who deserve better. I can't do that. I won't."

He backhanded her across the face, sending her sprawling. Drops of spittle flew from his lips when he leaned over her, his face ugly in the smoky light. "You're so stupid you make me sick! You want us to lose so we can congratulate ourselves on being honorable? Tell me if 'honorable' will replace my store. Will it, Les? Tell me if honorable will make us rich. Use your head!"

He jerked her upright and thrust his face so close that she could see the tiny broken veins fanning across his nose. "You don't have a choice. I told Caldwell that we'll do it, and gladly. You're going to lose some cattle, Les. That's how it is."

The blood drained from her face. "You shouldn't have done that because I won't help Lola win. Never."

He slapped her again, then his fingers bruised into her arms. "Yes you will." Fury glittered in his eyes. "Or I'll leave you, Les. I swear it."

Suddenly she hated him with an intensity that shocked her. She hated the physical violence, hated his threats and emotional blackmail. She hated a character so tarnished that he was willing to betray her sisters, Dal, the drovers. She stared into his eyes and didn't recognize anything that she could ever love or admire.

"Do it then," she said in a hard low voice. "Go. Leave and good riddance!"

His mouth dropped and for an instant he looked thunderstruck. Then he drew back with a venomous hiss. "I see. You Roarks are all the same. You think you're better than anyone else. Well, you should thank God that you have me to save you from your own stupidity! Do you have any idea how foolish and inadequate you are?" He grabbed her again, his fingers deliberately cruel on her flesh. "It was me, protecting your interests, who negotiated Caldwell's offer up to eighty thousand. But you don't appreciate what I do for you, or all the sacrifices I've made. You're a goddamned Roark, and the world should bow down and cater to you!"

"Let go, Ward." She said it quietly with no plea in her voice, no tears in her eyes. He expected her usual apologies and reassurances, but she was through debasing herself.

"What the hell has come over you tonight?"

"Let go," she repeated. Surprised, he lifted his hands from her upper arms. "You will never again strike me or hurt me," she said firmly. "You will tell Caldwell that I spit on his offer. If you can't agree to those two things, then I don't want you. Go ahead and leave."

She couldn't believe she was saying this, but it felt so good and so right. Neither of her sisters would have allowed a man to strike them or dictate their thoughts or behavior. Thinking about Freddy and Alex gave her the strength to reach deep for self-respect and clasp it hard.

"Be careful, Les," he warned. "You're past your prime. You're old, and you're not a beauty. If I turn my back on you, no one else will have you."

His cruelty hurt as much as her conviction that he was right.

"I may never marry or have a family of my own. But spinsterhood would be easier to bear than betraying people who care about me. I won't do that." Tilting her head, she looked up at the stars and felt a weight lift from her shoulders. Suddenly she felt taller and stronger.

Now that she had begun to believe in herself and feel her dependency dropping away, she marveled that she had ever accepted his suit. Wanting to slap at Pa for marrying Lola didn't explain everything. What disturbed her most was seeing her own inadequacies reflected by the choice she had made. Some weakness in her had responded to Ward's emotional and physical mistreatment. But a secret pride arose as it dawned on her that she would never have chosen him now.

"I can't marry you," she said, blurting the words. Marrying him would be the worst error of her life, a disaster. "I'm truly sorry that I didn't realize this sooner. I'll reimburse your losses when I receive my inheritance." That would assuage her guilt. She wanted to be fair.

Pulling her shoulders back, she felt as if she had suddenly grown up. She had stepped out of a trap and had done it herself without appealing to anyone else. A rush of pride and happiness erased the lines of anxiety between her eyes. She was free.

There was nothing more to say. It was finished, and thank God.

After looking at him for a moment, she walked toward the end of the gully, her thoughts jumping ahead. She was eager to tell Alex and Freddy that she had endured a confrontation and had not crumbled or backed away. She had stood up for herself and done what she needed to do.

The surprise of his hand roughly gripping her arm shattered her self-congratulations. Ward spun her around and hit her with his fist. When the blackness cleared from her eyes, she found herself lying on the ground near the lantern, watching his boot swing toward her ribs. Pain exploded through her rib cage. Moaning, she curled into a protective ball, her eyes stinging with shock and hot tears. This was the worst attack she had endured from anyone in her life, and she thought it would be the last. A glimpse of his face confirmed that his rage was so powerful that he could kill her. Convinced that he would, all she could do was pray.

When he jerked her onto her feet, she was so weak with relief that she could hardly stand. She didn't think his kick had broken any ribs, but the pain was intense.

She would have doubled over, if he hadn't gripped her so hard.

"No one walks away from Ward Hamm!" he snarled. "Oh, you'd like to humiliate me, wouldn't you? You'd like to walk out there and tell everyone that Ward Hamm isn't good enough for a Roark! Well, you're not going to use me, then toss me aside! I'll see you dead before I'll let you belittle me in front of everyone!"

He grabbed her chin so tightly that her lips puckered. "Listen and listen good," he said, hissing spittle into her face. "You aren't walking away—I own you. And I'll kill you before I let you cheat me out of my money. I swear it, Les. I earned that money, and I deserve it."

Terrified, she stared into his eyes, and she believed him. Her heart slammed against her battered ribs and she couldn't speak.

"So help me God. If you try to cut me out of what's mine, you'll drown in what looks like an accident. You'll burn in a prairie fire. You'll fall off your horse and die of a broken neck." His fingernails dug into her flesh. "You *will* do as Caldwell tells you. And if you ever defy me . . ."

He threw her to the ground, then picked up the lantern and walked out of the gully without a backward glance.

Defeated and hurting, Les lay on her back, blinking up at the black sky. As her shock faded, hopelessness settled on her like a slab and helpless tears streamed down her cheeks.

If she told Dal about this, he would immediately throw Caldwell off the drive. And Ward too, most likely. She would be rid of him.

But Ward would never forgive her. She didn't doubt

for an instant that he would make good on his threat. He would find a way to kill her. She would spend the rest of her life looking over her shoulder, and one day Ward would be there. He would never let her go. And eventually he would put her in a grave.

No, she couldn't tell anyone what he'd done. She had to pray that she could find another solution.

Curling protectively around the pain in her side, she closed her eyes and wept. Instead of escaping her trap, the trap had turned lethal.

CHAPTER 18

The days and nights were warmer now. Wildflowers dotted the range with glowing jewel colors. Bluebonnets, wild golden mustard, scarlet paintbrush. Ahead lay green waves of billowing open prairie that offered good grazing and frequent, easily forded creeks.

Dal rode point, enjoying a feeling of content and control. The herd was moving well, there hadn't been a stampede in a while, his drovers were rested after the stop outside Fort Worth, and the two days that Freddy and Les had been riding flank had justified his confidence in them. They squeezed down the herd when they had to, strung them out when needed. He shook his head and smiled, thinking how far they had come in a short time.

Lifting his face to the morning sunshine, he inhaled the warm scents of late spring and green grass and cowhide, listened to a serenade of meadowlarks off to the right. It was a good day, the kind of day that made a man glad to be alive.

There were only two things worrying him. Jack Caldwell, and Frederick Roark.

He hadn't forgotten the warning he'd received in the bathhouse. And he didn't doubt that Lola and Jack would sink to rustling. As a precaution, he kept the herd away from stands of trees that might provide concealment for outlaws. He didn't want to lose any more cattle between here and the Indian Territory.

That Caldwell might have arranged trouble wasn't Dal's only problem with the bastard. Caldwell might have thrown his cards in with Lola, but he hadn't forgotten Freddy.

Gripping the seat of his saddle, Dal turned to look over his shoulder and spotted her about a quarter of a mile behind him. Grinning, he watched her gallop after a muley who had decided to head for open spaces. She cut off the escape and deftly turned him back where he belonged.

In every way, she was a magnificent woman. Strong and spirited and beautiful. And damned if she wasn't turning into a cowboy.

In the beginning she'd done just enough to get by, but that had changed. Before the drive began, she'd been playing a role; now she was living it. Maybe she hadn't guessed her own strengths back then. Perhaps she hadn't understood that her nature was to give more, not less. And she did give more. She was tougher, gentler, more understanding, braver, and more uninhibited than he had ever imagined she would be.

She was becoming the kind of woman who turned a man's thoughts toward settling down.

Frowning, he released a string of cusswords. What in the hell was he thinking? He and Freddy mixed as well as silk and rawhide. She dreamed of big-city theaters and waves of applause. He dreamed of high mountain pastures and solitude. She had hated ranching and cattle all of her life. He thrived outdoors and preferred the company of longhorns to that of most men he knew. They didn't fit into each other's worlds.

He couldn't believe he was wasting time considering a future with her. He must be experiencing an attack of chivalry. A decent man didn't despoil a good woman without reflecting on his responsibilities, which meant an offer of marriage. This obligation accounted for his settling-down thoughts. That and an urge to put his brand on her every time he saw Jack Caldwell look in her direction.

Jerking off his hat, he pulled a sleeve across his forehead and swore again. If he mentioned marriage to Freddy, she would laugh her head off, and rightly so since they were such an unlikely match. She would guess that he proposed out of a sense of duty. And because, bastard that he was, he wanted to bed her again. She would be right about that. Making love to her again was all he could think about.

The ironic thing about their conflicting dreams was that Freddy's dream was destined to fail. She might go to San Francisco and buy herself a fancy playhouse, but she would never be the famous actress she longed to become.

Dal had observed her performances around the campfire at night, had watched her emote in the affected manner she unconsciously assumed when she was acting. The inescapable fact was that Fancy Roark was a lousy actress. She just wasn't good at it.

The kindest thing he could wish for was that she never discovered how bad she was at the one thing she wanted most. He cared for her enough to hope her audiences were as appreciative as the drovers and as equally lacking in critical judgment.

Alex spent the afternoon jerking meat, a disgusting chore that she detested. When she finished preparing the jerky, she hobbled around the chuck wagon on her crutch, draping thin strips all over the sides to dry in the hot sunshine.

Today she was very aware of the empty space beneath her right knee. She kept wanting to step down on that side and discover a miracle had occurred and her leg and foot were restored. "Stupid," she muttered, shaking her head. She was never again going to plant two feet on the ground and feel her hips align, or stand straight and tall. Never, never, never again.

"Sit down and rest. You look plumb wore out," Grady ordered, bringing her wheelchair up behind her. "I got good news and bad news. Which you want to hear first?"

"I'm in a low mood anyway, so tell me the bad news," she said, sitting down.

"The cooney's empty and there ain't a stick of wood within five miles of here. I got a horse needs doctoring so I can't go looking for prairie coal for you. It's gonna be that way for most of this week."

She sighed and blotted perspiration from her throat. The rest of this afternoon and all the afternoons of this week would be spent struggling to shove her chair over rough ground looking for dried cow pies. If nothing else, this cattle drive was teaching her humility.

"What's the good news?"

Grady nodded his hat brim toward the range. "Your mute friend is back."

Her head jerked up, and her heart skipped a beat. Shading her eyes, she peered across an ocean of grass and saw him walking toward the wagon, followed by his three cows. He was dressed this time, but it was John. Without thinking about her reaction, she pulled off the man's hat she wore and smoothed back tendrils of hair that had escaped the bun coiled on her neck.

"Why is that good news?" she asked Grady, feeling a blush heat her skin.

"I got eyes in my head," he said, grinning at the color in her cheeks.

His comment embarrassed her. But she had indeed spent a lot of time thinking about John, missing him since they parted company in Fort Worth. And that was so wrong of her.

Oh God, she thought, dropping her head. Was there no end to her disloyalty to Payton? First the crutch, and now an attraction to another man. What kind of terrible person was she?

Pressed by guilt, she fetched the spike and bag and shoved herself toward the open range and away from John McCallister. She knew how awkward and unappealing she looked, hunched forward, her arms akimbo and flapping when she pushed the wheels of her chair. This was her punishment, to sweat and grow red-faced from exertion, to look foolish and clumsy to a man whose gaze had made her feel beautiful again. To roll away when she wanted to rush forward.

She had traveled farther from camp than she usually did before she turned and saw him walking past the chuck wagon, heading toward her. Resisting an urge to pat her hair and smooth her skirt, she gripped the sack of cow pies in her lap and watched him approach.

She loved the lean tall look of him, the way he strode forward with easy grace as if the ground were not as rough as she knew it to be. She loved the strong square line of his jaw and his steady grey eyes and the elegance of his hands. Doctor's hands, according to Dal.

Now she knew how John could touch the stump left by another doctor and not be repelled. A hundred times she had visualized him near death in a Union prison and tried to imagine the terrible things he had witnessed. It was no wonder that he didn't speak. Somewhere she had read about hills of amputated limbs growing outside the medical tents. Surgeons had worked while standing in lakes of blood. What would such horrors do to a sensitive man's mind? Now she understood that John was as crippled in mind as she was in body.

When he reached her, he knelt beside her chair, smiled into her eyes, and raised a hand to her face. Surprise lifted his eyebrows as he brushed a tear from her cheek with his thumb.

"Oh, John," she whispered. "I'm so confused. I'm glad to see you, but I shouldn't be." Lowering her head, she gently pushed his hand away, then pressed her fingertips to her damp eyelids. "I know that doesn't make sense to you." He had returned because of her, she knew that as surely as she knew her joy in seeing him. "I can't . . . you and I, we can't . . ."

Leaning forward, he touched her tears, then he put his arms around her and guided her head to his shoulder. And she wept as she had not wept since Payton's funeral. She couldn't have explained why except she felt the same deep aching loss.

Finally the storm passed and she wiped her face with her handkerchief then placed a trembling hand on his cheek. "I'm sorry for losing control, but you can't stay with us, John. It would be too hard on me." She drew a breath and let her shoulders collapse, fighting a fresh onslaught of tears. "I know you don't understand," she repeated helplessly.

She knew so little about this man, and yet she knew him utterly. How that was possible, she couldn't imagine. It simply was. She knew his compassion and gentle touch. She knew the shape and texture of his skin and body. She knew the man he must be to have devoted his life to healing. And she guessed the horrors he must have observed and experienced during the war, horrors so painful and appalling that he had walked away from life and humanity.

He stroked her hands, then took the sack from her lap and the spike and walked away from her, hooking up cow pies. Watching him, she felt like crying again.

When the sack was filled, he pushed her back to the chuck wagon and would have kindled the fire but she reminded him of the rules. And she had to remind him not to help her up when she tried to stand with her crutch but instead fell at his feet. Knots rose along his jawline and his hands opened and closed at his sides, but he respected her wishes and stood clear as she struggled to rise. Mercifully, he left her to prepare supper and walked over to Grady's remuda. Grady, she noticed, displayed no compunction about accepting John's help with the injured horse. Remarkably she managed to cook an entire meal without giving it two complete thoughts.

When Dal rode in, he shook hands with John, and Alex saw him look from John to her with a knowing smile. Pink blazed across her throat. Was there anyone in this camp who hadn't noticed the peculiar bond between herself and John McCallister?

Apparently not, she decided when Freddy came to the wagon to drop her plate into the wreck pan. Freddy slipped the vial of rose perfume into Alex's apron pocket and smiled. "It appears you might be needing this."

"What is that supposed to mean?" she snapped, bearing down on the rag she rubbed briskly over her work space.

"It means I'm grateful that you didn't judge and you haven't asked any questions about Dal and me. It means that I want to repay your thoughtfulness by doing the same for you."

The fight went out of her stiffened shoulders. "I'm sorry," she whispered, balancing on her crutch and leaning against the worktable. "It's just . . ." She frowned toward the fire, where John was sitting with Dal and the drovers.

"There aren't many secrets on a cattle drive," Freddy said gently, reaching to smooth a tendril of Alex's blond hair behind her ear. "We all know John is here because of you."

"He'll leave in the morning."

Freddy studied her. "He doesn't have to. He could join the observers . . ."

Alex shook her head. "I know you mean well." Surprisingly, she did know. "But you don't understand." She gazed into Freddy's eyes. "There are reasons why I can't let myself . . ."

"Your leg? Alex, the man was a doctor. If he cared about your missing leg, he wouldn't have returned. You're beautiful and courageous and caring. That's why he came back."

Lord, the tears flowed close to the surface today. She blinked hard. "I'm courageous and caring?" How odd to discover how deeply she craved her sisters' approval and admiration.

"Yes," Freddy said firmly. Embarrassed, she grinned and reached for a coffee cup. "And you fry a fine steak. Tonight's supper was almost edible."

Alex laughed, her eyes shining with unshed tears. "Thank you," she said, wishing she had two legs to stand on so she could give Freddy a hug without falling. Such a gesture would have shocked them both. She glanced toward John. "There's another reason why I can't . . ."

Freddy waited then she said, "If you ever want to talk about that reason . . ." she drew a long breath, "I'd like to hear it. Sometimes talking helps. Or so I've heard."

She thought about Freddy's offer while she finished cleaning up, and again when John pushed her chair to the shadowy line between light and dark. He removed a thin cigar from his vest pocket, sat down, and looked up at her, then when she nodded permission, he lit it.

"Payton smoked a pipe," she said as a beginning, her gaze following the smoke floating in the night air. She had to tell him. Speaking around long choked pauses, she made herself begin the story by relating how she had met Payton at a lecture in New Orleans. "I don't think he believed me when I promised I would run away and join him in Boston." Looking back, she couldn't imagine where she had found the courage to defy her father and run off to marry a man she scarcely knew. "To outsiders I suppose my elopement seemed romantic."

But this was John, and tonight she would tell the truth about her marriage for the first time. Swallowing, she twisted her handkerchief between her fingers and continued, feeling his gaze on her face. "Payton was incredulous when I showed up on his doorstep. I knew at once I'd made a terrible mistake." Tilting her head, she blinked up at the stars. "But he did the honorable thing. He married me." These few statements glossed a universe of pain and humiliation.

"As you might guess from such a beginning, ours was a troubled marriage." Another long pause elapsed. "But I enjoyed living in the East. I felt I'd come home. And I thrived in the closed society of academia. I believed my skills could be helpful to Payton in that regard, believed I could advance his career through social conquest. I wanted to feel necessary in his life, wanted him to be glad we had married." She shook her head. "Maybe things would have been different if we'd had children, but we weren't blessed that way." She pulled at her handkerchief. "We argued about the cost of entertaining, about servants, about buying a carriage as opposed to hiring . . . Nothing was too insignificant to provoke a disagreement," she added softly. "From the first, we seemed to bring out the worst in each other.

"Then, early last year, we received an invitation to dinner at the home of the University's president. This was a triumph I had been striving to achieve for years." She balled the handkerchief in her fist, and her voice sank to a strangled whisper. "Payton had a fever that night and wanted to send regrets. But I feared we wouldn't be invited again if we declined. I argued, insisted. And finally, though he was ill and should have stayed in bed, Payton angrily agreed.

"I have relived that argument a hundred times. If only I hadn't been so selfish . . . if only I'd thought more about him and less about myself . . . If only I hadn't been so ambitious Payton would still be alive." Struggling, she swallowed the lump in her throat. "It was raining and dark that night, and the driver's cautious pace made me feel frantic that we would arrive distressingly late. I harangued Payton into ordering the driver to greater speed."

She lowered her head. "And that is why the accident occurred. Because I forced my ill husband to go out when he did not wish to and because I insisted on speed when the road conditions urged caution. Because of me, my husband died that night. I killed him."

When John tried to take her hands, she pushed him away, her eyes hot with anguish. "I wish I had died that night and Payton had lived. That's how it should have happened. That would have been just. But he paid the price for my foolishness, and I lived. I can hardly bear it."

John's grey eyes filled with sympathy and compassion. He tried to take her hands again, but she would not permit it.

"My punishment is here," she said, touching her right knee. "And here." She touched her temples. "And here," she whispered, placing her palm against his chest. "I can't live as if that night were just an accident, because it wasn't. It was a tragedy that didn't have to happen. My husband died because of me."

And she could not forgive herself. Could not permit herself to seek happiness now or in the future. Each time she made things easier by using the crutch, she rewarded herself when punishment was what she deserved. Every time she enjoyed something or forgot herself and laughed, she trivialized her husband's death. And when she gazed at John McCallister with longing in her eyes, she betrayed the husband she had killed.

"That is why you cannot stay. You tempt me with happiness that I don't deserve and will never have." Finally, she let him take her hands and she clasped his fingers. "If you care for me a little, then please, I beg you, leave." Gently he withdrew a hand and touched his fingertips to her lips. Alex pulled away, tears glistening in her eyes. "You touch me and I feel . . . guilt," she whispered. "I look into your eyes and ache with despair. Please. The only way I can atone for what I . . . I mustn't think about . . ."

Blinded by tears and pain, she gripped the wheels of her chair and savagely thrust forward, running away from him toward the bedroll that Grady had laid out for her. Long after the rest of the camp slept, she lay awake, staring through the darkness at the figure sitting on the grass where she had left him. Weeping silently, she prayed he would be gone when she awoke at dawn.

But he wasn't. After breakfast, John climbed up on the chuck wagon beside her. He touched her hand and smiled.

"How is it possible to be happy and this miserable at the same time?" she whispered.

"You're worrying me," Freddy said before she swung her saddle up on Walker's back. Reaching beneath him, she caught the cinch and buckled it tight. "You ought to be happy now that we're off drag, but you seem," she frowned, "about as unhappy as a person can be."

Les closed her eyes and leaned her forehead against Cactus's warm side. "I'm sorry I shouted at you last night. I'm just . . . I have a lot on my mind."

Not an evening went by that Ward didn't slap her or hit her when he discovered she hadn't lost any longhorns. And God help her, there were times when a muley peeled out of the herd and she was tempted to let it run off just to spare herself one night of rage and bruises. Shame colored her cheeks that she could even think for one small moment about betraying her sisters to save herself a little pain.

Freddy placed a boot in the stirrup then swung into the saddle and Walker reared and bucked and raced away from the remuda, kicking his heels and doing his best to fling Freddy into the dirt. When she rode back toward Les, flushed and laughing, she looked pleased that she'd kept her seat.

"You know, I've been thinking," she said, studying Les. "There's something I assumed you knew, but maybe you don't."

"Is it about Ward?" Les's stomach tightened in dread.

"I've been noticing the way Luther looks at you, and Les, he's always looked at you that way. Luther loves you, and I suspect he always has. Did you know that?"

"Luther?" Her mouth fell open, and she stared at Freddy in astonishment.

"If you could see your face!" Freddy laughed, then she turned Walker in a circle and rode out toward the herd.

Luther?

"Oh, my God." Her hand flew to her lips and her eyes widened in shocked understanding. The young lady who would have considered Luther too dull and too old, the young lady who had accepted someone else . . . she was that young lady.

A sudden tumble of memories overwhelmed her. Luther giving her flowers on his way into the house to see Pa on business. Luther bringing her a book from his library, his face turning pink with pleasure when he learned that she had enjoyed his choice. Luther, watching her dance with the young swains of Brush County, his expression wistful, or gazing soft-eyed at her across a formal dining table. Blushing violently red when he accidentally touched her. Stammering when she smiled at him.

She sagged against Cactus. How could she not have guessed?

Because, she thought, staring at the ground, he had been right. Since she hadn't dared hope that someone like Luther would be interested in someone like her, she'd made herself think of him as her father's business associate, and as a friend. Not as a possible suitor. After Pa married Lola, she'd turned her gaze to younger men, and she had not seen Luther.

And now it was too late.

Raising her head, she looked toward the observers' camp. Both Ward and Luther were standing near the coffeepot, but it was Luther she saw.

He was taller than Ward, and ten years older. He never thrust himself forward, never bragged about his accomplishments, which were considerable. He was unfailingly thoughtful and kind, considerate and fair. Respected by all who knew him. Les usually thought of him as retiring, but that wasn't entirely true.

It had been Luther who pulled Ward away from her and hit him in the mouth the night everyone had seen Ward strike her. Luther who had restrained Dal on at least two occasions that Les could recall.

Suddenly she remembered Prince Charming coming into her tent to hold her hand and whisper words of love. Had she dreamed that incident, or had it been . . .

Despair washed over her in a wave of blackness, and she stumbled against Cactus's side, blinking at tears.

She wished Freddy hadn't told her.

Riding flank position was a hundred times better than riding drag, Freddy decided, enjoying the morning. When she thought of Charlie and Peach eating dust and trying to nudge Mouse and Brownie into keeping up with the herd, she laughed out loud. But she missed Les. Except for the times when Dal circled the herd, she rode alone all day.

Thinking about Dal took the edge off of her good mood. And of course she thought about him morning, noon, and night. It hurt and annoyed her that he hadn't referred even once to their night together in Fort Worth. Nor had he attempted to touch her or kiss her again.

Looking ahead, she fixed her gaze on his back. He

was easy to spot as he rode the tallest in the saddle and wore his hat at a jaunty, arrogant angle.

As she did a dozen times a day, she tried to figure out why he seemed to be avoiding her. He knew she had gone unwillingly to the hotel; therefore, he might reasonably suppose that he had discharged his duty, that was the end of it, and that's what she preferred. Maybe that was it.

On the other hand, he *had* to know that the night in Fort Worth had been the most thrilling experience in her life, had to sense that she wanted to be with him.

Or maybe he'd looked beyond Abilene and saw himself riding toward Montana, where she didn't want to go, and imagined her boarding a train for San Francisco, where he didn't want to go. At no point did their futures intersect.

Without a future, theirs could only be a relationship of brief duration. But no decent woman entered into an affair knowing that was all it could ever be, and she was Joe Roark's daughter, a decent woman. She was also a woman on fire with desire, and there was the dilemma.

Looking ahead through the light haze of dust that existed even on flank, she remembered his hard-muscled body and his mouth crushing hers and the warm texture of his skin. She remembered his rippling flat stomach and his hands and his tongue on her body and . . .

"Stop this," she muttered sharply.

Squinting, she spotted the chuck wagon and the observers' wagons up ahead. In the distance, she saw Alex out on the range hooking up cow pies. Alex had wandered far from camp, undoubtedly because the cooks with the outfits ahead of theirs had already stripped the ground of dried pies closer in.

Then she saw something that she didn't at first recognize as trouble. Five men suddenly appeared, galloping up out of a deep gully. Still not alarmed, Freddy watched them speeding toward her and the herd. She hoped they had the sense to rein in, hoped they knew better than to charge the herd and risk startling the beeves.

When she saw them pull up bandannas to cover their faces and draw their pistols, she sucked in a sharp breath. Instantly she stiffened, and her hand dropped to the six-shooter at her waist. But she stopped in a panic of indecision. If she fired a warning shot to alert the other drovers, the sound of the shot would stampede the herd.

The decision became irrelevant when one of the men shot at her. The bullet whizzed past Freddy's ear, close enough that she heard the whine and felt a streak of heat. She had a second to snap a glance over her shoulder and see one of the beeves drop, then the stampede began.

Two thousand cattle simultaneously went mad with fear. In the blink of an eye, they were running crazily, fleeing an unknown terror. Freddy's job in this situation was to gallop alongside the crazed steers and try to hold them together until the point men could turn the seething, clacking, pounding maelstrom into a mill. Her instructions didn't cover what to do when outlaws were firing at her during the stampede they had started.

Figuring things couldn't get worse if she fired her six-shooter now, she leaned over her horse's neck and fired at the outlaws through clouds of billowing dust, wishing she were a better shot. She didn't have much hope of hitting moving targets, but she sure as hell tried.

When she ran out of bullets, she gave up on the out-

laws and concentrated on trying to squeeze down the
herd and keep the steers from fanning out. Then she
made the mistake of glancing ahead, and her heart
stopped on a spasm of icy horror. She had been wrong.
Things could get much worse.

Instead of curving to the right and away from camp,
the herd had veered left, away from the outlaws and
gunshots. Two thousand maddened steers were bearing
down on Alex, who was alone in their path and helpless
in her wheelchair.

CHAPTER 19

At first Alex didn't understand what was happening. The ground was bumpy and pocked with holes. Her first thought was that she must have braked on a small ridge or at the edge of a prairie-dog hole and an unstable position explained why her chair began to shake and vibrate. Then she registered the thunder of running hooves and an explosion of gunshots. The gunshots didn't make sense, but the growing rumble did.

Her heart leapt into her mouth and her hands shook violently, but she managed to wrench her chair around then wished she hadn't. Horror widened her eyes and scalded her chest. The herd had swerved toward her, was perhaps half a mile away and closing the gap fast. Gripping the wheels of her chair so hard that her palms bruised, she swung a panicked look toward the chuck wagon and understood at once that she could never reach it in time.

Terror blotted her vision, and her heart shuddered with fear. She couldn't escape. The rampaging steers would trample her. She would die an ugly death alone on the prairie.

Dizzy with horror, she stared at the oncoming tide of destruction and for one terrible instant, she couldn't think, couldn't breathe. And then a numbing calm stole across her mind.

So be it.

Resignation relaxed her fear-clenched muscles and the terror slowly faded from her eyes. She released a low breath of acceptance. She'd had a year longer than she should have had and she had used her time well. She had said good-bye to her father, had gotten to know her sisters, and she had known John. Her only regrets were that she would never have the chance to tell her sisters that she loved them, and that she had not met John McCallister at another time in another place under different circumstances.

Before the maelstrom of thundering hooves drowned his voice, she heard Grady scream, "Run!" Luther and Ward added urgent shouts to Grady's. But she couldn't walk, let alone run. Certainly she couldn't push the unwieldy and heavy chair fast enough to save herself, even if the ground had not been shaking as if an earthquake rocked it. "Run, you son of a bitch, run!"

The crazed steers were close enough now that she could see sunlight sliding along their pointed horns, could smell the fearful stink of them and feel their heat rolling toward her. They would be upon her within minutes.

Folding her hands in her lap, she bowed her head and calmly began to recite the Lord's Prayer, but a flash of white caught her eye, coming up fast on her left. When she raised her head and saw John running toward her, an electric jolt of horror replaced the serenity of acceptance. Heart slamming against her chest, she gripped the wheels of her chair and screamed frantically. "No! No, go back!" Oh God. Oh God, no. "Don't do this, no! Go back! Go back!"

When he reached her, he spun in front of her chair, planted his legs wide and swung a rifle to his shoulder, firing into the onrushing destruction. The noise was monstrous now, a roaring hellish din. The ground shook so violently that John lost his footing and fell, rose to one knee and fired again. One steer dropped. And then another, so close to them that the horns furrowed the ground not eight feet from where John knelt, firing continually.

The herd split around the fallen steers, and a foaming sea of animals swept past them, surrounded them on all sides. The hot stink of fear and chaos and animal hide thickened the air. Alex's ears rang with the hideous sound of horns clacking and crashing and knocking together, with the sound of heavy snorting and blowing and hooves tearing up the ground. Her wheelchair toppled on the shaking earth, and she sprawled on the grass, immediately snatched into John's arms. He caught her up upright against his chest, clasping her tightly, his face in her hair, his breath against her cheek, holding her as the cattle pounded around them.

Alex clung to his neck, screaming, crying, praying they would miraculously survive this horror, praying that she would not be responsible for the death of another good man.

And then finally, finally, after a nightmarish eternity, it was over. The massive animals raced past them, the stampede rampaging toward the open range, fanning out in all directions. Still clinging to John, Alex watched with dazed wet eyes as the drovers galloped past in pursuit. Freddy and Les reined in, their faces white with fear, looked at her, then spurred their mounts and chased after the drovers and steers.

As the blood returned to Alex's face and her arms and leg began to tingle, Grady, Luther, Ward, and even

Jack Caldwell ran across the trampled ground. Luther picked up her toppled chair and Alex collapsed into it, shaking so badly that her teeth chattered and she couldn't speak.

Grady stared at John. "That was the goddamnest thing I ever seen in my life!" Turning, hands on hips, he stared at the dead beeves that had saved their lives. "You can shoot a tough old longhorn six or seven times and not even slow him down. But you got three of them! Well sheeeeit. 'Scuse me, Alex. That was some shooting, son! You had to place those shots just right, and you sure enough did!"

John came to her and knelt beside her chair. Lifting her icy hands from her lap, he glanced at the abrasions she'd received on her palms when she spilled out of the chair, then he rubbed her fingers, trying to restore the circulation. White-faced and trembling, Alex gazed into his steady grey eyes. She couldn't articulate what she felt; mere words couldn't possibly convey the emotion swelling her heart. Fear, gratitude, awe. And an odd fringe of regret. There had been a moment when she welcomed the fact of her death and found relief in knowing her punishment would end.

And she felt love. Looking deeply into John's eyes, she saw what she had never seen in Payton's gaze. Hot tears burned her throat, and she covered her face with shaking hands. The sudden intensity of emotion confused and exhausted her.

Luther gripped the handles of her chair and pushed her toward camp. Grady remained behind, shaking his head over the dead steers. Jack strode back to camp. Ward walked on one side of her and John on the other, his comforting hand gentle on her shoulder.

"It's a miracle the two of you weren't killed," Ward

remarked, turning to inspect the cattle running across the range in all directions.

A glance at John's frown told Alex that she hadn't imagined Ward's disappointment. And she wasn't imagining the concern in John's eyes. She covered his fingers with her own and smiled.

"I'm fine," she assured him softly, knowing she didn't look fine. Her skirt was soiled and torn. Her hair tumbled around her shoulders. "My hands and knees are scraped, but that's the worst of it. After some coffee and a few minutes to collect myself, I'll put some beans on the fire. They'll hold until the boys come in."

"Alex, for God's sake." They were the first words Luther had spoken. "You don't come that close to dying, then minutes later prepare a meal as if nothing happened."

She agreed with Luther, but she knew Dal wouldn't. And she had grown enormously since the day she'd set her skirts afire. She would find the strength to do what she had to do. "If you want to help," she suggested to Luther and John, "I'd appreciate it if you'd collect some prairie coal for the fire." She'd lost her bag and stick. She couldn't imagine herself ever again searching for cow pies if a single longhorn were in sight. But she would.

She had always been a woman who set standards of excellence. The change that had occurred during this drive was that now her standards concerned character. The realization made her smile. Her new standards were infinitely harder to meet.

While she drank a cup of black coffee and tried to calm herself, she remembered John's strong arms crushing her close to his body. Pink infused her cheeks when she realized that would be her strongest memory. Not a near brush with death, not her terror, but John's arms around her and the thrill of his warmth and strength and touch. She didn't realize something had happened until she heard John draw a sharp breath, saw him set down his coffee and stand up beside her.

When Alex followed his gaze, her breath hitched and stopped, coffee spilled across her skirts. Dal was riding into camp, leading Freddy's horse. Freddy lay crumpled over the horse's neck, blood pasting her shirt to her shoulder and arm.

"The damned fool took a bullet in the shoulder, but she rode out anyway to round up steers," Dal snapped, his face clamped in a scowl. He reined in front of Alex. "Have you ever removed a bullet?"

"Good God, no," she whispered, her eyes fixed on Freddy. There was so much blood.

John's hand clamped down on her shoulder, then he pointed to Grady and jerked his head toward the water barrel. Alex understood at once.

"Grady. Put a pot of water on to boil. We'll need bandages. John, the medical box is in the large bin on the left of the chuck box. I hope to heaven we have whatever you need. Grady, when you finish putting on the water, erect one of the tents." When she saw a flash of indecision in Dal's eyes, she hastily assured him, "We're not breaking any rules. John is our guest and we're fortunate enough that he's a doctor. There are no rules about doctoring in the will." Her gaze swung to Jack Caldwell, who hurried forward to catch Freddy in his arms as she slipped off her horse.

That's when she became aware that John had not moved after his initial impulsive action. He stood stock still, his gaze focused somewhere in the past, and a tremble passed through his body. Alex could only guess what he was seeing and remembering, the sights and sounds of men shot and sliced on a field of battle. She slipped her hand in his and gently pressed.

"John? The war is over. This isn't a battlefield. That is my sister and I love her and I'm frightened for her. I don't know what to do." He looked down at her, struggling to return from dark memories. Alex held his hand and his gaze. "If you cannot do this, I will understand. But if you can, please save Freddy, too."

For one endless moment, she thought he would refuse, thought he would retreat into the safe blank spot he had built in his mind. She feared he would walk away from her, from humankind, and return to the range. He gazed at the prairie, then he looked down at Alex and touched her cheek with trembling fingers.

When he took Freddy out of Jack Caldwell's arms and into his own, Alex gasped softly, and a rush of hot tears spilled over her lashes. She had watched a turning point. His healing would not be easy, but now it would begin.

Dal swung down from his saddle, strode forward, and smashed Caldwell in the mouth hard enough to knock him down, bloody his nose, and crack his lip. "Get up, you worthless cheating son of a bitch!"

Fury shook his body and reddened his mind. He wanted to kill Caldwell, and he wanted to do it with his bare hands.

Caldwell stayed on the ground. After touching a hand to his mouth, he glanced at his bloodied fingertips, then up at Dal. Dal threw off Luther's restraining hand. "Caldwell hired a rustler named Hoke Smyth. That's why today happened. That's why Alex almost died, and Freddy might die." His fists opened and closed. "Get up you fricking coward!"

"Is that true, Caldwell?" Luther demanded. "Did you endanger everyone in this outfit?"

"Frisco can't prove a goddamned thing." Sitting up, Caldwell rubbed a sleeve across his bloody nose. "I don't have to hire any two-bit rustlers, Frisco. Not when I can depend on your incompetence."

Dal ground his teeth and pushed a fist against his palm. "Were you and Lola thinking I was incompetent back when you offered to double my fee if I'd make sure we didn't deliver two thousand steers? Is that why you've started stampedes, drowned cattle, and hired rustlers, you whoreson, because I'm incompetent?" From the corner of his eyes he saw Luther staring at Caldwell.

When he realized Caldwell was not going to get up, was too cowardly to fight, his chest tightened with frustration. "If Freddy dies," he snarled, "I'll kill you, Caldwell. Nothing will stop me."

"That's what this is about," Caldwell said, sliding a calculating glance toward Luther. "It's Freddy, isn't it?" He smiled. "Didn't like to discover that someone else got there first, did you?"

"You lying son of a bitch!" He would have torn Caldwell into bloody pieces if Luther and Ward hadn't grabbed him. Even that wasn't enough. Grady had to jump in before he stopped struggling to reach Caldwell and rip his throat out.

"You can sort this out later," Grady said quietly, looking into his eyes. "Right now, you got a herd scattered all to hell and back, and only about six hours of daylight left." A scream spiraled toward them and they all looked toward the hastily erected tent where John McCallister was removing the bullet from Freddy's shoulder. "That little gal was out there rounding up beeves with lead in her shoulder," Grady said evenly. "If you want to help her, get out there and get your herd back together. That's what's important to her. Not this snake in the grass." He turned around and shot a wad of tobacco juice toward Caldwell.

The red haze of rage slipped enough for Dal to understand that Grady's advice made sense. Killing Caldwell wouldn't change anything. What was needed now was to mop up the mess, take a count, and discover how much devastation the son of a bitch had inflicted.

"This isn't finished," he said, a promise glittering in his icy eyes.

Then he followed Freddy's screams to the tent, steeled himself, and looked inside. John had tied her to a board so she couldn't hit out or thrash while he probed her wound for the bullet. He'd ripped her shirt open to expose an ugly raw opening that bubbled red. Dal watched the cords rise on Freddy's throat as she arched her neck and screamed, and he felt sick to his stomach. John didn't look up, but Alex glanced toward him, her face the color of whey. Her hands were bloody.

"She'll be all right," Alex whispered. But the fear in her eyes told him that she was saying what she needed to hear, not what she knew as a fact.

Freddy's screams cut through him like a hot knife. He'd seen men shot before, had heard them scream. Hell, he'd been shot himself. But nothing had been as painful to witness as this. If he could have, he would have traded places with her in an instant.

Shaking with helplessness and rage, he swung up in his saddle and lashed the reins across the horse's flanks. If she died . . .

But she couldn't. She wouldn't. That was Joe Roark's daughter back there in the tent. She could be as tough as nails when she needed to be. He hoped she remembered that and pulled through, because he needed her.

He loved her.

It was after midnight before Dal returned to camp. Alex offered him a plate of food, but he was too exhausted, too worried to eat, and he waved aside the beans and fried meat. Picking up a lantern, he walked directly to Freddy's tent and stepped inside. "You idiot," he said, looking down at her. Grady had set up the cot they used in cases of serious injury or illness, and he'd fashioned a makeshift pillow. Her hair covered the pillow like a dark cloud, and her left arm was bound in a sling that rested on top of a light blanket.

"Feels like I'm floating," she murmured, reaching for his hand.

"That's the laudanum John gave you." He sat on a low stool beside her. "What in the hell did you think you were doing? Chasing beeves when you had a bullet in your shoulder? If you weren't already shot-up, I'd shoot you myself for being so damned dumb."

"Didn't want any to escape." She started to shrug, then sucked in a breath and winced instead. "How many?"

"It's bad, Freddy."

"How many?"

"We lost fifty-eight." John McCallister had shot three. There were four dead cattle on the range, two of which he'd put down himself when he saw they wouldn't recover from bullet wounds received from the outlaws' guns. Fifty-one additional longhorns were missing. Some might still be found in the morning if they hadn't joined another herd by then, or found a hiding place in the brush. He figured the rustlers had made off with the rest while he and his drovers were chasing down the stampede. Closing his eyes, he pulled a hand through his hair and swallowed the bitter taste of frustration and fury.

Reason told him he shouldn't blame himself, but he did. Haltingly, he told her about his bathhouse conversation and the probability that the rustlers had been hired by Caldwell. "I should have pulled a couple of the boys off the line and sent them out to watch for strangers." He had assumed any attack would come at night, and he'd beefed up the watch. Now they were paying for his error.

Freddy's eyes sharpened through the pain and laudanum. "This was Jack's fault, not yours."

"The problem is proof. There isn't any proof."

Wetting a finger, he rubbed a speck of blood off her throat before he drew a long breath, held it a minute, then took her hand again. "We'll stay here until noon tomorrow, but I can't give you more time than that, Freddy. I'll put you back on drag, that's the best I can do." She was going to have an agonizing few days, and he couldn't do a damned thing about it.

"Don't worry," she murmured, her eyelids drifting shut. "You always said the horse does most of the work anyway."

He stayed with her after she slept, blowing out the lantern and sitting in the darkness listening to her breathe and holding her hand. She had calluses now, something he hadn't noticed that night in Fort Worth. He ran his thumb over the rough pads on her palm. And he wished he had killed Jack Caldwell.

Fifty-eight. He was down to a margin of ninety-one.

He stared out the tent flap at the boys gathered around the campfire drinking coffee. Everyone was too worked up to sleep. He doubted the drovers on night watch would have to rub tobacco juice in their eyes to stay awake tonight; the day's excitement would reverberate well into tomorrow.

Ninety-one. And Red River wasn't far ahead; he'd heard it was swollen and running fast with the worst of the spring melt. Even in the best of conditions, it was a rare boss who didn't lose a few beeves crossing the Red River. Christ. Dropping his head, he rubbed his forehead.

If he was going to win their inheritance for three women who had earned it and deserved it, he needed to be luckier than he'd ever been before.

"Dal?" When he lifted his head, he saw Alex pushing her chair through the soft summer darkness. "May I speak to you a moment?"

Stepping outside, he put his hat on and looked down at her. She had pinned her hair in place and found a minute to mend her skirt. She didn't look like a woman who had been caught in the center of a stampede and lived to tell about it. Had in fact gone from surviving almost certain death to helping remove the bullet in Freddy's shoulder and then prepare supper for twelve men. "Are you all right?" he asked, his gaze softening with admiration.

"I've had better days," she said with a wan smile. "There's coffee on my worktable."

Nodding, he moved around behind her and pushed her back toward the chuck wagon, remembering that day—a century ago—when he had refused to assist her with her chair. None of them had been the same people then. He gave her one of the coffee cups and took the other, leaning against the side of the wagon, feeling the fatigue in his shoulders and thighs.

"Luther told us what you said, about Caldwell and Lola making you a dishonorable offer. I'd like to hear more about that," Alex said quietly. "And I'd like to tell you how my heart stopped beating when I saw you bring Freddy in off the range. I'd like to know if Grady is right and Caldwell is responsible for most of our large losses." She gazed up at him with a lifted eyebrow, firelight dancing across her complexion.

"We lost fifty-eight," he said, anticipating her next question.

She nodded grimly and glanced down at the handkerchief she was twisting in her lap. "It's been a long rough day and we're all tired, so I'll save the questions for another time. I just want to tell you that Freddy will recover." Her eyes briefly closed then opened. "And there's something—"

"John McCallister," he guessed.

"Yes." Bright pink flooded her face, obvious even in the glow of flames reflecting across her throat and forehead. "I don't know what to do," she said softly. "He won't leave."

They both looked up as John walked out of the darkness. He reached up on the side of the wagon, then removed a tool that he handed to Dal. Dal recognized the King's Walk branding iron.

Turning the iron in his hands, he studied McCallister's face. The blank, almost dreaming look was gone. McCallister's gaze connected now. He carried himself differently.

"I think he's giving us his cows," Alex explained quietly.

"I'll take them," Dal said promptly. "I don't believe there's any prohibition against accepting cattle as a gift, but I'll check with Luther."

John nodded and stepped back, dropping a hand to Alex's shoulder. Alex gazed at Dal. "When you speak to Luther, please ask him to add John to our list of observers," she requested in a low voice, raising a hand to cover John's fingers on her shoulder.

Dal had seen this coming, had thought about it. "John's expenses will be deducted from your share of the inheritance. If we don't deliver the right number of beeves," he shrugged. "Then the widow Roark gets stuck with the extra expense."

Alex smiled and nodded. Her next words, Dal suspected, were meant more for John than for him. "John and I will part in Abilene. But for the moment, we enjoy each other's company."

Dal extended his hand and clasped John McCallister's palm. "Thank you for everything you did today. I'm glad you're with us."

Sensing they wanted privacy, he walked away. He didn't feel like joining the drovers gathered around the fire, didn't feel like riding out to check on the night watch although he would later. Glancing toward the observers' campfire, he noted that no one slept there either. Les and Ward sat silently beside the embers. He spotted Luther and Caldwell hunched over coffee.

Straightening his shoulders, he adjusted the pistol on his hip, then crossed the grassy patch separating the two camps. Eyes burning down on Caldwell's scabbed lip, he told them both about John's three cows and Alex's request to add John to the observer list.

Luther shrugged. "There's no mention in Joe's conditions prohibiting someone from giving cattle to the drive."

Caldwell faced Dal. "If there isn't a ruling against it, there should be."

The red fell across his vision like a curtain and he wanted to slam his fist in Caldwell's face. "If we can accept strays, we should be able to accept a gift."

Luther glanced at their expressions, then stepped between them. "That's correct. I'm ruling that you can accept McCallister's three cows."

"I want to file an official protest," Caldwell snapped, staring at Dal.

"Your objection is noted," Luther answered. His gaze was cold. "As for Alex's request that I add McCallister to our list of observers . . . it doesn't appear that McCallister intends to leave in any case," he observed drily.

"Three cows aren't going to help you, Frisco," Caldwell said with a sneer. "We both know you're going to lose that many and more crossing Red River."

He did know. His hands felt hot, tingled with the urge to smash the smirk off Caldwell's cracked lip. He started to walk away, then stopped and looked back. "No one was there before me," he said softly. "If I ever again hear you malign the lady, you'll wish to hell you hadn't."

A dark flush rose to surround Caldwell's pale mustache. "I'm getting tired of your threats, Frisco."

"Then let's take it out there," he said, nodding toward the starlit range, "and settle things right now."

When Caldwell only stared, Dal let his gaze drop to the scab on Caldwell's lip and he smiled before he returned to check on Freddy. Then he rode out to join the night watch.

The broken country in the Red River valley was the most beautiful land Les had yet seen. Stands of pine and cottonwood sprang up in clumps, spring rains had polished the range to an emerald green sparkling with wildflowers.

She would never have seen this beauty if Joe hadn't structured his will as he had. She would have missed so much if Pa had just handed them his fortune with no strings attached.

She wouldn't have learned to ride, would never have slept beneath a starry sky, would never have enjoyed the burning shine of sunlight on her face and hands. Never would she have learned to admire or respect the steel-hooved longhorns that Pa had taken such pride in.

Gazing ahead, she watched the herd plodding along ahead of her, tails curled over their backs, their long heads swaying. She would never have believed that she could develop something approaching affection for the bony, coarse-haired, narrow hipped, big-eared cattle. She suspected that's what Pa had hoped for, that she and Alex and Freddy would learn to care about these contrary animals as he had.

Most of all, if Pa had simply given them his fortune, Les would never have gotten to know her sisters. Or learned to love them.

After wiping sweat from her forehead, she rode over to Freddy and turned Cactus up beside Walker. "How are you feeling today?" she asked, glancing at the dusty sling cradling Freddy's arm close to her chest. "Better?"

"Well enough that I don't need a nursemaid anymore," Freddy said with a smile. "But it was nice of you to request drag so you could keep an eye on me." She sighed. "This still hurts like a bugger. Les, did you ever think that we'd come out of this with actual scars?"

Keeping an eye on the stragglers and occasionally nudging them to a faster pace, they rode together, comparing their wounds, talking about rabbits and coyotes they'd spotted, speculating about Alex and John. Les would have given everything she owned to tell Freddy about Jack Caldwell's offer, and how Ward was threatening, hitting her, and insisting every day that she "lose" some beeves. But Freddy would have exploded. She would have told Dal no matter how strongly Les pleaded with her not to. Freddy wouldn't mean to, but she would set in motion a chain of events that would end in Les's murder. Despairing, she tried not to think about any of it.

"Les?" Freddy said in a low voice as they drove their stragglers onto the bedding gounds at the end of the day. "Getting shot scared me. It made me think about dying and . . . you know, things." She looked down at her sling and a flood of pink rose from her throat. "I just want you to know . . . I'm very glad we had this time together. I haven't been much of a sister or a friend to you in the past, but I want to be in the future."

An answering pink invaded Les's cheeks. "I've said so many awful things to you."

"If I remember right, you had provocation." Freddy looked embarrassed. "I got my licks in. I've said some awful things, too, and I regret that, Les."

Maybe they would never be able to say the words aloud, but the emotion was there and Les felt it. Needing to state her own version of I love you, she drew a breath and looked ahead, watching Dal ride toward the campsite. "He's a good man, Freddy." A wistful desperation ran beneath her tone. "I hope things between the two of you work out the way you want them to."

"I don't know if that's possible." Wincing, she adjusted her sling, then watched Dal riding toward the chuck wagon. "But I've decided life is short, and I'm going to live it the way I want to, not the way other people think I should. Do you understand what I'm saying?"

Les did understand. Freddy intended to follow her

Maggie Osborne

heart even if the road was a short one that ended in Abilene. Once Les would have taken a high tone of moral superiority, would have snapped out a judgmental and scathing reply. Now, she examined her own heart and tried to be as honest as she could. "What you do doesn't change who you are," she said finally. "And who you are is a sister I admire and respect."

Tears glistened in Freddy's eyes. She had waited years to hear those words.

CHAPTER 20

Initially Alex had feared Jack Caldwell would register
a protest when John took over her doctoring duties, but
after Caldwell asked John to treat his cracked lip, her
concern abated. Without discussing it, everyone accepted John as the outfit's doctor and the drovers
brought him their injuries, mostly of a minor nature
such as small burns, lacerations, cuts, and sprains.

The worse injury had been Freddy's wound, and removing the bullet from her shoulder had been profoundly disturbing for John. Performing the surgery
had forced him to face the reasons he had retreated
from civilization. He had been different since that
night. Alex would have said that he'd become quieter
if that statement could be applied to a man who didn't
speak.

But that's how it seemed to her. He rode beside Alex
on the seat of the chuck wagon but oftentimes he was
miles away in another time and place. At other times
she noticed him examining his long slender fingers
with a frown. Twice the drovers had brought him
wounds to tend, and she had seen him instinctively balk
and withdraw in his mind. Both times he had treated
the men, but she had witnessed the inner battle he

waged before he could force himself to do so. He was winning his war, but the victories came hard.

Alex slowed the mules after the pilot waved her off near the head of a small creek. There was no hurry to set up the nooning camp, as she planned rabbit stew using cooked rabbit leftover from the previous night. The meal would come together quickly. Personally, Alex didn't care for rabbit, but the drovers were happy to receive a little variety, thanks to Luther's hunting skills.

Easing the mules to a walk, she smiled up at a hot cloudless sky. Oddly, the open spaces didn't alarm her as they once had. Perhaps it was because they were seeing more timber now, passing stands of oak. Or possibly it was because she had confessed her secret to the people who mattered most, and she didn't feel the need to hide as she had when they began this journey.

So many changes had occurred since they all rode away from King's Walk. Occasionally she thought about her father and believed she understood why he had insisted on the cattle drive. She and her sisters were no longer the frivolous soft women they had been.

"Win or lose, I'll always be grateful that I had this experience," she said, after sharing her thoughts with John. "Without it, I would have missed so much. I would never have known Freddy or Les or myself. Or you," she added in a softer voice.

She braked the wagon near the willows lining the banks of the creek and reached for her crutch and her pistol. Ready for the noon snake hunt, a chore she truly enjoyed, she prepared to climb down from the seat, but John placed his hand on hers.

Ignoring the tingle in her fingers, she turned to smile at him, drinking in the sight of his deeply tanned, strong face and the grey eyes that could say so much.

Before meeting him, she wouldn't have believed that a man who didn't speak could offer such depth of companionship. Nor would she have believed that she could ever feel this powerful a connection to a man.

Placing his hands on her shoulders, he turned her to fully face him. The expression in his eyes, on his lips, was one she hadn't seen before. "John? Is something wrong?"

Then she understood and her breath caught in her throat. He was going to kiss her. Her first confused thought was: *Why here and why now?* Followed swiftly by: *No, I can't allow this.*

But she couldn't move away from him. The only sound she heard was that of her heart pounding rapidly in anticipation of a kiss she had both dreaded and longed for. A hundred times she had wondered how she would respond if this moment ever arrived.

There was no doubt what she should do. She should remember Payton and that terrible night. Payton would never again experience the thrill of a kiss, would never enjoy any of life's pleasures. And neither should she.

But heaven forgive her, she yearned for John's mouth on hers, had dreamed of his arms around her since the stampede. She couldn't make herself resist. Helplessly, she watched as his gaze lingered caressingly on her lips then traveled up to her eyes. "I thought if this happened, it would be at night," she whispered, trembling beneath his hands on her shoulders, "not in the full blaze of the noon sun."

His hands slid down the sleeves of her shirtwaist and gently he guided her into his arms, pressing her against his chest. A low sigh escaped Alex's lips and sudden tears sparkled on her lashes. It felt so good—so wonderfully good!—to feel his strong body pressed to hers, to feel his arms holding her. Winding her arms around his neck, she closed her eyes. To be embraced, safe in a man's arms when she had never expected it to happen again, this would be enough.

Time sheltered their embrace, enfolding them within a summer-scented capsule that felt endless and theirs alone. The fragrance of grass and sunlight and nearby water sweetened each breath. Theirs was the music of birds and the lazy buzz of insects and the beating of two hearts. Yes, she thought, she didn't need more. This would be enough.

Raising his hands, John tenderly framed her face, his fingertips as light on her skin as the caress of a breeze. He gazed at her, and no words had ever been as eloquent as the message she read in his eyes. He loved her. This splendid wonderful man loved her.

Leaning forward, he touched his mouth lightly to hers, enough to taste her without startling her. Alex's breast rose, and her heartbeat quickened. A sound that was almost a sob, almost a gasp, sighed past her lips, and she leaned into him, supporting her body against his chest. He loved her. Helplessly, she parted her lips and her head fell back.

This time his kiss was full and provocative, summoning sensations she had believed, had hoped, were submerged too deeply to be awakened. But his fingers on her face, his mouth, his lips, stirred slumbering emotions and coaxed them to life. His hands moved to cup her head, to spread across her spine, and he crushed her against him as their kisses deepened.

Only when the pounding hooves of the remuda penetrated their absorption in each other did they ease apart and stare at each other.

"My God," Alex whispered, lifting trembling fingers to her lips.

Payton had never kissed her as John just had. No

man had kissed her like that. His kisses had blended tenderness and passion, emotion and desire.

"Well gol-dang," Grady shouted as the remuda trotted past the wagon. "Ain't you two got nothing better to do than sit and admire the scenery?" He scowled at Alex's bright cheeks. "You got some hungry punchers coming along not far behind me."

She peeked at John's grin and laughed. "Almost caught." Reaching for her crutch, she poked at the grass to scare away snakes, then hurried to her chores with a smile on her lips.

The day was glorious. The hot sun felt wonderful on her face, and she hardly noticed the ubiquitous mosquitoes that plagued her whenever she was in camp. All she could think about was John's lips on hers, the solid heat and power of his body. And what she had read in his eyes.

In retrospect, it was inevitable that her happiness could not last. The instant she looked down at her worktable and saw her wedding ring, reality and guilt brought her crashing to earth.

Because of how he had died, she would always be Payton Mills's wife.

Until death do us part did not apply to a wife who had caused her husband's death. She was tied to Payton forever, bound more tightly by guilt than they had been bound in life.

The gold band on her finger caught the sunlight and flashed accusation at her.

Swaying, she gripped the worktable. When the dizziness passed, she lifted her head and cast a frantic glance around the noon camp, looking for John. She had to tell him that he must leave. The temptation was too great. Being near him was too heavy a punishment to bear.

But she didn't see him. For the last ten days, he had mysteriously vanished during the noon meal, off doing something he clearly did not want her to know about. Frustrated, she struck the worktable with her fist. Already she felt a wave of weakness submerging her resolve.

When Freddy came past the worktable and held out her plate, she paused and peered at Alex's face. "Are you all right?"

"It's John," she said, staring down at a skillet of biscuits. The urge to tell someone, to say the words aloud overwhelmed her. "Oh, Freddy, I love him."

Freddy's eyebrows shot up, and she smiled broadly. "That's wonderful!"

"It's the worst thing that could have happened to me!" Taking up her crutch, she gripped the handle and stumbled toward the creek to be alone with her conscience.

"I'm worried about Alex and Les," Freddy commented, carrying her plate of beans away from the noon fire. Beans and bacon were a staple of cattle drives, but she had reached a point where she would have been happy never to see another bean.

"What's going on?" Dal asked, walking beside her.

"I think Alex is going to end up making a sad mistake," she said, frowning. "As for Les, something has changed."

"Is Ward beating her?" Dal's tone was sharp though he seemed distracted. As always, his eyes were not still. He scanned the herd, glanced toward the other two outfits waiting to cross the river.

The Red River was in full rampage, flooding its banks. One herd camped ahead, another had backed up behind them. Everyone waited for the spring floodwaters to recede, but they couldn't delay more than another day before the range would be grazed out. Tempers frayed as drovers fought to keep their stock from mingling with other herds, worried about quicksand and the upcoming crossing.

"I don't know," Freddy said. Rolling her eyes in disgust, she poured the rest of her beans on the ground. "Les has always seemed apprehensive toward Ward, but lately she seems almost terrified."

Dal's gaze sharpened. "Has he hit her again?"

Freddy was sure of it. She'd seen bruises on Les's chin, had noticed Les wincing with pain. "When I asked, she denied it, then started crying and begged me not to mention anything to you." They walked toward a low bluff overlooking the rushing water.

"Do you want me to speak to her? Throw Ward off the drive? I'd be happy to."

Freddy put her hand on his arm, drawing a soft breath at the powerful feel of iron muscle. "Don't. I'm just expressing my own frustration and concern." When a tingle leapt from his body to hers, she dropped her hand and frowned down at eddies of swiftly flowing water. "It's funny how things change. I used to resent it that Les looked to everyone else to solve her problems. Now I'm upset that she won't let anyone help her."

"Gunderson is going to take his herd across tomorrow," Dal said, changing the subject. "We'll go the day after." He jerked off his hat and raked a hand through his hair. "The question isn't whether we'll lose beeves, the question is how many."

Freddy looked down at the tossing, raging river. "How deep is it?"

"Too deep to walk. The cattle and horses will have to swim."

"Swim *that?*" she asked in disbelief. As she watched, a small tree floated past, tossing and whirling in the rapid, churning currents.

"We're damned if we do and damned if we don't," Dal said, his voice rough with frustration. "We lost two beeves in the quicksand last night. It's a miracle we haven't lost more."

A powerful thunderstorm had rumbled through, sparking stunning displays of cracking lightning. All the waiting herds had stampeded, and all had lost beeves to the quicksand, the bluffs, or the river. The King's Walk outfit had been lucky not to lose more than two, but it had taken all night and most of the morning to sort things out and retrieve their cattle from other herds. James and Peach had provoked a fistfight with the drovers from the herd behind them, and both had black eyes and bruises to show for it.

Adding to the general dissatisfaction, the Red River Station had nothing to offer but one outfitting store and one crowded saloon. Luther—Luther!—had almost gotten into a fight when he drove his wagon to the store to buy supplies for Alex.

Everyone was edgy about swimming the floodwaters, and tempers boiled near the surface.

"How will Alex get across?"

"Luther will pay the six-dollar ferry charge for Alex and the chuck wagon. And Luther will keep Caldwell away from the herd. The rest of us will ride through." He cast brooding eyes on the swollen river. "Including that idiot, Ward. He'll send his wagon on the ferry, but he's decided to save two dollars by riding across."

"I think Ward has some foolish idea that he can do whatever you can do." Trying to imagine swimming her horse across the cold floodwaters frightened Freddy. The last time they swam the herd, it had scared her badly when her horse's hooves left the ground and she knew her life depended on Walker's ability and power to swim against the currents and emerge on the opposite bank. That river had been deep, but not raging in flood. The Red River would be much more dangerous.

Dal placed his hand on her arms. "Are you up to this? I can send you with Alex on the ferry if your shoulder is still giving you trouble."

The temptation was great to accept his offer, but that would place an extra burden on the other drovers. The crossing would be difficult enough without attempting it shorthanded. "I'm on the mend." Her shoulder still ached, but today, she wasn't wearing the sling. She was trying to work the stiffness out of her sore muscles.

Gazing up at him, she wondered how she had ever imagined that his eyes were cool or cold. Now she saw warmth and a flicker of desire that made her stomach tighten and her breath quicken, made her long to step forward into his arms.

"I didn't want to say this, but . . . I miss you," he said gruffly.

The heat of his large, callused hands on her arms made her remember his fingers teasing along her naked skin. "I didn't want to say it either, but . . . I miss you, too."

"Sometime soon, Freddy, we're going to have to talk about you missing me and me missing you." His gaze dropped to her lips.

"What do you want to do about it?" she asked, feeling herself go weak inside.

"There's the dilemma." Shoving his fingers into his back pockets, he stepped up on the bluff and looked down at the rushing, tossing waters. "I think about you all the time. It's like you've possessed me," he said without looking at her. "You know damned well what I want."

Relief sapped the strength from her knees. She hadn't been sure, had needed to hear him admit it. "I can't stop thinking about that night in Fort Worth." She'd even dreamed about being with him, the dream but a pale version of reality.

"Hearing that only makes it worse." When he looked at her, his expression was almost savage. "I want you all the time. I wake up wanting you and go to sleep wanting you."

"I thought you were avoiding me."

"I have been. You're a hell of a woman, Freddy. And I respect you too much to take advantage of you. I don't want you to walk away in Abilene thinking I used you or acted selfishly. I don't understand this myself, but your good opinion is important to me. I need your respect more than I need your body." He looked surprised and then amused to hear himself admit such a thing. "Which is saying a whole lot."

No one had ever told her that she was a hell of a woman, and a lump of gratitude rose in her throat. "Thank you for saying that." Before she could tell him that he had earned her respect regardless of what happened between them, he turned abruptly and strode away from her.

As she walked back to camp it struck her as ironic that she'd complained bitterly for a very long time about men treating her as if she were one step above a doxie and now she was upset because Dal insisted that he would not treat her that way.

After pouring a cup of coffee, she watched Alex shape sourdough biscuits in between slapping at mosquitoes, and asked, "Where's John?" Usually he wasn't far from her sister.

Frowning Alex pushed a lock of hair off of her forehead. "John's been acting very mysteriously since the stampede." Freddy didn't have to ask which stampede. "He's spending more time by himself." Alex paused. "Removing the bullet from your shoulder was a big step for him. I think he laid to rest a lot of painful memories that night, and it's given him much to think about. He's changing, trying to return to the world."

Freddy took one of the biscuits and tossed it in her hand. "Are you worried about crossing the river?"

"No. Are you?"

"No."

They looked at each other and burst into laughter.

Then shyly and with many embarrassed pauses, Freddy did something she had never dreamed she would. She told her older sister about being a virgin, about the night in Fort Worth, and about her current dilemma. "You're shocked, aren't you? You think only a harlot would consider accepting a man on a temporary basis."

Alex laid her crutch aside and sank into her chair. She wiped floury hands in her apron then waved Freddy down beside her. "Before this trip, I might well have . . . " The color deepened in her cheeks. "But I've learned a few things. One of the truths I've learned is that life is uncertain." She leaned her head back. "There are so many things in life that we have to do, must do. And so many rules either real or self-imposed against the things we want to do. Are you asking my advice?"

"No," Freddy answered, smiling. "But I'd like to hear it anyway."

"Whatever you decide about Dal, you'll have to live

with the consequences for the rest of your life. And that might include a child. Will you look back and regret giving yourself to this man? Or will you look back and regret that you didn't? No one can make the decision for you," she added gently. "But if I were offering advice, I think I'd say follow your heart."

Surprise was followed by quick tears. "I've been so wrong about you."

"No, you weren't." Tears swam in Alex's eyes, too. "I've been a hypocrite." She drew a long breath. "There's something I've been meaning to tell you and Les." Speaking slowly, she told Freddy the truth about running away to Boston, her life there, and how Payton had died. "So you see," she said at the finish, "I have no right to judge anyone."

"The accident wasn't your fault," Freddy objected earnestly. "You didn't make it rain that night or cause the slippery road. Payton could have insisted on staying home. You're wrong to blame yourself."

"Thank you," Alex whispered, covering her face. "More than I can ever express, I appreciate hearing you say that. Even if you're wrong."

"I'm not wrong. If John could speak, he'd say the same thing."

They sat together, feeling closer than they ever had before. The moment would have been perfect if Les had been with them. But Les was at the observers' camp, sitting with Ward and Jack Caldwell. She looked miserable and utterly hopeless.

Waiting to cross the river gave Alex time to do some baking ahead, time to do laundry, and enjoy some rare leisure time. She and John had picked wild plums most of the afternoon, and she had baked plum pies. If she'd

had the faintest idea how to make jam, she would have
been tempted to try.

After putting away the pies, she lit the lanterns on
the back of the chuck wagon, then smiled. "You've
been so restless." Usually, John was a man who didn't
display much agitation, but today he'd been edgy and
he'd glanced at the sky a dozen times, as if wishing the
day would hurry past. In the light of the lanterns, she
gazed at his mouth and then away.

They hadn't kissed again because she hadn't permit-
ted it. And to make certain that her resolve remained
strong, she had stopped wearing gloves. The gleam of
sunlight on her wedding ring kept Payton in front of
her mind even while her body longed for John. Being
an observant man, John had noticed that she preferred
blisters and calluses to wearing her gloves, and she
didn't doubt that he had guessed the reason why.

"Thank you," she said gratefully, as he pushed her
chair up behind her and took the crutch from her hands.
She'd been on the crutch most of the day, her arm
ached, and her leg was tired.

Like everyone, she supposed, her thoughts had
begun to turn toward the end of the drive and what it
would mean. Her mind shied from saying good-bye to
John; she could not bear to imagine that moment. But
she'd begun to think about returning to her wheelchair
full-time. She would abandon the crutch she had come
to depend on so strongly. That had been her decision
from the beginning, and she intended to honor it.

"It's a lovely evening," she murmured, wrenching
her thoughts from the future.

John touched her shoulder, then pushed her toward
the spot where they usually sat after she had cleaned
her worktable for the night, close enough to the camp-

fire to enjoy the songs and tall tales, but far enough away that they felt a measure of privacy.

Tonight, to her surprise, he pushed her past the outer reach of the light and into the darkness beyond. "John? What are you doing?"

He didn't reply, of course, but the answer became obvious a few minutes later. When he set the chair's brake, she saw that he'd chosen this site earlier. He'd spread a blanket over the soft grass in a spot where the air was scented by wild plums and they could hear the murmuring whisper of the river. In the light of a half-moon, she noticed a basket placed beside the blanket and a long narrow package.

At once, she knew what he intended.

Nervously, she wet her lips and felt her heart flutter, then sink. *Please,* she silently prayed. *I'm not strong enough to refuse him. Help me.*

Walking around her chair, John knelt before her, his hands on the arms of her wheelchair, his expressive eyes on her face. Alex sucked in a deep breath and held it until her lungs burned. Tears pricked her eyes because tonight would destroy them. Once and for all, she had to reject him, had to make him understand that she had no right to take the happiness he was offering. When he finally accepted there was no place for him in her life, he would leave. She had so hoped they would have a little more time, that they could stay together until Abilene.

Placing a trembling hand on his cheek, she gazed deeply into his eyes, her own eyes sparkling with tears. "I can't," she whispered. "I'll always be married, John. You know why."

But God help her, that wasn't the only reason for refusing him. There was another, equally compelling reason, one that propped her obligation to Payton.

Once she'd had a lovely whole body that she had been shyly proud of. Now her body was mangled and incomplete. She didn't want John to see her naked, it would shame her. That above all made it possible for her to refuse something she tried to pretend she had not dreamed of.

He reached for her hand and gently removed it from his cheek. And then, before Alex realized what he intended, he slipped the gold band from her finger. Shock rendered her speechless. Stunned, she gripped the arms of the chair as he stood, having no idea what he would do. Then she cried out, and her hands flew to her chest when he brought back his arm and threw her ring toward the willows and plum bushes lining the banks of the river.

"Oh my God!" Trembling and white-faced, she stared up at him in the moonlight. "How dare you . . . you had no right! No right!" Shock and outrage widened her eyes. Shaking violently, she dropped her hands to the wheels, fumbling to release the brake. "I'll never find it! Oh God. How could you do that? How could you dare *do* that?"

Dropping to his knees in front of her, he caught her hands and held them so tightly that she couldn't struggle free though she fought him and tried.

"I love you, Alex."

Her heart stopped. She couldn't believe that he'd spoken. Thunderstruck, she stared into his steady gaze.

"You're not married. You haven't been married for over a year."

His voice was hoarse and strained from disuse. But when he became accustomed to speaking, his voice would sound exactly as she had imagined, deep and quiet and thrilling. Bittersweet tears swam in her eyes.

The words that broke his five-year, self-imposed silence were a declaration of his love for her.

Tears glistening in her eyes, she leaned forward to wrap her arms around his neck. "I'm so glad for you!" They hadn't needed words between them, but she understood that silence had been the last barrier between John and the world he rejected. Now that barrier had dropped, and he would be whole again. With all her aching heart, she wished that she, too, could be whole, for him.

His hands slipped around her waist and he stood pulling up her upright with him. Alex gasped, feeling the sudden open space beneath her right leg, and she clasped his shoulders to steady herself. "I can't," she whispered. "Oh John, please understand. I can't."

He molded her body to his and another gasp tore at her throat. She had never expected to be held in a man's arms again. Hadn't dared to hope that she would ever stand chest to chest, hip to hip with a man who desired her. She had truly believed lovemaking was a pleasure she would never again experience in her lifetime. That was her choice and her destiny.

His hands moved from her waist to her face, and he kissed the tears shining on her cheeks and eyelids. "I love you," he whispered. "I have loved you from the moment I saw you."

Standing on one leg made it impossible to step away from the solid heat of his body and the tender kisses raining over her face. Closing her eyes, arching her throat, she clung to him for support and struggled to breathe, wanting this moment and his kisses to endure forever. "I can't do this," she whispered helplessly. "You're taking advantage of me."

"Yes," he murmured, smiling against her lips.

His hands returned to her waist and he held her

tightly, securely against his thighs and chest and she swallowed a sob when she felt the power of his arousal. This wonderful man desired her. How was it possible? Didn't he know how ugly and scarred the hated stump was?

Of course he knew.

Taking her hands, he moved them to his neck, and then he kissed her, his mouth gentle and unhurried, warm and unbearably sweet. Her arms tightened around him and she parted her lips when his tongue explored her mouth then slipped inside to taste her.

There was one last moment of reason when she still could have refused. Drawing back, she gazed into his eyes, struggling against heart and body, and the moment hung between them. She knew without doubt if she gave herself to him, guilt would damn her all her days. But if she did not, regret would poison the rest of her life.

They both recognized the moment, and knew when it rushed past them.

His kisses deepened, and Alex returned them with the fervor of a woman who had discovered a passionate nature too late. In her heart, she knew tonight would be her last physical experience—it would not happen again. There would never be another man like John. She would never love this deeply, this completely. She would make her time with him a memory to hold tight and cherish, would make of tonight all it could be and had to be to last the remainder of her life. As for her wedding ring . . . she would think about that later. Not now.

When her leg began to tremble violently, he grasped her hands and swung her down to the blanket, the gesture surprisingly graceful, and he sat beside her, gazing at her face in the moonlight. "Take down your hair," he requested softly.

Not looking away from his beloved face, she lifted her arms to remove her hairpins. Skeins of golden hair cascaded over her shoulders and down her back. He filled his hands with her hair and let the silken strands flow through his fingers.

Shyly, her fingers quivering, she opened his shirt and slid her hand inside against his hot skin, drawing a soft quick breath. His skin was smooth, the muscles hard beneath it. Leaning forward, she kissed the spot she had bared and heard him groan, then whisper her name.

But when he reached for the row of buttons running down her bodice, she caught his hand and gazed into his eyes with a plea for understanding. "Please, John. Must we undress?"

Speaking was new to him and he didn't answer but reassured her with his gaze and his hands on her buttons. Heart beating wildly, she closed her eyes and caught a sharp breath as her bodice opened and she felt the brush of warm fingers against the swell of her breasts.

Her distress was severe enough that she would never remember removing her shirtwaist and skirt or her petticoats. But she would always remember the strange freedom of being naked in the open night air, and the dizzying, wrenching need to cover herself and shield her legs from his eyes. Shamed, wanting to hide, she dropped her head and did not look at him until he spoke.

"You are so beautiful," he breathed. Standing over her, rampant in the moonlight, he gazed down at her body. "You are as lovely and as perfect as I imagined you would be."

Afraid to believe, afraid to trust, she dared a look at him and felt her heart wrench when she read his expression and understood that she truly was whole and beautiful in his eyes. She was as magnificent to him as he was to her.

"Oh, John," she whispered, choking. Unable to speak further, unable to see him through a blur of tears, she opened her arms and he came to her. Kneeling, he clasped her tightly against his chest and she sucked in a hard breath when her breasts touched his naked hot skin. She hadn't beleived she would ever again know the touch of bared hearts meeting, would never again experience the thrill of a man's quickening breath and mounting passion or her own.

Gently, he eased her back on the blanket and warmed her from the night breezes with his body and his kisses and his hands. Unhurried, they explored each other with growing passion and joy. When his fingers and kisses traveled to her right leg, she tensed and would have pushed him away, but he would not allow it, would not permit a single inch of her body to go unloved, unworshiped.

Ceasing to resist, she lay back on the blanket, tears of gratitude and love brimming in her eyes. Then her insistent fingers teased him back up beside her and she began her own exploration with lips and hands and caressing fingertips. When they were wild and trembling with need, drunk with deep intoxicating kisses, John came to her. Gazing into her eyes, he thrust within her and Alex knew a joy that she had never dared imagine. This, then, was what it could be when two people gave of themselves entirely. This was what she had always longed for and had never known in the fullest sense.

Because it had never happened to her before, she didn't recognize the sweet, almost unbearable tension building between her thighs. Each fevered kiss, each powerful thrust increased her pleasure, and the strange frantic tension raised a patina of perspiration to her skin and turned her wild beneath him. And then it was as if a wave crested and swept her away on a flooding sea of sensation and pleasure more intense than anything she had ever experienced.

When the wave subsided and she could breathe again, she stared up at him in gasping amazement and wonder. "Good heavens!"

Laughing, he bent to kiss her, then he allowed his own burst of pleasure. But he didn't release her. Rolling to one side, he held her while a breeze played over their cooling bodies, drying the dampness on their skin. If Alex could have been granted one wish, she would have wished that these moments in his arms would never end.

"I was a captain in the Confederacy," he said against her hair. "A surgeon."

Holding her, speaking softly, he told her about his practice before the world went mad, and then he spoke of the horrors he had witnessed during the war. He remembered young men with shattered limbs and broken chests, and the despair of knowing he could not save them all. How he had almost welcomed his capture by the Union as an escape from the death and destruction he dealt with every day, and his own bone-deep weariness. But there had been horrors in the Union prison, too. When the final release came, he'd weighed 105 pounds, and the atrocities he had witnessed had seared his mind.

"I returned to my home in Atlanta, but there was nothing left. The foundation still stood, everything else was gone."

"Were you married?" Alex asked. It was the first she had spoken in an hour.

"Elizabeth died before the war," he said, stroking her hair. "My son and parents died the night Atlanta burned."

"I'm so sorry." Now she understood why he had chosen solitude and open spaces far from the company of men.

Easing away from her, he sat up and reached for the basket beside the blanket. He offered her a plum and a canteen of water. "It's not very romantic," he said, smiling at the canteen, "but the best I could manage in the circumstances."

Laughing, Alex sat up, astonished that her nakedness and his did not embarrass her. She couldn't have dreamed this would be possible.

"But I did bring you a present."

"A gift?" she asked in surprise, wiping plum juice from her lips.

He reached to the side of the blanket and lifted the long narrow package she recalled seeing earlier. "Every person in the outfit helped with this. Dal bought the hickory at the Red River Station. Freddy cut a piece of canvas from her tent. Les found the padding among items in Ward's wagon. Grady cut and cured the rawhide for the straps. I did the carving. There wasn't a man in the outfit who didn't help with the smoothing and polishing, including Luther."

Alex blinked at the package and horror dawned in her eyes. The plum fell from her fingers, and she clutched the blanket with both hands. "John, no! I'll never wear it."

He untied the string and opened the cloth wrapping. She stared in revulsion at moonlight gleaming softly on the wooden leg. In a horrible way, it was a work of art, she could see that. Knowing anatomy as he did, John had shaped the wood to approximate an actual leg. At the top was a padded canvas cup with a harness contraption that would hold the leg firmly in place. At the bottom was a large wooden knob.

She scurried backward on the blanket as if he held a snake in his lap.

He caught her icy hands in his. "Alex, please listen." Ashen-faced and trembling, she jerked free and clapped her hands over her ears. "I can tell you a hundred times that Payton's death was not your fault, but you'll never believe me. So I'll tell you this. However Payton Mills died and for whatever reason, you have punished yourself enough. Nothing you do will change what happened that night. You can confine yourself to a wheelchair and shrink the world around you. You can deny yourself convenience and happiness. You can seclude yourself and define your life by the stairs you cannot climb, by the pleasure you will not allow yourself. And Alex? None of your misery or self-punishment will bring Payton back or change one minute of that night."

"Payton would be alive if it weren't for me!"

"The time has come to forgive yourself and go on. Would Payton want you to punish yourself for the rest of your life? Was he that kind of man? I can't believe it, Alex. You wouldn't have chosen a cold, vengeful man for a husband."

She had always assumed that Payton would be as unforgiving as she was of herself. Odd that she could forgive others, but not herself. Never.

"I can't," she whispered, staring with abhorrence at the wooden leg. "I'm sorry, I just . . . I can't."

John caught her hands and stroked them. "Alex, I beg you. Put the past behind you. Do you really think you were spared that night so you could live in misery and blame? Is that why you didn't die, too? So you could make yourself unhappy for the rest of your life?"

White-faced and choking, she jerked her hands out of his and reached for her clothing. "I don't want to hear this!"

"I love the woman who had the courage to face down a stampede. I love the woman with the determination to pick herself up every time she falls. I love the woman who drives those stubborn mules and shoots the snakes. That is the woman I want to build a life with. Not the woman who wants to retreat to her wheelchair when this cattle drive is over."

"You don't understand. No one does." Hurrying, she dressed herself and fastened her buttons with shaking fingers. She had longed to hear him speak, imagined it a hundred times. But now all she wanted to do was escape the torrent of words. Her need was so intense that she would have crawled to her chair if John hadn't stood, pulled on his pants, then pushed the chair to her.

"Please, my love. Stand upright and give us a future. Live again." He met her eyes in the starry light as she rose to her knees and gripped the arms of the chair. "Walk into my arms and let me love you forever."

"Please. Just take me back to camp."

He stood behind her for a long moment, his hands on her shoulders. Then he silently pushed her back to the campfire. "John . . . " she said, when they reached the chuck wagon. But she couldn't tell him that she loved him. He would interpret her love as a promise for a future together.

But they had no future. He could throw away her ring, but not her obligation to Payton. Not her guilt. Tonight, she had betrayed Payton in a way she had never dreamed she would. It was madness to consider even for an instant that she would reward her betrayal by walking upright again.

"Please," she whispered, rolling away from him toward her bedroll. "Burn that thing."

In the morning, she found the wooden leg on her worktable. Furious, she would have hurled it into the campfire except Caleb and Dal were already up and waiting for their coffee. They watched her with smiling expectation and she remembered John explaining that everyone in the outfit had helped craft the hideous appliance.

Tears glistened in her eyes as she threw the leg into the bed of the wagon, then concentrated on preparing breakfast.

"The worst thing that can happen is if the cattle panic and go into a mill in the water," Dal warned, addressing them all. "We've got solid footing on either side, and we won't have the sun in our eyes. The point steers will follow a horse, so I'll lead us in and we'll swim the herd as a unit. If we break into smaller bunches, we'll never get the beeves to enter the water. Keep the herd compact and don't allow any gaps. Keep them moving."

His gaze found Freddy and Les. "Three cowboys died last week crossing this river. This one is dangerous even for experienced hands. I want both of you to ride the forward swing today. And the sooner you're across, the easier I'm going to breathe. Any questions?"

Les had a thousand questions, but her mouth was too dry to speak.

"All right, then." Dal settled his hat on his head

and flexed his shoulders, his gaze lingering on Freddy. "We've done this before. Good luck everyone. Let's move 'em out."

Les wet her lips and mustered a ghostly smile for Freddy. Since Freddy's arm was still weak, Freddy would ride on the upstream side of the herd. Les had agreed to take the more dangerous position on the down side. If she was swept off her horse, there was nothing to catch her, nothing to prevent her from being swallowed by the violent river. Suddenly, her boots felt as if they weighed a hundred pounds. She wasn't a strong swimmer in the best of circumstances; weighed down with boots and clothing, if she fell into the water, she was dead.

Ward intercepted her on the way to the remuda. Clasping her arm, he leaned close to her ear. "You heard what Frisco said. Do something to start a mill in the water. Do it, Les! I'll be watching." He increased the pressure on her arm. "I'll cross about a half hour behind you," he warned. "If you don't do as I've told you, you're going to be very sorry."

Without speaking, she jerked her arm free and found her saddle, taking extra care today with the girth cinch before she swung up on Cactus. Farther upstream she could see Alex's chuck wagon already on the ferry. Luther and Jack Caldwell stood beside their wagon, waiting their turn to cross.

It was a beautiful morning, clear and dry, but a tense excitement quivered in the air. Some of the Red River Station people lined the bluffs to watch, knowing the potential for disaster was high. After murmuring a quick prayer that everyone in their outfit would cross safely, Les urged Cactus forward and swung into position alongside the herd. Freddy rode on the other side of the longhorns and forward, the drovers spaced out to provide as much coverage as possible.

When the drovers were in position, Dal rode past Les waving his hat, pointing it north. He cut in front of the lead steers and moved toward the riverbank. A good trail boss never let his stock trot, and Dal didn't allow it today, but he set a brisk pace. He wasn't going to give the leads time to think about entering the turbulent waters. If the lead steers went in without balking, the rest of the herd would follow.

Les lost sight of him when he rode down the bank, and she didn't release her breath or her grip on the pommel until she saw him reappear in the river. Water churned around his waist and all Les could see of the buckskin was his head. Behind Dal came two sets of horns, then the rest of the herd. That's all Les could see of the swimming animals, just their horns bobbing up and down above the surface of the rampaging waters.

But the lead steers had not balked. The herd was going in smoothly. She released a breath, then gasped as one set of horns began to drift away from the line of animals crossing the river. As she watched, the horns turned form north to west and swiftly flowed downstream. An instant later, the horns sank and were gone.

All too soon Les saw Freddy set her mouth in a grim line and urge Walker into the heaving waters. Off to her left, she noticed a longhorn mired in quicksand. He wasn't bawling yet, but he would be soon and that would make it difficult for the drovers behind her to hold the herd squeezed down. There wasn't time to worry about it.

Suddenly the floodwaters tossed in front of her. She felt Cactus tense beneath her and hesitate, then she swallowed hard, dug her heels into the horse's flanks, and they plunged into the violent waters. To her right were floating horns and the eerily silent animals straining against the currents. To her left, a cottonwood gave way and crashed into the river. One of the steers turned his head, eyes wild, but Les's body blocked his view. "Keep going," she crooned, her voice shaking. "Nothing to fret about, old boy. Keep swimming."

Cactus's legs were off solid ground and cold water swirled up around her waist. Leaning forward, as frightened as she had ever been, Les wrapped her arms around the horse's neck and clung for dear life, struggling against powerful currents that plucked and snatched at her. An eternity elapsed before she felt Cactus's hooves strike solid ground, then they were coming up out of the water dripping on the muddy, trampled north bank, the steers struggling out of the river alongside her.

She waved her hat in the air and it was all she could do not to release a relieved and exuberant shout of triumph. Freddy twisted around in the saddle to give her a thumbs-up sign, then they drove forward, running the glistening cattle into the main herd.

Dal was waiting, grinning when he saw their wet clothing and wide smiles. He nodded to Les. "I know you're worried. Go back and watch Ward cross, then get your butt back here." He called to her before she was out of hearing. "Stay well downstream so you don't spook the herd."

She cut west and found a low spot with an unobstructed view. Slipping off Cactus, she walked to the edge of the boiling floodwaters to watch. In a way there was something beautiful about the steady stream of cattle coming down the bank and entering the water, the drovers beside them. Sunlight flashed on bobbing wet horns that appeared to float across the river. The water sparkled and hurled bubbles of foam into the air.

Then she saw Ward. He'd spotted her and was frowning angrily. By now he knew that none of the steers in her charge had drowned. She narrowed her gaze. By his hesitation at the edge of the raging waters, she could guess that he was having second thoughts about crossing on horseback. Dal had told him not to, but he'd stubbornly refused, insisting no one had the right to stop him. His mount backed away from the water, moved forward, backed away again. Pride would take him into the flood. He wouldn't ride away and choose the ferry, not after watching her cross. But she could see that he was frightened and regretting a foolish decision.

A great weariness settled on Les's shoulders as she thought ahead to the punishment she would face tonight. They had lost one steer to the quicksand and one to drowning and more would be lost before the crossing was accomplished, but none of the losses could be attributed to her. Ward would make sure she paid for that omission.

She had started to turn away, deciding she didn't want to watch him cross, when his horse reared and plunged into the tossing river. White-faced, Ward fell forward and grabbed the horse's neck even before the churning waters whirled up around his waist.

And then something happened in the middle of the floating horns. The center seemed to collapse as the animals there broke the line and spun into the downstream current. Gasping, Les stepped forward, smothering a scream. The horns swept toward Ward, struck him, and his horse sank beneath the surface. Thrashing in the water, unseated, he tried to grab at the horns around him. Then, he was tumbling in the violent currents, and all she could see were flashes of his arms and legs. Voices screamed on the shore, but Les didn't hear anything except the rush and roar of the river. The steers that had been swept out of the herd vanished beneath the waves, but Ward was struggling to swim, to break free from the deadly current and thrashing animals and angle toward the bank. He was whirling toward her.

His head bobbed above the surface about twenty feet from where she stood, and his eyes met hers. His mouth opened and he shouted something, but she couldn't hear. He stretched a hand toward her. Their gazes held as he sped abreast of her, then the current hurled him downriver and dragged him underwater. Dashing forward, Les scanned the turbulent surface and her heart slammed against her chest. Frantically, she searched for some glimpse of him, but there was nothing.

The greatest horror came when she looked down and saw her rope in her hands. She might have thrown him a lifeline, might have saved him, but she hadn't even tried.

CHAPTER 21

The Webster brothers found Ward's body two miles downstream from the point where the disaster occurred. Numb and dry-eyed, Les watched them bring him into camp, draped across the back of Caleb's horse.

Stumbling, she headed toward a clump of blackjack oak, feeling sick inside. The last thing she wanted was company, and her heart sank when she heard the creak of Alex's wheels.

"Peach and James are digging a grave," Freddy said, setting the brake on Alex's chair.

"Luther has agreed to say a few words. If there's anything you want, a special hymn . . ."

Freddy touched her cheek. "We're sorry for your loss, Les."

Hysteria choked her. "My loss," she repeated. Sinking to the ground, she buried her face in her hands. "I could have saved him, but I didn't." She kept remembering him reaching out to her. He would have seen the rope in her hands. "I just stood there and watched him drown."

Freddy placed an arm around her shoulders. "No one could have saved him, Les. He was lost the minute his horse went under."

Sobbing, she told them about the evening in the gully, about Caldwell's offer, about Ward's threats to kill her and the beatings she had endured. At the end, she lifted a tear-streaked face. "Don't you see? I hated him! When I saw his horse go under I was glad! All I thought about was me. That I was finally free. He wouldn't hit me ever again. I wouldn't have to marry him, wouldn't have to be afraid. And God help me, I was *glad!*" She stared at them. "What kind of monster am I?" she whispered.

Freddy studied the anguish in her eyes, then she silently rose and walked away, heading toward Grady's remuda.

Les thought her heart would break. Shoulders heaving with fresh sobs, she sagged against Alex's chair. "Do you hate me, too?"

Alex stroked her hair. "Freddy doesn't hate you. I don't know what she has in mind, but trust her."

They both looked toward the soft thud of hooves as Freddy rode toward them, leading Cactus. Wiping at her eyes, Les tried and failed to make sense of what she was seeing. Freddy wanted her to ride somewhere?

"Come on, Les," Freddy said firmly. "We have enough light left to try an experiment." She glanced at Alex. "I know what I'm doing."

Alex nodded and leaned forward, pushing Les to her feet. "Do as Freddy says."

Too wrung out to resist, Les swung up in her saddle. Riding with her head down, she didn't look up until she heard the roar of tossing violent water. "What is this?" she asked sharply, reining in. The river was the last place she wanted to be. "I'm going back."

"No, you aren't." Riding up beside her, Freddy grabbed the reins out of her hands and lead her to a low spot much like the place where she had stood motionless and let Ward die.

"Oh God." She didn't want to relive this. When Freddy tied up their horses, she refused to get out of the saddle. "Why are you doing this to me?"

Freddy looked up at her. "I'm going to walk upstream a ways, and I'm going to toss branches into the river. You stand at the edge of the water and try to hit the branches with your rope." Green eyes narrowed and flashed at her. "Get off that horse."

They stared at each other, both suddenly angry. "You always have the answers, don't you? You always have to make a drama out of every damned thing!"

"Do you want to spend the next twenty-five years like you've spent the first twenty-five? Feeling afraid and sorry for yourself? Poor Les, who everyone picks on. Poor Les, the monster who let her son-of-a-bitch fiancé drown without lifting a finger! Is that what you want? Do you get some kind of pleasure out of seeing yourself as a victim?"

"Shut up! Shut up!"

"Get down here. Show me you have the courage to discover the truth."

"I hate you! I don't have to show you anything!"

"Then show yourself! If you don't find out the truth, you'll lose everything you've gained. You'll go back to being the kind of woman who lets a man hit her. If you can't find a man to punish you, you'll punish yourself! Maybe you could have saved him, Les, and maybe you'll have to live with that. But I'm betting that you couldn't have done it, and you have nothing to blame yourself for." Turning on her bootheel, Freddy stalked away, pushing through the willows.

Crying, Les watched her go. When Freddy disappeared into the foliage, she climbed off her saddle with the intention of untying her horse and leaving. Then she saw the first branch go bobbing past in the river waters.

Frozen, she stood beside her horse and waited for the next branch. When she saw it rush by her, she dropped her head and felt the weight of the rope coiled on her hip. Did she have the courage to seek the truth? Did she want to know?

Freddy was out of sight and would never know the results. Only Les would know. Suddenly, urgently, she needed to learn if she could have saved him.

Taking the rope from her hip, her breath hot and fast, she made herself approach the water's edge. The next branch that came tossing and swirling in the foamy water, was closer than Ward had been and she believed it would be easy to lay the rope right on top of the wet leaves.

She was wrong. Her rope hit the water behind the branch, which had already swirled past her. Clutching the rope in sweaty hands, she waited for the next one. This time her throw landed short. By her seventh attempt, she understood she could not have saved him.

She gave it one more try, straining to anticipate the speed and power of the current. This time she came close. If she'd had the time to make a calculated judgment, if she could have practiced, if Ward had caught the rope at the precise moment, maybe . . . But there were too many ifs. In the end, Freddy was right. Ward had been doomed the instant his horse went under.

Her hands went limp and the rope played out through her fingers, dragged into the flood by the currents. She watched until it disappeared, then she ran crashing through the underbrush, shouting Freddy's name. When she found her, she threw herself into Freddy's arms. "Thank you! Oh, Freddy, thank you!"

Freddy held her and let her cry it out, then she eased back and smoothed a strand of hair off of Les's cheek. Finally she smiled. "If you're ready, let's ride back and watch them plant the son of a bitch. It's over, Les. You're free."

The trail wound north through the Indian Territory, over high, rolling prairies. Water was plentiful along heavily wooded streams, the grass thick and lush. Dal camped near Stinking Creek the first night after crossing the Red River.

As he rode into camp, he could see Monument Hill, a flat-topped mesa strewn with slabs and boulders of sandstone. Early trailblazers had marked this section of the Chisholm with red stones off the mesa, creating piles almost twelve feet tall.

After supper, he and Freddy walked out on the range, and he showed her the rocks. "The piles are about three hundred feet apart across this section of the trail," he explained. "Somewhere in one of those piles is a stone with my initials. Shall I carve yours?"

"Thank you." The setting sun bathed her tanned skin in tints of gold and orange. "And Alex's and Les's, too, if you don't mind."

Kneeling, he removed his knife and leaned over the soft sandstone. "How is Les holding up?" As he carved the initials, Freddy told him Les's story, and his face turned grim. "It worked out for the best," he said finally, standing away from the rocks.

Now that he'd folded his knife away and his hands were unoccupied, it was harder to be near her. He couldn't look at the smooth column of her throat without remembering where it led. Couldn't glance at her slender waist without recalling the delights above and below. When he saw the curve of her buttocks beneath her trousers, his palms grew moist. Desire was no stranger, but it had never been this consuming, this intense and constant.

Freddy held a wild daisy in her hand and plucked at the petals as she spoke. "How many beeves did we lose during the crossing?"

All day the drovers had been asking the same question, and each time the answer stuck in his throat. "Twenty-three." He did the math for her. "Our margin is down to seventy-one."

"Will that be enough?" she asked, raising eyes that looked like jade in the glow of sunset.

"I sure as hell hope so," he said thickly, staring at her mouth. Something about this woman and this woman alone sang to his mind and body, calling to him like the sirens of myth. When she looked at him a dozen emotions churned inside his chest. He wanted her, wanted her to admire him. He wanted to be twice the man he thought he was for her sake. He wanted to win the inheritance for her, wanted to slay a dragon and lay it at her feet. He wanted to put his brand on her for the world to see, wanted to hold her close and never let her go.

"When you look at me like that, I can't think," she whispered. The daisy fluttered from her fingers.

"We should go back," he said hoarsely.

"Is that what you want to do?"

A groan scraped his throat when he glimpsed the tip of her tongue. "I don't want to take advantage of you, Freddy. I don't want you to ever think I used you."

"I appreciate that." Then she surprised him by stepping close and winding her arms around his neck. "Now I need to know how offended you would be if I take advantage of you, and use you." A mischievous grin curved her beautiful lips.

For an instant he didn't think he'd heard her correctly. Then he laughed and pulled her roughly against his body. "I think I could put up with it." Cupping her buttocks, he held her close and let her feel what the touch of her did to him. Then he said what he had to before he lost control. "We want different things, Freddy, different lives. I can't promise you a future. Hell, I can't promise you anything."

"Just give me now," she murmured, lifting her lips.

When he kissed her, he forgot about everything except her body curving into his and the womanly scent and heat and sweetness of her. A deep hunger shook his body and mind, and he could not have stepped away from her if his life had depended on it.

They came together with fire and urgency, needing each other and the joy they could take and give. Wild with desire, they sank to the soft grass beneath the high pile of sandstone and tore at each other's clothing, frantic for the warm touch of smooth skin.

Dal told himself that he wanted to be gentle and tender with her, wanted to tell her all the things he could not say except through lingering caresses and long, slow kisses. But they had been too long apart, and the urgency to melt into each other ran at fever pitch.

They tore at each other's boots, then threw off shirts and trousers and fell backward in the grass, locked in each other's arms. He didn't notice the small rocks beneath his bare knees, didn't hear the distant notes of a harmonica drifting on the evening breeze. The only thing he saw were her eyes looking up at him, filled with desire and as green as the grass that surrounded her cloud of dark hair. All he heard was the music of their quick, ragged breath and the cadence of two hearts pounding as one.

When he entered her and felt her bare legs wrap around his waist, he paused and gasped and knew he would never come closer to heaven than he was this minute.

Later, Freddy lay in his arms, her fingers idly combing the hair on his chest. "When did it get dark?" she asked softly, laughing. "I didn't notice." After a moment she posed a serious question. "Dal? What will you do if we don't win?"

He pulled a long strand of dark hair across his throat, enjoying the silky feel on his skin, then he tightened his arms around her. "Maybe I'll go to Montana anyway. See if I can hire on somewhere. What would you do? Join up with an acting company?"

She was silent so long that he wondered if she had fallen asleep. "I've never told anyone this," she said finally. "I didn't return to Klees because I came to my senses or because Pa ordered me to return. I went home only because the Maestro sent me packing. I tried three different companies and—this is so hard to say—they all let me go."

She spoke so softly that he could hardly hear her although his ear was only inches from her lips. "I'm sorry, Freddy."

"Do you know what it's like to want something with all your heart, but know that you aren't any good at it?"

He had hoped she didn't know. Hearing her confide that she did hurt him inside. "Maybe the Maestros didn't recognize good acting when they saw it."

Leaning, she kissed him, then sat up and gazed into the darkness. "I'm good enough to act scenes for Peach and Drinkwater and the rest. But I'll never be good

enough to perform for a real paying audience." She
paused and her head dropped. "I wanted it so bad. I
loved the applause, and I pretended it was for me. But
it never was. It was for the other actors."

There was something so dejected and vulnerable in
the naked curve of her spine that his chest ached just
to look at her.

"Riding night watch gives a person a lot of time to
think," she said, tugging at the prairie grass. "I've been
fooling myself. Reading scripts and practicing scenes.
I'm never going to be a great actress." Her shoulders
collapsed, and she sat very still for a moment before
she reached for her shirt. "The best I can hope is that
we win and I can build a theater house. That way, at
least I'd be close to the stage and greatness. I don't
know what I'll do if we lose."

"You could come to Montana," he said lightly,
touching the back of her neck.

She arched her throat and leaned back against his
hand. "I saw snow once. I didn't like it much. I think
Montana is for you rough, tough cowboy types, not for
failed actresses." She didn't look at him. "Have you
ever thought of trying your luck in a place like San
Francisco?"

"What would a man like me do in a big city? All I
know is cattle and ranching." Gently, he turned her to
face him. "Freddy, I've listened to you recite around
the campfire, and I think you're a fine actress," he lied.
"Owning a theater is a good second choice, but maybe
you're giving up the dream too soon."

"Liar," she said softly, but he saw a glisten of gratitude in her moist eyes. "The worst of it was I shamed
my family, hurt my pa, ruined my reputation and destroyed my future, all for something I'm no good at."
A bitter smile curved her lips. "I wouldn't admit it,

even to myself. But this . . ." She waved a hand to include the land, the steers, the campfires, and the people around them. "It's all so real. There's no room for pretense out here. You can't hide in a role. The drive scrapes people down to their core and makes them take a hard look at what's inside."

He put his arms around her and held her close. "What's inside you is good, Freddy Roark. You don't have to pretend to be anyone else." Staring toward the range over her shoulder, he ground his teeth together and silently swore he would get two thousand cattle to Abilene if it killed him. She would have her grand theater in San Francisco.

It wasn't going to be easy. Last year, a party of Cheyenne had stampeded a herd of longhorns in the Indian Territory and made off with all of them. Later it came out that the trail boss had refused to give any beeves to the Indians who came into camp begging for meat. The raid had occurred in retaliation. The lesson? When begging Indians appeared, give them a steer. The next three weeks were going to seem endless.

So many steers were footsore that Dal announced they would rest the herd for two days beside the flooding Washita River and wait for the high water to subside. No one wanted a repeat of the Red River catastrophe. Fine tall grass swayed in a light breeze flowing down the Washita Valley. The water was clear and sweet, good for drinking, bathing, and washing clothes.

Freddy draped a wet shirt over the willows lining the red-clay banks, humming under her breath. It was amazing how a bath and clean clothing could improve a person's spirits.

She was smiling as she walked back to camp, but

her smile vanished when she noticed a tall Indian man and a boy. Slowing her steps, she watched Dal rope one of the footsore steers, and lead it toward the Indians, his expression tight. This was the third steer so far that the Cheyenne had demanded as tribute for crossing the territory.

What she saw next infuriated her. The man and the boy left camp, leading the steer, and Jack Caldwell followed. She could guess what Caldwell was saying to the Indian.

Fists clenched, she stormed onto the range, anger blazing in her eyes. She intercepted Jack as he was turning away from the Indians, a satisfied smile on his lips.

"If I were a man, I'd kill you," she said, spitting the words.

"Now, Fancy honey, why would you say a thing like that?" He smiled, his gaze lingering on the silky fall of hair that dropped almost to her waist. "You look beautiful today."

"Did you tell them to come every day and demand a steer? Did you tell him to send his friends here to beg for meat?" She knew that's what he had done. "You make me sick!"

Caldwell fell into step beside her as she whirled. "It's not too late, Fancy. The offer is open. You can come out of this with something to show for it."

"Even with all your cheating, at the last count we still had enough steers to win!"

"Why, darlin', you've cut me to the quick." Grinning, he placed a hand on his chest, then his expression sobered. "You aren't going to win." He grabbed her arm, but she shook off his hand. "I don't care about the others, but I'd hate to see you go through this ordeal, then end up with nothing." Stepping in front of her, he touched her face. "I can't get you out of my mind."

Freddy slapped his hand away. "Don't touch me," she warned, letting him see the frost in her eyes. "I have no feeling for you. None. You don't want to know what I think of you."

"If you're betting on Frisco, you're putting your money on the wrong man."

"I'm putting my money on the best man," she snapped. "I love him."

It was the first time she'd spoken the words aloud and they rang in her ears. Surprise stiffened her shoulders, then her body relaxed. Fighting a fact didn't make it less true. But admitting something she'd been trying to ignore didn't make her happy either. Her gaze swung toward the remuda, where Grady and Dal were talking. Loving him complicated everything.

"By Wichita, the inheritance will have been decided," Caldwell said. "Let me tell Lola that you've earned the money we're offering you."

Putting all her strength into it, she slapped him as hard as she could. Then she spit on the ground, sorry she missed his boots. "That's my answer."

From there, she went directly to Luther and told him her suspicions. "He might even have suggested a raid," she said bitterly. "Luther, you *know* Jack and Lola are cheating!"

"I happen to agree with you," he admitted. "Did you actually hear Caldwell suggest anything to the Indian?"

"No," she conceded, her heart sinking.

Luther spread his hands in a gesture of frustration. "Then all we have is more speculation. Caldwell may or may not have deliberately arranged for the loss of several cattle. And he may or may not have done so with Mrs. Roark's knowledge."

"Several? Luther, Jack is directly responsible for the loss of well over a hundred steers! The number is approaching two hundred!"

After examining her expression, he kicked a rock. "I'm supposed to be impartial, Freddy, but I'm not. I want to see you and Les and Alex win what I think is your rightful inheritance. If there was the slightest proof that Mrs. Roark and Caldwell are cheating as we all believe, I'd disqualify her this fast." He snapped his fingers.

"I know you would," she admitted with a sigh. "Damn, cheaters aren't supposed to win!"

"They haven't won yet," he reminded her firmly.

But the contest was over in Jack's mind. By the time they passed through the Indian Territory and entered Kansas, Jack believed Lola would be a clear winner. He'd make sure of it.

Before she headed for the remuda, she placed a hand on Luther's sleeve. Like all of them, he had changed during the trip. "This is none of my business, but I'm going to say it anyway. You let Les get away once. Don't do it again. She didn't love Ward, and she's not grieving his death."

His brow lifted and he stared. "Ward was . . . surely you must be wrong."

"I'm not. Ask her."

"I couldn't inquire about something that personal, it's none of my . . ." Biting off the words, he studied her face and a red tide spread from his ears to his throat. "I'm too old for Les. Too dull and set in my ways. She couldn't possibly be . . ."

Freddy rolled her eyes. Men were the most exasperating creatures in creation. "Why don't you let Les decide? Maybe you'll be happily surprised. I can tell you this. A faint heart never won a fair maiden." As usual, she couldn't recall the quotation exactly. "Things haven't changed so much that Les is going to come courting you. You'll have to make the first move."

Feeling his thoughtful stare on her back as she walked away, she found Dal and Grady and repeated her suspicions about Jack's latest ploy.

Grady threw his hat on the ground. "This ain't right! Did you tell Luther?"

"He can't do anything without proof," she said, speaking to Grady but watching Dal.

She loved the bronzed hard look of him, the ice in his eyes when he swung to look toward the observers' camp. She loved his rough brown hands and graceful wiry body. Loved the way his pants hung low on his hips, loved the purposeful way he moved. She loved his determination and the way he expected the best from the people around him. She loved everything about him.

"When you look at me like that, I can't think," he said gruffly, after Grady stomped away.

"You have changed my life," she whispered, staring up at him, marveling at the truth of it.

He had taken three pampered, self-absorbed butterflies and molded them into efficient, competent women. He had demanded they be the best they could be and refused to accept anything less. He'd shown them their abilities and courage, had stripped them to basic values that none of them had examined before this drive. Win or lose, when they rode into Abilene, she and her sisters would be stronger, more confident, and better equipped for life than they would have been without Dal Frisco.

"I love you," she said softly, drowning in his eyes.

She had never dreamed that she would say those words standing beside two dozen smelly horses, sweating in the hot prairie sun. And she had imagined the man would say them first.

He stared at her, his hands opening and closing at his sides, "Damn it, Frederick, you just wrecked my life."

"By telling you that I love you?" Stung, she blinked hard. "I'm not asking anything in return, if that's what you're worrying about. No promises, remember?" Embarrassed and angry, she started to back away, wishing to hell that she'd kept her impulsive mouth shut.

"No promises? The hell there aren't. Loving never comes without promises." Gripping her arms, he leaned forward. "If you hadn't said what you just said, I could have ridden away and told myself that you and me weren't meant to be. Maybe I would have believed it someday. Now I've got to figure out how to mesh two incompatible dreams in a way that won't make one or both of us miserable for the rest of our lives. And frankly, I'm not convinced that's possible."

She returned his scowl. "You don't have to figure out anything. Pardon me for wrecking your life and creating a problem. Just forget I said a word. Stupid me. I thought it might make you happy to know that I love you!"

"You come sashaying over here and tell me the damned Indians are going to strip away our margin one beeve at a time, then right out of the blue you say, by the way I love you." He glared into her blazing eyes. "Now that's a hell of a thing. You couldn't do this at a more appropriate time, could you? When I'm not worried half to damned death about the Indians and crossing the Washita, or when we could talk about this without the whole outfit watching."

Jerking away from his grip, she tossed her head and lifted her chin. "There's nothing to talk about! I changed my mind. I'd have to be an idiot to love someone like you."

Blinking rapidly, she headed to the river and the willows strewn with her clothing, intending to cry in private. By the time she reached the swollen banks of the Washita, she'd reviewed every word of their conversation and reached a startling conclusion.

Dal loved her, too.

She gazed at the sparkling water foaming past the tips of her boots, then lifted her face to a hot sky as blue as his eyes. He hadn't said it as clearly as she had, but he'd said it.

But the way he had said it checked the joy that suddenly warmed her body.

Sitting down on the red bank, she drew up her knees and watched the tossing water. Dal was right. A theater in San Francisco didn't mesh with a ranch in Montana and never would. One of them would have to surrender his or her dream. If that happened . . . how long would it be before resentment began to chip away at love? Before regret and misery set in? A year? Two years?

A tear dropped on her knee. The misery was already starting.

As the days slipped past, Alex believed that John would begin to understand and accept that she would never wear the wooden leg. Each morning she awoke with her heart in her throat, wondering if today was the day she would discover he had slipped away during the night and was gone. When she found him after a frantic scan of the camp, she closed her eyes and thanked God for one more day with him.

Sometimes discovering that he hadn't left her filled her heart with so much emotion that she ached with pain. And sometimes she threw out her hands and laughed at the frustrating discovery that John was as stubborn as she was.

But things had changed between them. By unspoken agreement, they had not sought to repeat their night of lovemaking, and John had borrowed a horse from the remuda. He no longer rode in the wagon with her.

He still sat with her every evening, and they talked softly in the warm darkness, discussing the day's events, filling in their history for each other. John's thoughts had turned to the future, and occasionally he spoke of establishing a medical practice back East, of building a home, of reentering the world.

"How will you afford such things?" Alex asked, inhaling the scent of his cigar and a hint of the aloe paste he'd rubbed on Freddy's sunburn. He never mentioned her in his plans for the future, and she was grateful for his consideration. But the omission also broke her heart and made her feel as if she were strangling.

"My father was a prudent man. Long before others began to predict the South would end in ruin, my father had shifted his fortune to Northern banks and investments and advised me to do the same." He stubbed out his cigar and took her hand. "Does it surprise you to learn that I'm wealthy?"

Alex blinked hard at the lanterns glowing on the sides of the chuck wagon, then she dropped her head and lifted a hand to her forehead. She knew what he was telling her. Even if they failed to deliver two thousand cattle in Abilene, she would never have to worry about money again. If only. If only she could forget the husband she had killed and the debt she owed him. If only she could strap on a wooden leg and pretend that the carriage accident had never happened, pretend that she was blameless and deserving of a life with John. But she couldn't.

"Why won't you ride in the chuck wagon with me?" she whispered. She missed him like she missed her leg, the loss an empty space inviting despair.

He raised his knees and wrapped his arms around them, turning his face toward the drovers singing around the campfire. "I used to think about all the boys who died in my medical tent. I saw their faces in the clouds and reflected in the rivers, and I flogged myself that I hadn't been able to save them. I remembered every bloody body, every failure. And when that pain became familiar, I thought about my father and my son and told myself I could have gotten them out of Atlanta if only I'd been smart enough not to get captured by the Union."

His grey eyes turned to her and softened. "And then one day, I met a beautiful courageous woman. Your touch was the first soft thing I'd experienced in years, my love. And you were the first person in years to look at me and see a man instead of an eccentric husk." He took her trembling hand between both of his. "A man—or a woman—cannot change the past or live in it. Eventually the moment comes when it is time to put on one's clothing and move toward the future." She stared at him, knowing his definition of clothing was broad enough to include a wooden leg.

"You helped me recognize that moment. I hoped I could do the same for you."

"Oh, John. Don't you understand that meeting you has made me question everything in my life?" She'd never been as confused or as profoundly disturbed. Before John strode into her life, she had accepted her obligation to Payton and her punishment. Her decision never to walk again had not changed, but loving John made accepting her penance so hard.

"I love you, Alex," he said quietly, gazing into her eyes. "I want to spend my life with you. But I won't share our life with Payton Mills. And this chair," he touched the hard rubber rim of the wheel, "is your shrine to Payton and the suffering you think you owe him. The day you put the chair away, I'll know you have chosen the future instead of the past."

"And if that day never comes?" she whispered.

His eyes closed briefly, then he brought her hand to his lips. "I will spend the rest of my life seeing your face in the clouds and in the morning mist. I'll hear your voice in the breeze, and I'll grieve for what might have been." He kissed her palm, then pressed it to his cheek.

After he pushed her back to camp, they gazed at each other in silence, not needing words to express their pain. Alex understood that he was waiting for her to make a decision. But she had made that decision the night Payton died.

Blinded by tears, she almost ran into Freddy as she rolled through the darkness toward her bedroll. "I'm sorry," she murmured, dashing a hand across her eyes. "I didn't see you."

Freddy stood in front of her, hands on her hips, a frown tugging her lips. "I can't stand it another minute. Every person in this outfit helped make your new leg, and every one of us comes to breakfast every day expecting to see you standing there without your crutch. I can't begin to count how many hours John worked on that leg. We all did. So why aren't you wearing it?"

"You know why." She placed her hands on the wheels of the chair. "Please let me pass."

"You aren't going to wear it?" Freddy's eyebrows

rose and she stared. "Is that why you and John are fighting?"

"We aren't fighting." She should have known everyone in camp would notice that John no longer rode with her in the wagon, would feel the tension between them.

"Alex, for God's sake. John loves you, and you love him. Put on that leg, and—"

"If you don't step aside, so help me, Freddy, I'll run over you. Tell everyone I appreciate what they tried to do, and I'm sorry their effort was wasted." For a long moment she and Freddy stared at each other, then Freddy swore and walked away into the darkness.

Alex sagged in her chair and closed her eyes, rubbing her ring finger. Her wedding ring was gone, but she still felt it squeezing her finger and her spirit like a manacle tethered to Payton Mills and the obligation she owed him.

As Freddy had predicted, the Indians came every day. Frustrated and feeling helpless, Dal gave them a beeve, sometimes two, depending on the size of the begging party. It was never enough. They followed the herd, demanding tribute during daylight hours, coming like ghosts in the night to steal more cattle while the camp slept. He doubled the night watch, cut himself to two hours of sleep, and still the Indians slipped in and out, taking two or three steers every night.

"I don't know how they do it," he said wearily, clamping his hands around his coffee cup. The embers of the fire cast rusty shadows across the sober faces of the drovers.

"What's our margin now?" Les asked anxiously, looking at him across the fire pit.

"Thirty-one." A hissing sound went around the fire

as everyone sucked in a breath. He felt Freddy's eyes on his face and looked up to meet her gaze. "Here's the problem. If we don't give the Indians a beeve when they come begging, they might attack and steal half the herd."

"They're stealing us blind anyway," Freddy said.

The drovers nodded. "If the Indians attack, we'll drive 'em off," Peach stated firmly.

Dal examined the faces around the campfire. "People get killed in Indian raids."

Caleb Webster laid a hand on the butt of his six-shooter. "So do Indians, boss. I say we take our chances. Maybe one of the Indians will put an arrow in that card fanner's chest."

The animosity toward Caldwell had begun long before they'd reached the Indian Territory and had hardened during the last weeks. There wasn't a man in the outfit who didn't bitterly blame Jack Caldwell for shrinking the margin. Dal knew his men and he knew every one had rejected Caldwell's offer of corruption and every one of them had come to admire the Roark sisters.

"All right," he said, standing up. "We're agreed. We won't give away any more longhorns. We can't stop the night raids, and we'll lose a few more before we get out of the territory. So let's pick up the pace and get this herd to Kansas as fast as we can. We'll ride sunup to sundown." He waited until the men nodded before he left the campfire.

A consistent twenty-mile-a-day pace would result in saddle-weary drovers and footsore longhorns and horses, but he had no real choice. Thirty-one. The number ran through his mind waking and asleep.

He knew when Freddy came up behind him. Without a word, she slipped her arms around his waist and pressed her cheek against his back. Her presence wasn't enough to end his frustration, but he felt himself relax against her.

"I thought you weren't having anything to do with me," he said gruffly. Her arms around him felt so damned good. He'd missed making love to her during the last two weeks, but more than that, he'd missed talking to her and just being with her.

"I wrecked your life, remember?" she murmured against his spine.

"Yeah, you have," he said, covering her hands at his waist with his own.

"So of course I've been ignoring you. Why should I want to be with a man whose life is wrecked?" She pressed her breasts against his back and adjusted her cheek on his shoulder.

"If I were you, I wouldn't. When I haven't been worrying about Indians, I've been worrying about you. We can't work this out, Freddy. There's nothing long-term here, and short-term isn't honorable." She snuggled closer to him, and her warmth made the stars seem brighter and the night better. Damn, he'd missed her.

"One of your worst qualities is making decisions for other people," she murmured. "I'll decide what's right for me. And I've decided to take what I want even if it is short-term."

He owed her better than that, but he couldn't find a solution. A hundred times a day he thought about her saying she loved him, and it started a fire in his belly because he wanted a future with her, but he couldn't see any way to have it. No matter what happened in Abilene, they were headed in opposite directions.

Pulling her around in front of him, he told her his conclusions. "I took something I had no right to take, and I've gone on taking it because I couldn't stop myself." She was so beautiful in the starlight, she took his breath away. "Then you said what you said, and I had to take a look at what I was doing. I've done you wrong, Freddy. That's why I've been keeping my distance."

She pushed his hands away and stepped up close to his body, resting her head on his chest. "Dal? Are you ever going to say the words?"

The touch of her ignited his blood and incinerated his resolve to stay away from her. His arms came around her, and he buried his face in her hair. "Oh, hell. I love you," he murmured hoarsely. "Damn it, Freddy, we have to stop this. A man doesn't bed a woman when they both know he can't do right by her." He'd been over and over it in his mind. He'd never go to San Francisco. She'd never go to Montana.

"We don't have much time left," she whispered, lifting her hands to the buttons on his shirt. "Right now, I love you, and you love me. For the moment, nothing else matters."

When she lifted her lips and breathed his name, his good intentions fled. His arms tightened around her, and he kissed her hard, trying to tell her with his hands and body that saying good-bye to her was going to be the hardest thing he ever did.

They were naked and in each other's arms when a dozen painted horses galloped between them and the herd. Startled, hearts pounding, they jumped to their feet, swearing and grabbing for their clothing.

"Indians!" Freddy shouted toward the camp.

But the warning came too late. The Indians fired their rifles in the air, and an instant later the herd was in full stampede.

CHAPTER 22

The contest was over. The inheritance had been decided.

After conferring, Dal and Luther returned to the main camp where everyone had assembled. Caldwell staggered behind, wearing a gloating expression, but he didn't speak. If Caldwell had uttered a single word of self-congratulation, Dal would have killed him. He wouldn't have been able to stop himself.

The herd was grazing now, but it had been a long night. No one had slept. The sun had climbed well into the sky before they finished rounding up the scattered steers and took a count.

Habit carried Dal to the coffeepot above the fire and he poured a cup before he looked at the worried faces watching him. His gaze rested a moment on Freddy's weary expression, and his chest tightened with bitterness. She would never have her grand theater in San Francisco, would never stand in the wings close to her dream. Maybe Luther would declare his obvious feelings for Les, or maybe he wouldn't. Maybe Alex would bury the past and accept John, or maybe she couldn't. He didn't know what would happen to them.

He squared his shoulders then cleared his throat.

"The good news is that no one got killed or seriously injured. The bad news is that the Indians stole forty-two steers. During the stampede, five beeves drowned, and one was lost in quicksand. Two broke their legs, and we had to put them down." His jaw clamped so tightly it was an effort to speak. "That's fifty. The herd now numbers 1979."

A soft sighing sound whispered through the camp as breaths released and heads dropped. Someone said, "Son of a bitch!" Another voice protested, "It aint fair!"

"We oughta walk away right now," Grady snapped. He threw a bitter look at Jack Caldwell. "These aint our beeves anymore. Why should we take 'em in for the widow? I say we just turn 'em out on the range and ride away."

"I've never abandoned a herd, and I'm not going to start now." Turning the herd loose wouldn't hurt Lola or Jack, wouldn't affect the outcome. But it would place a stain on the reputation of every man in the outfit, and Dal owed his drovers more than that. Raising a hand, Dal kneaded the tension in his shoulder. "We're about two and a half weeks out of Abilene. Let's get those beeves moving."

Silently the drovers filed past him, dropped their coffee cups into Alex's wreck pan, then headed for the remuda to saddle up. They flung black glares toward Caldwell and cursed his name. Drinkwater and Caleb spit in front of his boots.

On her way to the horses, Freddy stopped in front of Dal and stroked his cheek. "It's not your fault," she said softly. Les pressed his hand and nodded. "You did everything you could."

Standing next to Alex's chair, he watched them mount, then ride toward the herd. When Alex took his hand, he frowned down at her. "No man could have done more than you did, and no man could have done it better. You aren't to blame." She gave him a little push. "Go on now. They need you at the river."

He watched Freddy and Les riding toward the drag, felt Alex's hand in his. It was one of the worst moments in his life.

Needing some time alone, he rode out on the range where he could see the herd beginning to move out, and he dropped his head and rubbed a hand down his face.

Like the gracious, honorable women they were, each of the sisters had offered *him* a word or a touch of comfort. They hadn't wept, hadn't blamed. They hid their despair and accepted their defeat with grace. He hoped Joe Roark was watching today, and he hoped the bastard was proud of the strong fine women he'd raised. Sons could not have done better than his daughters had done, couldn't have worked harder or given more.

Raging inside, he lashed his reins across the buckskin and cantered toward the river. The crossing proceeded as smooth as glass, and they didn't lose a single beeve.

It didn't matter anymore.

In the following days, they forded the Salt Fork and Pond Creek, passed large colonies of prairie dogs, and once they had to hold the longhorns while a herd of buffalo ran west across the trail. Tomorrow they would enter Kansas below Bluff Creek and Fall Creek.

"Are we finished with Indians?" Les asked Grady as she pulled her saddle off Cactus.

"Might see some Osage, but mostly they'll ask for

tobacco. Sometimes they'll beg a steer, but mostly the Osage got more pride than those thieving Comanche." He spit in disgust.

"If they need the meat, we might as well give them a beeve or two." Now that the cattle were Lola's, she could be generous. The thought raised a bitter smile.

"Well, gol-dang. Look what's coming your way, Missy."

Les placed her saddle on the ground, then stood up, rubbing her hands on her trousers.

Luther strode toward her with a grimly determined expression and a bouquet of wildflowers clutched in his hand. But it was a Luther that Les hadn't seen before. His hair was slicked back with oil, he was clean-shaven, and he wore a dark suit, vest, and tie. His hat was brushed and his boots polished.

"A man don't get all slickered up like that unless he's coming a-courting," Grady said. "You got to ask yourself if that's the worst sunburn you ever seen, or if he's feeling mighty nervous."

"Go away," Les said, feeling nervous herself. She had hoped he would come to her, but she'd begun to think it wouldn't happen. "Help Alex or cut some firewood but go away." She had time to knock the dust off her pants and smooth her hair before he reached her.

"Here." Removing his hat, Luther thrust out the wildflowers. "These are for you."

"Thank you." As far as she knew, there wasn't a vase within twenty miles of camp. "You look very nice tonight." Her comment brightened the red pulsing on top of his ears.

"So do you," he said, looking at her.

Les doubted it. She was dusty, sweat-stained, and sunburned. She needed a bath and a hair wash. This moment would have been better if she'd been wearing a nice dress with her hair curled and a tiny packet of violet sachet pinned inside her corset. Instead, she wore a sun-faded shirt with a hole at the elbow and pants smeared across the thigh with horse slobber.

Luther pulled at his collar. "Would you do me the honor of joining me for a short stroll before supper? There's a prairie-dog town not far from here which you might find entertaining."

He was so Sunday perfect while she smelled of horseflesh and cowhide and a day's labor. At least she could wash her face and hands. "Would you give me a moment first?"

He looked stricken. "I'm sorry. I . . . of course you need to think about this. I should have inquired before I . . . damn, I'm no good at this." He started to back away. "I apologize. I didn't mean to impose."

Instinct warned that Luther would approach once and once only, and that it had taken enormous courage to bring him this far. If she let him walk away, he would not return.

"Luther . . ." Crimson rushed into her cheeks as she marshaled her own courage. "I think I have loved you since I was fourteen or fifteen years old."

"I can see this is an inconvenient . . ." He stopped and stared at her. "What did you say?"

"I didn't think you noticed me. I thought you brought me books and talked to me because I was the silly young daughter of your client. You called on Pa, not me. You didn't dance with me at socials, didn't invite me for a ride in your buggy." Stepping up to him, she tucked her arm through his and turned him toward the prairie-dog village. He looked dazed. She was a little dazed herself. "So I stopped hoping you might be a suitor, stopped thinking about you."

"You couldn't be more wrong," he said, staring down at her. "I invented reasons to call on your father so I could see you. I wanted to dance with you, but I'm so poor at it I thought you would refuse me. Les, I can't remember a time when I didn't love you."

She faced him, sudden tears glistening in her eyes. She had waited a lifetime to hear a man say those words to her. No, she had waited for Luther to say those words. Until Freddy opened her eyes, she'd considered her feelings for him so hopeless that she had pushed them far far away. Eventually, she had turned elsewhere and had almost made the worst mistake of her life.

Gazing at each other in amazed delight, they stood on the prairie, their hands lightly touching. "Oh, Luther. I'm so happy." And then began the rush of lover's questions.

"When did you first know . . . ?"

"How could I not have guessed?"

"What if . . . ?"

"I almost spoke that time you . . . "

And suddenly it was dark. Supper had come and gone, the drovers had drifted to their bedrolls. And still they had not said all there was to say. Les suspected they never would.

Blazing with surprise and happiness, feeling the rightness of him, of them, she clasped his hands and gazed into the love shining in his eyes. "Luther? Are you ever going to kiss me?" The brazenness of the question shocked her, then she let it go. She was not the same timid, unsure girl she had been before this journey. A woman had replaced that girl, a woman who knew what she wanted and was not afraid to reach for it.

Grinning, he pulled her close. He kissed her tenderly, gently, as if she were a fragile porcelain creature who might shatter if he applied too much pressure. When he eased back, anxiously scanning her face, Les sighed. She was going to have to lead him every step of the way. Rising on tiptoe, she wound her arms around his neck, pressed her body hard against his, and kissed him with all the fire and passion she had been saving for a lifetime. This time when their lips parted, he looked stunned. But only for a moment. His hands tightened on her waist then slid to her buttocks and he caught her up against him. When his lips crushed hers, his kiss was as passionate as she had dreamed, a kiss like none other she had ever received.

Breathless and feeling her heart beating hard against her chest, she blinked. "I think we're getting the hang of this."

Laughing, he folded her into his arms and pressed her against his heart. "Say you'll marry me, Les, I beg you. I want this to be the shortest courtship on record. I've waited long enough."

Easing back in his arms, she lifted her fingertips to his lips. "Luther, will you ever wonder if I accepted you because we lost the contest, and I had no way to support myself?"

"Is that why?"

"No. I want to marry you because I love you."

He cupped her face between his hands. "Oh, my dearest. Then you *will* marry me, and make me the happiest man on earth?"

"Oh yes," she said, laughing and throwing her arms around him. "Yes, yes, yes!"

Someday she would tell him about Ward. What their relationship had been, and all that had happened. But not now. Tonight was for love and the wonder of discovery.

An hour before dawn she stumbled toward her bedroll, and as she sat down to jerk off her boots, she suddenly remembered her shift on night watch. With a
guilty start, she began to rise, then Freddy pushed up
from her pillow and squinted at her.

"I took your shift," she muttered sleepily. "Are you
still a virgin?"

Shocked, Les stared at her. "Of course! You are so
vulgar, Freddy."

"Too bad," Freddy said, dropping back on her pillow. "About the virgin part, I mean."

Laughing softly, Les crawled into her blankets and
smiled up at the fading stars. Freddy's rude question
kept returning to her mind, making her feel warm all
over and remember Luther's kisses. He was right. The
wedding needed to be very soon. Perhaps in Abilene.

"Pa?" she whispered, looking up at the velvety sky.
"Thank you. This cattle drive is the best gift you ever
gave me." She'd found something far better than an
inheritance. She'd found herself. And her sisters. And
Luther.

"You know," Freddy said, striding up to the chuck-
wagon table. She slid her noon plate into the wreck pan
and watched Alex cut chunks of meat for their supper
stew. "I used to think you were smart."

"Is that right?" Alex asked drily. "So what happened to change your mind?"

"The stupid way you're behaving. For a person who
has to be right all the time, you're wrong about a lot of
things. Maybe it's time you thought about that."

Alex looked up from her worktable and frowned in
surprise. This was a familiar argument with roots twisting into their childhood. She'd believed this hard jour-

ney had changed her relationship with her sisters and laid to rest old conflicts. "What are you talking about?"

Freddy lifted a hand and ticked down her fingers. "Here's a few of the things you've been wrong about just since you returned to Texas. You were wrong when you insisted that you didn't need to know how to shoot a weapon. You were wrong about Les loving Ward. You were wrong not to interfere when we heard Ward slap Les."

"You didn't interfere either!" she said, feeling a flush of embarrassment rise on her cheeks.

"We're not talking about me. You were wrong every time you said, 'I can't do this.' You were wrong when you thought you were going to die in the stampede. You were wrong about that, too," Freddy said, nodding at the crutch leaning against the worktable.

She put down her knife and wiped her hands on her apron. "So I've been mistaken about a few things," she snapped. "What's your point?"

"First, let's talk about the past. You were wrong to go chasing after Payton, and wrong to pretend it was a marriage made in heaven. You were wrong to insist on going to that party and wrong to urge the carriage driver to drive faster in the rain."

"How dare you!" she said furiously, her voice low and shaking. Heat burned on her cheeks and her hands trembled badly.

Freddy leaned forward with narrowed eyes. "You're wrong about a lot of things, Alex. So what the hell makes you think it's the right decision to give up John, a good future, and, instead, sit down in that clumsy, confining wheelchair and live the rest of your life as a miserably unhappy recluse?"

"Shut up!" Shaking so badly that she feared she

would fall, she reached for the crutch and slipped it under her arm. "You . . . you . . ."

Freddy waved an angry hand toward the drovers sitting on the grass eating their noon meal. "Every man in this outfit worked on that wooden leg, Alex. And every one of them thinks you're wrong not to wear it. But you think you're right. Now, why is that? Do you prefer to feel crippled and helpless? Does it feel good to be dependent and imagine that strangers feel sorry for you? Because that's the only reason I can think of to explain why you're being so stupid."

Alex gasped. The blood drained from her face and pain tightened her chest. "Why are you saying these hurtful things?" she whispered. She had believed that she and Freddy were friends now, that they cared about each other.

"You think you killed Payton. You're wrong about that. But you *are* hurting a good man who loves you. Is that what you stand for, Alex? Is it right to sacrifice yourself for a dead man, but cause a living man pain? John turned himself inside out for you. He faced his past and put it behind him, because he loves you. But you won't do that for him, will you? Is guilt easier to live with than love? Is it easier to make a prison out of that damned chair than to strap on your leg and take two steps toward the man you told me you love?" Her lip curled. "I looked up to you, Alex. I thought you had courage. I never thought you'd throw away your life just to prove that you're right, and that's really what this is all about."

"You don't know what the hell you're saying!" she shouted, fury blazing in her eyes.

"Wrong again," Freddy said quietly. She reached for Alex's hand, then dropped her arm when Alex jerked back. "You aren't going to let John walk away because of some deranged need to punish yourself for Payton's death. That isn't the reason. If you retreat to that chair, it will be because you can't admit that you made the wrong decision when you decided to spend the rest of your life atoning for another wrong decision."

"Get out of here and leave me alone!" She was shaking violently, so angry that she was stuttering.

"In a few days we're going to ride into Abilene and John is going to get on the train and you'll never see him again." Freddy grabbed her hand, and this time she wouldn't let Alex shake her loose. "You can go with him. Or you can spend the rest of your life regretting two wrong decisions. Payton's death and rejecting John. Think about it, Alex, and think fast. Time is running out."

Tears of pain, outrage, and fury blurred Freddy's form as she walked toward the remuda. Alex wanted to scream at her, throw something, say something, but she was so deeply upset and furious that she couldn't speak or move. When she regained a semblance of control, she dropped into her wheelchair and shoved savagely at the wheels, lurching out onto the grassy prairie. Facing away from camp, she dropped her head and buried her face in her hands, gulping deep breaths and shaking. Finally, she made herself think about what Freddy had said.

And, oh God, Freddy was right.

She had been wrong about so many, many things, had made so many bad decisions.

Staring at the vast space in front of her, she thought about her life. And in the end she understood that she had been deceiving herself. Confining herself to a wheelchair wasn't an attempt to atone for Payton's death; it went deeper than that. She was running away from past mistakes and the fear of making more in the future. Not Payton, but pride and fear would make a recluse of her. Her punishment was not for setting in motion a chain of events that had led to her husband's death and the loss of her leg. Her punishment was for all the wrong decisions.

Shrinking into her chair, she hugged her arms around her trembling body.

Less was expected from a woman in a wheelchair. There were fewer opportunities to make wrong decisions. Her chair was safe and familiar, a shield between her and a world full of expectations and wrong decisions that could lead to disastrous consequences.

But she loved him. She loved him so much that it was tearing her apart.

Covering her face, sitting alone on the prairie, she wept until no more tears came.

It was easy to be right. But it took courage to live with mistakes, with being wrong. Alex didn't know if she possessed the courage to take that kind of risk again.

Time was running out.

They crossed the Chikaskia River, Slate Creek, the Ninnescah, and camped alongside the Arkansas River outside Wichita, Kansas.

Like all the boom towns along the trail, Wichita was wide-open with more saloons and gambling halls than churches or harness shops. Strung out along a bluff overlooking the wide, shallow Arkansas, Wichita was a good place to fatten weary stock on lush sedge grass and provision the outfit for the last push into Abilene.

Dal crossed his arms atop the pommel and let his shoulders slump as he watched Jack Caldwell canter toward town and a rendezvous with Lola. Lola was going to be very happy today. The injustice of it stuck in his craw like bitter fruit.

Clicking his tongue, he urged his horse into a circle around the King's Walk herd, warning himself not to count the longhorns, but he did. And each time the number came up the same. Acid poured into his stomach, and he ground his teeth.

He knew Lola, and he'd recognized Caldwell for what he was. From the beginning he had known they would cheat. He had *known* this, but hadn't been able to stop it. He had been counting on Emile Julie to arrive, kill Lola, and solve his problems.

For the rest of his sorry life he was going to blame himself that the Roark sisters had not won their father's inheritance. He'd let them down, and he'd let Joe down. Dal couldn't believe that Joe had wanted Lola to have his ranch, his stock, and all his holdings. Joe had gone to his final reward hoping his daughters would inherit their birthright. Wanting it to happen that way.

They would have if Dal had been better and smarter.

By the time the sun set, he was as low as he'd ever been. He had failed in every way a man could fail. He'd failed the woman he loved, he hadn't done the job he was hired to do, and he had failed himself.

Damn, he needed a drink. The craving gnawed at him, turned his mouth as dry as a desert floor. What the hell did it matter now if he found some relief? He'd fallen as far as he could. What was one more failing?

Without a word to anyone, he rode away from his herd and headed for the lights of town.

The saloons were crowded, but he'd expected that. Several herds camped along the Arkansas, and the cowboys were spending their wages and cutting up along Main. Eventually, he found a saloon that wasn't as jammed as the others, took a stool at the bar, and ordered a whiskey.

The hot pungent aroma strung his nostrils and he swallowed hard, gripping the shot glass and a promise of oblivion. He inhaled deeply, anticipating the long burn followed by an explosion of heat in his belly. One shot wouldn't be enough, it never was. Escape required a bottle, maybe two. Surrender would be costly and would take most of the night.

Turning the whiskey glass between his fingers and staring down at the surface, he thought about that. Giving up. Worse than giving up was acknowledging himself as a quitter. If he swallowed this whiskey as his mind screamed at him to do, then the drive wouldn't end at Abilene, it ended right here. He ended right here.

One swallow, he thought. That's all it would take, and his problems dissolved. He looked at his fingers straining around the glass and saw the future. He'd smuggle some bottles back to camp. He'd be drunk when the herd entered Abilene. That way, the count wouldn't matter. It wouldn't matter when Freddy walked away from him. He wouldn't give a damn that he'd failed to stop Lola and Jack or that he had quit when it looked like he was beaten. Nothing would matter, not the past, the present, or the future. And he wouldn't matter, not even to himself.

Raising the glass to the light, he contemplated the golden promise inside. Surrender.

It was that, or . . . keep fighting. Refuse to give up.

He still had a week. The contest wasn't lost until the longhorns were counted by the officials in Abilene. Unless he took the first swallow. Then, he was beaten.

He slammed the shot glass down on the bar. Lola was not going to win. It wasn't over yet. Disgusted that he had skirted so close to ruin, he turned his back to the bar.

That's when he spotted her, dressed to the nines, sashaying through the saloon doors with a fancy man on her arm whose most interesting feature was that he was not Jack Caldwell. Lola saw Dal the instant he saw her. Leaning to the ear of her escort, she whispered something then walked toward Dal, swinging her hips.

"Well, well, if it isn't my favorite cowboy," she said with a gloating smile. "Bartender? I'm a rich woman now and I want to buy this puncher a drink. Give us both a whiskey."

"Where's Caldwell?"

"Him?" Her husky laugh turned a few heads. "Why, Dal honey, Jack didn't work out. You can tell Luther that I fired Jack as my representative. Now that my prospects have improved, I don't need a two-bit gambler helping me spend my money."

He hooked his elbows on the bar and regarded her with interest. "You always planned to double-cross him, didn't you?"

"That's such a harsh way to put it, honey." She tossed back the whiskey and signaled the bartender for another. "Let's just say Jack's usefulness ended." Looking into the mirror on the back bar over Dal's shoulder, she patted her curls and preened. "The poor boy took it real hard," she said with a laugh.

Now, he smiled. He had anticipated this moment for years. "Enjoy it while you can, Lola honey, because you've got trouble coming."

"My only problem is figuring how to spend all the money Luther is going to give me."

"I sent a telegram to Emile Julie from Fort Worth. Told him where you were and where you were heading. I figure if Julie and his men left immediately, they should be in Abilene by now, waiting for you. Or maybe they're working their way back along the trail." He scanned the crowded saloon, running a lazy gaze over the faces. "Julie's men could be here now, looking for a chance to slip a knife in your cheating heart."

Whiskey slopped down the front of her gown. "You son of a bitch!"

"You aren't going to live long enough to spend Joe's money."

"The hell I won't," she snapped. "I'll instruct Luther to pay Julie out of my inheritance. All I have to do is put out the word that I'll pay what the bastard thinks I owe him."

"Luther isn't going to release a penny until after the herd is officially counted. A lot can happen in a week." And this conversation had given him an idea. Pushing away from the bar, he stood, enjoying the ashy paleness beneath her rouge. "You can go on into Abilene where I can guarantee Julie's men are waiting to kill you. Or you can disappear from here."

"You're right. I could tell Luther to send my money to a safe place."

He nodded, smiling. "You could do that. If you think Julie won't be watching the telegraph office or the post office or Luther. If you think Julie isn't smart enough to follow the money. If you believe he won't track you out of here. Personally, I think you're dead."

She screamed at him, her face pulsing scarlet. "You son of a bitch!" She flew at him, but he grabbed her wrists.

"When a woman starts repeating herself, the conversation is over." An icy smile curved his lips. "Rest in peace, Lola." He flung her away from him and walked toward the door and out onto the noisy boardwalk.

Now all he had to do was find Jack Caldwell.

CHAPTER 23

He found Caldwell in a less-crowded saloon on a side street off Main, brooding in front of a bottle and a deck of cards. Dal pulled up a chair and rested his elbows on green felt.

"I just talked to Lola," he said.

Caldwell refilled his shot glass. "She double-crossed me." He tossed back the whiskey. "I won't get a plugged nickel of the money that bitch wouldn't have if it wasn't for me. If it takes the rest of my life, I'll find a way to get even."

"It won't take the rest of your life. You can get even right now. Tonight."

"What the hell are you talking about, Frisco?"

"How good are you with those cards?" He nodded at the deck on the table.

Without looking down, Caldwell fanned the cards in one hand. He stared. "I'm good enough to beat you any hour of any day."

"This town is overflowing with cowboys and trail bosses. If I point out the trail bosses, can you beat one or two of them?" His expression hardened. "What I want is cattle, Caldwell. I want you to win twenty-five beeves. What the Roark sisters need plus a couple extra."

Caldwell stared then fell back in his chair with a growing smile. "Sweet. I get what I want, revenge when Lola loses. And you get what you want, sixty thousand dollars." He riffled the cards between his fingers. "Split the sixty, and you got a deal."

"We split nothing. What you get is revenge, plus you stay alive," Dal said flatly, his eyes cold. Pulling his pistol from the holster, he laid it on the table. "Here's how tonight is going to go. I ride out of here with twenty-five longhorns in my pocket, or I put a bullet between your eyes. It's your call."

"Put the gun away, Frisco," Caldwell said after a moment's thought. He fanned the cards across the table. "All right. I'll give the outfit enough beeves to win Roark's money. And I'll do it for the sheer satisfaction of making sure that Lola doesn't get one cent of Roark's money. The more I think about this, the better I like it."

Disappointment twisted Dal's lips. He wasn't a killer, but he'd never wanted to shoot someone as much as he wanted to shoot Jack Caldwell. His eyes narrowed, and his grip tightened on the butt of the pistol. "I'm pissed, and I'm losing patience. Let's go."

Standing, Caldwell flexed his fingers and straightened his shoulders. "You point out the sheep. I'll fleece them."

It took all night, but when the sun popped over the horizon, Caldwell had collected IOUs for twenty-five longhorns. He and Dal stepped out of the last smoky saloon, filled their lungs with cleaner air, and looked at each other with fatigue-reddened eyes. Dal folded the IOUs into his vest pocket.

"The losers promised delivery before noon," Caldwell said. "And before noon the widow Roark is going to know she won't get a cent. She double-crossed the wrong man." He watched Dal walk away. "Frisco? Tell Freddy these cattle are for her. Tell her I bet on the wrong filly."

Frowning, Luther watched the last trail boss deliver ten longhorns for branding, then ride away. "Someday," he said to Dal, "I want you to tell me why Jack Caldwell chose to give the drive enough steers to beat Mrs. Roark."

"In case you need reminding, you already made a ruling that the drive could accept a gift without violating the terms of Joe's will." His drovers were cheering so loudly that Dal could only hope they heard Grady ordering them to fetch the irons out of the chuck wagon and slap the KW brand on the fresh additions. The bosses hadn't given away prime stock. They'd paid their gambling debts with skinny, footsore beeves, but he wasn't complaining. He'd take them.

"The ruling is documented." Luther thrust out his hand, and a wide grin spread across his face. "I don't know how the hell you accomplished this, but congratulations."

Freddy and Les ran up to him then, their eyes shining. Alex followed, rolling forward in her chair.

"Is it true?" Freddy asked, clutching his arm and searching his face. "And how in the world did you manage this? What on earth did you say to Jack?"

"I'll tell you later. The important thing is you're going to have that grand theater in San Francisco," he said, not surprised that her dream had become more important than his. Maybe that's what love was, when a man put a woman and her dreams above everything he had once thought was important to him.

"San Francisco?" Les asked, frowning. She and

Alex looked back and forth between them. "But I thought you two . . ."

"We can't seem to reconcile our dreams," Freddy said softly, looking at him with anguish in her eyes.

"There aren't words to express my gratitude," Alex said. Her words were sincere, but she wore a distracted expression, and she scanned the campsite, looking for John, Dal guessed.

Les rose on tiptoe and kissed his cheek. "How can we ever thank you?"

"By getting back to work," he said gruffly. The smell of scorched cowhide hung in the air, and the branding was almost finished. "You cowboys have a herd to move."

He held Freddy's gaze for a long moment, then he turned on his heel, unable to bear the tears glittering in her emerald eyes, and he walked to the remuda and saddled the buckskin. He should have been happier, damn it. He'd won everything he wanted. Except the woman he loved.

They skirted east of Newton, and crossed the Cottonwood River, heading north.

Three more days, Alex thought. She finished washing the supper dishes, then dried her hands on her apron and leaned against the worktable, watching the sun flare into a glowing disk and sink into the horizon. Three more days and the most profound experience of her life would come to a close. Would she drive into Abilene the same woman who had driven away from Klees? Or would she be someone new? It was time to face her choices.

"A penny for your thoughts," John said, coming up behind her.

He didn't touch her because touching her was too painful. She knew that. He didn't touch her, didn't kiss her, no longer spoke of the future. His eloquent grey eyes told her that he thought placing a distance between them would make saying good-bye easier.

"I've been wrong about so many things," she murmured, watching the sun set.

"Don't," he said gruffly, running a hand down his face. "You don't have to explain."

He thought she meant she had been wrong about him. She turned to correct him, then stopped and stared into his beloved face. Golden light bathed his cheekbones and the mouth she longed to kiss, illuminated the steady love glowing in his eyes.

"Would you do something for me?" she whispered.

"Anything you ask."

"Would you fetch my bedroll out of the wagon?"

He glanced at the sky, judging the time, surprised by her request. "Of course."

"Put it over there, beside the women's latrine tent, please." Gripping the crutch, she swung forward. "And then, please leave me."

He stiffened and turned away, but not before she saw the pain in his eyes. "Good night, my love. Sleep well."

Dropping to her knees on the grass, her heart pounding and her hands shaking, she untied her bedroll and checked to see that everything she wanted was there. When she was sure, she dropped her head and touched her fingers to her eyelids.

"I can. I'm not wrong about this. I've never been so right."

* * *

Freddy sat next to Dal, their shoulders touching, looking across the campfire at Les and Luther. Les and Luther held hands, gazing into each other's eyes wordlessly. Seeing them put the sweet into the bittersweet thoughts that drew lines across Freddy's forehead.

She didn't want the drive to end.

Never again would she know the thrill of chasing a tough old longhorn, or sleep in the open air beneath a starry sky. Never again would she tuck into a raw steak and a charred biscuit and think she was dining on the food of the gods. She'd never again pick at calluses on her palm, or feel the warm power of a cutting horse between her thighs. Or lie in the arms of a man that she loved with all her heart and soul.

She leaned against Dal's shoulder and closed her eyes. There had to be a way they could find a future together without giving up their dreams, without making each other miserable. Why couldn't they find a solution?

Dal dropped an arm around her. "Are you all right?" he asked in a low voice.

"I feel as hopeless as John looks."

John sat across from them, cradling an empty cup between his hands, staring into the flames licking the bottom of the coffeepot. For the past week he'd been almost as silent as he'd been when he came to them.

"Where's Alex tonight?" Dal asked, frowning and looking toward the chuck wagon.

"I don't know. I haven't seen her in a couple of hours."

Then she heard Drinkwater gasp, and one of the other drovers dropped his cup. Dal's fingers tightened on her shoulder, and she heard him draw a sharp quick breath. When Freddy followed their stares, she saw

Alex standing beside the chuck wagon lanterns, lean-ing on her crutch.

But it was an Alex that Freddy had not seen in sev-eral months. Her luxuriant blond hair was dressed high and scattered with tiny wild roses. She wore a blue silk dress that matched the color of her shining eyes. She was as elegantly beautiful as Freddy had ever seen her.

Looking at John, she came forward on the crutch. And Freddy rose to her feet as the drovers slowly stood, watching. The hush was so absolute that she heard the crackle of the campfire, heard the longhorns settling down out on the bedding grounds.

When John came to his feet, Freddy sucked in a breath and held it, feeling a lump rise in her throat. Understanding blazed in his expression, and his hands opened and closed at his sides. Moisture glistened in his eyes.

Alex came to the fire and scanned the faces staring at her until she found Freddy. "Thank you." Her soft voice sounded loud in the silence. "I love you."

Freddy nodded and smiled, and blinked hard. She clutched Dal's hand so tightly that her knuckles whit-ened.

Then Alex drew a deep breath, and tossed her crutch into the flames. The drovers made a hissing sound be-tween their teeth, and Freddy gasped, but Alex didn't fall. She pulled back her shoulders, standing straight and tall, her head high, her hips aligned, her shining eyes on John McCallister.

When he started forward, she smiled and shook her head. Then, pressing her lips in determination, she took the first step toward him, wobbled and threw out her arms for balance, then steadied her gaze on his face, and took another step. And then another.

Dal threw back his head and shouted the Rebel cry.

The drovers erupted in applause and wild cheers as Alex stumbled and fell forward into John's arms. He caught her and swept her into a fierce embrace, burying his face in her hair. Coffee cups lifted in shouted toasts, hats sailed into the air, and everyone rushed forward to pat Alex and offer encouragement and congratulations. In the melee, Freddy spotted Les sobbing happily against Luther's chest. She, too, was weeping.

Dashing at the tears swimming in her eyes, Freddy watched as John led her sister away from the fire, seeking privacy. Arms wound around each other, gazing into each other's eyes, they walked north, toward the future. And Freddy didn't doubt that Alex would master the wooden leg as she had mastered so many other things.

Dal wrapped his arms around her waist and rested his chin on top of her head. "Whatever you said to her, however you helped . . . I'm glad."

"Me too," she said softly, watching as Alex stumbled and John caught her. She heard them laughing, saw them turn to each other and melt into one silhouette. Dropping her head, she blinked at Dal's hard brown hands clasped at her waist.

Alex had John. Les had Luther. Freddy had a few more days.

The long hard journey was over.

They bedded the herd on the banks of the Smoky Hill River, two and a half miles outside of Abilene, Kansas. In the morning, they would lead the longhorns down the town's main street to the Great Western loading pens, where the cattle would be counted, weighed on a pair of ten-ton Fairbanks scales, then loaded into railroad cars bound for Chicago.

It was tradition to spend the last night sitting around the campfire, reminiscing about the high and low points of the drive, laughing at exaggerations and the beginnings of new tall tales that would be told around other fires on other drives. Freddy listened as long as she could, then she realized the tears hanging in her eyes were putting a damper on the last-night frivolities.

Silently, she left the campfire and walked out on the range, wanting to see the dark silhouettes of the cattle one last time, wanting to listen to the soft sound of chewing cuds and occasional blowing.

As she had hoped, Dal followed her into the darkness, coming up behind her and slipping his arms around her waist. Together, they listened to the night watch singing end-of-the-trail laments in low melodious voices to the dozing animals.

Each night since Wichita, they had walked away from the fire in search of a place to be alone together. But their lovemaking had possessed a desperate quality that wasn't wholly satisfying. Tonight, Freddy knew, would be the worst. Tonight would be the last time. Closing her eyes, she leaned against his chest and warned herself not to spoil the last night with tears. There would be time for tears later.

"Dal? I could go to Montana. I'd like ranching, I really know I would. It isn't like before. Now I know longhorns, and I know what ranching is all about."

He lowered his head to her ear and kissed her temple. "You'd hate the snow and cold winters. There's no town large enough to support a theater, Freddy." After a while, he said, "There must be some ranches near San Francisco." When she told him she thought the land was largely agricultural, he fell silent for a period. "Maybe there's something I could do in town."

"Nothing you would love like you love ranching and

cowboying." It was hopeless and they both knew it. They'd had this conversation before and were just repeating what had already been said, looking for an answer they might have overlooked.

"I love you, Freddy. This is killing me."

"Oh, Dal. I'm no good at acting, and owning a theater is a stupid idea anyway. Let me come with you to Montana. I can give up everything but you."

"Freddy? Dal?" Les walked out of the darkness, pushing Alex in her chair. "We want to talk to you." Freddy reluctantly stepped out of Dal's arms. "Alex? Tell them what we decided."

Moonlight gleamed in Alex's hair as she leaned to set the chair's brake. "First, I haven't had a relapse, I just didn't want to go stumbling across a dark prairie on a new leg looking for you two and falling down every two minutes."

"They don't care about that," Les said impatiently. "Ask them."

"Ask us what?" Freddy said, frowning.

"I'll tell it my own way," Alex said to Les. "John and I will leave for Boston from Abilene, as soon as Luther finishes the paperwork involved with the final settlement of Father's will. We hope to visit the West from time to time, but we'll make our home back East." She glanced at Les. "Les and Luther plan to enlarge Luther's home and raise their family in Klees. This leaves us with a problem, because Les and I don't want to sell King's Walk. Father built the ranch, and he loved it. He set up this drive, I think, because he hoped we would learn to love ranching, too. Les and I do, and Freddy, we think you do, too."

Oh God. She caught a glimmer of where this was leading. Standing up straight, she fixed her gaze on her sisters' smiles.

"Les and I want to keep King's Walk in the family, but John is a doctor, and Luther is an attorney, and neither wish to give up satisfying professions to become a rancher. So, we need the best boss in Texas to run the ranch. Dal, we want you to take over King's Walk. If it should happen that my sister decides Klees might appreciate a theater more than San Francisco, which has plenty of them, and if it should happen that the two of you recognize you belong together and want to live on the ranch, that would make us very happy. Regardless, Dal, if Freddy agrees, we'd like you to take over King's Walk. Unless, of course, you have your heart set on setting up your own spread in Montana."

Freddy peered at his face through the starlight. "My God," she breathed. "Why didn't we see it. A theater in Klees would be a success before the first curtain ever rose. The closest competition is a hundred miles away." Her eyes sparkled. "The same people who snubbed me will love me for bringing them a theater, Shakespeare, and some culture!"

He stared back at her. "I could spend a lifetime and not build a ranch as fine as King's Walk. The minute I saw Joe's spread, I knew that's what—"

Freddy jumped on him and kissed him hard on the mouth. "I want you in the front row for the opening night of every new play. And I want to go with you on at least one drive a year."

Dal pulled her to her feet and swung her in a circle that ended with him crushing her against his chest and kissing her long and deep. "We're going to build the best damned theater Texas ever saw!"

"And the best damned ranch west of the Mississippi!"

"I believe they have accepted our offer," Alex said drily.

Laughing, Les released the brake on Alex's chair, then gripped the handles. "As Freddy would say if she wasn't kissing and carrying on, I believe it's time to exit this scene."

They had almost reached the campsite before Freddy caught up to them. She dragged Les around to the front of Alex's chair and fiercely hugged them both, laughing and crying. "Thank you! I don't know what we would have done if you hadn't . . . I love you both so much!"

Caressing their hands, their dear faces, she tried to tell them what knowing them meant to her, and how much she loved them both. "Alex! Promise that you and John will come home at least once a year. And Les, we won't let anything stand in the way of seeing each other once a week!"

Alex gripped Freddy's and Les's hands, tears sliding down her cheeks. "I'm going to miss you both like life itself. As soon as John and I establish our home, you must come—"

"Frederick Roark!" Dal shouted. "Get your fanny back over here. A naked cowboy wants to talk to you about a wedding!"

They looked toward the bedding grounds and laughed. Freddy embraced her sisters, holding each of them next to her heart for a long tearful moment. She kissed them both, then ran into the darkness toward her future and a man she could not live without.

There was no desperation in their lovemaking tonight. There was passion and tenderness and joy and promises and love enough to fill the vast prairies.

The last day dawned hot and bright. Excitement quivered in the air as the last campfire was smothered, the chuck wagon was packed for the last time, and the drovers cinched up their saddles for the final short drive.

Dal cantered around the herd, taking one last count, making sure, then he made a decision he would be proud of for the rest of his life. Smiling, he instructed Grady to saddle another horse and he beckoned a puzzled Freddy and Les to follow him. He trotted to the chuck wagon and reined in beside Alex, who was seated with the mule's reins in her lap, ready to drive out.

"Ladies, you've been shot, gashed, almost trampled. I've asked a lot from all of you on this drive, and you've never let me down." He looked at Alex. "I'm about to ask one more thing. You told me you used to ride. Can you do it again? Do you think you can stay on a horse for two and a half miles?"

"Mr. Frisco," Alex said softly, and with obvious affection, "by now you should know that my sisters and I left the words 'I can't' way behind us. We can do anything."

"Here's what I want you to do . . ."

Freddy listened, and tears sprang into her eyes. She would love him for the rest of her life, but she couldn't imagine ever loving him more than she did this minute.

Alex's face lit in a radiant smile. "Thank you, Dal. I'll always be grateful for this."

The outfit waited while John helped her mount, then Dal shouted to his drovers.

"Caleb and Bill, you ride swing. Drinkwater and Charlie and Peach, you take the flanks. Dan and James, pick up the drag." He waved his hat and pointed it north. "Let's move this herd."

"Who's taking the point, boss?" Grady called with a grin that said he knew.

"Joe Roark's daughters will take 'em in."

Dal held his hat against his chest as the drovers cheered. There wasn't a man in the outfit who didn't recognize that Joe's daughters had earned the right to take the point, not a man who didn't remove his hat in respect as Freddy, Les, and Alex cantered to the front of the herd.

Riding abreast, tall and proud in their saddles, the Roark sisters led two thousand Texas longhorns into Abilene, Kansas, and down the main street. No one who saw them that day ever forgot them.

A Special Note
from
Maggie Osborne
to You

Dear Reader,

THE BEST MAN is a book I've wanted to write for a long time since I can identify with the Roark sisters in many ways.

Two years ago my husband and I moved to a twenty acre horse farm. While this has been a long time dream of my husband's, we're both city kids and living in the country has been a challenge. There have been times when I've thought: I have suits and sequined gowns in my closet—how did I end up on a farm? And how is it possible that I now own two pairs of overalls and love them?

I'm not as ignorant of horses as Freddy, Les, and Alex, but almost. When we first moved here, every time one of the horses lay down, I thought he was dead. Then he'd come back to life, and another one would lay down and die. This went on all day and worried me so much that it was hard to concentrate on writing. After I'd phoned the vet twice to come out here and check a dead horse, my husband and I agreed that I should ignore the dead horses and leave them for him to deal with when he got home from work.

This summer I discovered I've come a long way from the days when I thought a resting horse was dead. One night our horses and the mule got out of the pasture at midnight. My husband and I ran out of the house, our bathrobes flapping. Horses were running and rearing in the darkness. It was chaotic and a little frightening. But at the end, I'd managed to lure the horses into the corral while my husband was still searching for the mule. I felt like my flying bathrobe was Superman's cape. I felt a little like Alex must have felt after surviving the stampede.

Like the Roark sisters, my husband and I have had to learn new tasks we previously hadn't thought about: pasture management, irrigation, bucking hay. And like the Roark sisters, we're taking great pleasure in discovering new strengths and skills. Another thing we've discovered: Irma Bombeck was correct. The grass *does* grow greener over the septic tank.

As many of you have noticed, I like to write about women who through choice or circumstance find themselves in situations outside the mainstream of their society. While I've spent most of my life within the mainstream, I'm drawn to stories about women on the fringes. It seems to me that all of us have experienced flashes of feeling different, feeling a little out of step with those around us. We know how uncomfortable and vulnerable that perception makes us feel. I think the women who for one reason or another are outside the mainstream flow must have those feelings most of the time. And this tugs my heart.

I like to explore how such women came to be where they are in life, and where they are going. And I believe in the healing and freeing power of love. These two elements can be found in most of my books.

Certainly that's the case in A STRANGER'S WIFE, my next Warner's release, due out in December, 1998. Lily Dale is definitely a woman on the fringes of her society. When the book opens, Lily is being released from the Yuma Women's Prison, after having served five years for shooting a man. She's a hardened woman with a past and no future when she meets Quinn Westin, a man with a future and past he must hide. When these two collide, you can be sure a few sparks will fly.

Lily interests me in several ways. She's a survivor. And like all my heroines, she has an inner core of integrity regardless of her circumstances. Plus, she is a dead ringer for Quinn Westin's mysteriously missing wife. I've always been intrigued by the idea that somewhere in the world we each have a double. What would it be like to step into another woman's life? To live with her mistakes . . . and her husband. Her friends . . . and her lover?

Perhaps this book had it's genesis years ago when I dated a man who had an identical twin brother. I told myself, of course, that I could tell the twin brothers apart. I knew who I was dating, didn't I? Years later, I discovered I had attended a

prom with the second brother. I felt
deceived, angered by the deception . . . and
a little fascinated. And I wondered what it
must have been like for the brother,
stepping into the middle of on-going
conversations, pretending to be someone he
was not. Did he feel good about deceiving
me? Or a little guilty?

These are some of the questions I
enjoyed working with in A STRANGER'S
WIFE. And I enjoyed watching Lily Dale
grow and move closer to the mainstream.
Like all my heroines, Lily will never fit
exactly into the mainstream of her time, but
she's a little closer by the end of the book.
As for Quinn Westin, picture a tall, great-
looking cowboy type, tortured by secrets
and a web of deception. Imagine a
forbidden love and . . .

Better yet, read A STRANGER'S WIFE.

Maggie Osborne